Bijoux

Also by Meredith Rich

LITTLE SINS

VIRGINIA CLAY

BARE ESSENCE

Bijoux

MEREDITH RICH

Doubleday
New York London Toronto Sydney Auckland

PUBLISHED BY DOUBLEDAY
A division of Bantam Doubleday Dell Publishing Group, Inc.
666 Fifth Avenue, New York, New York 10103

DOUBLEDAY and the portrayal of an anchor with a dolphin
are trademarks of Doubleday, a division of Bantam Doubleday
Dell Publishing Group, Inc.

*All of the characters in this book are fictitious,
and any resemblances to actual persons, living or dead,
is purely coincidental.*

Library of Congress Cataloguing-in-Publication Data
Rich, Meredith.
Bijoux / Meredith Rich. — 1st ed.
    p.   cm.
ISBN 0-385-18425-5
   I. Title.
PS3568.I296B55   1989
813'.54—dc19   88-27159
                                                            CIP

DH

India, my jewel,
this one is for you,
with all my love forever

Acknowledgments

Thanks to Elaine Giovando, Bonnie Knickerbocker, and Eric Shelton for the information they supplied. And thanks to Barbara Lowenstein, Abner Stein, Loretta Barrett at Doubleday, and the people at Collins for waiting so patiently for this one.

Prologue

1988

"Hell, I don't have *time* for this!" Jewel Prescott muttered, although no one was within earshot.

She let her head drop forward over her desk, closed her eyes, and growled out loud. Kneading her knuckles hard into the back of her neck, Jewel tried to unlock the tension in her pressure points. The muscles fought back, refusing to budge. Her long neck stretched out painfully, slowly to the left, backward, to the right, forward. Her brain was signaling for a break; it was time to shut down her mind, her thoughts. But hell, she couldn't give in to the stress.

Jewel found herself back at work on the spring catalog. What had started out to be a simple, classic sales device seemed to become more complicated and annoying every season. Of course, it all came with success. In the beginning she had made all the decisions. It was a snap. Now, heading the jewelry empire that she had founded, Bijoux International, she had a number of department heads who deliberated for weeks on matters that she had once settled in minutes. And, of course, paying her staff the fortune she did, she was obliged to listen to what they had to say. Even take their advice often enough that they wouldn't quit and go to work for the competition. Happy workers didn't scatter secrets in the marketplace. So Jewel listened to their ideas and paid them whopping salaries, in return for their allegiance.

Jewel was aware of her reputation; she *was* difficult to work for. Temperamental, quixotic, aloof, those were descriptions of Jewel Prescott that the press had bandied about over the years. Also: talented, savvy, original. *Oh, for the good old days,* she sighed out loud. And then thought better of it. *No, cancel that . . . cancel.*

Jewel closed her green-contact-lensed eyes. Cupping her hands over them, she opened her eyes again, seeing only darkness. The darkness alleviated the ache in her head and the pressure that pounded behind her eyes, but it produced an anxious panic in some other part of her psyche. A feeling of claustrophobia.

"Jewel? Are you okay?" Meg Higdon, her assistant, stood in the doorway, tall and splendidly leggy in a black chamois skirt cut nine inches above her knees.

"Yeah. Just the usual headache. Get me a couple of Tylenol, would you? Extra strength."

Meg brought the Tylenol and set it, along with the photographs and layout for the February ads in *Vogue* and *Town and Country,* on Jewel's desk. "Check this a.s.a.p. Mike needs to know before five." She shook two tablets out of the bottle and poured a glass of Evian water. "It's been a high-stress week for you."

Jewel shrugged. "No worse than usual. Not enough sleep. This weekend I plan to make up for it."

Meg looked puzzled. "But aren't you flying to Rome Friday?"

Jewel stared at her assistant. "Rome?" Then she laughed, covering. "Well, that's what I mean. I'll get plenty of rest on the plane."

After Meg had gone, Jewel swallowed the Tylenol and sat for a moment, staring out over St. Patrick's Cathedral and waiting for the pain in her head to recede. The trip to Rome . . . Jewel wondered how it could have slipped her mind so completely.

While Señor and Señora Gomez-Archuleta chatted in rapid Spanish with some friends who had dropped by their table at Odeon, a perennial late-night hot spot in downtown Manhattan, Allen Prescott, Jewel's husband, turned to her, his smile fading.

"Christ, Jewel, what's going on? You haven't said two words all evening. I was counting on you to chat up Olga while Giulio and I talk around a price on the Monet."

Jewel looked at her husband. Her attractive husband. Her attractive, once-wealthy husband who was now art poor. His vast fortune hung on the walls of their Fifth Avenue apartment and the house in Connecticut. There was also a storage loft somewhere in lower Manhattan for which Jewel paid an astronomical annual rent.

Allen Prescott acquired. He never disposed of his acquisitions. And so, having swept through a vast inheritance—Oklahoma oil money— he now relied on Jewel to write the checks. Jewel admitted, in rare moments of charity, that it was probably fair; she owed Allen a great deal. Once she had even been proud of his art collection. His gee-whiz enthusiasm was what had impressed her most about him in the beginning. But art had become his obsession. Buying from private collectors, buying at auction, buying from the artists themselves; that was how he spent his days, and most of his evenings.

"I don't have anything to talk to Olga about," Jewel said sotto voce. "Do you see what she's wearing? That Cathalene Columbier necklace is obscene. Emeralds and aquamarines, with gold *and* stainless steel panels? I didn't think even Cathalene could turn out something that atrocious. Anyway, I have a headache. I just want to get this over and go to bed."

"For a change," Allen said. "Why can't you just make an effort and try to help me?"

"Help you! When have I not?" she hissed indignantly. "You owe me a hell of a lot."

Allen gave Jewel's foot a swift nudge under the table as the other couple breathily said their farewells, full of hugs and "lunch soon," to the Gomez-Archuletas.

Jewel flashed Señora Gomez-Archuleta a dazzling smile. "I was just chatting with Allen about your necklace, Olga. It's one of Cathalene's pieces, isn't it?"

"Oh, yes. She is so *very* talented," Olga Gomez-Archuleta gushed, fully aware of what she was saying; it was no secret that Jewel Prescott and Cathalene Columbier were bitter rivals. "It is beautiful, isn't it? Giulio gave it to me as a little gift for having my appendix out."

"How sweet," Jewel smiled. "And how appropriate! Tell me . . ."

The suite at the Hassler, overlooking the Piazza di Spagna in Rome, was one of the few that the hotel had not redecorated in the past few years. The rooms were an anachronism, from a time that Jewel had never experienced except in books—an era when young American heiresses were escorted to Europe on the Grand Tour, prior to engagement, marriage, and a lifetime of devotion to children, charity, large staffs, and palatial homes.

Her lover, Mike Marshall, thought the rooms somber and depressing, not romantic enough. He wanted to switch to a smaller suite on the fifth floor that was bright white with a balcony overlooking the Spanish Steps and Bernini's fountain. Mike's style was clean-cut and contemporary. He liked the Rome that translated into the clothes of Giorgio Armani, the textile patterns of the Missonis, the Italy of twentieth-century fashion.

The designer in Jewel agreed. But the part of her that had grown up poor craved the splendor of days past, the elegance that her own heritage lacked. Grand hotels such as the Hassler made up in some small part for Jewel's poverty-ridden childhood. Of course, most people did not know about that childhood. She told Mike that this particular suite brought back memories of her seventh birthday.

"Jewel, darling," Mike said as his hand gave up on caressing her breast, "sex takes two people, unless one of them is a corpse."

Jewel smiled apologetically. "I'm no corpse. My back hurts too much. Unless it's rigor mortis. Would you be a love and rub it, darling?"

Mike was Bijoux's art director as well as her lover. She had hired him because of his impressive background with Saatchi. But it did not hurt that he was young and tall and called to mind the youthful Clint Eastwood.

"All right," he sighed. "Turn over. I'll rub your back. Then you can rub some part of me. Your choice."

Jewel stretched out her naked body and turned over. Mike dug strong fingers into her shoulders. "Hmmmm . . . that's . . . good," she moaned.

"At last we're getting somewhere. You've got to snap out of this depression, Jewel," Mike said as he worked up and down her neck. "You haven't lost it. And anyway, even if you coasted for years on what you've already designed, no one would notice. Rich women will keep buying Jewel's bijoux until their husbands divorce them for somebody younger. And then the new wives will head straight for Bijoux. It's kind of like the food chain."

"Hmmmm," Jewel mumbled, her face buried comfortably in the soft down pillow.

"I'm hooked on you, Jewel," Mike whispered. "Why don't you leave Allen? We make a great pair."

"Let's not talk about it now," she forced herself to say. "Darling, could you move down to my lower back?"

Mike worked his way down to Jewel's buttocks. She was the only woman he had ever known who could turn him on by being passive. He pressed his erection against her thighs as he leaned his face down into her short blond-streaked hair and kissed behind her ears. "I love you," he whispered. "Tonight I'm your Roman lover. *Carissima . . .*"

Then he became aware of her even, rhythmic breathing. "Jewel . . . *amore mio?*"

But Jewel was asleep.

Jewel sat in a maroon leather wing chair in the parlor of the Sheldon Arms School. The chair emanated the stuffy, stifling atmosphere of generations of proper girls being educated for matronhood. Jewel could not have imagined herself lasting a semester there. But it was the Right Sort of Place, and Jewel was determined that her daughters would have the advantages that Sheldon Arms could provide. And it was less than an hour's drive from her house in Washington, Connecticut. At one time that had seemed like a marvelous convenience; now she spent so little time there that it hardly mattered.

Jewel waited impatiently, sipping Constant Comment tea as she checked out the other parents gathered in the well-worn room for parents' weekend. They were, by and large, a conservative, cashmere-and-tweed group. Most of them, Jewel was sure, had attended Sheldon Arms when they were young. They seemed content and secure to be back in the hallowed halls.

Content and secure, that is, until their gaze met Jewel Prescott's. When old money meets new money that blatantly flaunts it, old money generally feels threatened. Under Jewel's unsmiling inspection they began to look ill at ease. Jewel—wearing an outrageous Christian Lacroix suit, with blood-red lipstick, and her own gold-and-ruby earrings and necklace—looked as if she could devour any of them. Her hair, now auburn, was very short, and slicked down behind her ears with Tenax. Today's contact lenses were tinted violet.

"Mummie!" Beryl Prescott called out as she burst into the room, flinging her arms around Jewel. "You look wonderful! Oh, I'm so glad to see you! Amber said you wouldn't make it, but I told her you would. You promised to come."

Jewel smiled. "I wouldn't miss it for anything. Where *is* Amber?" she asked her youngest daughter, who was now fourteen and a freshman. "I sent Miss Foulke to find both of you."

"Oh . . . well, she must still be getting dressed," Beryl smiled. "Her skin is really clearing up . . . you'll be so pleased. And she's making much more of an effort this year than she did at Dalton. She's a writer on the yearbook staff."

"I'm glad to hear it," Jewel said. "She needs to become more enthusiastic about things. Boredom is an indulgence." She looked at her watch. "But if she doesn't hurry up, we'll miss our dinner reservation at the Yardley Inn. It was completely booked. Meg had to beg and cajole them for a table. The only time they had open was six-thirty. Uncivilized, I'm afraid, but it's the only decent place for miles."

"But didn't they know who you were?" Beryl asked.

"Well, apparently not. Or at least not the person who takes reservations. This part of Connecticut is very comme il faut. They still wear their ancestral diamonds. I'm not in vogue up here."

Beryl laughed. "That's silly. There was that huge spread in last month's *New York* magazine."

"Ah, but this is Connecticut, darling," Jewel said with a smile. "Well, let's think of where else we'll eat if your sister doesn't show up soon."

"I'm here, Mother."

Jewel turned to see her fifteen-year-old daughter, Amber, looking pretty much the same as when she had left for school two months before: a mess. Her shirt was tucked carelessly into an unflattering pleated skirt and partially hanging out at the back. Beryl had been kind to say that Amber's acne was improving. Her face was a mine field of erupting spots, and her oily hair looked as if it had not been washed for days.

Jewel, however, took a deep breath and smiled, reminding herself that she must bite her tongue rather than criticize. Amber's therapist in New York had put all the blame on Jewel for her daughter's problems. "God," Jewel had told Allen, "one would think shrinks would have the good sense to realize who pays the bills." Nevertheless, Jewel was not one to be intimidated into feeling guilt.

"Amber, darling!" Jewel said, embracing her daughter while trying not to let her cheek brush against the small, greasy hills on Amber's face. "You look wonderful. I thought we'd go and have lobster at the Yardley Inn."

"Shellfish is bad for my skin," Amber said.

"Oh, well, whatever. But we'd better hurry or they'll turn us away at the door."

"When were you ever turned away?" Amber said. She was tall, with good bone structure, but at present all possibilities for attractiveness had gone awry, out of willful neglect. "Where's Daddy? Didn't he come?"

"He's off at an auction in London," Beryl said enthusiastically. "I told you, remember? And there's going to be a big one at Sotheby's over Christmas. Some duchess's entire collection of art and antiques. He promised he'd take me. Maybe we could all go! It's really interesting. Daddy knows so much."

"Yes," Jewel said, "he knows a great deal about art."

At the Yardley Inn, Jewel was recognized after all, and they were seated immediately. After ordering a martini and two ginger ales, Jewel dutifully began quizzing the girls about their classes and teachers and extracurricular activities, exuding as much maternal enthusiasm as she could muster under the circumstances.

It had been a hell of a day. Things at Bijoux International were starting to unhinge because Jewel was having trouble handling the stress. The deal to open a store in Atlanta had dissolved because she had lost her temper with Travis Peterson, her would-be partner on the project. Peterson thought Jewel was a brilliant designer but did not want her to have control over every business aspect of the Atlanta store. Jewel, of course, could not let go a minutia of control over *any* of her stores. She *was* Bijoux. So, in a fit of temper, Jewel had told Travis Peterson to take his money, roll it into a fat wad, and shove it up his wife Antonia's ass.

Well, not having a store in Atlanta wasn't the end of the world. But allowing herself to lose her temper that way, that was something to come to terms with.

And, of course, there had been the quarrel with Anna McNeill Ferguson, a head-on collision after all these years. That had really ripped Jewel open, to discover that Anna still hated her so much for what she had done.

The past. You couldn't get rid of it, no matter how hard you tried. But what was the lesson?

"Mummie!" Beryl was saying, indicating the waitress standing by their table. "She wants to know if you want another martini."

"What? Oh, no thanks. Why don't you bring me a club soda?" She had work to do later, at home. "I'm sorry, darlings, I'm just a little preoccupied."

"For a change," Amber said, glaring at her mother with the petulant sulkiness that Jewel had come to expect from her.

"Let's talk about what you two want to do tomorrow," Jewel said, trying to sound perky. "I thought we might go shopping and see a movie."

"Oh, let's talk about what *you* want to do tomorrow," Amber whined.

"Oh, Amber! Mummie's just making a suggestion," Beryl said quickly. Even though she was a year younger than her sister, she had assumed the role of family peacemaker; she did not want this evening to turn into a scene between her mother and Amber. "I think it'd be fun to go shopping, Mummie. And there's a movie with River Phoenix playing in Danbury. Come on, Amber, what do you say?"

"I have to stay at school and work on my history term paper," Jewel's elder daughter said. "I don't need any clothes, and I heard it wasn't a very good movie anyway."

Back at her house later that evening, Jewel headed upstairs to try to get some work done.

"Oh, Miss Jewel, I thought I heard you come in," Nushka Krupa, the housekeeper, said, emerging from the kitchen. "How was your evening with the girls?"

"Oh, fine," Jewel said. "Beryl seems to be doing wonderfully. Amber's just scraping by, as usual. They'll be spending tomorrow night here, by the way, after the parents' dinner."

Nushka nodded. "Is there anything I can get you, Miss Jewel? You look tired. A cup of tea?"

"Sure, Nushka, that sounds great. And maybe a few crackers. I'm working late tonight."

Up in her room, Jewel got a sketch pad out of her briefcase and optimistically propped up the pillows on her bed. She turned on the television, flipped around the dial, and stopped at an Errol Flynn swashbuckler. Then she slipped on her nightgown and snuggled into bed with the sketch pad on her lap. Closing her eyes, Jewel conjured up images of faceted pink tourmalines. But all she could picture were loose stones glistening against a background of dark green velvet. Loose stones were not what she needed to think about. The cut gems had to transform themselves into jewelry so sparklingly unique that each piece would fit the image of Bijoux.

Her creativity had vanished months ago; it had seemed to disappear overnight. She was faking it now, coasting on variations of her old designs. No one had noticed so far. At least, nobody had had the guts to mention it, except Mike. But they would, if she could not regain the magic soon.

Jewel opened her eyes and tried to let her imagination enter the world of the pirates in the film on television. Seventeenth-century Spain, it looked to be. She thought of the Spanish Queen, whichever one it was, and what her vast collection of jewels would have been like. She began sketching, concentrating on the old-fashioned look of ornately scrolled gold, paired with more modern tourmalines, and perhaps peridots or tsavorites.

But it was no good. There was no inspiration behind the drawings. Jewel tossed aside her pencil with a sigh. Her head hurt again. *What's taking Nushka so long with the tea?* she wondered.

Closing her eyes with a sigh, she tried to sort through things. How sweet her daughters had been as babies, yet how difficult Amber was now. How gallant Allen had been when they were first together; how desperately she had needed him then. What a great friend her partner Edward Randolph was, and how snappish she was with him these days.

Her mind flickered to her old friend Anna McNeill, who now hated her enough to want to see her dead. And Hadley McNeill, Anna's brother, the great love who had disappeared from her life. There was, of course, Cathalene Columbier, who would love nothing better than to dance on the grave of Bijoux International. And Sascha Robinovsky, the romantic, impossible father of her daughters, who was threatening to upset her equilibrium again. What had happened in her relationships with all these people? Where had all the feeling gone? She thought about what a sexy lover Mike Marshall had been, how bored she was with him now, and the tireless loyalty of Meg, her assistant.

And what a total bitch she herself had become.

Now, with her fortieth birthday looming around the corner, Jewel wondered what was she going to do about herself and her life. Something had to give, if for no other reason than to keep Bijoux International from sinking under the weight of her enormous ego. There had to be an exciting new world to conquer, to stave off boredom. And, Jewel realized, she had to reconcile herself with the world she inhabited now. She had everything, but she *enjoyed* nothing.

If only someone could open up her head and pour in some emotion, some warmth. Her soul was as dead as her creativity. Jewel wanted to be able to care again, about herself and the others with whom she shared her life. No, that was another aspect of the problem: she didn't share her life. She *controlled*—her own self as well as others.

All of a sudden, a wave of nausea swept through Jewel. She dashed for the bathroom. Her first thought was that she must have eaten a bad cherrystone clam at dinner. Food poisoning.

As she reached the bathroom, a strong attack of dizziness overtook her, and a grayish cloud passed before her eyes. She grabbed the sink and, heaving, willed her way toward the toilet. Before she made it, her knees buckled underneath her and she crumbled onto the white-tiled floor. Helpless, she could feel her consciousness falling down something dark and bottomless, sinking deeper and deeper. Then the nausea and dizziness went away, and a strange, disoriented euphoria took their place. In the darkness, she could feel warm, golden light bathing the inside of her head.

She could hear someone calling her name: Maddie . . . Maddie . . .

Then she blacked out completely.

Book One

1960 — 1978

1

1960

"Maddie . . . Maddie? I'm afraid you have to run along home now."

Madeleine Kathleen Dragoumis looked up from the book she was reading. "Oh? Is it late, Miss Lathem? I guess I lost track."

Jane Lathem smiled at her small, thin fifth-grade pupil. Maddie was an enigma. She was a quiet, reclusive child whose academic skills were more suited for a grade or so lower. But she was obviously so determined to improve that the teacher had resisted sending her back. Maddie read voraciously, anything she could get her hands on, yet, when it was time to write a story, her spelling was appalling and her grammar awkward and inadequate. But she was good at math and seemed to enjoy numbers, especially when Jane Lathem had the class perform exercises where they were given a certain sum of pretend money, to learn how to budget. Maddie always figured out how she would spend her money, to the penny, before anyone else in class.

More than anything, Maddie enjoyed reading books and magazine stories about rich and successful people. She loved the idea of money. It was obvious to Jane Lathem from the way Maddie dressed that the child had not seen a great deal of it in her life. Not that many of the kids at the Green Mountain School had, but Maddie seemed worse off than the others. There had never been a high level of income in that corner of Pennsylvania. Now that the only factory in town had shut down, nearly everyone was desperate. Many families were moving away to search for employment. Jane Lathem herself had spent the past few weeks sending off letters applying for teaching jobs in more affluent parts of the state.

"Well, it's four-thirty, dear. I'm afraid we have to close up shop now. Come on, I'll drop you off. You can take that book with you, if you've finished the rest of your work."

"Oh, thank you, Miss Lathem. But I think I'll walk."

"You'll do no such thing. It'll be getting dark soon, and you live clear across town, don't you? Come on, get your things." Jane paused. "Actually, I'd like to have a talk with your mother."

"Oh, well, er . . . she won't be home yet. She got a job waitressing over in Thomasville."

Jane Lathem locked the classroom door behind her. It was almost Thanksgiving and Maddie was wearing no coat, only a dingy-white nylon sweater over her cotton dress. "What time will your mother be home?"

"Oh, soon. By dinnertime," Maddie said quickly.

The teacher shrugged. "All right . . . I'll meet her another day. You tell her to call me and make an appointment. But I *will* drop you off. It's far too cold out for you to walk, dressed like that."

Maddie did not want her teacher to know where she lived. But it *was* cold, and she didn't relish the walk. To solve the dilemma, she accepted the ride with gratitude but asked Miss Lathem to drop her at Johnny's Cash Store, a couple of blocks from where she lived. Maddie told her teacher that she had to buy groceries for dinner.

As soon as Miss Lathem's car was out of sight, Maddie skittered home the back way, through shadowy alleys, to her house. "House" was a more than generous term, although that's what it had once been. Currently, it was one of a row of condemned structures, the best of the row, and Maddie shared it with a stray cat she had found and named Scrappy. Occasionally, a bum would wander in for the night, and she and Scrappy would hide quietly in their secret room in the basement until daylight came and she could sneak off to school. Nowadays, with the town so poor, she usually had the house to herself. Bums traveling east or west on the train did not bother to get off at Green Mountain; they knew there were no handouts there.

Maddie knew it too. Of course, there were a few shopkeepers who always gave her some nearly perished food at the end of the day—

Maddie told them she needed it for her family's dogs and chickens—but she was careful never to go to any of them more than once a week, for fear of overstepping her welcome. The lady at the Salvation Army had known Maddie's mother, and she always set aside the best clothes she got in Maddie's size. But in a poor, mostly Catholic town where the citizens had large families, the pickings were slim. The Salvation Army was fixing to close down too.

No one, however, not one person in town, knew that the ten-year-old girl had been living alone, with Scrappy, for over four months.

Maddie got by. Children at school made fun of her clothes, which never fit because she was so bony. They also had caught her between periods stealing parts of lunches—an orange here, a cracker or half of sandwich there—and had threatened to report her to the principal. But when her eyes had welled up with terrified, heartfelt tears, even the least charitable child had felt sorry for her. Maddie continued to steal food from lunch boxes, but the children pretended not to notice. She was quiet, and there was a sweet sadness about her that kept the biggest bullies from teasing her. For the most part, Maddie kept to herself and the kids ignored her.

Nobody could understand how Maddie happened to appear so poor when she was always telling Miss Lathem about her mother waitressing, and her father working in a "big, important job" in New York City. Eventually the kids figured out she was lying about her father, which she was. They weren't sure what the truth was about her mother. Neither was Maddie.

Maddie's father—there really had been a legitimate father—had taken off only weeks after her birth. Maddie's mother carried around a small photograph of him in her wallet. Maddie loved to look at it: he was a large, handsome man with dark wavy hair and intense Greek eyes. Maddie had seen his name, Nick Dragoumis, typed on her birth certificate. She never knew what happened to Nick. Her mother refused to talk about him.

Maddie believed, with no evidence at all to go on, that he went to New York and became rich and famous. One of her favorite fantasies —one of her *many* fantasies—had it as only a matter of time before Nick Dragoumis would long to see his beloved daughter whom he had deserted at birth. Then he would send for her. After their loving reunion, Nick would take her to live in an elegant town house in

some beautiful neighborhood, and she would be the best-dressed girl
at her private school.

Maddie's mother, Lulu Fleishman, had grown up in another ham-
let in the area, poor and from a large family. She was plain, but made
up for it with the opposite sex by having large breasts and a slim,
supple body. At sixteen she left home and went to Pittsburgh, where
she struggled for two years to make ends meet. When she met and
married Nick Dragoumis, a bartender at the rough neighborhood bar
where she worked, she thought her life had changed for good. But
she got pregnant right away, and although Nick stuck around for her
nine months, he didn't hold an image of himself as a father. So he left.

Lulu was a waitress, that part was true. She supplemented her
income by becoming a hooker, although Maddie didn't know that
was the name for what her mother did. After Nick deserted her and
the baby, Lulu left Pittsburgh, for reasons known only to herself, and
began drifting around western Pennsylvania. There were relatively
few clients in any small factory town, and they were mostly married
with not much extra money to throw her way. Still, Lulu never went
back to live with her family, nor did she return to Pittsburgh.

Lulu took care of Maddie reasonably well until the child was nine.
It was then that they wandered into Green Mountain and began
living for free in one of the condemned row houses. At that point the
dismal quality of her life began to overwhelm Lulu. She slipped into a
deep depression and spent most of her time looking out the window,
crying. Occasionally, she would get herself together enough to go out
at night and return the next morning with some money.

Maddie found the local elementary school and, after several
months, managed to drag Lulu over to enroll her. Maddie got a
Saturday job sweeping up for Mr. Vlasic, who owned a small grocery
store that specialized in his homemade sausages. On Saturday evenings, Maddie and Lulu would dine on bratwurst and sauerkraut,
compliments of Mr. Vlasic. They would eat in the boarded-up back
room, indulging in candlelight instead of going to bed just after dark.
On those Saturdays Maddie could almost trick herself into believing
that she and her mother were a normal, happy family.

One day, while Maddie was at school, Lulu took off, simply up and
left town. She wrote a note to her daughter, telling Maddie that she
had gone to visit relatives and would return soon. She cautioned
Maddie to stay put and not tell anybody that she was alone, on the

threat of severe punishment when Lulu returned. Pinned to the note were two ten-dollar bills.

During the day, surrounded by her classmates and made brave by her secret hardship, Maddie was pragmatic about her life. Nights were horrible, though. She did not feel the least bit brave, alone in the dark, surrounded by spiders and mice and strange creaking noises. Maddie cried often, confused and scared, totally bewildered by her mother's sudden departure. She told herself that something important must have happened, that Lulu would probably return with enough money for them to live in a real house. Better yet, Maddie liked to fantasize that Lulu would return with Nick Dragoumis. These thoughts carried Maddie through the first night and many subsequent ones, although she often cried herself to sleep, clutching her cat tightly for comfort and courage.

Maddie accepted the day-to-day scramble for food (the days she didn't ask for handouts, she stole, but only from the one supermarket in town that was part of a big chain). She and Scrappy became content enough with their living arrangements, at least until Lulu returned and they could move. The basement of the house was dry and warm enough. She had dragged old mattresses from upstairs to insulate the little basement room (and taken several cans of Lysol from the janitor's closet at school to make them smell decent). Every week or so, Maddie stole clean sheets from clotheslines around town, and returned them dirty a week later. She did that with socks and underwear too. At school, after all the children had gone home for the day and she had the bathroom to herself, she washed herself and brushed her teeth. Maddie often borrowed Miss Lathem's scissors, when she wasn't looking, and kept her hair cut very short because it was easier to keep clean and dried faster in the chillier weather.

Once or twice, Maddie made plans to go search for her mother. But when it was time to turn the plans into action, the child realized that she had no idea where to begin looking. Except for telling Maddie that she had been born in Pittsburgh, Lulu had never divulged even the tiniest snippet of information about her own past. Every so often Maddie had asked Lulu if she had grandparents and where they lived. Lulu had only answered, "As far as you're concerned, you don't."

Scared as Maddie was, as much terror as she felt when she woke up in the middle of the night and realized that the worst nightmare imaginable—that her mother was gone—was *real*, she was determined that no one discover her situation. That kept her from trying to make friends with whom she might have gone home occasionally to have dinner or spend the night. Friends' parents would pry, and Maddie knew she could not risk that. They would send her off somewhere, to an orphanage. And how would her mother—or her father —ever find her then?

"Maddie . . . your mother never called me for an appointment. Did you give her the message?"

Maddie looked up at Miss Lathem. "Er, well . . . I guess I forgot."

Jane Lathem smiled. She was a strong-featured woman, in her midthirties. A nose that was too long and thin kept her face from being pretty, but her skin was rosy and flawless and her hair was always shiny-clean and curled into a neat pageboy. She wore matching skirts and sweaters, always accessorized with a scarf around her neck or a belt. To Maddie, Jane Lathem was beautiful and the most stylish woman in town.

"It's not that I have anything bad to say about you, Maddie," Jane assured her. "You're working hard. Your spelling and grammar are improving. I enjoy meeting the parents of my pupils, getting to know them a bit. Maybe I'll stop by this weekend."

"Oh, gosh, we're going to Harrisburg," Maddie said quickly. "To visit my grandparents."

"Well, that's nice, Maddie. I'm sure you'll have a wonderful time."

"Yes ma'am, I will. My grandfather owns a movie theater, and we're going to the movies . . . and *out* to dinner in restaurants every night."

Jane Lathem nodded distractedly, searching for a mislaid spiral notebook. She had been frantically busy the past month. Her class was too large for one person. The ten-year-old boys were a rowdy handful, and she was still trying to find another job for next year. Putting her hands on the notebook, it occurred to her suddenly that she had let her initial concern for Maddie slip away with the weeks; Maddie was there, waiting, when she arrived at school in the mornings and the child was always the last to leave. Maddie never complained, but it was as if she dreaded going home.

"I'll drop you off today," she said. "Perhaps your mother will be there."

"Oh, no . . . I don't think so," Maddie hedged, "Thursdays she works late."

"You mean she won't be home to fix your supper?"

"Well, she always leaves something for me. Cold chicken or beef stew or something."

Jane Lathem nodded. "Well, I think maybe I'll buy a sandwich and eat with you. A child your age shouldn't be all alone after dark."

Maddie swallowed, her throat dry. A terrible panic wedged itself into the pit of her stomach. "I just remembered. She *is* coming home tonight."

"Then I'll stop in and say hello."

"No! I mean, the reason she's coming home early is 'cause she's having a party. It's a surprise birthday party for one of her friends. I have to help her get ready."

"Maddie," Jane Lathem said firmly. "I am taking you home. If your mother isn't there yet, I'll wait for her. If she's busy I'll merely say a quick hello."

As Jane Lathem's emerald green Dodge crossed town, Maddie searched her brain for a solution. She could jump out of the car at the next red light and take off down the street, but Miss Lathem would never give up after that. Maddie would have to stop going to school to avoid Miss Lathem's persistent probing. On the other hand, her teacher was so intent on learning the truth that Maddie considered coming clean about the situation. But what would happen then? Miss Lathem would undoubtedly be required to report Maddie's predicament to someone. Then everyone would know. The whole town. The humiliation accompanying that thought was unbearable. Even worse, she would be carted off to some foster home where they probably would not want Scrappy.

As the car neared Johnny's Cash Store, Maddie felt more and more panic-stricken. Suddenly, she knew what she had to do. The car slowed down, then stopped at the small intersection across the street from the grocery store.

"Which way now?" Jane asked.

"Oh . . . could you wait here a minute? I have to run into the store and buy some Coca-Cola. I'll be right back."

"Do you have money?"

"Oh, yeah. Mama gave me five dollars this morning."

Maddie walked slowly across the street and into the store. She looked back at Miss Lathem and waved. She said hello to Johnny, the middle-aged owner, and headed quickly through the store to the back exit that led to an alley. She ran all the way home, her heart beating wildly. When she got there, she slipped into the dark house through a back window and grabbed Scrappy, holding him close up against her face until her breathing returned to normal. This was it. This was the end. Miss Lathem would not be able to find her tonight, but Maddie knew she could never show her face in school again without facing a barrage of questions that she would be forced to answer.

"We've got to move, Scrappy. I know Mama's not coming back. She would have been here by now if she planned on coming. So what we've got to do is pack up our things and sneak onto the ten o'clock train. You know, it's funny, Scrappy," she said, tears trickling down her face into the cat's fur, "hearing those trains all the time. I don't even know where the ten o'clock goes to." She squeezed the cat so tightly it meowed and tried to pry itself loose from her grasp. "Well, it'll be a surprise, won't it? An adventure."

She put the gray cat down before it scratched her. "Okay, you stay here while I go over to Mr. Vlasic's and see what kind of food we can get. I'll get a jar of water too."

As she headed for Vlasic's store she peeked around the corner to see if Miss Lathem's car was still waiting in front of Johnny's. It was, but Miss Lathem wasn't in it. Probably she'd gone in to find out what was taking so long. Maddie scurried away in the other direction, trying to invent a story to convince Mr. Vlasic to part with more food than usual.

Maddie was so preoccupied as she crossed the street that she did not notice the maroon car speeding up the street toward her until it had screeched to an ear-piercing halt to try to avoid hitting her. The front bumper knocked her off balance and jolted her back to reality. She fell to the ground in front of the tires, stunned but, as far as she could tell, unhurt.

"Oh my God . . . my God!" the man who was driving the car wailed as he leapt out of his Plymouth. "Little girl . . . I didn't see you. You darted out in front of me. Help! *Help!* Somebody! Help . . . call an ambulance. The child is hurt!" he screamed into the darkness of the empty street.

Maddie scrambled to her feet, more scared by the fuss he was making than by her own near-death. "I'm okay . . . really. You didn't hit me. I lost my balance *after* you stopped the car," she stammered. "Really, I'm fine. I don't need an ambulance."

But people had begun swarming out into the street from nearby houses. The ambulance had been called, she heard someone say, and the police. Someone else threw a coat over her shoulders and sat her on the hood of the car. The crowd huddled around her as the man tried to explain what had happened. Maddie's leg hurt a bit, but she knew it didn't hurt enough to be broken. She kept insisting to everyone that she was fine. All she knew was that she had to get out of there, over to Mr. Vlasic's before he closed up for the night. But how could she get away now? Some woman was insisting that she be taken to the hospital for observation. Someone else was asking whether her parents had been called.

And then, horror of horrors, Maddie looked up to see Jane Lathem's emerald green Dodge turn the corner and head down the street toward the commotion.

This is the end, Maddie thought, trapped. *It's too late to escape.*

2

1968

"And graduating with highest honors, with a scholarship to the University of Colorado, it is my great pleasure to award this diploma to the class valedictorian, Madeleine Kathleen Lathem."

Ernest Johnson, the robust principal of the Pine Ridge High School in Pine Ridge, Colorado, twisted his mouth into a broad smile. "We're proud of you, Maddie," he continued over the loud applause that bounced off the walls of the school auditorium on the stifling, early June day.

Jane Lathem, sitting in the third row, bit her lip hard and tried to fight off the tears that were gathering behind her eyes. She might as well have tried to stop the rain that was falling outside.

Dammit, she thought, *I swore I wouldn't do this.* And then she thought, *What the hell, why shouldn't I? Maddie's my child as much as if I had given birth to her myself.* And she let them run down her cheeks, tears from a heart bursting with love and pride.

Jane reached for a tissue, and blew her nose discreetly. She was not the only parent in the room who was crying. A burst of pleasure engulfed her. She was indeed a parent. Maddie was her daughter, as far as anyone in Pine Ridge knew.

Later, while Maddie dressed for the prom, Jane Lathem tried to focus and store away every moment of this special day. It was hard to believe that she and Maddie had been together for seven years. And now it was almost over. Maddie would be leaving for college.

If Doctor Evans was right, Jane would be leaving too.

But this was not the day to think about that. This was Maddie's day. Maddie didn't know anything about Doctor Evans's diagnosis. There was no reason for her to know, not for a while yet. Maybe not at all. Maybe the doctor was wrong. Maybe she'd live to see Maddie's college graduation, see her married, grandchildren . . .

Seven years. The time had sped by in what now seemed like an instant. In the very beginning the going had been rough financially. Jane's salary was low, and Maddie—after years of near starvation— was an eager mouth to feed. But Jane did not deny the child anything. She tried hard to make up for the hideousness of Maddie's life before she came to live with Jane, that night after the car had nearly killed her, so long ago.

Jane knew about emotional pain and physical hardship firsthand, having been orphaned herself in her teens, when her parents and brother were killed in a boating accident. Her parents had been in debt, overextended in the small laundry they owned. In the months after their deaths, Jane saw everything she thought she had inherited slip away to settle their estate. She was left with nothing except for her personal belongings and a few mementoes.

Fortunately, being an excellent student, she had been awarded a full scholarship to the University of Pennsylvania. Unfortunately, her luck did not improve beyond that. Jane fell in love, but her boyfriend got her pregnant the first and only time she slept with him. Gerald was on scholarship too, and planning to become a lawyer, which meant six more years of school. He and Jane could not afford to settle down and have a child.

Jane had been raised a Catholic. But there was no choice. If she had the child alone she would be forced to give up her scholarship and dreams of having a good education. Even if she had the child and gave it up for adoption she would miss school and perhaps lose her scholarship. So Gerald raised the money and drove Jane to the squalid two-story house where she submitted to the moral and physical horrors of an illegal abortion, performed by a "doctor" who smoked a cigar while he tormented her uterus.

Afterward Jane felt unbearably guilty. She told Gerald that she could never see him again. And then God punished her for her sin.

Like some other unlucky young women of the time who were forced to have abortions under unsanitary conditions, Jane developed an infection that eventually led to her sterility.

After that, it seemed that every young man Jane dated seriously wanted to get married and have a family. Knowing that she could never provide the family, she always broke up with them, on one pretext or another, never admitting the truth. Then she accepted a teaching job in Green Mountain, where there seemed to be no eligible young men at all. At thirty-four, Jane forsook all hope of ever finding a husband who would accept a barren wife.

Then, miraculously, God had a change of heart and forgave her: Maddie appeared in her life, needing her desperately. Soon after the child moved in with her, which was the very night of the accident, Jane landed a teaching job in another part of the state. Still, she hired a private detective to track down Maddie's mother. It was an expense Jane could barely afford, but she felt that was her obligation. If she had brought in the police they would have taken Maddie away from her, and the courts would have awarded the child to a foster family. Jane was sure they would never have given Maddie to her, a single woman living alone.

After months went by with no trace, Lulu Dragoumis began to fade from Maddie's memory. Finally Jane told the detective to call off the search; she had done her duty and by then could not bear the thought of giving Maddie up. But she lived in terror that one day Lulu Dragoumis would reappear and demand her daughter back. Jane decided that she and Maddie had to leave Pennsylvania for good and go to another part of the country.

On the enthusiastic advice of a friend who had gone to Denver, Jane decided to move to Colorado. It was a healthy place to bring up a child, and the chances of Lulu Dragoumis showing up there were next to none. Jane took night courses to get her Colorado teacher's certificate and got a job in Pine Ridge, a small town north of Pueblo. They rented a stone house by a lake, surrounded by aspen trees and unlimited sky, and at last felt a deep peace settle over their lives.

When they moved from the East, Maddie took the name Lathem and posed as Jane's real daughter. It was easier that way, and no one questioned the relationship. Maddie and Jane were both slim, with brown hair and blue eyes. They *looked* like mother and daughter.

Seven years. Beyond compare, they had been the best seven years of Jane Lathem's life. And if Doctor Evans was right, and they turned out to be the last ones as well, at least she could be grateful to God for the timing. He had kept her together with Maddie while the girl had needed her most.

Now that Maddie was graduating and heading off to college, well . . . if God was ready to call Jane, she would greet Him with a prayer of thanks on her lips.

"Mother? Are you all right? You're staring into the onions."

Jane glanced up, startled, from the chili she was preparing.

Maddie was in the kitchen doorway. Her hair was ironed straight and hung almost to her waist. She was wearing a shocking-pink strapless taffeta gown that she had found in a resale shop in Denver. It had been ankle length, but Maddie had cut it off and refashioned it so that now it billowed out from midthigh. It was the sort of outfit that *Vogue* showed models wearing in New York. Miniskirts for evening were a style that had not heretofore made their debut in Pine Ridge. But Maddie had always been independent of mind and fashion. That's how she made up for not being able to afford the classic clothes that everyone else wore. She simply created her own style, on the limited budget she could afford.

"My goodness, look at you! The dress turned out great. You're beautiful, darling."

Maddie smiled, pleased. "Do you think Tommy will like it?"

"If he doesn't he's either blind or brain dead," Jane snorted. With the corner of her apron she brushed at her eyes. "Onions," she muttered. Then suddenly she gasped. "Oh . . . I almost forgot. Wait right here. I have a present for you."

She ran upstairs and was back in a moment with a small box wrapped in pink tissue paper with a white bow.

"Happy graduation," she said, handing it to Maddie. Her eyes glistened. "I'm so proud of you!"

Maddie kissed Jane, then accepted the box. They had always lived on a tight budget. Maddie knew that Jane could not afford anything expensive. But when she opened the box, she gasped.

"An opal pin!" It was in the shape of a heart. "It's beautiful! I'll wear it tonight. Right here." She pinned it to the waist of her dress. "Oh, it's perfect!"

Jane smiled. "I'm glad you like it. I was really lucky. I unearthed it at the church rummage sale. I took it to the jeweler in town and he cleaned it up for me. The opals are absolutely real, he told me. I know girls don't wear pins very often nowadays. You might want to make it into a pendant sometime."

"Don't start apologizing. I love it just as it is. You know, this is the first real piece of jewelry I've ever owned." Maddie gave her a big hug. "This is the best day of my life . . . next to the day I moved in with you."

By the time summer had ended and Jane had driven Maddie to Boulder to get her settled, Jane knew that she had inoperable cancer. But Maddie was so happy—on the brink of college and dating Tommy Morgan, the local bank president's son—that Jane could never seem to find the right moment to break the news to her. Not telling Maddie seemed to make Jane stronger, and Doctor Evans marveled at her determination.

Maddie had no idea of Jane's condition, except she noticed that Jane had lost weight and seemed to go to church more often than usual. But Maddie thought nothing of it . . . until later.

It happened around Thanksgiving. Doctor Evans called Maddie the day Jane was admitted to the hospital. Maddie was distraught. The doctor was surprised that Maddie still had been told nothing of Jane's condition.

Tommy Morgan drove Maddie to Pine Ridge at once. There she stayed, by Jane's side at the hospital, for fifteen days.

During that time, Jane was sedated and in terrible pain, but she made great effort, in her lucid moments, to help Maddie prepare for the future.

"Work hard at the university," Jane counseled. "No matter what, get your degree. I know you want to be an artist, but a degree's still important. Artists have to eat . . ." Jane closed her eyes from the effort of speaking.

"I'll be fine," Maddie tried to assure her. "Just rest now, and don't worry about me. I mean, I can always marry Tommy. He's going to be a banker like his father."

Jane squeezed Maddie's hand. "Don't marry him . . . unless you're sure it's the right thing to do. Don't give up your dreams."

"Oh, don't worry. I'm going to be famous! You wait and see . . ." Tears welled up in Maddie's eyes. She wanted so badly for Jane to be around to see her become famous. Jane was her family, and her best friend. It didn't seem fair that she had to die now, when there should have been so much time left.

"Oh, Jane . . . how can I thank you for all you've done?"

"Thank me?" Jane whispered. "You don't . . ." she trailed off.

"You know," Maddie swallowed, afraid of the silence, "sometimes I try to imagine what would have happened to me if you hadn't come along when you did that night. Where I would have ended up."

"Do you," Jane struggled to get out the words, "ever think about . . . your real mother?"

Maddie shook her head. "Not really. Except to wonder what happened to her. And out of curiosity, what sort of traits I've inherited from her. A long time ago I used to think about what I'd do if she suddenly appeared and wanted me back." She squeezed Jane's hand. "But I knew the answer, even then. I would've stayed with you. You're my mother now. There's a connection between us as strong as blood." Tears came to her eyes and she sniffed and swallowed quickly so that Jane would not see her cry. But Jane's eyes were closed. She was breathing evenly, asleep.

"A few years ago . . ." Jane said sometime later, after she had dozed a bit, "I took out a life insurance policy. It's in the drawer by my bed at home. You . . . are the beneficiary . . ." She closed her eyes for a few moments, then opened them again. "Promise me, Maddie . . . that you . . . will never spend the money unless you . . . have no other choice. Save it for an emergency. Invest it . . . save it . . ."

"I promise, Mother," Maddie whispered. "I promise."

Jane's eyes drifted shut again, and her light grip on Maddie's hand fell away. She lived several more days, but it was her last conversation with Maddie.

Maddie stayed by Jane's bedside until the end.

The week after Jane Lathem's funeral was spent in a blur of financial legalities, all the inevitable things involved with closing out a life. The hospital bill, fortunately, had been covered by Jane's teachers' group-insurance policy. The life insurance money came to fifteen thousand dollars, and Maddie put it into a savings account at the bank until she could figure out the best way to invest it. Then she slowly, painfully, went through Jane's clothes and belongings. Except for the furniture, some photographs and books, Jane's Timex and some costume jewelry, Maddie donated everything to the Salvation Army. She could not afford to pay storage on the furniture, an ill-matched assortment at best, so she sold the lot of it to an auction house for two hundred dollars.

Once all that had been taken care of, Maddie had to decide what was to happen to Scrappy, her beloved cat, the remainder of her family. Maddie couldn't bear to part with her old friend. On the other hand, she wasn't allowed to keep a pet in the dormitory at school. She thought about sneaking Scrappy in, but the cat loved to roam the outdoors. He would be miserable, confined to a small room with a litter box. One of Jane's friends, an English teacher at the high school, had been taking care of Scrappy during Jane's illness. And so, in the end, Maddie arranged for Ellen Peterson to keep the cat.

"Don't you worry, Scrappy. I'll be back," she promised, hugging him before she left. "I'll come first chance I get."

But even as she was saying it, Maddie knew in her heart that she would never return to Pine Ridge. And perhaps Scrappy knew too, for the cat squirmed in her embrace, jumped down, and walked stiffly away.

Before taking the bus back to Boulder, Maddie walked over to the empty house by the lake and sat on the floor of the vacant living room, quietly trying to assess the impact all this had on her life. If anyone had a reason to cry, she did, abandoned *and* orphaned, but her well of emotions had dried up.

The house had been rented, and a new family would be moving in before Christmas. So fast. It was amazing that someone's entire life could be disposed of so quickly. In scarcely more than three weeks, Jane had gone into the hospital, died, and now there was nothing left of her at all. Except a few photographs and Maddie's memories.

Maddie had been unbelievably strong, all of Jane's friends and associates at school had said so at the funeral. And she had remained strong while she dispassionately handled the details surrounding Jane's death. One thought, though, nagged at her consciousness and would not leave her alone. Not actually a thought: an emotion. And that emotion was not grief, but anger.

Maddie was furious that Jane had not told her she was ill. Everything that Maddie had done at college that autumn mocked her with its triviality as she replayed it against the backdrop of Jane's suffering and slowly dying . . . alone.

"You could've told me, Mother," she said aloud, softly. "You *should* have told me. I could have missed school. I could've missed one lousy semester, to be with you!" The words came louder and faster, tumbling out in anger and frustration. "You always told me to tell the truth. Why couldn't *you* tell the truth? *Why?* Don't you see *you* were important to me? Not school, not— I shared your life, Mother, why couldn't you have let me share your illness?"

Her words seemed loud in the bare room, and she stopped suddenly, feeling guilty and terribly confused.

Maddie got up and walked from room to room in the empty house, almost in a trance. She tried to imagine the new family moving in, what they would be like. In a couple of weeks the house would be full again, decorated for Christmas. New voices would fill the rooms.

The tears came, at first slowly, then in a downpour. Maddie leaned against the kitchen counter and cried and screamed hysterically for over an hour. In her misery, Maddie cried for Jane, for Scrappy, for the empty house.

And for herself, for being left alone again.

3

For the rest of the year at the university, Maddie never seemed to catch hold of the momentum. On the surface things seemed fine. She attended classes, turned in papers on time, maintained an honors average, and continued to go out with Tommy Morgan, the boy she had dated since sophomore year of high school. Inside, however, she felt undefined and dull, as if she were gliding through her life, not living it.

Just before the end of the school year, Maddie broke up with Tommy. It had been coming for months. At Pine Ridge High, the two of them had shared many interests. But at Boulder, Tommy had become totally engrossed in the party scene. Maddie had found, over the long winter, that they had had little to talk about anymore. Their friends were his friends, and she considered them immature. Finally, she realized that she was happier during her time apart from Tommy than with him, and decided to call it quits. When she suggested that they begin seeing other people, Tommy took the news well, so well in fact that Maddie realized that she was no longer what he wanted either. She had changed too. Since Jane's death, she had lost the ability and desire to enjoy herself.

When summer came, the summer of '69, Maddie decided to remain in Boulder to take several business courses, as a practical counterbalance to her major in art. She looked for a part-time job and finally found one that appealed to her: working in a jewelry shop.

It was better than a waitressing job; Maddie had morning classes most days and the shop's hours were from noon to seven. Even though she would make less money than waitressing, she would have more time to study. And, in lieu of higher wages, the shop's owner had agreed to teach her about jewelry design, the area of art that had begun to capture her fancy.

Maddie had loved jewelry since she was a small girl and used to pore over magazines to see how rich people lived. Over the years, for holidays and birthdays, she had almost always made some sort of trinket for Jane to wear. Their first year together, when they had been so poor, Maddie had given Jane a bracelet made of dyed string, masking tape, and feathers plucked from the school janitor's feather duster. Another year she gave Jane a necklace of acrylic-painted safety pins. Maddie loved to collect old beads and rhinestone buttons and string them with unusual things, such as plastic hearts or soldiers out of Cracker Jack boxes. The idea of working in a jewelry store excited her enormously.

The shop's owner and chief designer was a young man named Brady Gardner. Actually, Maddie was not crazy about his designs, although he was a skilled craftsman. His work was too elaborate, she thought, bordering on the tacky. But it was popular, both with the tourists and with a regular local clientele. The shop had a continuous flow of activity.

Brady Gardner's studio was directly behind the shop, connected by a glassed-in walkway filled with English ferns and bougainvillea. Often Maddie would come to the shop early and wander out back to watch Brady work before it was time to open up. By the end of her second week, however, Maddie realized that this was not going to be much of an apprenticeship. Brady Gardner jealously guarded his work. He was too busy to take time to show her even the simplest techniques.

Gardner had an enormous ego about his work. A bachelor at twenty-eight, he also held a high opinion of his looks and sex appeal. Hidden away in the back of a drawer, he kept a secret notebook with the names of all the women he had slept with, beginning at the age of fourteen. It gave him great pleasure to get out the book after each new conquest and enter the name. The last name he had entered was number three hundred, even. He hired Maddie because she was pretty and unattached. Mentally he was already penciling her in as number three hundred and one.

"What are you going to do with this turquoise?" Maddie asked. She had just locked up the shop and had ventured back into Brady's workroom to collect her paycheck.

"Turquoise?" he said with disgust. "Here, *look* at it. It isn't at all like turquoise. It's malachite and azurite, put in a tumbler for two weeks to get that sheen."

"It's pretty," Maddie said, ignoring the insult. "What are you going to do with it?"

"Haven't decided. Mo just brought it to me today, along with some Mexican opals. I have to sit with the stones and see what they say to me. Hey! Don't touch."

"I was only looking."

Brady scooped up the tray of stones and put them into his safe. When he had finished, he looked at Maddie and smiled. "Oh, it's Friday. I guess you want some money."

Maddie nodded.

"Doing anything tonight?" He undid the rubber band of the ponytail that kept his hair out of his way while he worked, and shook his head briskly. His sand-colored mane fell loosely beyond his shoulders.

"Studying. I have a test in accounting in the morning."

"Jesus, don't you ever have fun?"

"Of course. But I have this test." In truth, Maddie couldn't remember the last time she'd enjoyed herself. One's college days were supposed to be a kick, but thus far Maddie had felt the kick only in her backside. The pressure to maintain her grades and her scholarship was always with her.

"You know," Brady said, turning off the light over his worktable, "you're too serious."

Maddie shrugged. "Maybe."

He grabbed his denim jacket from a hook next to the door. "I'm knocking off early tonight. Why don't you let me buy you some dinner. You have to eat."

"No, I don't . . ."

Brady fixed his eyes on her, cajolingly. Maddie had known that it was only a matter of time before he made his move. His friend and gem supplier, Mo Steiner, had warned her about his reputation as a womanizer, but she didn't find him tempting. Brady, with his perfect features and long-lashed blue eyes, was far too good-looking. Maddie did not like men who were prettier than she was. Not that she was bad-looking, with her thick, shiny brown hair that hung below her shoulder blades, and her clear blue eyes, full mouth, straight nose, and high cheekbones. But she wore no makeup, convinced her features were too exaggerated to accentuate them more. Jane, and others, had told her she had the basic potential to be a model. And she did, although she did not believe it.

"I won't take no for an answer," he said.

Well, Maddie thought, *what the hell.* She was hungry. Having a decent meal with Brady Gardner was better than her usual Pepsi and Hershey bar out of the dorm's vending machines. "All right, why not?"

"I love your enthusiasm," he said. "Maybe you should take etiquette instead of accounting."

"Look," Maddie snapped. "I'm tired. I don't need this."

"Need what?"

"Your fucking condescending attitude. You talk to me like that all the time. Like I'm some . . . dumb bimbo! Like you're doing me a favor to even let me work here." She walked past him, out the door and down the pathway that led to the street.

"Hey, wait! I'm sorry." Brady caught up with her. "I was going to take you for pizza. But to apologize, how about a steak and some wine?"

"Let's get one thing straight," Maddie said. "It's just dinner. That's all."

"Hey . . . it's fine with me," Brady said offhandedly. "Dinner is all I want."

Brady took her to a new French restaurant near the university, and insisted she order the chateaubriand, the most expensive item on the menu. He selected a bottle of Nuits-St.-Georges.

"This is very good," Maddie said simply. The wine was far better than any she had ever tasted, but she was afraid of overpraising. She lived in fear of betraying her unworldliness.

Brady glanced around the intimate room, waving to several friends. He was pleased that his pretty employee seemed impressed by the restaurant, and hoped a couple of glasses of wine would loosen her up a bit. He had seldom seen a more uptight nineteen-year-old in his life. There was a real air of self-preservation about her—a guarded resistance to divulging anything of a personal nature.

"Tell me about yourself. The only thing I know is that you want to be an artist. Or maybe a jewelry designer?"

"Maybe. I haven't decided yet."

"Well, tell me your life story. Like, where you come from. What your favorite hobby is. Who you like better—the Beatles or the Stones. Anything you want to lay on me, I'll listen to."

"I don't like to talk about myself," she said truthfully, an old habit that years with Jane had not erased.

"I've noticed." Brady decided to stop trying to make conversation. If she wanted to talk, fine. If not, they'd sit and eat in silence. Maybe he could smoke her out that way. Maddie was an enigma to him; she was intriguing. It made the game more fun.

They sipped their wine in silence. Finally, it occurred to Maddie that Brady really was not going to talk anymore unless she opened up. He wasn't happy merely discussing movies or books or even talking about himself, the way most men seemed to be; he appeared to want to get to know *her.* Of course she knew Brady could not possibly be interested. It was just his form of seduction.

The steak arrived, with pommes frites, and haricots verts sautéed in garlic. Maddie dug in hungrily. She had never been to such an expensive restaurant before, and she knew this meal would cost Brady a lot of money. In spite of what she thought of him, he was making an effort. There was no point in acting shitty because he had a reputation as a ladykiller.

All Brady had asked her to do was talk about herself. An innocent enough request. Except she couldn't do it. Telling about her past seemed more intimate and embarrassing to Maddie than stripping off her clothes in a public place.

Suddenly, she had an inspiration.

"Well, I guess I have to tell you sometime. It might as well be now," Maddie said, after she had bolted half of her steak. "My father died in prison. For being a spy. He was a scientist at Los Alamos, and I don't know what happened, really. He wrote me a letter from prison one time, swearing he was innocent, that he was framed."

She ate a few pommes frites and took another sip of her wine. The waiter came over and refilled her glass. "My mother was humiliated. We moved to Los Angeles and changed our name. We started a new life. She married a movie producer and had four more children. I'm kind of an embarrassment. When she sees me, it reminds her of my father."

Maddie looked into Brady's eyes. It was going well. She could tell that he believed every word. It was so easy. And so much fun, to make Brady think she was baring her soul to him. But he was being nice to her, and lying like this, easy as it was, made her as uncomfortable as telling the truth. Of course, if he found out she was lying, what difference did it make? He probably lied to women all the time.

Except it made a difference to her.

"No . . . I just made all that up. I'm an orphan . . . that's the truth. And I really don't like talking about it," Maddie smiled, self-consciously. "My favorite hobby is reading. And I like the Stones."

Brady put his hand over hers. "I like you, Maddie. You really are different."

Maddie did not, true to her word, go home and sleep with Brady Gardner that night after dinner. But after that evening, Brady's attitude toward her began to change. He became kinder at work. He was no longer abrupt when he was busy. He took her out to eat fairly often, after work. He even began to instruct her in the lost-wax method of jewelry making. Finally—three weeks after their first date —Maddie decided it was time to let him seduce her.

Maddie was not a virgin. She had slept with Tommy Morgan for the first time when she was a junior in high school. By the time they had broken up, it was as if they were an old married couple. Most of the nights they had spent together during the last semester had been merely to sleep.

The truth was, Maddie did not like sex. She didn't hate it. She wasn't repulsed. She just did not think it was all it was cracked up to be.

That was why she had not been anxious to go to bed with Brady, even after she began to find him more attractive. Finally, though, she knew she had to deliver. She could not expect to dine out with him forever without eventually picking up what was clearly expected to be her share of the tab. Besides, and more important, she was getting valuable instruction from him in jewelry design.

And so Maddie felt it was time to give him her body.

"Here . . ." Brady said, handing her the joint. "Want another toke?" It was a hot evening, and they were lying on a mattress on the screened-in porch of his house.

Maddie shook her head. "If I mellow out any more, I'm afraid I'll fall asleep."

Brady tossed the joint in the ashtray and leaned over and kissed her. "We certainly don't want that to happen. At least not now."

"You know, Brady, you've turned into a pretty decent guy."

"Jesus, listen to the way she hands out compliments. I meant it about etiquette school." He reached out and smoothed her straight, long brown hair with his hand. "I really do like you just the way you are. I never know what to expect. I think I'm falling in love."

"Oh, Brady . . . please. I'll sleep with you. But not if you tell me you love me. I know your reputation. I've heard about that little notebook with all the names."

Brady sat up, annoyed. "What? How? Have you been snooping?"

"Mo Steiner told me. One day he was in the shop and things were quiet. We started talking. He warned me about getting involved with you."

"Mo? That fucker. Jesus! I thought he was a friend."

"Don't tell him I said anything! He was just trying to be brotherly with me."

"He was just trying to put the make on you," Brady said. "Jesus, you can't trust anyone these days."

"Least of all you," Maddie smiled, unbuttoning her blouse. She could no longer remember much about her real mother, but her large breasts were Lulu's greatest gift to her. Maddie's face was prettier, but her body was identical to Lulu's . . . thin everywhere except for her breasts. Maddie, embarrassed when she developed so quickly in the eighth grade, had always tended to wear loose clothing to conceal her body.

"Hey . . . I'm as nice a guy as you're ever likely to find," he said. Then Maddie, without fanfare, took off her loose-fitting blouse and skirt. "Oh my God, your body is outta sight."

Brady quickly undressed, and when Maddie got her first look at him, she whistled. "You're not so bad yourself. I mean . . . you're so big. It's funny, I wouldn't have guessed. You're kind of skinny, and short . . ."

"God, who *did* teach you to deliver compliments?" He reached out for her. "Come here, Maddie, I've wanted to do this since I first saw you."

They made love intensely the first time; and then again more slowly, until daybreak. Brady took his time with her, coaxing her to relax and let go of her inhibitions. He found pleasure points in her body that she had never known existed. She came for the first time in her life and discovered that sex *was* what it was cracked up to be.

Poor Tommy Morgan. After being with him, in and out was what Maddie had thought it was all about.

Anna McNeill had red hair, an acerbic wit, and white skin dotted with freckles. Even with freckles she managed to look glamorous and not cute. She was from New York City and had more clothes, more *expensive* clothes, than anyone else in the class of '72 at the University of Colorado. She had been very popular in the dorm the previous year, but Maddie had never liked her—possibly because Anna and her clique did not pay any attention to Maddie, who kept to herself studying most of the time.

And so Maddie was surprised, when she looked up from her desk one evening, to see Anna McNeill standing in the doorway.

"Hello, Maddie," she said. Her accent was Eastern preppie. "It seems we're in the same boat."

"Hmmm?"

"Both our roommates got knocked up over the summer. So I was wondering if you want to share my room with me. It's a corner one . . . bigger and brighter than this."

"I don't think so," Maddie said. "I'm all settled in . . . and I don't even know you. We might not like each other."

Anna broke into a smile and seemed instantly easier to like. "The girls told me you were blunt. But I like that. I mean, people should always say what they really think. Most people don't." She pulled a pack of Marlboros out of the breast pocket of the Brooks Brothers shirt that belonged to her boyfriend. "Mind if I smoke?"

"No."

"Want one?"

"I don't smoke. My mother died of cancer."

"Oh . . ." Anna said, blowing out the match before she lit her cigarette. "Golly . . . I didn't know. I'm sorry."

"You can smoke, if you want," Maddie said. "It wasn't lung cancer."

Anna started laughing. "You're amazing. You don't say anything expected. I think I'm going to like you. What about it? My room? They're going to make me share it with somebody; it's too big for one. I mean, Harriet Jackson's dying to move in, but she's such a cow." She put her hand over her mouth. "Oh God, that's not nice." She went over and sat on Maddie's bed. "You see? Being around you is going to be good for me. I was brought up to always say the perfect thing . . . no matter what you're thinking. It's so hypocritical."

"So you figure I might be better than Harriet, even though you don't know me?"

"Well, all last year I'd look at you and think, she's so attractive. Or at least she could be . . . with some makeup and maybe a few blond streaks in her hair."

"I don't think you need blunt lessons. You're doing fine," Maddie said straight-faced. And then she laughed, in spite of herself. "Okay, I'll go look at your room. But I have to warn you . . . I might move out before the end of the semester. My boyfriend wants me to live with him."

"Well, I spend a lot of weekends with *my* boyfriend. Long weekends. He's a senior at Princeton."

"Princeton? That's kind of a long drive, isn't it?"

"Well, Daddy has a business jet that I use. Maybe you'd like to come to Princeton sometime. Randy can fix you up. Unless you're madly in love."

Maddie shook her head. "I don't know. I can't decide." She told Anna briefly about Brady. "All right," she said finally, "let's go check out your room. It might work. I've always wanted one of those corner rooms. One thing though, I'm here on a full scholarship . . . I study a lot."

Anna laughed. "Well, I suppose I can live with that. *My* grades are awful. But you can leave the light on all night, if you want. I can sleep through anything."

"Don't you care about getting a good education?"

Anna seemed taken aback. "Well, yes, but college is to have fun. I mean, I don't want to come off as really spoiled, but I'm not really going to have to work afterward. Randy and I'll probably get married and . . . Oh God, I sound like a total nerd."

Maddie smiled. "Well, I guess there's nothing wrong with not having to work for a living. It's just not in the cards for me."

"It's not as if I won't have a career," Anna said defensively, "but what I want to do doesn't pay much. I'm going to work with retarded kids. I'm majoring in Abnormal Psych. My youngest brother, David, was born severely brain-damaged. He's in an institution."

"Oh. I'm sorry."

"Yeah, it really devastated Mummie," Anna said. "I don't think she's ever recovered. She wanted to keep David at home . . . but there was no way. He'd require constant attention. Daddy convinced her that she'd be taking away from the rest of us if she tried to do it. But sometimes I think Mummie regrets her decision."

"Do you regret it?" Madeleine asked.

"Heavens no," Anna replied. "David's in terrible shape. I want to work with children who have . . . *hope*. You don't think that's callous of me, do you? I mean, you have to start somewhere."

Maddie nodded in agreement.

"So . . . what about it?" Anna asked. "Sharing my room?"

"Well, I guess so . . . if you're sure you want me."

"Yes, I'm quite sure," Anna said. "I think we might even become friends. And we're about the same size. You're welcome to borrow any of my clothes. Mummie sends me new shipments every month."

Maddie smiled. "A bigger room and a new wardrobe. I'll go get my stuff."

Maddie was happy that fall and felt special. She and Anna McNeill not only became friends, they were inseparable, except when Maddie was with Brady and Anna was off for her long weekends at Princeton.

Anna was the kind of girl that Maddie had fantasized about as a child—sophisticated, beautiful, intelligent. Of course, Maddie was already intelligent. After Anna finished playing Pygmalion, teaching her new makeup tricks, Maddie was also beautiful. Maddie figured the sophistication would come eventually, if she hung around her new best friend long enough.

As she got to know Anna better, Maddie learned that a great deal of Anna's outer sophistication was merely a protective shell. She was tremendously close to her family and idolized her handsome father, Wyatt McNeill. Anna kept a photograph of the two of them in a silver art deco frame on her desk, and she had long conversations with him on the phone several times a week.

47

Maddie was evasive when it came to talking about herself. Around Anna she knew she could hold her own in terms of wit and intelligence, but her background was not up to snuff. Anna was always talking about who people were, their breeding. Maddie was forced to face up to the fact that she lacked the sort of breeding Anna and her friends had. If Jane Lathem hadn't stepped into her life, there'd be no telling *where* she'd be now. Certainly not sharing a room at the University of Colorado with the wealthy Anna McNeill. And so she said as little as possible to Anna about her past.

Maddie's relationship with Brady Gardner continued smoothly that fall. As far as she could tell, the great womanizer was being faithful to her. After moving past their initial impressions of one another they had become friends, as well as lovers.

Everything remained perfect with Brady until Anna invited Maddie to spend Christmas in New York with her family. Maddie was ecstatic. She had never been to New York, even though she knew it was where she wanted to live when she finished school. But she felt a bit torn. Earlier in the fall she had vaguely agreed to spend the holidays with Brady.

Ultimately the idea of turning down Anna's invitation—and the chance to fly to New York in Mr. McNeill's private Gulfstream jet— was unthinkable. When Maddie broke the news to Brady he was predictably furious. Assuming that they were spending the holidays together, he had arranged to rent a deluxe condominium in Aspen.

"Brady," Maddie sheepishly tried to explain, "you've just got to understand. I'm *really* sorry. But this is such a great opportunity for me."

"Understand?" he shouted, losing his temper with her for the first time. "Fuck you! I thought we were going to spend Christmas together. I had the whole trip planned. Doesn't that mean anything to you?"

"Yes, I told you I'm sorry." She went over and put her arms around him, but he turned away sulkily. "I really am. But, I mean, we never made *definite* plans. You sort of assumed I'd spend Christmas with you when I said I didn't have any plans . . ." "Look . . . let's go to Aspen for semester break. Oh, Brady, *please* don't be angry. You told me your family wanted you to visit them. Now you can. You're lucky to have a family that cares about you."

Brady, his feelings hurt, wheeled around to face her. "You really are something else. What, I'm not sure, although a few names come to mind." He stared at her. "You know, Maddie, I really loved you. I was even going to ask you to marry me."

"Oh, Brady, I *care* about you a lot. But you're turning this all into such a big issue. It's *only* Christmas."

"Fuck you, Maddie. You're one fucked-up person."

"Shit, Brady. I'm not fucked up because I want to spend Christmas in New York. It's the first time in my life I've gotten a chance to go there. I mean . . . *New York!*"

"You don't even hear what you're saying, do you? How could you love me and act like this? I've spent all these months patiently teaching you about jewelry making, and you've never once thanked me. You *take*, Maddie, but you don't give," he said quietly. "This is it. I don't want to see you when you come back. There's no point."

"Oh, Brady . . ."

"Get the hell out of here, will you? I've got work to do."

Brady turned away and began setting an amethyst cabochon into a silver ring setting. There was nothing else she could say to him now. Brady was angry, but he'd get over it. She would bring him a nice present from New York. In a few weeks, after he had cooled off, everything would be back to normal, she was sure of it.

On the walk back to her dormitory, Maddie replayed their argument in her mind, allowing herself her turn to get angry. Brady was wrong about her. How could he say she took but never gave? How dare he, a man who had slept with hundreds of women?

Then she thought about the past months with Brady. He had shown her jewelry-making techniques and patiently explained gemstones to her. He had lent her books to read. He had taken her out to dinner two or three times a week, or cooked for her at home. He quizzed her before tests. In fact, Brady Gardner had not acted at all like the man she had been warned about. On the contrary, he had shared every aspect of himself with her.

Could Brady actually have been right? Did she take more than she gave? Had she, since Jane's death, without realizing it, become afraid of loving again? Somewhere Maddie had read that in every relationship one person loves more than the other. Certainly Brady loved her more.

49

Would Maddie ever release her guard enough to give herself completely to anyone?

She was sure she would eventually. But at this point she was not ready to worry about that. Maddie was going to see New York City for the first time in her life.

And that was all she cared about.

The dining room of the Wyatt McNeills' rambling duplex on Park Avenue in the seventies was painted buttercup yellow. The color had been chosen by Elizabeth O'Hara McNeill's decorator—an Englishman who also dabbled in color therapy—for its reputed ability to stimulate conversation. A perfect choice, since the McNeills were lavish and frequent hosts to a coterie of friends from business to society to the arts, who had scaled the heights of Manhattan's summits. Twenty-four Sheraton-style Regency chairs—covered in a Chinese floral brocade—flanked three round mahogany dining tables. Over each hung a Russian rock-crystal chandelier that bathed the room with romantic, simulated candlelight. An eight-paneled Ming Dynasty folding screen covered the wall at the far end of the room. The china, which changed according to the guests and mood of the evening, was always Tiffany, the crystal and silver, heirloom Irish, from Elizabeth McNeill's family.

Maddie could not believe that she was there, sitting with the McNeills at the centermost table, looking at Anna across an arrangement of flowers so exotic she had never even seen pictures of them before, much less heard their names. An air of unreality surrounded it all. After the first day of being nervous and on guard, however, she had begun to relax under the family's unpretentiousness. She was Anna's new best friend, and they treated her accordingly.

Through the windows that overlooked the avenue, Maddie kept stealing glances at the blizzard that raged outside in the glow of the city's street lamps. Perfection. Everything was more ideal than Maddie had imagined it would be.

"See . . ." Anna gloated as if she herself had arranged for the snow, "I told you we'd have a white Christmas. In honor of Maddie."

"Then let's drink a toast to Anna." Hadley McNeill, Anna's younger brother, raised his glass. "To the McNeill family's chief meteorologist."

"We're having a special treat tonight, Maddie. Roast pheasant," Anna said, pointedly ignoring her brother. "Daddy shot it upstate somewhere."

"I've never had pheasant," Maddie said.

"It's okay," Hadley said. "Tastes like chicken."

"Isn't that what they say about everything? Rattlesnake and all that?"

Hadley nodded. "The only thing that doesn't taste like chicken these days is chicken. They pump it so full of chemicals."

"Oh, please, darling, let's not get into all that," Elizabeth McNeill said. "At least not while we're eating."

"But Mother, this is the perfect time to talk about it!" Hadley argued. "What better opportunity to discuss how we're being slowly murdered by what we put in our bodies? Nader eats only cantaloupe. It's the only thing with skin thick enough that chemicals can't seep through."

Hadley was a freshman at Yale. Over the previous summer he had done volunteer work for Ralph Nader. Although he had not actually been one of "Nader's Raiders," and indeed had never met the man, the summer had convinced Hadley to devote his life to saving the environment.

"Yes, yes, Hadley . . . we know all about it. And we agree. But," Wyatt McNeill said, anxious to avoid one of his son's inevitable diatribes on the rape of the land by big business, "I want to talk to our houseguest."

McNeill turned to Maddie. It was hard for her to realize that someone's father could be so attractive and youthful. The fathers she knew back in Pine Ridge were thick around the middle and looked older than they probably were. Was it living in Manhattan or being so rich that made Anna's father different, Maddie wondered.

"Elizabeth tells me you want to be a jewelry designer, Madeleine," he said. The McNeills, with the exception of Anna, had insisted on addressing her as Madeleine ever since she arrived. "Such a beautiful name," Anna's mother had said. "Let's *use* it!"

"Yes. Going around Tiffany's and Cartier and Harry Winston . . . it was like being hit by lightning," Maddie exclaimed. "Suddenly, I had no more doubts. I *am* going to be a jewelry designer."

"Hear! Hear!" Elizabeth McNeill said. She was a beautiful woman, also incredibly young-looking, with the same red hair as Anna, cut very short by Vidal Sassoon. Her skin was porcelain clear; there was no sign of makeup, except for mascara and lipstick. "I'm all for that. And of course when you're famous you'll give us all discounts."

"Of course," Maddie laughed. "And thank you again for showing me all the stores. This was one of the most exciting days of my whole life. Fifth Avenue is even more elegant than I imagined. And the Christmas tree at Rockefeller Center, with the ice skaters dancing below! I've seen postcards of it, but I never dreamed it would be so dazzling."

"I loved taking you around," Elizabeth said. "Anna's bored with all that, has been for years. I guess it comes from growing up in the city." She lit a cigarette. "I was born and raised in Shaker Heights, Ohio. And I think Manhattan will send a thrill through me till my dying day."

"Yes . . . that's exactly what I felt! *Thrills.* The energy—the *glamour*—of Manhattan is unbelievable."

"Well, it's good to hear you're not disappointed," Wyatt McNeill said as the butler cleared away the soup course, "New York gets so much bad press these days."

"Oh no, I love it here."

"I'm glad." Wyatt McNeill paused. "Madeleine . . . Anna hasn't told us much about you. You grew up in Colorado?"

Maddie felt a sudden panic. She had invented a bit of a story for Anna. Nothing elaborate . . . but Anna's impeccable credentials had made her feel like such a hick. And, after all, she was an orphan; there was no one to dispute anything she made up.

"Well . . . my father was a ski instructor . . . a fantastic skier. He would have been a medalist in the Olympics . . . but he broke his leg . . ." She trailed off. Her head felt light. She reached slowly for her water glass, raised it to her lips, and took several swallows.

"Madeleine," Elizabeth said with concern, "Are you all right?"

"It's just . . . I'm sorry, I feel a bit dizzy." Her cheeks burned, and her stomach was doing little flips. She had come clean with Brady, but somehow the idea of telling the McNeills the truth was unthinkable.

And yet, Anna's family had treated her with such warmth and generosity. How could she lie to them? Some instinct in Maddie told her that *this* was where her real life would lie—in the polished wood and marble of Manhattan with people like the McNeills, not with Brady in a little Colorado shop with a studio in back. A tissue of lies here was something serious that she would have to live and deal with for a long time to come. She could not bear to tell them the truth, but she was terrified to go on lying. Maddie opened her mouth, and even she did not know what was going to come out.

But it was Elizabeth McNeill's voice that she heard, not her own.

"You poor thing, you're shaking." Anna's mother came and put an arm around Maddie and helped her from the table. "I do hope it's not the flu. I'll bet you're just exhausted. Hadley, dear, go ask Lucille to send up a cup of tea. Come along now, let's get you to bed, Madeleine." Gratefully, Maddie let herself be mothered. She felt deeply ashamed to be counterfeiting for these people who had shown her nothing but kindness. At the same time, she felt a tremendous strength-robbing sense of relief. It was as if she had received an eleventh-hour pardon on death row from the governor. She was safe this time.

She might not always be so lucky.

As it turned out, Maddie spent the next week, including Christmas Day, in bed with the recurring fever and chills of an honest-to-goodness flu. The McNeills showered her with attention, coming in to chat or read to her, bringing her books, nursing her first with tea and toast and later, as her strength returned, with tempting goodies from the kitchen. Madeleine loved being treated as part of the family; she felt a real sense of belonging.

By New Year's Eve, Maddie was herself again. To bring in the year 1970, Anna and her boyfriend, Randy Ferguson, fixed Maddie up with Randy's Princeton roommate. His name was Win Burgess. Win had a girlfriend, Anna explained, but she was spending the holidays in Gstaad. Maddie did not care. She was so in love with New York that she did not yearn for additional romance.

The four of them—Anna and Randy, Maddie and Win—started out

the evening at a dance at the Plaza, given by one of Anna's childhood friends. After the New Year was ushered in, they became bored and headed downtown to hear some jazz at the Village Vanguard. By that time, they had gone through four bottles of champagne.

The others seemed accustomed to drinking so much, but Maddie was not. Her light-headedness turned into fuzzy-headedness, and she wished she could go home to bed. But it was not very late, and Win Burgess was putting the make on her. At midnight, when they were still at the Plaza, he had kissed her passionately. He had continued to try to kiss her during the long cab ride downtown. Now his hand was trying to snake up her thigh, under the table at the jam-packed, smoky Vanguard. She kept pushing Win's hand away and he kept putting it back. But, other than physically, Win made absolutely no effort to relate to her.

Maddie did not like anything about Win. In fact, she would have much preferred spending New Year's Eve alone with a good book. But here she was, trying to sneak glances at her watch to see how much longer she had to endure.

"Win," Maddie said, removing his hand once again, "when are you going to start taking the hint?"

"It's New Year's . . . come on," he put his arm around her shoulders. "Get in the spirit. I thought Western girls were wide open," he chuckled. "I really like you . . ."

"No, you don't. We haven't anything in common. You've hardly bothered to say three sentences all evening."

"How can we have a conversation over this noise? We'll talk later, baby . . . when we're alone. But now we have to party. Hey . . . waiter!" he called out. "Hit us with another bottle of the good stuff."

Over the holidays, Maddie had begun to discover that, while she loved Anna and the McNeills, she was not taken with Randy or any of Anna's other friends. They were sophisticated in that they dressed expensively and went to all the right restaurants and discos, but they seemed so inbred. Maddie was made to feel—and she knew it was not her imagination—like the outsider she was. Anna's New York friends had all known each other forever, it seemed. They were always referring to past shared escapades, and to prep schools Maddie had never heard of, such as Kent, Madeira, Choate, Exeter, and St. Paul's. Anna, to her credit, tried valiantly to keep bringing Maddie into conversations, but Randy wanted to monopolize Anna. And they all drank so much.

After another glass of champagne, Maddie's tongue felt swollen and she had trouble getting out even the simplest sentence. She felt dizzy and knew that she could not last much longer. How could the others drink like this and not feel it, she wondered? They certainly acted fine. Anna and Randy were holding hands and gazing lovingly into each other's eyes. Win's hand continued to wander up under Maddie's short sequined skirt. Maddie kept her own hand poised to fend off attack.

Maddie looked around at the other tables. Everyone was having a wonderful time. She was spending New Year's Eve with a drip who treated her like a piece of meat. She thought longingly of Brady and wished she were with him tonight, the two of them alone together in Aspen. It was two hours earlier in Colorado. If she got home soon there would still be time to call and wish him a happy New Year.

"Listen," she told Win, speaking with an effort to sound normal. "I really don't want to spoil anyone's fun, but I don't feel well. I think I'm going to head back to Anna's."

"But I want to stay and hear the next set," Win said. "Here." He grabbed the bottle of champagne out of the cooler and poured some into her glass. "Have some more."

"No, really . . . I've got to get out of here! *You* don't have to leave. I'm perfectly capable of making it home by myself."

"No," Win blinked. "I'll take you." He pushed his chair back and threw a hundred-dollar bill on the table. "This'll cover me," he told Randy. "Maddie and I are going."

"Oh . . . is everything okay?" Anna asked.

"Sure. I'm just tired. I'll see you later," Maddie said.

Out on the Avenue of the Americas an icy wind blew into their faces.

"Really," Maddie said, "you go back inside. I'll be fine. I just want to go to bed."

"Sounds good to me," Win leered, putting an arm around her and waving in vain at a passing off-duty taxi.

"No, Win. Just me." But if he heard, he did not seem to pay much attention.

All the cabs that headed uptown, however, were packed with

merrymakers. Maddie and Win waited for fifteen or twenty minutes and then began walking uptown. Around Fourteenth Street a cab pulled up to the curb to let somebody off and they grabbed it.

By that time, from the walk and the bracing cold air, Maddie's head had begun to feel clearer. Her mind raced to think of ways to get rid of Win when they got to Anna's. She knew that, having brought her uptown, he would insist on being invited in. He was already warming up in the cab, nuzzling and groping and burrowing with hands that, like sharks, seemed obliged to keep moving or die.

"Boy, what a great pair of tits," he murmured in champagne-induced rapture. Irritably she pushed his hands away, for the hundredth time that evening.

"Win, dammit, I said *stop!*" she hissed. But Win feinted low, a hand sneaking suddenly up to the dry coolness of her panties; and then, when she went to defend this position, he pawed triumphantly again at her bosom.

She parried as best she could, embarrassed to scream at him as she would have liked to, because of the driver. Finally, the cab turned the corner onto Park Avenue and slowed to a stop in front of Anna's building. Maddie opened the door quickly and jumped out.

"You keep the cab and go back downtown. I can see myself in from here. Good night, Win," she said briskly, slamming the cab door in his face and rushing inside, past the doorman who could not move fast enough for her.

When she had walked through the lobby to the elevator, she looked back outside through the glass doors. The cab was still sitting there. Win was obviously trying to decide whether to let her get away with the brush-off. Finally, leaning forward, he said something to the driver and the cab pulled away.

Maddie knew that Win was furious, but she could not care less. There was no chemistry between them, no spark of basic friendship. Why go through all the motions when they meant nothing to each other? In the stuffy elevator, the claustrophobic sick feeling returned. By the time the elevator man opened the door to the McNeills' hall, Maddie could barely keep from retching.

The key. She didn't have it; Anna did. She'd have to ring the bell and wake someone. Ordinarily, rather than do that she would have sat in the chair in the vestibule and waited for Anna. But now she was desperate to get to the bathroom. She pushed the buzzer and waited.

No one answered. After another minute, she rang the bell again, more insistently.

Wyatt McNeill finally opened the door, looking sleepy, in a silk paisley robe. "Why, Madeleine! Where's Anna? Is everything all right?" He stood aside to let her enter.

"Yes. It's just that I felt bad and left early . . ."

Maddie dashed across the hall toward the stairs. Wyatt McNeill was in her wake, to help her. Before she could reach the first step, nausea overtook her.

She threw up on the marble floor, in front of him. It was the most embarrassing moment of her life.

By then Elizabeth McNeill was heading barefooted down the stairs.

"Oh dear. Too much champagne, I imagine . . . on top of the flu. Let me get you upstairs and into a bath, Madeleine. Wyatt dear, wake Emory and have him mop the hall."

"No, I'll handle it. You look after Madeleine."

"Oh, I'm so sorry," Maddie managed to say.

"Don't try to talk. Let's get you into a hot tub," Elizabeth McNeill said. "Now, take hold of the bannister . . ."

Later, after she had thrown up again, soaked in a hot bath, and Elizabeth McNeill had tucked her into bed—between cool linen sheets—Maddie began to feel better.

"Thank you. I'm so sorry," she kept saying to Mrs. McNeill.

"Don't worry. It happens to everybody, at least once in their life. Those kids drink far too much. It bothers me about Anna, but she gets mad when I say something to her. You just aren't used to the pace, thank God. You're lucky," she said. "Now, close your eyes and get some sleep. You'll feel fine tomorrow."

Maddie nodded. How could she face Wyatt McNeill in the morning? She wished she could talk to Brady. But it was too late to call him now.

A little later, Maddie came out of her heavy sleep long enough to notice that the room was bright. She opened her eyes, shielding them with her hand. The light was on. Anna was standing naked in front of her dresser, looking through her drawers.

"Hi," Maddie said huskily. "You're home."

Anna turned around, startled. "Oh! Yeah, I'm having trouble find-ing my nightgown. The black lace one." Her words sounded slurred.

"It's on the hook behind the bathroom door. I saw it earlier."

"Oh, yeah," she hiccuped and stumbled into the bathroom, to get ready for bed. Maddie forced herself to stay awake while her friend brushed her teeth and removed her makeup. Finally, Anna weaved back into the room.

"Did you have fun? I'm sorry about leaving like that," Maddie said.

"Win was furious," Anna giggled. "But that's okay. He's just used to women falling all over him. He'll live." She came over and stood by Maddie's four-poster bed. "Are you ready to see something?" she asked with vinous drama.

"Sure . . . what?"

Anna stuck out her left hand and wiggled her ring finger. "Look!"

On her finger was a three- or four-carat, marquise-cut emerald, flanked by small diamonds. "Randy just gave it to me," Anna said breathlessly, sinking onto the bed beside Maddie. "We're engaged!"

"Oh, Anna!" Maddie gave her friend a big hug. "I can't believe it!" As Anna gushed on about Randy's proposal—in the hansom cab he had hired to bring them uptown from the Village—a feeling of ap-prehension settled in the pit of Maddie's stomach.

"When do you think you'll get married?" she asked, trying to muster enthusiasm.

"Oh, we've figured it all out. Summer. Probably August. It'll take that long to get everything arranged." She threw her arms around Maddie. "Oh, isn't it *too* exciting!"

"Yes, it's . . . fabulous," Maddie smiled. "I'm so happy for you."

Of course Maddie was not happy for Anna. This meant that after the next semester Maddie would be losing her roommate and best friend. And she hated the idea that Anna was actually marrying Randy Ferguson. Anna was too good for him, Maddie thought, and too intelligent. She had the money, and the ability, to do something far more worthwhile with her life than organize charity balls.

But, for once, Maddie kept her mouth shut.

The next morning, New Year's Day, Maddie woke around nine with an overpowering headache. She brushed her teeth, took an aspirin, and then settled back woozily in her bed with a copy of *War and Peace*. Anna was still sound asleep. Maddie did not want to go downstairs and have to face Wyatt and Elizabeth McNeill, after having woken them up and puked right in front of them.

The aspirin began to work its miracle, and she read and dozed for several hours. Anna did not stir. Finally, around noon, there was a light tap on the bedroom door. Maddie went and opened it.

"Oh, you're up! Good." Elizabeth McNeill said. "Are you feeling better?"

"Yes," Maddie whispered, "but Anna's still asleep."

Elizabeth swept by Maddie. "Well, she has to get up. We have brunch at the Madisons'. We're due there at one. Darling," she shook Anna. "It's time." She turned back to Maddie. "Well, have you heard the news? Anna woke us when she came in."

Maddie forced herself to smile. "Yes! Isn't it wonderful!"

"Oh God, Mother," Anna groaned. "I don't want to go to Aunt Franny's today. I'm too exhausted."

"You have to. As your godmother, Franny'll be devastated if you don't tell her about the engagement yourself. Come on now, shake a leg."

The brunch they were heading off to was to be given by Peter and Frances Madison. Frances Madison, besides being Elizabeth McNeill's best friend and Anna's godmother, was the famous Broadway actress, Frances Barry. Maddie had been looking forward to the party, to meeting the famous actress in her own home. Now, however, after last night, she did not feel as if she could face anyone at all.

"Er, Mrs. McNeill? I still don't feel well and I . . . I wondered if I could stay here while you go to the brunch. Would that be all right?"

"Of course, dear," Elizabeth said. "You must be sick to death of meeting all these new people. I'm afraid if you get hungry you'll have to fend for yourself. Everyone has the day off."

"Oh, that's okay. You don't mind, do you, Anna?"

Anna had roused herself and was now rummaging through her closet. "I'm only going for a few minutes myself. Just long enough to show Franny my ring. Then I have to meet Randy at the Carlyle for drinks with his father and stepmother, to tell them the news." She smiled at Maddie. Her skin was pale but otherwise she showed no aftereffect from all the champagne she consumed the night before. "You know, I think getting married is going to be the most exhausting thing I've ever done."

After everyone left for the party, Maddie stayed upstairs to read another chapter of her book. Then, feeling better and hungry, she decided to go and fix herself a sandwich. It was fun having the elegant, fifteen-room apartment to herself for a few hours, being able to pretend that it belonged to her.

Heading downstairs to the kitchen, she was startled for a moment to hear voices, then realized that they were merely coming from the television. She turned and headed for the library to turn off the set. As she entered, she jumped back with a surprised, "Oh!"

Wyatt McNeill was stretched out on the beige suede sofa, drinking a beer and watching a football game.

"Oh! I thought you went to the party!" Maddie exclaimed. "You scared me."

"I backed out at the last minute. Peter loathes football, so I knew I wouldn't get to see the game there. My alma mater's playing in the Rose Bowl." He indicated the vacant wing chair next to the sofa. "Care to join me?"

Maddie shook her head. "I . . . if it's all right . . . I was going to make myself a sandwich."

"Good idea. Make me one too, would you? Anything with plenty of mayonnaise, and lettuce." He held up his empty beer bottle. "And I could use another one of these."

Maddie went to the kitchen, feeling very uncomfortable. She had hoped to avoid a solo confrontation with Wyatt McNeill, not merely because of last night. She always felt ill at ease around him. She wasn't sure whether it was something to do with Wyatt himself, or fathers in general, never having had one herself.

And there was always the fear, whenever she found herself one-on-one with any of the McNeills, that the intimacy would encourage more questions about her background.

Maddie had already gotten in deeper than she liked. They knew her parents were dead. She had buried the ski instructor father in an avalanche in Switzerland late one night in a conversation with Anna. About her mother, Jane, she had been more factual, telling Anna that she had died of cancer, but managing to convey the impression that it had happened in a special sanitarium for musicians.

She knew Anna had passed this information along, and she hoped it would get her through the holidays. She did not have any more details ready.

After a thorough search of the kitchen, Maddie located a loaf of rye bread in the pantry and made sandwiches out of leftover roast beef. She found a jar of dill pickles in the refrigerator, and a bag of potato chips hidden away in a cabinet. Piling it all onto a tray, along with two imported beers, she headed back to the library.

"I hope roast beef's okay."

"Terrific. Great, you brought pickles. I love pickles," Wyatt said. "Here, have a seat." He swung his legs off the sofa and sat up.

Maddie took a seat, piled potato chips onto her plate, and pretended to take an interest in the game. "So who's playing?"

"Southern Cal and Michigan . . . my team. We're not doing well. Nearly halftime. Yep, there's the buzzer." He pushed a button on the remote control and muted the set. "This hits the spot, Madeleine. Thanks."

"Look, I'm really embarrassed about last night. I've never drunk so much that I've gotten sick before. I don't drink much at all, actually. Please forgive me."

"There's nothing to forgive. It's part of growing up," Wyatt laughed. "We're all human."

Maddie was starting to relax. Wyatt McNeill acted more like a person than a father. Maddie liked him, in spite of the initial awkwardness she had felt. "I guess you're happy about Anna," she said.

Wyatt shrugged. "Randy's a good enough kid. Good family. But Anna's twenty. I had hoped she'd finish school before she got married."

"Well, she told me this morning that they have it all worked out. She's going to transfer to Barnard while Randy goes to graduate business school at Columbia."

"Good. I'd hate for her to quit school."

They ate in silence for a few moments. Then Maddie said, "Do you mind if I ask you a personal question?"

"Of course not," Wyatt said. "Shoot."

"What is it exactly that you do . . . for a living? I mean, Anna's always so vague about it."

Wyatt McNeill laughed. "I used to have a full-time law practice. Now I'm a deal maker. I put people together, and if it works out, I take a percentage of the business. I travel a lot, all over the world."

"Well," Maddie said, "it sounds interesting." She smiled. "Not that I really understand any more than I did before I asked the question."

Wyatt broke into an amused grin. "Oh, you want to know facts. Anna's always been satisfied with the five-second explanation."

"Well, it's just that, I mean, I know you're successful. But I don't quite understand, and I want to. I don't mean to be rude," she said, thoroughly flustered.

Wyatt stared at her, his brown eyes still crinkled in amusement. "I wish Anna had more friends like you, Madeleine. You've got a good head on your shoulders. I enjoy talking to you." He helped himself to another pickle from the jar. "There are a lot of companies that could be a hell of a lot more profitable. I find the companies, and then I find the management or new ownership to help turn them around. My last deal was Flowers Chocolate Company. We took their candy bar image and turned it into a worldwide gourmet chocolate power. Now I'm working on a new deal . . . a boating company." He paused. "It *sounds* a bit boring. The *doing* is more fun. Putting together the pieces of a puzzle."

Maddie shook her head. "It doesn't sound boring at all."

There was something about Wyatt McNeill that made her like him more and more. What it was, she decided, was that he treated her like an adult, an equal. Jane had done that; they had been friends, above all else. But with Jane it had been different. As much as Maddie would have liked to view Wyatt as a friend, and not Anna's father, it was difficult. Wyatt *was* Anna's father.

Maddie, aware that Wyatt was studying her, began to feel nervous under the scrutiny. Glancing over at the television, she saw the teams lined up for the second-half kickoff.

"Oh, look," she said with relief, "the game's starting."

Wyatt turned up the sound, but looked at her instead of the television.

"I want to ask *you* something personal, Madeleine. Did your parents leave you any money when they died?"

"My mother did. Some insurance. Fifteen thousand dollars."

"And what have you done with it?"

"It's in the Pine Ridge National Bank. I thought about investing it. But I'm not quite sure how."

"Look, my stockbroker's son has just gone into the business. Graduated from Harvard, then graduate school at Wharton. He's a whiz kid, from what I hear . . . and the market's up. My broker doesn't handle such small portfolios, but his son'll do a great job with it. When

you get back to school, send me the money and I'll take care of it."
Wyatt paused, then broke into a hearty laugh. "From the expression
on your face, Madeleine, you look as if you think I'm going to steal
your life's savings. But Gary Pollock can quadruple your money in no
time at all. Trust me."

"My mother told me you should never trust people who say 'trust
me'."

"Madeleine, you keep me on my toes," Wyatt grinned. "I like that.
And I promise you won't lose your money. I just want to help you."

"But why? I mean, why should you be so nice to me?" Maddie
asked.

Wyatt smiled at her. "You're Anna's friend. And you're all alone.
Someone has to take an interest." He shook his head sympathetically.
"Hasn't anyone ever done anything for you just to be nice?"

Maddie swallowed, thinking of Jane. "Yes," she said. "Thanks."

So Wyatt McNeill felt sorry for her. Well, there was nothing wrong
with that. She needed all the help she could get.

5

Back in Boulder, after the electric atmosphere of New York City, things seemed to run at half speed. It was winter and very cold, but that wasn't the reason. The energy surrounding Boulder was diffused, unfocused. Madeleine, as she insisted her friends call her now, could feel the difference. She tried to hold on to the vigorous charge that had zapped her in Manhattan, but as the days passed, it became harder. The feeling of happy anticipation that she felt in New York slipped away, fading day by day, until it was only a memory.

Madeleine had hurried to see Brady at the shop as soon as she got back. He was waiting on a customer. His eyes flicked over her and then away, scarcely acknowledging her. Madeleine felt her stomach sink.

As soon as the door closed behind the woman, Madeleine threw her arms around him. Brady shrugged her off.

"Oh, Brady, please don't still be mad at me," she pleaded. "I missed you."

"Really?" he said coldly.

"Yes, really!" She squeezed his arm. "Brady, let's be together again. How about tonight? I want us to make up . . ."

"I'm busy tonight," Brady said shortly.

"Oh, please." Madeleine stared at him, hurt. She held out a gift-wrapped box to him. "I brought you a present," she said. "From Bloomingdale's. Merry late-Christmas. I love you."

"That," Brady said, "is your misfortune." He did not take the present.

Madeleine recognized the line. It was Rhett Butler's, from *Gone With the Wind.*

"Oh hell. Fuck you," she said, turning and huffing out of the shop.

She cried a little, off and on for the rest of the day. But she was not going to beg or humble herself to Brady Gardner. If that was what he expected, he would have a long wait. She decided to keep the shirt she'd bought for him and wear it herself.

After having spent time in New York, Madeleine was more fashion conscious than before. If she was going to achieve a "look" on her budget, she decided, it would have to be a personal, eccentric one. Always one to shop at thrift stores and rummage sales, she found that since Jane's death her mood had caused her to gravitate toward conservative clothes, skirts and sweaters and scarves. Now, her eye sought the outrageous—a clash of colors, a contrast of fabrics, the "found" accessory. She developed a taste for vintage clothing, silks and crepe de chine prints from the thirties and forties being her favorites.

As a Christmas gift from the McNeills, Madeleine's hair had been streaked with blond highlights at Kenneth's. With her jazzy hair color and eclectic way of dressing, she blossomed with new confidence in her attractiveness.

"You know, Maddie. I'm sorry, *Madeleine,*" Anna said one night when they had come back from the library, "you really could be a model if you wanted. You're so thin, but you can eat everything in sight. Your cheekbones are to die for."

Madeleine laughed. "Me? A model? You've got to be kidding. I'm not beautiful."

"You're crazy. I mean, you're not pretty in the Miss America way," Anna admitted, "but you have real style. Your features are strong, and you're very direct. When you talk to people, you look them in the eye. I think that's why older men like Brady fall for you. Boys your own age," she laughed, "*our* own age, are a bit intimidated by you, I think."

Madeleine shook her head in amazement. "Intimidated? I'm the least intimidating person I know."

"Well . . . to you, and me, because I know you so well. But

Randy's a bit afraid of you. That's why he . . . kind of ignores you. Because he's not comfortable."

Madeleine longed to launch into a candid discussion of what *she* thought of Randy. But she had sense enough to know it would come to no good. There was no point in giving Anna, now or ever, her opinion of Randy Ferguson. Still, to remain quiet while her best friend threw away her life. . . . Maybe it was worth testing the waters.

"You know, Anna," Madeleine said, handing her half of a Mounds bar, "I've been wanting to ask you if you're having cold feet at all . . . I mean, about getting married."

"Cold feet? Well, sure, sometimes. I mean, it's a lifetime commitment. But Randy's so sure I'm what he wants. He's got confidence for both of us."

Madeleine, the candy eaten, opened her drawer and pulled out a box of saltines. "Want one?"

"You know I can't stand boring crackers. Besides I promised Randy I'd lose five pounds before the wedding. He likes me lean . . . close to the bone."

"You don't need to lose an ounce! Honestly. Sometimes I think you give too much of yourself to Randy. *He's* graduating, so you're getting married. Why doesn't he wait until *you* graduate? Your degree is as important as his."

Anna had gotten her tweezers out and was plucking stray hairs from her eyebrows. "God, Madeleine . . . that's the most ridiculous thing I've ever heard. Of course it will be nice to get my degree—and I *will* get it—but it's not nearly as important as Randy's. I mean, he's got to support me."

"But don't you want to be a person in your own right?"

"I *am* a person in my own right!" Anna flared. "God, Maddie, I'll make worthwhile contributions to society . . . as Mrs. Randall Ferguson. I'll do the right things."

"But you have so much going for you. You're smart, you're beautiful. How can you want to live your life in someone else's shadow?"

"I'm not going to be Randy's appendage, you know," Anna snapped. "I'm going to be his other half. He *needs* me, Maddie. You don't realize how *much* he depends on me."

"I'm sure he does," Madeleine said, "but you don't *have* to need him. I'm not saying you shouldn't love him, or even marry him, if that's what you want. But put it in perspective. Think of yourself! What you want should come first."

"It does. I want Randy." She looked at her watch. "Oh, it's time to call him." Her eyebrows back in a perfect arch, she put away the tweezers and headed for the door. "You know, Maddie," she said, pausing in the doorway, "you're very jealous of Randy. You think he's going to block our friendship. But he won't. You don't give him enough credit . . . you don't give *me* enough credit. Nothing will ever come between us. You just have to adjust to the idea that many women feel fulfilled by being with men. You want to do everything on your own. But someday you'll fall in love too, and you'll understand what I'm talking about."

Anna rushed out to the bank of pay phones down the hall, leaving Madeleine without the last word. After conversations like this, Madeleine wondered what it was she saw in Anna McNeill. They were so different from one another. What *was* their friendship based on? Still, after all was said and done, they were friends, and friends put up with each other's annoying traits. Madeleine put up with Anna, and loved her in spite of everything. Anna probably did the same, although, in truth, Madeleine was positive that she was much easier to put up with.

At the university in 1970 it was a free and open time, a time of experimentation, a time of vocalization. People were banding together to protest the war in Vietnam and the United States government's escalation of it. And, in between demonstrations, peace marches, sit-ins, and rallies, all of Madeleine's other friends and acquaintances were falling in and out of bed with each other with astonishing regularity. Three to a bed, in varying combinations, and experimental orgies were as common as drugs. Marijuana, old hat by now, had given way to LSD, mescaline, and magic mushrooms. Boulder had become a pop-culture center during the psychedelic sixties; it was the hip place to be.

Madeleine, in the past, had protested the war. When she was with Brady, they smoked grass occasionally. But, other than getting high and the fact that he wore his hair long, Brady had little to do with the hippie scene. He was in his late twenties, had a heart murmur, and wasn't even worried about being drafted. So Madeleine stayed apart from most of what was going on. She was concerned with keeping her scholarship and didn't dare risk losing it.

Having always been a loner, Madeleine never felt the peer pressure to do anything she didn't want to do simply because everyone else was doing it. But, by spring, with Anna seldom around and Brady out of the picture, Madeleine began to gravitate toward the center of the scene.

It was time to experiment.

High-decibel Led Zeppelin was blasting from the record player. Red and green bulbs were screwed into all the lamps and ceiling sockets, giving an otherworldly appearance to the rooms of the old, rambling house near the university that several of Madeleine's friends from the art department had rented. Madeleine was there, sipping Gallo Hearty Burgundy with a guy named Peter Lane, who had been trying to get into her pants since the beginning of the year. Anna, back in Boulder to study for exams, had come along too; Madeleine had talked her into it.

"Hey, what are you doing this summer? Why don't we go someplace in the Caribbean . . . the three of us . . . and do weird things to each other with mangoes and suntan oil," Peter grinned, rolling a joint of Maui Wowie. He was a short, chipmunkish-looking guy whom Madeleine liked as a friend. There was no romantic interest on her part.

"We're going to New York," Anna sniffed. "I'm getting married."

"Married? You're kidding. Nobody gets *married* anymore. It's just a bourgeois trap, man." Peter took a long drag and passed the joint to Madeleine.

"If you only knew how *sick* I am of hearing that!" Anna snapped. She shook her head when Madeleine handed her the joint, and poured herself another glass of wine from the gallon jug that sat on the floor. "Marriage is never out when two people love each other. It's the ultimate commitment. And besides . . . if we're married Randy doesn't stand as much chance of being drafted."

"Hey, I hear you," Peter nodded. "But still . . . don't you want to sample from the menu of life before you make your order?"

Madeleine spoke up for Anna. "Anna's lived more than you, I bet. She's from New York. She *knows* what she wants. Not very many people do nowadays."

"That's right," Anna nodded in agreement.

"Okay, okay," Peter raised his hand in defense. "Two against one." He reached into his pocket. "Look what I scored today. Some psilocybin. It's organic. Really hard to come by, *very* precious." He looked at Anna and Madeleine, hopeful. "Wanna do it?"

"No," Anna said.

"Well, maybe another time. I've heard psilocybin is great," Madeleine added.

"It is. The absolute best. A totally different high from anything else. It's almost spiritual. I mean, people get into sex on mescaline, but this stuff arouses your soul. Not that sex isn't great too."

"How long does it last?" Madeleine asked. She was interested in trying it, but she knew Anna would never go along with the idea.

"Oh, five or six hours, I guess," Peter estimated.

"Haven't you taken it before?" Anna asked.

"Yeah, it's just that you kinda lose track of time. You go into a different dimension where time doesn't matter." He held up a small plastic bag that contained four capsules filled with a yellowish-colored powder. "Look, I'm gonna do it. You're welcome to join me. Or you can leave. I'm not into forcing anyone to do anything they don't wanna do."

Madeleine looked at Anna. "Why don't we? You have to try everything once. And before you know it you'll be married and totally away from this scene."

Anna refilled her wine glass. She clearly wasn't enthusiastic, but she couldn't think of a reason not to try it. She had never experimented with mind-expanding drugs: she supposed she ought to before she got married. After all, Randy had taken LSD at Princeton and said it was super.

"All right," Anna relented. "But you have to *promise* to take me immediately to a hospital if I have a bad reaction."

Peter nodded. "I promise. But you won't. This drug is the mildest of them all. Really far out. You'll love it."

He pulled two capsules out of the Baggie, opened them up, and sprinkled the powder into a glass of water, stirring it with his finger. The powder wouldn't dissolve completely. Tiny mounds, resembling powdered mustard, floated on top. "Here. We each drink about a third."

Madeleine drank first, then Anna.

"Ugh!" Anna said, chasing it down with wine. "It tastes horrible."

Peter drank the last third and went into the kitchen. He came back with a container of lemon yogurt. "Here," he handed it to Anna. "Both of you eat some of this. Shouldn't take drugs on an empty stomach."

Peter's German shepherd, Lady Soul, came into the room and perched by his chair expectantly. "Hey," Peter said, "let's take my friend here for a walk so I don't have to do it later. It'll take about forty-five minutes for this stuff to start working anyway."

They put on their coats and walked out into the cool, fragrant, early May night. Madeleine felt a rush of anticipatory excitement, but by the end of the walk, when nothing had happened, she began to forget that she had taken the drug.

Back at the house, Peter rolled another joint, and this time even Anna joined in. Slowly, Madeleine became aware of something happening. No major rush, more of a secure feeling of well-being.

"This hitting you yet?" Peter asked.

Anna nodded. "I *think* so. I mean, everything in the room looks a little different. All the colors are so vibrant. But it's very gentle. This isn't at all what I thought it would be."

"There's no jolt . . . no zings," Madeleine said, relieved and disappointed at the same time. "I don't have a feeling of 'Wow, this is it.'"

"That's what I told you. That's what it's all about," Peter reiterated. "What you feel now is about as strong as it gets."

"You're a good drug guru," Anna purred approvingly. She kicked off her high-heeled black boots and snuggled up in her chair. "I feel fabulous."

"Yeah," Peter said, "this is dynamite stuff." He stood and held out his arms toward Anna and Madeleine. "Come with me. Upstairs. I want to show you something."

"We're *not* going to fool around," Madeleine said.

"Who said anything about that? Just come up to my room where we can relax. My housemates'll be coming back from the movies any time now. Things'll get noisy. Come on. I have this far-out Chinese lute tape I want you to hear."

Upstairs, they lay around on Peter's bed and listened to the music. The airy Chinese lutes conjured up nightingales, cherry blossoms, pagodas.

"I'm in a Buddhist temple," Anna said dreamily. "You're right about this being spiritual. It's a major experience. I'm a Buddhist monk . . . I'm at one with the universe . . ." She raised her arms and moved them with the music. "I am all there is," she whispered.

A while later, Peter put on a new tape, Tchaikovsky's *1812 Overture*. While Anna and Madeleine listened, he disappeared downstairs, returning with cups of Red Zinger herbal tea and a bowl of sunflower and pumpkin seeds.

"Hmmm, this music changes my mood completely," Madeleine noted. "I'm not floating anymore. I'm very focused."

Picking up a handful of seeds, she began moving them around on the sheets, as if they were little armies. Anna and Peter grabbed seeds and joined combat. That led them into a discussion of the war in Vietnam.

"This is too heavy," Anna said after a while. "I'm too afraid of war. Please, Peter, please change the music."

He obliged. They listened to the Beatles and smoked another joint. Later still, the sexy whine of Paul Desmond's saxophone playing "Like Someone in Love" permeated the room. Peter nonchalantly removed his clothes and got back on the bed. Reaching out slowly, he ran his hand up and down Madeleine's arm, barely touching her.

"Why don't you get comfortable?" he suggested.

"I am," Madeleine replied. "Like this."

"But bodies are a lot more tactile when you're on this stuff. Sex takes on a whole new dimension. Not only sex. Just touching your own body . . . try it," he urged.

"Well, I suppose I've gone this far. Come on, Anna." Madeleine said.

"Okay . . . but one thing has to be understood. I'm in love and I'm engaged. Absolutely *no* fucking."

Peter rolled over onto his stomach. "No fucking. Just give me a back rub."

Madeleine and Anna took off their clothes, except for their underpants, and slowly gave Peter a deep back rub while he moaned his approval.

After a while he turned over. Anna became upset when she saw his erect penis.

"I said, *no* fucking!"

"Hey, okay. I can't help this, you know. Being in bed with two beautiful women with out-of-sight bodies does this to me." He sat up and readjusted the pillows behind his head. "Hell, I'll jerk myself off if you two'll hug each other for me. The idea of that turns me on a lot."

"No . . ." Madeleine started to protest.

"All right," Anna said unexpectedly.

"Far out!" Peter exclaimed, and grabbed hold of his erection. "Hey . . . I just had this great idea for a movie. Captain Ecstasy. He's a reporter for an underground newspaper, see? Then he becomes Captain Ecstasy by jerking off. Something in the magical self-contained circuit of his hand, his mind, and his cock working together for orgasm turns him into the greatest fighter against crime and injustice and sexual frustration the world has ever known . . ."

While Peter rambled off into fantasy and masturbation, Madeleine glanced uncomfortably at Anna. She had been surprised by her friend's reaction. Anna was not a touchy-feely sort of person. Even when they greeted one another, Anna never left her cheek in place long enough for Madeleine's lips to make contact. But the drug, or the mood of the saxophone music, seemed to have taken hold of her. Anna reached out her slim, freckled arms to Madeleine and pulled Madeleine toward her until their breasts touched.

Madeleine responded, tentatively wrapping her own arms around Anna's delicate, bony back. It was not that she was turned on exactly, but there was something so exotically different about feeling a woman's soft arms around her, about touching a woman's body. The ethereal quality, the fragility, of Anna's body touched Madeleine on a deep level. She comprehended, for the first time, the totality of the difference between men and women. It was profound.

Madeleine's and Anna's lips brushed together lightly, danced away and then back again. Slowly their mouths opened to each other. As their tongues embraced, Madeleine became aware of a sexual stirring in her groin, both exhilarating and frightening to her. It had never occurred to Madeleine that another woman could turn her on. She had never been excited by the idea of women as lovers.

It was the psilocybin, of course, that had opened them up to the experience. When the drug wore off, so would this feeling that they shared, Madeleine rationalized as her lips caressed those of her best friend.

Then Anna grabbed Madeleine tightly, kissing her more insistently. Madeleine let her hand trail down Anna's body, gently placing it on Anna's thigh. Outside of themselves, seeming very far away, Madeleine was aware that the mattress was bouncing up and down to the rhythm of Peter's hand, moving faster and faster. She heard him moaning, "Far out . . ."

The tape player clicked off. Paul Desmond was replaced by loud sounds of laughter wafting up from downstairs. The three of them seemed frozen in their positions.

The music was gone. So was the mood.

Anna pulled away quickly from Madeleine, suddenly self-conscious. "Hmmm, well, that was . . ." she trailed off, somewhat absently.

They looked at Peter, who was in the process of coming. Dispassionately, they witnessed the event, as if they had both seen men jerk off many times before.

"I'm freezing, all of a sudden," Madeleine said, reaching for her blouse. "Look, my teeth are actually chattering."

"So are mine," Anna realized. "It's cold . . . and I'm starving. What time is it anyway?"

Peter, still lying on his back with his eyes closed, slowly raised his arm and looked at his watch. "Around three."

"Wow, I can't believe it," Madeleine said. "You were right about time on this stuff. I thought it was about midnight. I had no idea it was so late."

"I think we should head back to the dorm," Anna said. "I feel like raiding the candy machines."

The girls finished dressing while Peter watched them from bed. Then they leaned over and each kissed him good-bye, on the cheek. He remained propped up against the pillows, smiling happily.

"Thanks," Madeleine said. "It was really interesting."

Peter nodded. "Yeah, it always is. It always is. Life's a trip, man."

Madeleine gave Lady Soul a hearty pat and headed out with Anna into the night. During the walk home, they tried very hard to appear casual and sober.

The next day Madeleine and Anna both overslept, missing all of their morning classes. Over a shared Pepsi and some saltines, which Anna deigned to eat because she was so hungry, they talked about the psychedelic experience of the night before—and the mind-expanding insights they had felt they had. Each was careful to avoid mention of the sexual part of the evening. Madeleine, in retrospect, had enjoyed it, but was confused by her feelings. She supposed that Anna felt much the same way. It was experimentation, after all.

And a subject best left undiscussed.

The next few weeks passed quickly in a race to complete term papers and cram for finals. Anna left school immediately after her last exam, in order to attend Randy's Princeton graduation and get ready for the wedding.

Madeleine was lonely, left in the room by herself, knowing that Anna would never be back again. Their friendship would never be exactly the same after Anna was married. No more staying up all night together, laughing and talking and eating Hershey bars. She knew that she and Anna would remain chums. But it would be different. For one thing, Randy would be around. For another, Anna would be in New York and Madeleine would still be in Boulder.

Before school ended, Madeleine tried LSD one night with another boy from the art department. He had insisted that he was experienced with drugs, but when the acid took effect, he freaked out and nearly killed himself by trying to fly out of a second-story window. Fortunately, he landed in some bushes, and Madeleine summoned one of his friends in time to administer vast quantities of water and niacin to help race the drug through his system without having to take him to the hospital. The incident scared Madeleine fiercely. It was a night she never wanted to repeat.

She had had it with the drug scene. It was expensive, not to mention illegal. And, at least as far as she was concerned, it wasn't enough fun to counterbalance the terrifying risks involved.

Madeleine remained in Boulder through July, working as a waitress until it was time to fly east to Anna's wedding. One night Brady Gardner came into the restaurant, his arm around a stunning Swedish woman whom Madeleine recognized as the ex-wife of one of her professors. Brady stared right at Madeleine, then turned away without bothering to speak. It hurt her that Brady still hated her so much he wouldn't even talk to her. She hadn't meant it to turn out that way; she had *liked* him.

That night, Madeleine cried herself to sleep, something she had not allowed herself to do very often since her early childhood. Her life in Boulder had turned hollow; she had botched things up. There was nothing, and no one, there for her anymore.

But she had promised Jane that she would finish school. How was she going to keep her promise?

6

The wedding of Anna Chipley McNeill and Randall Porter Ferguson III was a major event in the Manhattan summer social calendar.

Madeleine arrived in New York two weeks early (Wyatt McNeill had sent his Gulfstream jet for her) to join in the final round of prenuptial parties that had been flourishing since June. She had dreaded the inevitable first meeting with Win Burgess, Randy's roommate and best man, after the abyssmal New Year's Eve. But, to his credit, Win behaved politely, or more specifically, as if he had never laid eyes on Madeleine before, which suited her fine.

For the most part, the parties bored Madeleine, much as they had when she had visited over Christmas. Still, she was glad to be included in the wedding festivities. They gave her time to spend with Anna before she rounded the corner into matrimonial togetherness with Randy. And they kept her from having to think about the future.

Madeleine's main escort for the parties was Hadley McNeill, Anna's brother. He was quite full of himself after his year at Yale, but he made up for it by being caustically witty about the events they were forced to attend. He seemed to find them as tedious as Madeleine did, so they developed a common bond. After several evenings with him, Madeleine began to relish his black humor and sense of the ridiculous.

The weekend prior to the wedding, the party moved to the McNeills' summer place in Southampton for another round of fêtes.

On Saturday night, after a brunch, a sailing party, a cocktail bash, and a sit-down dinner for sixty, Hadley and Madeleine slipped away from the crowd at the Somebody Mellon's house. Like children, they ran giggling through a maze of landscaped gardens, into an oriental-style gazebo. Under the clear, starry sky, their party chatter lapsed into silence, and they gazed out at the ocean, each lost in thought.

"I'm champagned out. I'm talked out. I'm smiled out," Hadley said finally, wearily. "Want to take a walk along the beach and get even farther away from the madding crowd?"

Madeleine nodded. "You know, it's really exhausting, making endless small talk to people I've never seen before. *And* will never see again."

"Consider yourself lucky. I, you see, *will* see them again. And again. And again. These are people I knew in kindergarten. And after we've finished going to school with one another, we'll all work together, and have affairs with each other's wives. We'll get divorced, remarry, and wind up back here, drinking martinis, when we're eighty."

"You make society seem like so much fun."

"Hmmm. I always wondered why there are social climbers. I guess they're people who don't know any better," Hadley observed.

"Ah," said Madeleine wryly, "if us simple poor folk only realized how happy we really are."

"Now you've hit it," Hadley approved. "We could start a whole new direction in social climbing. Down."

"It's been done. It's called slumming."

"Damn! I always come up with these ideas a season too late."

"It didn't catch on. The thing is, nobody much seems to want to live there."

"You've got a point," Hadley admitted, seriously. He sighed. "Last summer the Pendletons gave a skid row party. Cost thousands. Everyone had a marvelous time. I found it totally disgusting. It turned my stomach." He was silent for a while. "Say you had tons of money, Madeleine. All you wanted. What would you do with it?"

"Well, all this has certainly opened my eyes. If I had the kind of money the people around here have I'd sure spend it on other things besides parties."

"Oh? Like what? Say you just inherited ten gushing oil wells. All your creature comforts are covered, expensively. What would you do?"

"Well, I'd . . . God, this is really hard!" Madeleine laughed, pausing to think. "Of course, I'd try to do worthwhile things: contribute to cancer research and do whatever I could to help people who were worse off. And then, well, I wouldn't sit around on my buns waiting for the cork to fly off the next bottle of champagne. I'd work even if I didn't need the money, because you have to produce, to create, to get a sense of your own self-esteem."

"That's important to you?"

"Yes, of course. It's *everything*. I want to be appreciated for myself, not for how big my bank balance is." She burst into giggles. "My bank balance, however, puts this entire conversation into the realm of high comedy. Let the rich worry about how they're going to spend their money with good conscience. I have to worry about making enough to keep me in SpaghettiOs."

Hadley looked at her, as if scrutinizing her from the vantage point of vast wisdom. "You'll do just fine, Madeleine. You'll get everything you want. You're focused . . . you're ambitious. I think whatever you set your sights on, you'll get."

"You make me sound very cutthroat. I'd like to think I come across nicer than that."

"You come across very nice," he said quickly. "What I mean is, you haven't grown up having it all, like Anna and all of us. So you both want things and despise yourself for wanting them. I saw you looking at Anna's wedding gifts. The expression on your face was a mixture of lust and horror."

"That's not true!" Madeleine shrieked. "God, Hadley, Anna's absolutely right about you! You make fun of everything and everyone. Can I help it if I grew up poor? I'm trying not to be dazzled by all this because it's all so unreal. But on the other hand it *is* dazzling."

"Hey." Hadley came over and gave her a hug, then brushed the top of her head lightly with a kiss. "I'm not putting you down, really. I'd take you over every one of those debs in there," he pointed back toward the beach mansion where the party was still in full swing. "You're real. That's all I'm saying. You're not contrived or artificial. I like that. I admire it. There's a lot more to you than meets the eye."

Madeleine smiled wearily. "All right. I'll say thanks, but let's just not talk for a while."

They took off their shoes and walked along the water's edge, letting the cold Atlantic waves roll over their feet. Madeleine considered what they had been talking about. In truth, she was in the midst of a great conflict, scorning all these people for their huge fortunes, yet coveting what they had at the same time. How she was going to come to terms with that, she wasn't sure. But the first step was to design fabulous jewelry and become famous and rich. Then she'd deal with the morality of the situation.

"You know what?" Hadley said after a bit. "You're the only one I can say this to, but I think Anna's a real ass to get married now. She has plenty of time. And Randy's so predictable. What possible excitement could there be in a lifetime with him?"

Madeleine nodded in agreement. "To put it bluntly, Anna's terrific and Randy's a bore."

Hadley laughed. "Right on. You know, my sister could take off if she wanted to. She has some money our grandmother left her. She should travel. People don't get married anymore—they live together. If she lived with Randy for a while, she'd get sick of him."

"I agree. I certainly don't plan to get married anytime soon. There's too much to experience."

"Exactly! Look, why don't we find Anna and talk to her?" Hadley said excitedly. "It's not too late! She *has* to call off the wedding. She can spend a year abroad. Hell, we'll go with her."

"Great idea!" Madeleine exclaimed. "Randy'll find somebody else."

"Unfortunately. Women drool over him, although I can't imagine why," Hadley said. He grabbed Madeleine's hand and took off across the sand. "Come on! Let's go steal Anna off into the night."

By the time they finally found Anna she was back at home, sitting on some cushions on the floor of the living room, hugging a bottle of champagne and crying.

"Anna!" Madeleine ran over to her. "What's wrong?"

"Everything!" she sobbed, looking up at them miserably.

"But you're home so early. Did you and Randy have a fight?" Madeleine asked, concerned.

"How could we fight? He hasn't said one word to me all day . . . except in front of other people."

"Well, it doesn't matter. Even when he does talk he doesn't say anything." Hadley sat down on the floor beside Anna, who glared at him with petulant hatred. He detached the champagne bottle from her grasp, took a swig, then passed the bottle to Madeleine, who set it on the coffee table without taking any. "Look," he said, "we came to convince you to elope with us to Europe. Don't do this ridiculous thing and get married."

"I *have* to get married!" Anna screamed. "I have to!"

"Hey, calm down . . . calm down," Hadley said, changing his tone to a more soothing one, "you don't have to at all. Just because Mother's made all the arrangements? It can all be canceled"—he snapped his fingers—"just like that!"

"No, it can't." Anna started sniffing again. Her face was red and splotchy and her nose was running. Madeleine grabbed a box of tissues from behind the television and sat close to Anna, on the other side from Hadley, gently dabbing her friend's face.

"You don't have to go through with it," Madeleine said quietly. "It's much better to call it off now than to get a divorce later."

"No, you don't begin to understand. I'm fucking knocked up!" Anna said through her tears. "It's just impossible, but it's true. I saw a doctor. I only messed up on the Pill once or twice."

"Hey, Sis, it's okay. This *is* the twentieth century, after all," Hadley said. "You can have an abortion. No big deal."

"That's what Randy said. That's what Randy wants."

"But you don't want to have a baby yet? So soon? *Do* you?" Madeleine asked.

"Yes! That's the thing. It *is* a big deal," Anna sobbed. "I've got this wonderful feeling inside of me. I *want* to give birth. I want to have dozens of children."

"Dozens of children? Anna, the peasant of Park Avenue? Really. I don't believe I'm hearing this from my sophisticated sister," Hadley said.

"Well, you are hearing it. And you'd better find Randy first thing tomorrow and talk to him. As my brother, it's your duty to . . ."

"Hey, wait a minute! *My* duty? I don't even *want* you to marry the creep."

"Creep? So *that's* what you think of the man I love!" Anna shouted. She made a fist and hit Hadley hard on his upper arm. He stared at her in disbelief but did not attempt to move away. "Get out of here!

Just get the hell out of here, Hadley! I never want to speak to you again! I mean it!"

Hadley stood and took another swig of champagne. He looked at Madeleine. "Okay, she's all yours. This is totally unreasonable. I'm going to bed."

Madeleine sighed and hugged Anna, left in the impossible position of having to calm her down as well as reassure her that nobody thought Randy was a creep. Well, what were friends for if not for times like this? Anna was definitely in a crisis situation, one that had to be dealt with.

"Everything will be all right," Madeleine said as she held Anna and soothed her. She repeated the phrase many times, as it was about all she could think of to say. At last, nearly an hour later, after Anna had gone through both the bottle of champagne and the box of Kleenex, Madeleine convinced her to go to bed; they would deal with it fresh in the morning. "Tomorrow's another day," she heard herself utter wearily, and knew it was time for both of them to get some sleep.

After Madeleine had steered Anna upstairs, and her friend had finally dozed off, Madeleine thought about Anna's predicament and tried to put herself in the same position. How would *she* handle it? Pregnant by a man who did not want her child. She really did not know what she would do. It was horrible. By next week at this time Anna was supposed to be married. What would happen between now and then was anybody's guess.

For the next few days, after returning to the city, Anna ate very little and kept to herself. She had never seemed more fragile or delicate to Madeleine. But she was so tense and snappish that Madeleine had trouble making even light conversation with her.

Wyatt and Elizabeth McNeill had no inkling of the drama that was being played out under their roof. They put down Anna's lack of appetite to nerves about the impending wedding. Hadley had a job during the day, working for a conservation group, so he was not around much. Madeleine, to give Anna time by herself, spent most of her time holed up in the library, reading.

On Wednesday morning Anna came into the library where Madeleine lounged with the morning's *Times* and a cup of coffee. Madeleine noticed that Anna's eyes were dark rimmed and haggard. But there was a bright glint in them.

"You look tired, Anna. Didn't you sleep?"

"No. Of course not!"

"I'm sorry." Madeleine had grown used to Anna's shortness. But there was a slightly different tone to her friend's voice that made her put down the newspaper and sit up. "What is it?"

Anna smiled tightly. Her face was very pale, so that her fatigue-bruised eyes and her lips stood out despite the absence of makeup. "I've decided what to do," she said in a hushed voice that made Madeleine's skin cold.

"About the . . . ?"

"Yeah, the baby."

Madeleine waited.

"I'm going to do what Randy wants. He's the man. He ought to make the decisions." Anna paused, and the same chill, humorless smile played at her lips for a moment. "And he should be ready to accept the consequences for them."

"What do you mean?" Madeleine asked uneasily.

Anna told her what she had planned.

The Bellavista was a tired and dispirited hotel in the Eighties, just west of Broadway. It was difficult to tell what the view claimed in its name might once have been. Now its entrance faced a small Spanish grocery, a Chinese laundry, and a Greek delicatessen, above which were abandoned apartments with broken and boarded windows.

The room, for which Madeleine had paid thirty dollars in advance to a desk clerk too bored even to smirk at the two pretty young women with one small overnight bag, looked out across tenements to a school yard on the next block. The chain-link fence had been rent with bolt cutters, probably long ago, and a dozen preteen boys were playing a noisy game of basketball on the blacktop.

The room itself was small, with a double bed, a bedside table, a bureau, a wastebasket, a suitcase stand with a broken strap, and a print of an Alpine scene bolted to the wall above the bed. There was a bathroom with a small stained tub, a toilet, a sink, and a cracked mirror.

"Oh, Anna—" Madeleine began, but Anna cut her off.

"What time is it?"

"Quarter of two."

"All right."

Anna set the overnight bag on the bedside table. She opened it and took out a white nightgown. She undressed quickly, tossing her clothes haphazardly toward the bureau. Before she put on the nightgown, she pressed her palms against the smooth white of her belly and moved her lips, murmuring something that Madeleine could not hear. Then she pulled the nightgown on over her head and turned down the bed.

"At least the sheets look clean," she said. She lay down and stared at the ceiling.

They waited.

At four minutes of two, there was a knock on the door.

"Who is it?" Anna said.

"Me. Randy. What the hell is this, for God's sake?"

Anna nodded at Madeleine. Madeleine opened the door.

"Jesus Christ," Randy swore as the door swung back, "what kind of a dump is—"

He saw Madeleine and stopped. "What are you doing here?" he asked.

Then he saw Anna lying on the bed.

"Hello, Randy," she said. He took a step into the room, and Madeleine closed the door behind him.

"I'm sorry, Anna, I don't get it." Anna did not answer. Randy looked at Madeleine for help. "You said on the phone she'd decided I was right."

"I said she'd decided to do what you want, Randy," Madeleine corrected.

"Well, whatever. But why do we have to talk about it in this shit hole?"

"You're not here to talk about it," Anna said solemnly.

"What then? What are you two up to?"

Anna reached over to the bedside table and opened the overnight bag. Inside was a jumble of what looked like surgical instruments.

"You're here to do it," Anna said.

Randy turned pale. *"What?"* he croaked.

Anna took hold of the nightgown and pulled it up above her waist. "You put it here," she said, keeping her bright eyes on Randy's. "If you don't want it, darling, you can take it away."

Randy shook his head incredulously. "No," he said. *"No!* Anna, you're crazy." He wheeled on Madeleine. "You put her up to this, didn't you?" he snarled.

Madeleine started to answer, but Anna's voice cut through sharply. "She had nothing to do with it, Randy. It was my idea. You find that so hard to believe? *My* idea. Madeleine tried to talk me out of it. But this is it. We have the baby, or you do the abortion. It's your decision, Randy. You're going to be my husband. I'll do whatever you want."

"Anna, baby." He sat on the edge of the bed and held her hand. His voice was coaxing. There was perspiration on his forehead and in spreading crescents under the arms of his seersucker suit. "I know a very good doctor. He's got a clean office on Park . . . he knows what to do. And he's very discreet, if that's what you're worried about."

Anna kept shaking her head, slowly, back and forth.

"You're mad!" Randy protested, his voice rising to a panicky falsetto. "Honey, I'd butcher you. I don't know what to do. You could die!"

Anna reached out and touched his cheek. "Our baby could die too. If that's what's got to happen, I don't want anybody else but you to do it. Madeleine will assist you. She doesn't want to, but she will because I asked her to. To be able to get help, in case . . . anything goes wrong." She stroked the sweat-soaked hair off his forehead. "It's not a pretty thing, Randy. I don't want it done in a pretty place. But if it's what you want, we're in your hands, darling."

Randy got up suddenly and backed away. "No!" he said. "I won't do it!"

Anna's voice rang out like a slap as his hand touched the doorknob. "If you go out that door, I'm having the baby! I'm not afraid to have it alone. The wedding's off. I couldn't marry a man who was so uncaring, who was so callous. I couldn't marry someone who wasn't man enough to take responsibility for the consequences of his own actions. If you go out that door, it's over, Randy."

Randy stood frozen with his hand on the knob. His shoulders began to shake, and a sob broke from his throat.

"All right." He crumbled. He threw himself down on the bed and hugged her, crying. "All right. You're right. We'll have the baby."

Over his shoulder Anna's eyes met Madeleine's.

"Take the bag," she mouthed.

Madeleine picked up the bag of surgical instruments from the nightstand and went out the door, closing it carefully behind her so that the latch barely made a sound.

The wedding service was held at St. Bartholomew's Episcopal Church at Fiftieth and Park. Besides Madeleine, who was maid of honor, there were nine other bridesmaids. They all wore apricot chiffon garden-party dresses, with crowns of cornflowers in their hair —Anna's only salute to the Bohemianism of the period. Anna herself wore a gown of the palest apricot satin and lace from Henri Bendel and carried jasmine, baby's breath, and cornflowers. With her red hair and pale skin, she was breathtaking. Everyone remarked that she and Randy were the handsomest couple they had seen in years.

The reception afterward at the Metropolitan Club was lavishly de rigueur. Madeleine thought she had grown used to excessive entertaining over the past weeks, but the McNeills outdid themselves. A thousand near-and-dear friends crushed into the ballroom, transformed for the occasion into an enormous tent of pale apricot silk, with hundreds of thousands of flowers—jasmine and apricot tea roses. They dined on rack of lamb, lobster, and an endless buffet of gustatory delights, wines, and nonstop Louis Roederer Cristal champagne. They danced to the music of Peter Duchin until early Sunday morning.

Randy and Anna were forced to leave at midnight. They wanted to stay—they could sleep together anytime, why leave a good party early?—but Elizabeth McNeill insisted, for convention's sake. In a flurry of tears and rose petals, the couple took off into the night in a limousine bound for the bridal suite at the Pierre. The next evening they would fly to Italy for a three-week honeymoon.

Back at the McNeills' apartment, a little after three, Hadley and Madeleine relaxed in the kitchen, leaning back with their feet propped up on the kitchen table, wolfing down milk and cookies.

"Well, that's that," Hadley said. "A month I'd never care to repeat."

"Until *you* get married," Madeleine teased.

"Me? Not on your life. I'll live with women but I'll never marry one."

"Why? Aren't we good enough for you?"

Hadley laughed. "Sure. But I don't want to get tied down. Besides, it sounds like Anna's going to have my ration of children. I'm an advocate of Zero Population Growth. The planet's getting too crowded. How are we going to grow enough food to feed everybody? And what food we do grow is contaminated by pollution and chemicals."

Madeleine yawned, got up, and set her glass in the sink. "On that cheery note I think I'll go to bed."

"I'll join you," Hadley said.

By that, Madeleine assumed that he meant he was going up to bed as well. But when she climbed the stairs to Anna's room, he followed her in and flopped his tuxedoed body down on one of the twin beds.

"I've wanted to make wild, passionate love to you since the moment I first laid eyes on you," Hadley said. "Thank God Anna's finally out of the way."

"What?" Madeleine said, grinning, puzzled. "You?"

"Of course me. I'm only a year younger than you. Surely you've noticed how smitten I am?"

"No, I didn't. I mean, I don't know what to say," Madeleine replied. Hadley had a great sense of humor. Was he joking, or not? She couldn't tell.

"Don't say anything. Just get out of that ridiculous dress and come over here."

Madeleine had not slept with anyone for months. She was totally exhausted, but she longed to have a man's arms around her, to feel a man inside her. It had never occurred to her to think sexually about Hadley. He was Anna's younger brother. That's all she had ever regarded him as.

But now she took time to study him from across the room. Anna looked like her mother, but Hadley took after Wyatt—over six feet tall, with the same dark brown hair and large, intense brown-black eyes. His nose was strong, but not beakish. He was thinner than Wyatt, and his cheekbones were extraordinarily well-defined for a man. He smiled at her, waiting expectantly. Nice teeth.

Hadley?

Hadley?

Hadley. Now that she was looking at him, really seeing him for the first time, she realized that it was because of him that she had been able to get through the past few weeks. Hadley had been there for her, at her side, getting drinks, rescuing her from endless conversations with tipsy dowagers, making her laugh, offering himself as a replacement for the loss of Anna to Randy. She just hadn't paid any attention.

"Hadley, forgive me. It never occurred to me that you . . ."

"If only you had looked you would have seen all the signals," he said. "I'm mad about you."

"Well, I guess there is sort of an inevitability about this," Madeleine said, confused about what it was she felt for Hadley. He had been conveniently filed away in her mind as Anna's brother, nothing more, as if that made him a nonentity. But here he was now, emerging as a person, a man who wanted her. She was flattered, but she felt something else: an attraction to Hadley. She realized suddenly that it had been there all along. Except, as Anna's brother, she had automatically put him off limits, as if being attracted to him was incestuous. But the fact that he was Anna's brother was merely that, a fact, not a factor in how she should feel about him.

"I'm beginning to see," she said.

Madeleine walked over to the bed and knelt down for him to unzip her dress. That done, she reached over and switched off the light before she began to undress.

Hadley turned it back on again. He stood in front of her and slipped her arms out of the apricot bridesmaid's dress and let the chiffon slide to the floor in a heap.

"Oh, Madeleine. I've wanted to do this for so long." He leaned over and kissed her bare shoulder. And then he undressed her the rest of the way, slowly and skillfully.

During the hours that followed, Madeleine discovered, to her delighted surprise, that Anna's younger brother certainly knew his way around women.

And she discovered something else. The passion she felt was accompanied by something that intensified the sex and totally engulfed her. It was so different from what she had felt with Brady or anyone else. With Hadley, there was an intense coming together of their souls as well as their bodies. There was a feeling of coming home that she had never experienced before. It was as if she had been waiting for him all along, without knowing it.

And then she realized what it must be: love.

Madeleine was falling, at last.

On Sunday, Madeleine slept until noon. Hadley was not there beside her when she awoke, and she missed him. She showered quickly, threw on jeans and a T-shirt, and found him downstairs at the buffet brunch that had been laid out in the dining room.

He came over, put his arms around her, and kissed her. "You looked so exhausted I tiptoed out so I wouldn't wake you. Good morning, my love."

"Hmmm, yes, it is. I feel like I'm in a daze. Did it really happen? Or was it all a dream?"

"It really happened. Oh God, Madeleine, I didn't know it was going to be like this."

"Like what?" she asked, afraid that he was regretting the night before.

He held her face in his hands. "I mean, all these weeks I've been lusting after you, waiting till the right time to make my move. I thought after the wedding would be safe. We'd get it on, and then you'd take off back to Colorado."

"Oh, thanks very much," Madeleine said, bristling. "God, if I'd known . . ."

"Shhh," he said, "hear me out. I had no idea that this was going to happen, but I'm in love with you, Madeleine. I may have been all along and just not realized it. But now I know, for sure."

Madeleine smiled, relieved. "Oh, Hadley, I'm as surprised as you."

"But how do you feel? I mean, do you love me too?"

"Yes," she nodded, "I do. And I feel wonderful."

After bacon and eggs for Hadley—Madeleine was too euphoric to eat—the two of them walked over to Central Park, holding hands the entire way. It was a hot summer day, and the park was full of sunbathers, Hare Krishnas, mimes, picnickers, musicians, children, dogs, and joggers. And other lovers, although Hadley and Madeleine were too absorbed with one another to notice. They walked slowly, their arms around each other. Every so often Hadley bent over and kissed her hair or her face.

Madeleine was completely happy. She had never before basked in a feeling this delicious. Love. It far surpassed lust.

Hadley, for all his wry, man-of-the-world wit, was totally taken with her. Madeleine had the feeling that he really liked women, more than any of the men she had gone out with. He wanted to know her opinion on everything; he seemed to want to get inside her head and see what made her Madeleine.

"You're so different from my sister," he said later as they headed back across town to Park Avenue, still holding hands. "I mean, you're very opinionated and frank. You get on the defensive sometimes. But deep down, you're a nicer person than Anna. I can't explain why, but I feel it."

"Oh, Hadley, I'm not! It's just that you and Anna are brother and sister. Brothers and sisters never see each other the way other people do."

"How do you see Anna, then?"

"She's funny and kind and giving. She's been so generous to me. She's my best friend for a lot of reasons."

"I'm glad you feel that way," Hadley replied. "I happen to think she's incredibly self-centered. But—I know—my opinion is prejudiced." He stopped and turned so that he could look at her directly. "How do you see *me?*"

Madeleine laughed. "If you'd asked me that yesterday my answer would've been very different from today."

"How so?"

"Well, today I'm in love with you."

"No, don't hedge the question. Love aside, how do you see me?"

"Well, I told you, before I never looked at you as a man, just Anna's brother. A sophisticated guy with a jaded sense of humor."

"Thanks."

"Oh, darling, you know my opinion's changed since last night. You're much warmer, much more open than I ever thought. You always seemed in some kind of protective shell—when I first met you, I think I found you a bit intimidating. I mean, you do tend to have a know-it-all side." She grinned and leaned up and kissed him. "But I've changed my mind. All that is just your form of self-protection. You're the most loveable man I've ever met."

He tightened his grip around her. "God, I wonder how Anna will react when she hears about us."

"I've thought about that. I don't know."

"Well, in the past she's been very jealous of my coming on to her friends. We had a big fight about it once. When I was fifteen, her friend Darcy developed a crush on me and Anna was furious. On the other hand, I've known Anna long enough to know that you can never count on her reacting the way you expect to any situation. Who knows what she'll think?" He shrugged. "I, for one, don't care."

"Well, I do. But then I care about you too. Besides, it'll all be fine," Madeleine dismissed it.

"Don't bet on it. I know my sister."

"Well, so do I!"

Hadley squeezed her again. "Let's not get into our first fight over whether or not Anna will approve of our relationship. Subject closed."

Madeleine nodded. "Subject closed."

"Let's hurry. My parents are going out for drinks. We'll have some time alone." He looked at his watch. "God, it's been nearly six hours."

By Sunday evening, everyone was exhausted. Elizabeth McNeill went up to bed after dinner. Hadley, who had to be at work early the next morning, followed soon after, with instructions for Madeleine to slip into his bed when the coast was clear.

Madeleine took her cup of coffee into the library, to read for a bit before heading up.

A little while later, the double doors to the library creaked open. She looked up to see Wyatt McNeill standing there with a snifter of cognac in his hand and a lost, rueful smile on his face.

"I can't get used to it," he said.

"To Anna being married? I know. I can't either."

"Mind talking?"

"No," she said, closing her book. "Of course not."

Wyatt moved through the room aimlessly. "Things are going to be pretty quiet around here from now on," he said. "I didn't think it would affect me so much. But tonight at dinner it finally dawned on me. Anna's gone." He settled himself in a leather chair by the fireplace. "Seems like yesterday," he reminisced, "that I was looking at her through the window of the hospital nursery. And now . . . she's completely grown up." He smiled apologetically. "An awful cliché . . ."

Wyatt stared down into his snifter, lost in thought. Madeleine quietly sipped her coffee. Then he looked at her almost sheepishly. "I'm sorry, Madeleine. Didn't mean to get maudlin."

"Oh, that's okay," she said. "I'll miss Anna too. Not that we won't still be friends, but it'll be different."

Wyatt nodded. "I know. I hope she's not making a mistake. And I certainly hope she's got sense enough to wait a few years before having children. To give herself time alone with Randy."

Madeleine swallowed. Of course Mr. McNeill would find out soon enough. It was not her place to tell him.

"Well," Wyatt continued, sighing, "life goes on. What about you, Madeleine? When does school start again? You'll stay with us until then, won't you?"

"Thanks, Mr. McNeill, I'd really like to." She wanted to stay more than anything, to be near Hadley before he went back to Yale.

But what was *she* going to do then?

Madeleine bit her lip. "Oh, Mr. McNeill, I don't know what to do. I don't want to go back to Boulder. Now Anna's gone, there doesn't seem to be anything there for me anymore. But I promised my mother I'd get my degree."

"Well, there are other schools. Why not transfer to New York? Barnard or N.Y.U. or whatever? You could even live here. I'm sure Elizabeth would love it—the place wouldn't seem so empty. And you'd be able to see as much of Anna as you like."

"That sounds wonderful," Madeleine said. "But the only places in New York I'd like to go are the Fashion Institute or Pratt. I called them last week. It's too late to apply for this semester. Besides, I'd have to get a full scholarship. And I don't know where else besides Colorado I could do that, at this late date."

Wyatt sat forward in his chair. "If you had your choice—of anywhere you wanted to go—where would it be?"

"*Anywhere?*" Madeleine thought for a moment. Of course, she'd like to go to Yale with Hadley. But she knew her grades, good as they were, were not good enough for the Ivy League. And there was a dream, one she had barely allowed herself to consider. "Well, I guess I'd have to pick Zurich . . . or Germany. The greatest jewelry-design schools in the world are there. My professor at Colorado says if you're really serious about becoming a jewelry designer then you have to go to Europe," Madeleine said. "But, of course, that's totally out of the question unless I dip into my savings. Well, I suppose I could do that."

Madeleine paused long enough to allow the possibility to become real to her. She had never considered it before. She had entrusted Jane's life insurance money to Gary Pollock, the ambitious son of

Wyatt's own stockbroker. But she could get it back. "I *could,* couldn't I? I'll have Gary sell some of my stock."

"You could. But I'd rather you kept that money invested. I'll lend you the money you need," Wyatt said, "against your future success."

Madeleine was astonished. "Oh no! I couldn't."

"You've become very dear to us, Madeleine. We care about you, and your future." He put down his glass and leaned forward. "I'll have my secretary get on the phone tomorrow. We'll see what we can do."

"You mean it?" Madeleine shook her head and looked deep into Wyatt's eyes to determine whether he was joking. The look he returned was very serious indeed. "I don't believe this is happening."

"Believe," he said, pouring himself another cognac.

7

God, did she miss Hadley. What was she doing here anyway? Why on earth had she told Wyatt McNeill that she wanted to study jewelry design in Europe? Why hadn't she just stayed in New York so she could visit Hadley on weekends? Now, they were separated by thousands of miles, and God, did she miss him.

The town of Pforzheim, West Germany, had been bombed by the Americans shortly before end of the Second World War, and much of it had been destroyed. Nestled in the beautiful Baden region on the northern edge of the Black Forest, the town itself was gray and ugly. Reconstructed under the Marshall Plan after the war, the new Pforzheim lacked all trace of its former character. Nondescript, hastily constructed houses and public buildings replaced the distinguished medieval stone architecture that had been blown to bits.

Before the war, as now, the city had been a major jewelry center. In fact, the only museum in the world devoted exclusively to jewelry, the Schmuckmuseum, was located there. But, during the war, the Nazis had enlisted the skills of the Pforzheim jewelers to make small mechanisms for bombs. That was why the jewelry center had been eventually targeted for bombing.

Now, behind the town, there loomed a giant artificial mountain—all the rubble of the bombing's devastation that had been later covered with dirt. The mountain, constructed out of man's destruction, was rumored to contain a fortune in precious metals and jewels. There was probably no truth to the rumor; no one spoke seriously of demolishing the hideous hill to recover the only treasures left in Pforzheim.

The war had been over for a quarter of a century but Madeleine felt awkward about being an American there. It was her country that had bombed this once-beautiful town, and she picked up confusing signals from the Germans she encountered. She noticed that some seemed to overreact to her being American: they appeared almost too impressed. Others, she could feel, still harbored resentment.

"Ich hätte gern einen schwarzen Kaffee, bitte," Madeleine said to the waiter in halting German. She took a seat at an empty table at the Schwarzwalder Konditorei—a plain, rather bleak café near school. It was *das Mittagessen,* the midday break that everyone at the institute took between eleven and two. Rather than choosing one of the more popular cafés where the students hung out, she liked the isolation of this working-class coffee and pastry shop. Sitting alone here was preferable to sitting alone surrounded by tables of students who already knew and liked each other.

Before leaving New York, after Hadley had gone back to Yale, Madeleine had taken an intensive crash course in German at Berlitz. Now she was being tutored at night by one of the associate professors at the trade school. But with the classes all in German, by midday Madeleine's brain was too tired to try to make conversation in German with her fellow classmates. She needed to get away.

The owner of the shop, a tall, careworn woman, brought her coffee. Madeleine ordered a pastry—a thin cake with chocolate and almond flakes—by resorting to sign language. After nearly a month in West Germany there were days when the language seemed to flow through her head easily. Then there were days like today, when her mouth and brain were not in sync and she felt as if she were the sputtering village idiot.

On such days she wondered whatever had possessed her to leave the University of Colorado. What on earth had made her think that she could take such an intensive course, taught in German at a German school? Until she enrolled at Berlitz she had never heard the language spoken, except in a couple of Rainer Werner Fassbinder films in a seminar she had taken. Everyone had told her it would be an easy language to pick up, what with the similarities to English and all. Easy for them to say.

"Excuse me, er, you are American, are you not?"

Madeleine looked up to see a tall, blond young man she recognized from several of her classes. "Yes, I am," she smiled. "I guess it's pretty obvious."

"But your accent is charming. You have a good quality when it comes to learning to speak a new language. You, er, jump right in, I think is the phrase. You are not afraid to make mistakes. That means that you will be speaking with fluency in not very long. Do you mind if I join you?"

"Please do," Madeleine said, grateful to be speaking English.

The young man signaled for the waitress and ordered a beer. "My name is Christof Von Berlichingen."

"Madeleine Lathem," she said, extending her hand. It impressed her that Europeans, even young ones, always shook hands when they greeted friends. "You speak good English. Did you learn it in school here?"

Christof nodded. "Partly. And I have traveled. I have a cousin who is English."

"Have you studied at the institute for long?" she asked.

"This is my second term. The work is difficult, is it not?"

Madeleine grinned. "That's an understatement. You know, it seems to me—when I'm in class—that I'm back somewhere in the Middle Ages. All those long tables, everyone measuring and cutting and sawing in silence next to one another. I really feel that an apprentice in 1500 probably had it pretty much the same."

"Ah," Christof nodded, "you are right. Germans respect tradition. Methods that we are learning have been handed down from generation to generation for many hundreds of years. But it is essential to know the old before we dare to seek the new. When we emerge from the institute, only then will we even begin to explore our creativity in a valid way."

Madeleine finished her coffee and began gathering up her books. "You're right, I guess, but it's overwhelming. There's so much to learn."

"Well, if you need any help with the work please come to me. I will be happy to assist. I felt the same as you in the beginning. But now every day becomes a little less difficult."

"Thank you, Christof, for the encouragement . . . and the offer. And for speaking English with me. I feel a lot better than I did half an hour ago."

Christof stood and shook her hand again. "It has been my pleasure, Madeleine. *Auf Wiedersehen.*"

"*Auf Wiedersehen,* Christof," she said.

Madeleine stopped off at a market and bought some apples before heading back to her boarding house. It wasn't actually a boarding house, but a rambling, Black Forest-style cottage belonging to a family named Fischer, who rented out two bedrooms, one to Madeleine and the other to a shy Danish girl who was a year ahead of Madeleine at the institute.

Herr Fischer taught advanced stone faceting at the institute. He was a small man with a forbidding manner who seldom spoke, even during meals. In contrast, his wife, Lisa, was an enormous, friendly woman, a wonderful cook. The Fischers had three children, ranging in age from seven to thirteen. Madeleine had never lived around young children before and she found them delightful. They were very patient with her German and were always willing to help her with vocabulary. At night, after supper, they loved to congregate in Madeleine's room, when she didn't have a German lesson, and play cards.

Madeleine opened the front gate. Frau Fischer was in the garden raking leaves. Madeleine greeted her as she headed to the front door.

"*Sind Briefe für mich da?*" she asked, hoping the day's mail had been delivered.

"*Ja. Aus den Vereinigten Staaten* . . . Con-nec-ti-cut!"

"*Danke,* Frau Fischer."

Lisa Fischer nodded excitedly and went back to her leaf raking. Madeleine had told Frau Fischer that her boyfriend went to a university in the state of Connecticut. Frau Fischer always seemed conspiratorially happy when Madeleine heard from Hadley.

Madeleine snatched the letter off the hall table and went up to her room to read it. She curled up on her lumpy single bed and gazed at the familiar handwriting. Hadley had been writing to her two or three times a week, and she looked forward to his letters more than she could ever convey to him. The past month had been the loneliest time she had spent since she was a child. Everything was so foreign to her—the language, the people, the teaching methods at the institute. Sometimes she went for days without talking to anyone except Frau Fischer and her children. She missed Hadley terribly. There were many days when she wished she had stayed in the States, to be near him.

Madeleine carefully opened Hadley's letter and pictured him writing it in his room in Saybrook College at Yale. His letters always cheered her up. Yale had gone coed the year before and was still adjusting. He wrote hilarious accounts of his encounters around campus with the opposite sex. Yale's superwomen, he wrote, were superintimidating. It was still hard for him, after a lifetime of all-male schools, to adjust to the idea of screwing a classmate. Of course, he assured her, he was merely joking. Yale's women did not interest him this year any more than last. He was being faithful to her.

Madeleine was not entirely convinced. Taking into account the distance that separated them, they had agreed that they would have an open relationship. It was unrealistic to expect that, out of loneliness, one or the other of them might not occasionally take solace in the company of another person. Thus far, Madeleine had not been tempted to date anyone else, although she did long for friendship. And while she was getting her footing at the institute it was a godsend to have wonderful, tender memories of Hadley—as well as his letters—to fall back on.

Hadley had not reacted well, in the beginning, to her announcement that she was going to school in Germany. But Wyatt McNeill had made him realize that it was a great opportunity for Madeleine. Hadley had not sulked for long. He was too enamored with Madeleine to spoil their last weeks together.

Anna, on the other hand, had been tremendously enthusiastic about Madeleine's school decision. Having just returned from her European honeymoon, she went on and on about what a tremendous growing experience it would be for Madeleine. Underneath that, Madeleine suspected, was relief that Madeleine and Hadley would be separated for the school year.

Hadley had been right about Anna's reaction to his and Madeleine's affair. Anna did not throw a tantrum or anything dramatic like that, but the news had been met by a definite coolness on her part. She could not believe it happened and kept insisting that Madeleine couldn't possibly be *in love* with her brother.

Yes, Anna seemed a bit jealous, but Madeleine pretended to ignore it. She assumed that Anna would adjust eventually to her best friend's relationship with Hadley. It was merely a matter of time.

"Madeleine! *Das Telephon!*" Frau Fischer called upstairs.

It was the last Thursday in November, and Madeleine suddenly remembered that, in the States, today was Thanksgiving.

Madeleine sprinted downstairs and took the phone into the hall closet, not so much for privacy as to be able to speak loudly. The connection, whenever Hadley called her, was usually terrible.

"Hello, love," Hadley said. "I'm home and the whole family's here to say hi. I'll get back on after."

"Hi, Madeleine! Happy Thanksgiving!" Anna's cheery voice came through. "Oh, I can't tell you how much I wish you were here with us. You should see how big I'm getting . . . five months. Mother had to have Lucille bake a separate turkey just for me," she giggled. She loved being pregnant. She had written in one of her letters to Madeleine, "For the first time since I was twelve I can eat whatever I want and it doesn't matter. This eating for two is fabulous!"

"Send me a picture of you and your belly. It kills me to think that you're going through your whole nine months without me. I really wanted to be your midwife," Madeleine joked.

"Next time, darling. Anyway, the time will fly by. We'll see each other this summer. Oh, hold on. Daddy wants to say something."

"Madeleine," Wyatt McNeill said, "I have to be in your neighborhood—Stuttgart—on business in a few weeks. Are you free to let me buy you a decent meal if I drop over to Pforzheim?"

"Free? I'm *never* booked. I'd love it! Especially being able to speak English for a whole evening."

"Wonderful. My secretary will let you know when my itinerary gets worked out. Then I'll give you a ring when I arrive and we'll make plans."

"Thank you. I'll really look forward to it."

"I'm back," Hadley said. "Upstairs, in privacy. Jeez, you should see Anna. She's gained about fifty pounds already. Puffed up like a gigantic hot-air balloon."

"Oh, you're exaggerating, Had. I'll bet she's absolutely glowing."

"Growing," he corrected. "In all directions."

"You're terrible. What is it with you and Anna?"

"Sibling rivalry. She got all the best toys," he quipped. "Anyway, look, Madeleine, there's something I have to tell you. We agreed to be up front with each other, right?"

Madeleine felt a sinking feeling hit her gut. She knew what was coming. "Absolutely," she said, forcing perkiness.

"Well," Hadley began, "I've had a couple of dates with someone, a girl named Lydia. So far it's platonic. But, Madeleine, the scene at school is so wild. Everybody's sleeping with everybody else. I was wondering if you'd mind terribly if I . . . I mean, this isn't love or anything. It's horniness."

What could she say? She supposed she could say no, but he'd probably sleep with Lydia anyway. "Sure, Had. Do whatever you want. We're not committed or anything."

"Yes, we are committed. I love you. I merely want to fuck her."

"Well, it's okay with me."

How could he ask her this? How could he be so stupid as to think that she'd give him her blessing? How could she be so stupid as to *give* him her blessing? She loved Hadley. She hated the idea of his being with another woman. But she couldn't *make* him be faithful to her; it was her fault that they were thousands of miles apart.

"Maddie, you're the best woman in the world. I love you. There's no one else. There never will be."

Madeleine was getting angry, but she didn't want it to show. "What, Had? Can't hear you . . . the reception's shitty. We'd better sign off. Love you."

She hung up the phone and fumed out of the closet and back upstairs. "Men!" she grumbled out loud as she slammed the door to her room. "Damn Hadley! Damn Germany!"

Perhaps she should pack it in. Quit the institute and take the next plane home. Wasn't Hadley more important to her than becoming a jewelry designer? Or was he? Was he worth blowing her opportunity to study with the best technicians in the world?

No, she was here. And here she was going to stay. If she was going to be the best, she had to study with the best. And if Hadley really loved her their relationship would survive.

Then she burst out crying. She had the feeling she was losing him, and there wasn't a damned thing she could do about it.

Three weeks later, there was a call from Wyatt McNeill.

"I've just wrapped up two days of meetings," he said. "I'm free until Monday morning. If you can spare the time I thought you might let me take you sightseeing around the Black Forest."

"That would be wonderful. I'd love it. I haven't been anywhere since I arrived here."

"Then we're on. Pick you up around six."

The chauffeured limousine arrived on time. Wyatt McNeill was dressed in conservative business clothes that somehow did not match his deeply tanned face. The tan, it seemed, had been acquired during a recent trip to Morocco. The suit was not like his elegant Italian-cut ones. He had bought it in Germany, he told her, to fit in with the people with whom he was doing business.

Madeleine was once again struck by what an attractive man he was. Of course, there was a strong resemblance between him and Hadley. As things now stood, she did not particularly want to be reminded of Hadley. Still, it was so good to see a familiar, friendly face again that she almost cried.

"We're going to stay tonight in Rastatt," Wyatt McNeill said, as the long Mercedes drove out of Pforzheim and along winding country roads. "It's only about twenty-five miles as the crow flies. Unfortunately the crows didn't plan the roads around here."

Madeleine, before Mr. McNeill's arrival, had been afraid that she might feel uncomfortable around him, but that wasn't the case at all. She felt easier with him here than she had on Park Avenue.

"I've booked rooms at the Adler," he told her. "Do you know it? It's a beautiful eighteenth-century inn."

"That sounds lovely, but any place would be fine. It's just so nice of you. To take time out of your meetings and all."

"I couldn't miss the opportunity of seeing you, Madeleine," he said smiling, patting her lightly on the knee. Then he leaned over to the bar. "Want a drink? I'm afraid after the negotiations this afternoon I need a stiff scotch."

"Nothing for me now, thanks." She watched him pour a neat shot. He raised his glass to her, and downed it in one belt.

"That does the trick," he said.

"Is anything wrong?" Madeleine asked. "I mean, did the meeting go badly?"

"Oh, you wouldn't want to hear about it. It would bore you."

"No, not at all. I'm interested . . . really."

"All right, but stop me if you want." He poured himself another shot of scotch. "There's a wealthy German named Karl-Heinz

Pschorn. Made his fortune in hotels. Now he wants to buy an American motel chain—the Happy Travelers' Wayside Inns.''

Madeleine giggled. "In Boulder everyone referred to them as the Wayward Inns. They were cheap, and popular for weekend rendezvous."

Mr. McNeill nodded. "Exactly. But Pschorn wants to revamp them into high-quality lodges. Figures it's cheaper to do that than start from scratch. Anyway . . . I'm representing Pschorn in his negotiations with the Brown family, who own the Wayside chain." He refilled his glass with scotch and took a sip. "The Browns are quite a clan. Family-owned business. The old man died five years ago and they still haven't sorted out who's doing what. Brother against brother sort of thing, *except* now that they're dealing with Pschorn they've banded together in greed. Our meeting today ended with Laird Brown getting so red in the face I thought he was going to have a heart attack. He's a huge man, extremely overweight . . ." With his hands he indicated Laird Brown's excessive girth.

"How could you think I'd be bored?" Madeleine laughed. "This is fascinating stuff. Real-life drama. It must be exhilarating, dealing like that. Getting into the dynamics of people, trying to read them. Trying to be fair, yet getting the best deal at the same time."

Wyatt McNeill gazed at her earnestly. "Very perceptive, Madeleine. Maybe you ought to go into business."

"I am. I'm not just going to design jewelry. I'm going to open a store. Lots of them."

Wyatt smiled. "So you have it all planned."

"All except how I'm going to finance it. But I'm not worried. I'll figure it out."

"I'm sure you will." He finished his drink and set the glass back in the bar.

They talked about Anna for the rest of the drive. She had decided to name the baby Randall IV, if it was a boy, and Olivia, if it was a girl. Mr. McNeill, too, expressed some concern over the amount of weight she was putting on. He was still upset that she would not be finishing school—at least in the foreseeable future—but he was glad that she seemed content with the prospects of motherhood.

As they arrived on the outskirts of Rastatt, Mr. McNeill launched into the patter of a tour guide, reading from a green Michelin guide on the area. "The city was once a residence for the rulers of Baden.

There are two huge palaces here—baroque and rococo . . . built sometime in the late seventeenth century. One is supposed to be bigger and grander than Versailles."

The driver turned off into a narrow street leading to the Rhine and pulled up in front of the Adler. By the time Anna's father had checked them in, it was nearly eight. They went quickly to their rooms, at opposite ends of the same hall. After they had changed— Madeleine into something more formal, Wyatt McNeill into something less—they met downstairs, to have dinner.

One of the great chefs of the area, Rudolf Katzenberger, owned the inn and presided over the kitchen. By the entrance to the main dining room was a display of old cookbooks. A fire burned in the hearth. There were chintz curtains at the windows, and paintings and wreaths of flowers and herbs on the walls. Old, rustic lamps hung from the wooden ceiling. The tables were covered with linen cloths and adorned with vases of fresh flowers, antique silver, and fine porcelain.

After they had pored over the menu, Madeleine ordered for them both, in German, and translated Mr. McNeill's questions about the wine list.

"I'm impressed," he said. "You sound like a native."

Madeleine smiled, pleased by the compliment. "It's been hard work. Of course, you pick it up fast when you hear nothing but German being spoken all day."

"Tell me, how's school?"

"Incredibly disciplined," Madeleine sighed. "Some of my classes go till seven at night. Before I came, I thought I knew a fair amount about jewelry design. But I didn't know anything . . . not anything classic, at least. And hardly any of the technical stuff. I didn't know flat-metal work at all. There's such a difference between that and the lost-wax method I learned in the States." She laughed. "Don't worry, Mr. McNeill. I'm not going to bore you with the differences. But at the institute I'm required to take an intensive technical course before I'm even allowed to *begin* design. Then there are two years of design, including sculpture, painting, technical drawing . . . and silversmithing, stone cutting and setting . . . electroplating . . . engraving. It's endless! Can you believe what I've gotten myself into?"

"You're not having second thoughts, are you?"

"No, never!" Madeleine said emphatically. "As hard as it is, this is what I want to do for a living. I'm learning my craft. I'm going to be the best . . . and that's exhilarating."

"I'm glad to hear it. Tell me, have you made friends?"

"A few. It's a very international group. There're two other Americans, but we're not in the same classes so I don't really know them. There are several Dutch girls I like. And a German named Christof helps me translate some of the difficult technical manuals."

"Aha! Does Hadley know about this?"

"Oh yes. I wrote Had all about Christof." Madeleine sipped the local red wine that the waiter had just poured in her glass. She did not want to talk about Hadley. "Anyway, Christof is just a friend. He's not my type, but he's very popular. He's absolutely the most fastidious person I've ever met. You can practically see him shudder whenever he comes over to my room to study. I'm a reasonably neat person, but he's obsessive. In fact, Christof told me, in all seriousness"—Madeleine sat up rigidly in her chair and took on a German accent "—whenever the affair is over, and the girl will go on to someone else, I feel good . . . that I am passing that girl on a little more organized . . . and a little more disciplined."

Wyatt laughed heartily. "Well, it doesn't sound as if Hadley has to worry about Christof."

And now the moment she had been dreading. "No, I doubt if Hadley gives it much of a thought." She raised her wine glass slowly to her lips and took a large swallow. "I thought you might have heard, but I guess you haven't. Had and I have broken up."

"Oh." He looked at her with sympathy. "Why?"

"I got a letter ten days ago. He's fallen in love with a Yalie named Lydia. Can you imagine?" she said, forcing a smile. "A Yalie named Lydia? Of course, he insists it's only temporary. But meanwhile, I'm over here, being faithful to him. And he's not coming over for Christmas like he planned." She had more wine. "Oh hell, it's impossible to keep up a relationship from this distance. I can't really blame him. The same thing could have happened to me."

"I'm sorry, Madeleine." But Wyatt McNeill's expression was a curious mixture of concern and relief. "Hadley *is* a bit younger than you. It's a fickle age. And you, I think, are remarkably mature for your age." He smiled. "Well, I'll do what I can to try to cheer you up."

"Just your being here cheers me up, Mr. McNeill. And speaking English."

Wyatt McNeill smiled. "I'm glad, Madeleine."

Dining on specialties of the Baden region—escargot soup, pheasant and roe deer pâté, pike in Riesling-and-cream sauce with noodles, honey mousse—the conversation between them drifted easily from one subject to another. Madeleine noticed how relaxed he seemed. It dawned on her that if he weren't Anna and Hadley's father, she might be attracted to him. But, of course, that was out of the question.

After dinner, along with espresso, Mr. McNeill ordered them each a glass of a one-hundred-proof eau-de-vie made from the Zibärtle, a wild plum of the region. Madeleine could not drink hers. It was far too strong and sweet for her taste. Mr. McNeill knocked his back in one gulp.

"I'm absolutely stuffed," Madeleine said as they finished their coffee. "I think I need some air."

"Good idea," he said. "I'll join you."

Madeleine stumbled on a step as they were leaving the inn, and Mr. McNeill caught her and put his arm around her.

They walked for several minutes, talking about the town, before Madeleine realized that his arm was still around her. Almost as if Wyatt McNeill realized at the same time, he removed it. They continued to talk nonchalantly as they strolled, and when they got back to the inn, he saw Madeleine to the door of her room.

"It's been a fun evening. Very relaxing after being with Pschorn and the Browns," he said, leaning his mouth down to brush hers, very casually. "Call me when you're up and we'll decide what to do."

"Okay. Thank you for dinner, Mr. McNeill. See you in the . . ."

"Madeleine, I wish you'd call me Wyatt."

"Oh, all right . . . Wyatt."

"That's better," he said, his eyes lingering on her before he turned and headed for his own room.

Something had happened between them that night, Madeleine realized. They had evolved from being father and daughter's friend, to friend and friend. Or something else.

She began not to feel as relaxed as she had earlier. There were two more days to spend alone with Mr. McNeill . . . Wyatt.

Anything could happen.

8

As it turned out, Madeleine's weekend with Wyatt was innocent. Nothing happened, although Madeleine detected subtle sexual undercurrents. Wyatt even mentioned that his marriage to Elizabeth was not as it appeared on the surface, but Madeleine had been careful not to pursue the subject.

Wyatt McNeill was an attractive and engaging man, and she enjoyed his company. That was as far as it went, or would ever go, she told herself. And to be safe, to avoid any further awkwardness on her part, she decided not to accept any more overnight invitations from him.

In truth, she still missed Hadley. He continued his affair with the femme fatale Lydia, although occasionally he dashed off impersonal jottings to Madeleine, determined that they would "remain friends." In turn, she sent him back funny clippings from German magazines, or sketched anecdotes about her professors and classmates. She was careful to keep it light because, deep down, she knew she had lost him for good.

Madeleine was devastated, having found love only to have it snatched away after a few short months. One minute she hated Hadley, the bastard, the next she yearned for him. So she threw herself intensely into her studies to avoid moping around or daydreaming that they would get back together.

For Christmas break, at the invitation of her new Dutch friends at the institute, Madeleine joined them in Holland, at a pacifist commune. There she was surrounded by a group of gentle people, about twenty of whom lived full time on the communal farm. Madeleine and her friends added another eight people, but no one seemed to mind. Many of them spoke English and insisted on practicing it with Madeleine.

Madeleine was relaxed with the friendly Dutch people, feeling completely at ease for the first time since her arrival in Europe. The days were full of activity. In the large rustic kitchen of the two-hundred-year-old stone farmhouse, Madeleine even helped make the cheeses and breads that they sold in Rotterdam to keep the commune going. One of the boys, Leo, taught her how to milk a cow, amazed that she had never learned in Colorado. On Christmas Day, Madeleine baked apple pies as her American contribution to the feast.

But in the evenings, tucked into her cot in the drafty barn where everyone slept dormitory style, it was a struggle to force thoughts of Hadley out of her mind. Some nights, no matter how tired she was from the farm chores, she couldn't sleep at all. Finally, determined to banish Hadley from her mind forever, she learned to will herself to sleep by keeping her mind blank and concentrating only on her breathing. If she breathed in and out evenly, not letting any stray thoughts take residence in her brain, eventually she drifted off. The more she practiced it, the faster she was able to fall asleep.

Back in Pforzheim after the holidays, Madeleine was proud that she had made such a strong effort to get over Hadley. It had worked. Although still a bit resentful, she felt as if she had come to terms with what had happened between them. He was out of her life forever.

She never wrote to him again.

Wyatt McNeill returned to West Germany several times during January and February. Although rushed, he always took time to come to Pforzheim to take Madeleine out to dinner. During those evenings, the mood remained casual. Madeleine discussed school, and Wyatt talked about the irritating negotiations that dragged on between Pschorn and the Brown brothers. The deal had taken much longer to put together than originally anticipated.

"The only saving grace," he told her, "is that it gives me a chance to check up on you and report back to Anna."

"I wish I could see her. The baby's due the end of next month. It'll be practically grown before I get to see it."

"I promise you," Wyatt laughed, "by summer it will still look and act like a baby."

Madeleine put down her fork. "I don't think I'll be back for summer. I'm doing well here, and if I work straight through, I'll be able to start design classes next year." She lapsed into silence for a few moments. "And quite frankly, there's nothing for me now in New York. I can't stay with you because of Hadley. And Anna's in the midst of redecorating and having a baby. I'd just be in the way."

Wyatt nodded. "Put like that, I see what you mean. But, Hadley or not, you're always welcome in our house. Perhaps I should talk to him."

"No, don't!" Madeleine snapped. "It's *completely* over between us. Over and done with."

Wyatt McNeill squeezed her hand. "I understand. Let me know how much money you'll need for your summer courses and I'll take care of it."

"Thank you," Madeleine smiled, grateful. "I'll pay back every cent."

"I know," he said. "But not until you're famous."

"You're so wonderful. What would I do without you?"

"Well, you needn't worry about that. I'm here whenever you need me."

The winter term at the institute proved easier, particularly since Madeleine was now more fluent in German. And she had adjusted to the strict discipline. Every assignment had to be executed exactly. "Almost" was not allowed. This often produced great frustration, but Madeleine thrived on challenge. Learning to measure and cut to the degree of an eighth of a millimeter had seemed impossible in the beginning. Now, she was starting to get it. There was an exhilaration in achieving the perfection that the students strived for and the professors expected. And in knowing that when she left Pforzheim she would be among the best-trained in her field.

The teachers at the institute were taskmasters. They were the best of the best: aloof, but kind and supportive. They had no time to become personally involved with any student. There was much work to be done, and they were rigidly demanding.

Madeleine's technical course focused on teaching her to saw and solder metals with absolute precision. One had to learn how to measure and cut exactly, how to join pieces together. Every line had to be perfectly straight, every piece perfect in height, thickness, and depth. If Madeleine missed by the slightest fraction of a millimeter she had to repeat an assignment.

Her main teacher—a thin, bald, middle-aged man named Herr Pfeiffer—would not let his students get away with anything.

For months the class worked only on sawing and soldering metals into exact degrees of thickness. As time went by, they were allowed to make small models of rings, square as well as round. Toward the end of the year they would graduate to bracelets and gold chains. At this stage of mastering technical precision, design played a very small part.

One day Madeleine worked painstakingly for seven hours on a model of a simple silver ring, measuring precisely, sawing the metal, then soldering it. When she had finished, she knew it was the most flawless piece she had ever crafted, and her cheeks flushed with satisfaction. As she was putting on her clear glasses to protect her eyes during the polishing process, Herr Pfeiffer came over to the table. Smiling courteously, he asked to see her piece.

Madeleine set it in his hand, nervously. She was filled with expectation of the praise he would lavish on her. She had worked hard; the ring was perfect.

"Ah, Fräulein Lathem," he examined the ring carefully with the jeweler's loupe he kept on a silver chain around his neck, then handed it back to her. *"Nicht schlecht, aber mach es noch einmal, bitte."* Not bad, but do it again, please.

How many times she heard those words come from his lips that year she could not begin to count. *Not bad, Fräulein, but do it again, please.* Still, reflected in his eyes and tone of voice, there was encouragement. Herr Pfeiffer never, even at the beginning of the year, made Madeleine feel incompetent.

Every assignment found Madeleine doing it again at least three or four times before she was allowed to go on to something new. The same held true for her technical drawing class. Over the months, she drew sprigs of flowers until she thought that, come spring, she could not bear to see buds blossom on the trees.

But, despite the frustration, she was learning. Enormous pleasure

109

came from the simple approval of Herr Pfeiffer. Madeleine derived a solid sense of accomplishment as she mastered skill after skill. She was doing what she wanted to do. She was on her way to becoming a jewelry designer.

Still, Madeleine longed to be able to toss her technical drawings into the trash and start designing. Whenever there was an exhibit of the work done by the older design students, it depressed her. The "older" students were all younger than she. Nearly all came from European families who had been in some aspect of the jewelry business for generations.

Madeleine's best Dutch friend Katrina's family owned a jewelry store in Amsterdam. Cristof's father and grandfather were stone cutters in Idar-Oberstein. Brigitte, the Danish girl who also roomed at the Fischers', would be the first stone setter in her family, but they owned an enormous foundry outside of Copenhagen. None of them had gone to college; instead they had started designing jewelry, sometimes in their early teens. Had they not opted for the institute, their alternative would have been an apprenticeship under the supervision of a master craftsman.

One thing bothered Madeleine. Her friends at the institute were not there only because they wanted to be, but because they were expected to be. At the end of their two-to-four years in Pforzheim (depending upon their degree of proficiency when they arrived) they would return home and go to work for their fathers, uncles, or cousins, in family businesses.

Madeleine was at the institute of her own free will. She had chosen jewelry-making because it attracted her. It was hard for her to accept that her friends were simply doing as they were told. She held her tongue for months, but one evening, over a sandwich and beer with Katrina, she decided to speak up.

"Katrina, I don't understand why you're here. You're beautiful. You told me you modeled in Amsterdam."

Katrina gave a wide, open smile. "But if I model for five years, then what? My beauty will not last forever. I think it is hard for you to understand, as an American. In Europe, there is great tradition . . . and great respect for one's family. That is the way it is. The way one grows up. And the jewelry business is very family oriented, as are many businesses in Europe. I have a friend in Holland who is the seventh generation of her family to run an inn. It would never occur to her to do anything different."

"Yes, but that's what I mean," Madeleine protested. "What about what *you* want? Where's your freedom of choice?"

"I am free to do many things with my life," Katrina said, spreading a dollop of mustard on her bratwurst. "But for my work I am to go into my family's business, and that's that."

"Of course," Madeleine said impatiently. "But why not model now and appease the family later?"

Katrina smiled, an expression of sympathy on her face. "Americans have a different point of view from Europeans. I am not unhappy with my life or with the plan for my future. I like the certainty of *knowing*. There is no indecision, no doubts."

"No doubts about what?" Christof and another German boy, Pieter, joined them, beer glasses in hand.

"Madeleine is acting like an American," Katrina laughed. "She thinks we are wrong to do what is expected of us, and not what we want to do."

"But my dear Madeleine," Christof said, "did Katrina not explain that we *want* to do what is expected of us?"

"It's beginning to sink in," Madeleine said, "but I don't know if I'll ever completely understand."

"You will one day," Christof said. "Now let's have another beer. Tomorrow's Sunday . . . no school. We could make a picnic if the day is sunny."

Another thing about the students at the institute, Madeleine had observed over the months, was how easy it was for them to enjoy themselves. Subjects weren't talked to death. Beer and laughter were what it was all about, the simplicity of having a good time. In other parts of Germany, and all over Europe, there was a great deal of political agitation going on, especially at the university level. But here the students were focused in their own world. Global problems were of little consequence to them.

Madeleine paid for the next round of beer and sat watching her friends. Pieter was telling a joke in German. Madeleine gave her mind a rest and tuned out. Although they were unsophisticated, they were balanced people. And, Madeleine thought, there was nothing wrong in the pride they took in knowing what they wanted to do.

Yes, Anna had been right: this year was definitely a growing experience for Madeleine.

One evening in early March Frau Fischer summoned Madeleine to the phone. It was Wyatt McNeill, calling from London.

"I'm meeting on Monday with Pschorn. I have time to kill in between. How about skiing the French Alps for the weekend?"

Madeleine considered it for a moment. In spite of her previous resolve, she longed to get away from the grayness of wintertime Pforzheim. But it was wiser not to. "Oh . . . no. I, er, we have exams and I have to study," she lied.

"Well, can I take you to dinner?" Wyatt's voice cooled. "Or shall we skip it completely?"

Madeleine did not want to hurt his feelings. "I'd like to see you for dinner. It's just that the whole weekend . . ."

"No problem. I understand."

When Wyatt's limousine, a tan Bentley this time, arrived to pick up Madeleine, she was surprised to see him in new jeans and a pale yellow crew neck sweater. He looked younger than ever.

"My, my . . . " She smiled, getting in. "I live in jeans, but I put on a dress in your honor."

"We'll get it coordinated one of these days," he said lightly. "Where would you like to go?"

"Anyplace, it doesn't matter," Madeleine said, relieved. She had been afraid that he might have checked and found out that she had lied about the exams.

"Then let's head for Baden-Baden. There's a wonderful restaurant just outside town. It has a bunch of stars from somebody or other."

"Sounds great. You'll turn me into a gourmet yet." Madeleine opened her handbag and pulled out a paperback book on wines of the region. "You see, I'm trying to take it all in."

"Oh, let me see it." He reached for the book and their hands touched briefly. The touch sparked a static-electric shock, reviving Madeleine's memory of the apprehension she had experienced during their weekend together before Christmas.

The town of Baden-Baden was world famous for its curative mineral waters, which people had been sipping and soaking in since the

Roman emperor Caracalla popularized the spa in the third century A.D. By 1500 there were twelve spas in the town. Later, European society moved in, to holiday lavishly while taking the cure. Besides royalty, Turgenev had had a villa there. Brahms composed there. Victor Hugo wrote. Dostoyevski gambled at the casino. But not everyone loved Baden-Baden. Back in the summer of 1878, Mark Twain wrote a humorous send-up of the town, which he later published in *A Tramp Abroad:* "It is an inane town, filled with sham, and petty fraud, and snobbery, but the baths are good . . . I fully believe I left my rheumatism in Baden-Baden. Baden-Baden is welcome to it . . . I would have preferred to leave something that was catching . . ."

The rich and powerful still frequented the spa for restorative holidays. Besides the waters, they came for the roulette and baccarat tables at the casino, built in 1821 and considered by many to be the most elegant in Europe. In high season, there were also concerts, horse races, and theater.

But on this March evening Baden-Baden seemed cold and drab as Wyatt McNeill's limousine pulled up in front of the Bocksbeutel, three miles out of town. The restaurant was located in an old ten-room inn that was nestled among vineyard-covered slopes. With cloudy skies threatening rain, it was too dark for Madeleine to see the vineyards or the view.

In the restaurant, adjoining a wine-cellar tavern, Wyatt requested a table near the fireplace, to take the chill from their bones. The waiter brought a bottle of Affenthaler, a light local red wine. Within minutes they were cosy and warm. Madeleine was starving, having missed lunch, and could not make up her mind what to have for an appetizer. Wyatt solved the dilemma by requesting that the chef prepare small portions of every appetizer on the menu for them to sample. After that, they launched into a pasta with white truffles, and grilled wild boar with juniper-berry sauce.

The dinner conversation was as general and relaxed as during their other few evenings together. Wyatt seemed in an especially good mood, glad that Madeleine was obviously relishing the meal. Over espresso, however, he slipped into silence. Madeleine told herself that it was a comfortable silence, but she knew better. She waited, almost outside of herself, watching the scene. She was afraid that the moment she had hoped would never present itself was now about to.

"Well, that was really delicious," Madeleine said, trying to sound casual. "But I'm afraid I'm going to have to eat and run. It's time to . . ."

"This *is* an attractive place," Wyatt McNeill interrupted. "Can't I lure you to change your mind and spend the night? Franz can drive you back to Pforzheim early in the morning so you'll have plenty of time to study."

"Oh no—I didn't bring anything with me. Besides, I really have to . . ." . . . *get out of this,* Madeleine thought nervously.

"I have an extra shirt you can sleep in. And you don't need makeup. Come on, you've been working as hard as I have. A change of scene clears the head."

A voice told Madeleine: *No, don't do it!*

"No, thank you," she said out loud. "Really, I can't."

"*Relax,* Madeleine. You have to learn to enjoy yourself. You're too tense. Come on . . . it's a long drive back. Say yes."

No! the voice shrieked inside her head. *No!*

But different words slipped from her throat. "Well . . . okay," she mumbled.

"Good. You're so serious most of the time, Madeleine. You need to unwind." He signaled the waiter. "I'm having a cognac. Will you join me?"

"All right." Madeleine fumbled through her handbag, pretending to look for a tissue, having second thoughts. "No, Wyatt," she said finally, looking up and taking a deep breath. "I can't stay."

He slipped his hand over hers. "I want you to, Madeleine."

Madeleine sighed again, not knowing what to do. The trouble was, she *liked* Wyatt. But he was Anna and Hadley's father. And he was married, even if there were problems at home, as he had insinuated. This was too heavy a scene for her.

The waiter brought two snifters of cognac and set them on the table. "I want you, Madeleine," Wyatt continued. "It's time. And don't worry. It's right for both of us."

"No, Wyatt. I can't get into this. Don't you see? I like you, but . . ."

"You can't see being with me because of . . . who I am," he said. "Of course I understand. But I'd hoped that over the past few months you'd begun to see me for myself. As the man, separate from the family. And what I told you about my marriage wasn't a line. It was over long ago. Elizabeth and I are husband and wife in name only. At first we stayed together for the kids. But now they're grown. There's no point in keeping up the charade."

Madeleine sighed. This was becoming so complex. "Oh, Wyatt, I've enjoyed our evenings together. I've looked forward to them. But anything more . . . for this to go further, it would be *wrong.*"

He squeezed her hand. "Madeleine dear, what I feel for you is real," he said softly. "I care about you deeply. But I'm not going to force you into anything. I want you to stay. If you don't want to, I'll have Franz drive you back tonight. It'll never come up again."

The intensity of his stare made Madeleine's body tingle. Had she been standing, her knees would have buckled under her. She should get up, walk out the door, get into the car, and go back to the Fischers'.

But she could not muster the courage to do it. Hadley was past history, and Wyatt was a dynamic man, rich and sexy, and he wanted *her.* She was attracted to him too. The attraction had been building over the last months, but she hadn't wanted to admit it to herself. She had blocked it out.

But now they were here. Wyatt was right. It had nothing to do with anything else. They were consenting adults, after all.

Tears welled up in her eyes. "I want to stay. I just wish it weren't so complicated."

"It's not complicated," Wyatt said, wiping a tear away from her cheek. "I want to be with you. To take care of you. This is between *us,* no one else."

"All right," she said so softly it was almost a whisper. She desperately wanted someone to take care of her. How soothing his words were.

He summoned the proprietor and inquired if there was a vacant room. There was, the proprietor assured him; there had been a cancellation.

Madeleine nursed her cognac as long as possible, nervous. By the time Wyatt had settled up the dinner bill and they headed upstairs, there were a multitude of butterflies in her belly. It was a dangerous situation, yet here she was, racing toward it with abandon; as if there were an inevitability about it all. Well, perhaps there was.

The bellboy arrived with Wyatt's luggage from the car. A maid was summoned to light a fire in the hearth and turn down the bed covers.

Madeleine, trying to seem nonchalant, wandered over to the fire-place to warm her hands.

Wyatt waited patiently until the activity subsided. When the maid finally left, he hung the Do Not Disturb sign on the outside knob and closed and latched the door.

He came over and stood beside her. The back of his hand brushed her hair lightly, and she responded with an inadvertant shiver. "Are you having second thoughts? It *is* over with Hadley, isn't it?"

"Yes, completely over. But I am having second thoughts. I want this, but I'm scared . . . of the situation. Aren't you?"

"No. It's going to be easy to handle." He kissed her forehead. "I've looked forward to this moment for a long time."

"You mean, you *knew* that I'd . . ."

He took her in his arms. "I hoped that we'd be together sooner or later. I'm falling in love with you. And I know how to get what I want," he added, matter-of-factly.

"But, what about . . ." Madeleine's words were cut off by Wyatt's lips pressing hard into hers.

The next thing she knew she was being swept off her feet, literally, and carried over to the white-lace-canopied double bed.

Wyatt lowered her gently. "We'll talk later. Now I'm going to show you how *much* I care for you, my darling," Wyatt said, kissing her neck.

Madeleine extended her arms and pulled Wyatt to her. A sigh escaped from her throat as the weight of his clothed body pressed against hers. It was good to be wanted again, cared about. So good that it had to make everything all right. This handsome, rich man wanted *her*. Nothing else mattered except the two of them.

And no one would ever know. This would be their secret.

9

True to his word, Wyatt kept Madeleine up all night, making love with the stamina of a college boy. Since he jogged and played racquetball, he was lean and strong. And except for the gray scattered through his black hair, Madeleine didn't think he looked at all his age, which was forty-three.

Wyatt McNeill, her mentor, now her lover. As well as Madeleine thought she knew him, after their first night together he became a different person. This person wanted her for *herself.* All previous connections between them were dispelled. Anna, Hadley, and Park Avenue were light-years away and had nothing to do with the two of them. She and Wyatt were operating within their own universe now.

Was *love* conceived in the dark hours before dawn? Madeleine did not know. Wyatt *said* he loved her. Certainly they both felt tenderness and mutual attraction. But Madeleine was so emotionally confused she wasn't sure how to sort out her feelings.

They slept late, then had coffee and sweet rolls in the room. Madeleine confessed that she had been lying about the exams; Wyatt was delighted that they would have two more days to spend together. He made a reservation for that evening at Brenner's Park Hotel in Baden-Baden, one of Europe's great old-fashioned luxury hotels. Franz was dispatched to move Wyatt's luggage to the new hostelry, then dismissed until Sunday evening.

The afternoon was spent walking around town, gazing at the splendid Edwardian villas, visiting the Friedrichsbad—the elegant nineteenth-century Renaissance-style spa—and having *Schlag* and Black Forest Cherry Torte at the Café König. The threat of rain had passed, and although there was a chill in the air, it was sunny. Early spring daffodils and crocuses bloomed in abundance in the magnificent Lichtentaler Allee park that stretched along the little river Oos. Madeleine and Wyatt chatted and behaved like two old friends as they walked around town. Once, Madeleine slipped her arm into his, but he subtly extricated it within moments. That was the way it would always have to be in public, she supposed. No physical contact, in case they might unexpectedly bump into a friend or business associate of Wyatt's.

Before heading back to the hotel, Wyatt took Madeleine into the elegant shops along the Kurhaus-Kolonnaden and the Lichtentaler-strasse. He insisted on outfitting her from head (two pearl-encrusted combs to pull her long brown hair away from her face, the way he preferred it) to toe (a simple pair of ridiculously expensive black suede Ferragamo pumps that could be worn day or evening).

In a lingerie shop, Madeleine was embarrassed because Wyatt selected extravagant lace-and-satin Christian Dior underthings, including a garter belt, excluding panties. At Étienne Aigner, he picked out a leather handbag that he insisted she have. Madeleine caught a look at the price tag and did some quick mental arithmetic; did the deutsche marks really exchange into over two hundred American dollars?

Exhorbitant price tags did not faze Wyatt. At one of the haute-couture dress shops he chose Saint Laurent and Pierre Cardin day outfits, and a black Valentino cocktail dress with a miniskirt, décolletage neckline, and puffy sleeves to be worn off the shoulders.

Every few minutes Madeleine protested and tried to stop him. But Wyatt was determined to dress her. He hated her vintage clothes, he told her, and if she ever wore anything hippie or tie-dyed around him again he would rip it off her and throw it into the gutter.

By the time they arrived back at the hotel, arms laden with shopping bags, Madeleine had calculated that Wyatt must have spent about five thousand dollars on her in less than two hours. Overwhelming, especially since she knew she would never wear these clothes except with him. The idea of her showing up in Herr Pfeiffer's class in a Pierre Cardin day suit nearly made her laugh out loud.

Before dinner Wyatt ran a bath for them in the enormous marble tub of their suite. While they soaked, they sipped Dom Pérignon from a single crystal-fluted glass. When the water began to cool, they raced with bubbly, untoweled bodies and threw themselves, giggling, on top of the brocade bedspread. For an hour or so they made unhurried love while a thrilling Mozart symphony played on the radio, full volume. Afterward, they dressed and went out for fettuccine Alfredo at the ornate Stahlbad restaurant. Then Wyatt insisted they try their luck at roulette.

"You must be kidding. I'm not the sort of person who could ever gamble. It's the same as throwing money away," Madeleine said. Having been poor for so long, the idea of losing money at whim disgusted her.

Wyatt shrugged. "True. But there's nothing more exciting than *winning.* And I feel lucky tonight." Even though they were walking in public through the colonnade near the casino, he bent down and kissed her cheek. "Don't worry, darling. You don't have to risk a pfennig. Just watch me."

The famous, white-columned casino was packed with big-league gamblers, an international crowd costumed by all the top fashion designers. The gaming rooms—Versailles inspired, created in the nineteenth century by a Parisian stage designer—glittered as much with gemstones as with gold and chandeliers. Madeleine had never seen so much jewelry, outside Tiffany's, in her life. She stared so long at one dowager's emerald-and-diamond necklace that the lady spoke to her companion, and Madeleine was afraid they would have her thrown out on the suspicion of contemplated jewel theft.

Wyatt selected a roulette table and confidently began throwing down thousand-mark notes. At first he asked Madeleine which numbers to bet on. She suggested several, and he lost each time.

"The numbers are sensing your disapproval," he laughed. "From now on I'm going with my own hunches." He put five thousand marks down on number thirteen, and won.

While Wyatt played the wheel, Madeleine wandered around the rococo casino, discreetly trying to check out the bejeweled ladies. It amazed her that people could be so rich. She overheard one woman (in sapphires) telling another woman (alexandrite and pearls) that a third woman (canary diamonds) had lost a hundred thousand dollars that night, but refused to admit defeat. Beautiful as these people were, Madeleine disapproved of them completely.

Then suddenly it occurred to her that if she was going to be a famous jewelry designer she *needed* these women. Once in business she would be forced to be nice to them. She would have to try to like them.

An orange-haired French woman, wearing a Plexiglas choker studded with ball bearings, looked up from a baccarat table and glanced at Madeleine. Madeleine smiled at her. The woman looked away, dismissing her. Madeleine felt that these people could see through her fancy veneer and know that she was not one of them. In truth, she was very young and attractive, a threat to every woman in the room.

Madeleine decided then and there that part of her education—almost as important as what she was learning at the institute—was going to have to be the study of the rich and famous. She would start by asking Wyatt to send her subscriptions to *Town and Country* and *Women's Wear Daily.*

From time to time Madeleine caught sight of Wyatt, who changed tables at regular intervals, part of his grand scheme. Every so often she returned to his side, but his betting so much money—even though he was winning—made her stomach turn. Nevertheless, standing beside him she noted that they were as attractive as any couple in the room. The difference in their ages went unnoticed. Rich men doted on younger women. Madeleine realized that the only person who objected to the difference in their ages was *her.* But that was because of Anna.

And Hadley. The hurt Madeleine had felt when he dropped her still pricked. Every so often Wyatt made a gesture or did something that reminded her of his son. It was a difficult situation. Being with Wyatt all day, as much as she pretended it was not so, made her realize uneasily that she was not completely over Hadley, even though she had thought she was. Of course, now she had to put Hadley out of her mind forever.

After an hour at the casino, Wyatt had recouped his losses on the shopping spree with Madeleine. Forty-five minutes after that he had covered the cost of the suite at Brenner's, as well as dinner at that night's starred restaurant.

At two in the morning, winnings in pocket, they walked back to the hotel and went to bed. Wyatt was too exhausted from gambling to make love, but at dawn he woke Madeleine, pressing a vigorous hard-on into her belly.

The next day was spent quietly: reading the Sunday *International Herald Tribune*, making love, sipping tea and munching pastries brought by room service, making love, and watching a production of *Aïda* on television *while* making love. At five they decided to pack their things and go for an early dinner before Franz drove Madeleine back to Pforzheim and Wyatt to Stuttgart, where he was to meet with Karl-Heinz Pschorn.

"This has been the best weekend I've spent in . . . I can't tell you how long. You make me feel twenty again," Wyatt said, putting his arm around Madeleine as they looked out their window at the view for one last time.

"It's been wonderful," Madeleine agreed, intoxicated by the high living, "but I wish you hadn't been so extravagant. The clothes are so expensive."

"It's the way I want you to dress all the time. With your bone structure and features, you have an aristocratic beauty. Why disguise it by wearing secondhand clothes and jeans?"

"But I'm not beautiful," Madeleine insisted.

"You're fishing," he grinned. "You're the loveliest woman I've ever known."

Madeleine pulled herself away from him. "Oh, Wyatt, I'm still confused. This *has* been a wonderful weekend. But—you and I—it's not going to work out."

"Of course it is. You're in Europe. The rest of my life is in New York. When the Pschorn deal is settled, I'll find some other excuse to get over here."

"Excuse? You don't mean that Pschorn . . . ?"

Wyatt smiled patiently. "If you hadn't been at the institute I probably never would have bothered. The Brown brothers are notorious for their slimy business tactics. But it was a challenge. Pschorn wanted me, and I wanted you."

Madeleine went over and sat down on the unmade bed. Was it true? That Wyatt had *planned* this, months ago? Back when she had first gone out with him, it had all seemed so innocuous. She had still been in love with Hadley then. This was *much* more complicated than Madeleine had thought. Did Wyatt McNeill *always* get what he wanted? And if he did, what exactly did he want from her?

"You know, Wyatt," Madeleine said, angry at herself and him, "I really feel cheap. This never should have happened. It's *wrong!* You're married. Anna's my best friend. Elizabeth was so nice to me. I feel like a fucking slut!" Tears welled up in her eyes. "I can't see you anymore . . . I'm sorry."

Wyatt was across the room and beside her on the bed in seconds. "Now . . . now. Don't feel that way. What we have is not like that at all." He wiped her tears away with his fingers. "I've told you—for years Elizabeth and I have gone our separate ways. We're good friends, nothing more. Hell, we've been together since college. But we haven't made love for over five years. It's *not* a marriage!" He wrapped her in his arms.

"Anna has probably told you about our youngest child, David," Wyatt went on, holding Madeleine tightly. "He was born when Anna was fifteen. He's severely brain damaged. I'm not sure whether it was because Elizabeth was thirty-seven, or whether it happened during delivery. She was in labor for twenty-one hours." Wyatt took a deep breath and expelled it slowly. "It doesn't matter really. The upshot was that Elizabeth was devastated. David had to be institutionalized . . . there was no way we could take care of him. Anyway, after that Elizabeth never slept with me again. She told me to do whatever I pleased as long as we stayed married until the children were grown."

When he finished, they sat quietly for a while, Madeleine still in his arms. Finally she decided to ask the inevitable question. "Wyatt, have there been a lot of other women . . . since then?"

"No," Wyatt said. "But I won't lie to you. You're the second."

"What happened to the . . . ?" she asked.

"It wasn't serious. We had fun. That's all it was. She got married." Wyatt cupped his hand under Madeleine's chin and centered her face in front of his. His eyes were haunting, sincere. "It was completely different. You see, I *am* serious about you, Madeleine. I love you. I want to take care of you. Don't you see I'm at a crossroads? The children are grown now. My marriage is over. I can't go on like this. I want to start again—with you. It'll take a while, but as soon as I can get it worked out . . . I want to marry you."

"Marriage? But what about Anna and Hadley? We could never . . ."

"Goddamnit," Wyatt flared, "we have to live our own lives, darling!

Life is too short to sidestep our own happiness for the sake of others . . . for the sake of propriety," he said adamantly.

"But Wyatt . . ."

"I know what you're thinking," he interrupted. "But I'm not being callous. Elizabeth is an attractive woman. She'll find somebody else. Anna will come around when she gets over the shock. So will Hadley."

The finality of this conversation filled Madeleine with panic. Wyatt may have worked it all out while he bided his time, waiting for the right moment to seduce her. But Madeleine had not adjusted completely to the idea of being with him, much less marriage.

"Wyatt, I'm really confused. This is all happening too fast." She sighed with frustration.

"Don't say anything. I'll put on the brakes. We'll go easy for a while, be discreet until the timing is right." He ran the back of his hand along the line of her cheekbone. "Oh God, Madeleine, I adore you. Every time I look at you I want you." He glanced at his Rolex. "Franz can wait," he said. "Just one last time before we leave? You don't have to undress."

Unzipping his fly, he pulled up her skirt, exposing the pink lace garter belt sans undies.

10

"Let's drink a toast to baby Olivia—exasperatingly late, but cute as hell." Wyatt clinked his wine glass to Madeleine's. A dozen snapshots of the infant, only days old, were spread out on the table at Wyatt's favorite Munich beer garden. Anna had given birth to her nine-pound-twelve-ounce daughter three weeks later than the obstetrician's original calculation.

"To Olivia!" Madeleine smiled wistfully. She was sorry not to be able to share the experience with Anna firsthand; now she wasn't sure she'd ever be able to be friends with Anna again.

Wyatt did not seem to feel the real world closing in, but Madeleine did. Sometimes at night, in bed at the Fischers', she wished things were the way they had been. Part of her thought she should end the affair with Wyatt. The other part depended on Wyatt and the fun they had together, traveling and staying at the most deluxe places, shopping, going to the ballet and opera. It was a glamorous world with Wyatt McNeill; she was no longer looking through the window from the outside.

"God, Wyatt," she said, suddenly feeling the difference in their ages, "you're a grandfather now."

"Hey . . . take it easy. I'm a very *young* grandfather. And you're only as old as you feel, my darling. When I'm with you I don't feel any difference in our ages." He grinned, squeezing her thigh under the table. "Do you think of me as an old man?"

"Yes, you're an old lech!" she joked, then softened, aware of the fragility of his ego when it came to his age. "I'm only teasing. No one in this restaurant would *believe* you're a grandfather if you told them. I'll bet you on that." Madeleine smiled at the relief on Wyatt's face and picked up one of the photographs. "Anna says Olivia looks like Randy. But I'm afraid she simply looks like a baby to me."

"Me too," Wyatt chuckled. "Anyway, I'm happy it's all turned out so well. Anna's taken to motherhood like a pro. She's upset you won't be coming to the christening."

"I'd love to, you know that. But under the circumstances . . ."

Wyatt squeezed her thigh again, this time tenderly. "I know, darling. But a year from now it'll be all worked out. Everything will be fine."

Madeleine felt the panic set in. Everything was fine with Wyatt until he brought up the future. She was having trouble enough dealing with the ambiguities of the present to allow herself to think ahead. "We aren't going to talk about that. You promised."

"I know. But I'm tired of hiding out in hotels . . . of having you for a few days every few weeks. I want you with me *all* the time," he pleaded.

"I told you, I have to finish school." Madeleine squirmed. "Please, be patient."

"Yes, yes, I'm being patient. I'll keep on being patient," he said, miffed. He picked up the menu and began studying it.

"Did I tell you?" Madeleine said, nervously changing the subject. "Herr Lippmann, one of the professors at the institute, is in the hospital with lung cancer. And he doesn't even smoke. I'm positive it's because of the asbestos pads we use for polishing. And possibly the cadmium and lead we work with in the gold solder. Anyway, Katrina and I are putting together a petition. To get them to stop using it. You know, they've been working with those carcinogens in the jewelry industry for hundreds of years. It's time somebody did something, and . . ."

"Why don't you have the grilled venison?" Wyatt interrupted, still annoyed. "It's one of the house specialties."

"I want a sandwich." She hated the way Wyatt overrode anything she tried to say unless it had to do with him. It annoyed her to play the role of the adorable nymphette. Wyatt claimed he loved her for her intelligence, then seemed uninterested whenever she tried to display it.

True to his word, when the Pschorn deal had been successfully completed, Wyatt became involved with another venture that brought him regularly to West Germany, this time, Berlin. That way, they logged about two weekends together a month. Sometimes Madeleine went to Berlin; sometimes they traveled to the various music, opera, or ballet festivals that were held around the country.

Wyatt continued to be frustrated that they could not be together all the time. Madeleine was relieved. Not that she wasn't fond of Wyatt; not that she didn't thrive on the attention he lavished upon her.

Most of her energy and concentration, however, were expended on her studies at the institute, not the affair.

Herr Pfeiffer had become increasingly encouraging with Madeleine, and her days were wrapped around her craving for praise from the austere German professor. She longed to be the very best student he had ever had. Like a dog waiting for a treat, she would sit expectantly as she handed him her latest assignment. "Not bad" turned into "Pretty good. Do it again." And now she was often made to do it again only once. At the end of the spring term, Madeleine was honored to be one of four students whom he invited to his home to have coffee and cake with him and Frau Pfeiffer.

When Madeleine was with Wyatt she wanted to talk about the institute, but he made it obvious that he was not interested. Oh, he seemed pleased that she was working hard and enjoying herself, but deep down, Madeleine sensed that Wyatt didn't take her ambition seriously. Although for the most part he kept his word about not discussing the future, Madeleine was sure that Wyatt assumed she would be too busy fulfilling her duties as his wife to have time for a career.

There were definite problems with their relationship. For one, Wyatt wanted to take care of her. That was nice, in part, but Madeleine told him that she was not a flower, that she wanted to make her *own* living. She didn't believe that Wyatt thought she would actually open her own jewelry shop.

Another problem was Wyatt's bossiness. They visited the sights *he* wanted to see, saw the operas *he* liked, ate at the restaurants *he* chose. Madeleine dressed for *him.* He bought her gifts he wanted her to have, regardless of whether she liked them or not.

Madeleine was anything but spineless, but Wyatt wore her down. Often it was easier to give in to him than to fight. And even after a quarrel, they usually wound up doing things his way. Once, Madeleine accused Wyatt of being selfish, and he slapped her hard across the face. Hurt and furious, she told him she never wanted to see him again. To apologize, he showed up at the Fischers' house with an expensive gold chain bracelet with diamonds in it. The bracelet he *knew* she coveted was a contemporary design made of blue Czechoslovakian glass and silver; it was far less expensive.

In bed, however, Madeleine reigned. Wyatt was an accomplished lover and gave her enormous pleasure. Still, she figured out that her youth gave *her* the upper hand. Wyatt wanted her all the time. Madeleine found that she derived great satisfaction from holding back. When she finally let Wyatt have her, he was wild with lust. It was her way of keeping him from calling the shots completely.

But was it love?

On Wyatt's part, it appeared to be. He wanted to start over, have a second family, enjoy himself this time around, now that his fortune was made. But Madeleine slowly admitted to herself that her fondness for Wyatt, her delight in their affair, was not ripening into anything deeper.

It had a lot to do with the guilt she felt. She maintained a sharp definition between her life with Wyatt and her long-distance friendship with Anna. When Madeleine wrote to Anna, she simply did not allow herself to think about Wyatt being her friend's father. She almost convinced herself that Wyatt *was* someone else. In letters, Wyatt turned into Christof, Madeleine's blond German friend. Everywhere she went and everything she did with Wyatt she ascribed to Christof Von Berlichingen.

Anna wrote that she could not wait to meet the handsome Christof: he sounded like a dream.

Then out of the blue, in early June, Hadley McNeill called her. It was a Sunday night, and she had just returned from spending the weekend with Wyatt at the International Music Festival beside Lake Constance.

"Hi, Madeleine," he said. "Surprise."

"Well, it . . . it certainly is. Er, where are you?" she stammered, afraid that he was somewhere nearby.

"New York. Just got out for summer break. I'm on my way to D.C. next week to spend the summer lobbying against the pharmaceutical companies."

Madeleine smiled in spite of herself. "Good for you, Had. You don't ever give up, do you?"

"Not until they dump me in the ground and cover me up," he quipped. "Look, I, er, I'm sorry about what went down between us. I mean, Lydia and everything. It was just something that got out of hand. You weren't around and . . ." He trailed off. "But it's over. Completely. And I wanted to apologize . . . for acting like such an ass."

Oh God, Madeleine thought, *why is this happening now? Just when I thought I had you out of my mind.*

"Well," she managed to say, "things happen sometimes . . . for the best."

"Oh, Madeleine, I know you're angry, and that's cool. I don't blame you. But I've been thinking lately, about us and what we had. Actually, I've been thinking about you a lot." He hesitated, and Madeleine could hear fragments of someone else's conversation intruding through the crowded wires. "Anyway, I want to see you again, Madeleine. I was wondering, what if I come over this week before I start work? We could talk and . . . Oh hell, Madeleine, I miss you. Lydia and I broke up two months ago, but it's taken until now for me to get up enough courage to call you."

Madeleine sat listening, unable to respond. Why *was* this happening now? Months ago she had fantasized that Hadley would come back. Now, and for all time, it was too late.

But it was so good to hear his voice.

"Madeleine, are you there? Say something."

She sighed. "Hadley, I'm afraid you're too late. I'm involved with someone else."

"Yeah, I know. That German guy from your school. Anna told me. But can't we just spend some time together? Won't you give me a second chance?" he pleaded. "I want to make it up to you. At least *see* me again. Listen to what I have to say."

All the old feelings came rushing back. "No," she forced herself to say. "It's too late. It's over between us, and there's nothing to talk about." She swallowed to dissolve the lump in her throat. "I'm sorry, Had, but you have to understand. Life goes on."

"Yeah, I can dig it," he sighed, "it does, doesn't it? Well, sorry to bother you."

"No, Had, you didn't *bother* me . . ."

But he clicked off, unable to tolerate more embarrassment.

"Shit!" Madeleine said into the dead connection. "Why did you have to do this to me?" She hung up slowly and wiped the tears from her eyes before heading upstairs.

In her room, she flopped down on her bed, clutching a pillow to her chest. Hadley wanting her back was the last thing she had ever expected to happen. It threw a wrench into the confusion she already felt about her relationship with Wyatt.

Had Wyatt been a substitute for Hadley all along? She had thought that he wasn't. But now, hearing Hadley's voice, she was no longer sure.

Madeleine forced herself to get up and retrieve a small photo album out of her desk drawer, then sat back on the bed to look through it. It was filled with snapshots of her and Wyatt on their various trips together over the past months. She turned to a close-up of Wyatt to scrutinize the handsome, confident man who had everything, yet wanted her. He was wealthy, intelligent, caring . . . everything any woman would want.

She walked back over to the desk and fished out, from the very back of the top drawer, a picture of Hadley that she had been unable to throw away. She hadn't looked at it for months. Now, seeing his handsome face, together with the fresh memory of his voice, made her heart break.

No! It was Wyatt with whom she had cast her lot. There was no turning back. He offered her more than Hadley ever could.

Madeleine looked at Hadley's picture one more time, then slowly ripped it into confetti. Never in her life would she be able to love him again. She was so upset she couldn't even cry.

Well, she had been right about one thing she said to Hadley: life goes on.

If Hadley only knew how messed up it could get.

Despite her feelings, the fact that she loved the son more than the father, Madeleine continued the affair with Wyatt on into the summer. She knew that it would have to wind down eventually. But it seemed to have a life of its own; she let herself be carried up in the

momentum. It was the path of least resistance, and Wyatt entertained her royally; he kept her from being lonely. So she forced all
thoughts of Hadley from her mind, as she had done in the past. And
all thoughts of tomorrow.

For her birthday, in late July, Wyatt flew Madeleine to Venice, to a
suite at the Cipriani on Giudecca Island, four minutes across the
lagoon from piazza San Marco. At dinner the first night—in the
Cipriani's intimate main dining room, bedecked with Murano glass
chandeliers and floor-to-ceiling windows flanked by Fortuny draper-
ies—Wyatt presented Madeleine with a small Chinese lacquered box.

"A birthday gift?" Madeleine asked, surprised. "On top of all this?
You spoil me, Wyatt."

"That's the idea," he said. "I love you, darling. Happy twenty-first
birthday."

From the look of the box, Madeleine suspected jewelry. Secretly,
she hoped that it would not be too expensive or too conservative.
Wyatt's taste was so different from hers.

"Well, aren't you going to open it?"

"Yes. I'm trying to guess what it is."

"You'll never guess."

"A bracelet?" He shook his head. "A necklace? Ring? A watch?
Hair clip? Earrings? An anklet?" Wyatt kept shaking his head and
smiling.

"Just open the box," he said, enjoying her.

"All right . . . here goes." Madeleine geared up her smile for an
appropriate reaction; she was sure, whatever it was, she'd have to
pretend to like it. Instead, as she lifted the top of the box, her jaw
dropped. "Oh my God! This is unbelievable! I mean, thank you . . .
thank you!"

Inside, shimmering out from little black velvet niches, was an
entire handful of semiprecious gemstones, cut in varying sizes up to a
carat: purple amethysts, pink kunzites, ruby red spinels, white zir-
cons, olive peridots, emerald green diopsides, burgundy garnets,
blue topazes, yellow citrines.

"I'm overwhelmed!" she exclaimed. "This is fabulous! Think of all
the jewelry I can make!"

Wyatt was pleased by her obvious delight. "That's the idea. This is
to get you started."

"I know I'm not allowed to display affection in public, but by mental telepathy I'm giving you a big kiss."

"Hmmm, not bad," Wyatt said. "But I think I opt for the real thing. After dinner we'll go back to the room. You'll take off your clothes and let me cover your naked body with these jewels."

"Oh, Wyatt, you're insatiable." She rubbed her knee seductively against his. "Thank you. This is a really wonderful present."

"You're a really wonderful person," he said. "I want you to select your favorites and make an engagement ring out of them." Wyatt's dark eyes gleamed with happiness. "A year from tonight you're going to be Mrs. Wyatt McNeill. That's a promise."

Madeleine's excitement evaporated. Of course, she knew that married men often say they will leave their wives and seldom do. Wyatt might be saying it too, wishing it, without ever intending to leave Elizabeth. But he had talked so earnestly about starting over that she believed he *might* leave Elizabeth. And she couldn't let him do that, not for her. Eventually she was going to have to end things, and she dreaded it. She did not know how Wyatt would react; but she guessed he would hate her. No matter what, she would lose either Wyatt's friendship, or his children's. It was a no-win situation, and she had walked into it with her eyes open.

Madeleine gazed back down into the box of glittering gemstones. The rich certainly knew how to exploit one's weaknesses. But that wasn't fair. Wasn't Wyatt operating out of love for her? Perhaps it was *she* who was using *him.*

Why had she allowed her life to become so complicated? And how was she going to get out from under all this without everybody hating her?

Every problem had a solution. That's what Herr Pfeiffer always said at the institute. And there *was* a solution.

If only Madeleine could figure it out before things got completely out of hand.

Back in Pforzheim, after the weekend in Venice, Madeleine decided that the first thing she would create with the gems Wyatt had given her was a bracelet for her godchild, Olivia, with one of each of the stones in it, in a rainbow of colors.

After painstakingly making a cardboard prototype of her design, she crafted the bracelet at school, during the midday break, for several weeks. Finally, when she was satisfied, Madeleine showed it to Herr Pfeiffer.

"Ah, Fräulein Lathem . . . very nice. This is perfect," he said in German, kissing both her cheeks.

Perfect! Madeleine walked on air for the rest of the day. When it was time to take the bracelet to the post office, she almost couldn't bear to send it off. She hoped that it would please Anna, and that it would be something that Olivia would save for her children and grandchildren—an early piece by the famous jewelry designer, Madeleine Latham.

One Thursday afternoon in mid-August Anna McNeill Ferguson was left alone in Manhattan with baby Olivia; Nanny Williams had gone to visit relatives in Kew Gardens. Ordinarily Anna enjoyed the afternoons when Nanny was off. It was peaceful to have the apartment to herself and Olivia. Today, however, Anna was regretting her decision to put off going to the Island until Friday. The heat in Manhattan was oppressive. Air conditioners whirred in every room of the apartment, but still the air remained stale and warm. But here she was: some friends of Randy's were in from out of town, and she had promised to save Thursday evening for them.

Still paying for overindulgences during her pregnancy, involving chocolate ice cream, Godiva truffles, and jelly doughnuts, Anna fixed herself a salad with lemon juice dressing. There were forty pounds to go before she could fit into any of the clothes she had worn last summer.

After forcing down the salad—she hated dieting—she took her glass of iced tea to the library, and settled in to read *The Sensuous Woman,* by J.

Just as Anna had become absorbed in her reading, little Olivia began crying from the nursery. Anna looked at her watch.

"Shit, you're a half an hour early," she said to herself. Why did this always happen? Nanny Williams had Olivia eating and sleeping on a schedule that was precise to the minute. But Olivia always seemed to sense when Nanny was gone and Mummie was in charge. With Mummie running things, they never ran like clockwork.

Anna put down her book and went into the nursery. The baby broke into a big, gummy grin when she saw her mother. Her legs began to kick excitedly.

"Well, well, look at you!" Anna said, smiling. "Oh no! Your bed's soaking wet . . . so is your shirt. No wonder you woke up early."

Anna picked up Olivia, careful not to get her own dress wet, and carried her over to the changing table.

"It's such a miserable day, why don't we skip our walk in the park and go shopping? Don't you think that would make us feel better?"

The baby gurgled as Anna performed the diaperary functions.

"Good. I knew you'd go for that idea. Maybe we'll find something fabulous for you to wear to Lily Henderson's christening this weekend."

Anna powdered Olivia and changed her into a strawberry-appliquéd cotton sundress with booties and sunbonnet to match. She got the baby's jewelry box down from the shelf.

"Here, let's show off the bracelet Auntie Madeleine made for you," she said, slipping it on the baby's chubby wrist. "Isn't it pretty? It has all the colors of the rainbow." The baby raised her wrist to her mouth and tried to gnaw the gold. "No! It's not to eat . . . it's for decoration. I want to take a picture of you wearing it to send Madeleine."

Anna took Olivia into the kitchen and fed her a bottle of formula that Nanny had prepared. Then she took a couple of snapshots of Olivia and filled another bottle with apple juice for their outing.

Heading down Madison from Eighty-sixth Street, they stopped off at Eightieth and bought Olivia some little French T-shirts and a baby bikini, on sale, and a pink lace tea dress for the christening party. On Seventy-eighth, they picked out a sterling silver picture frame and had it sent, as a christening present. Then they headed for the grown-up shops that were Anna's reward for being such a good, organized mother.

Mother and daughter had barely gotten their bearings at Metamorphosis—a new boutique that Anna had been dying to check out —when Anna began to detect an all-too-familiar baby odor.

"Oh no, Olivia. This is the *third* time today! Okay, kid," Anna said, pulling Olivia out of the stroller. "It's time to hit the powder room." She reached into the pocket of the stroller for a diaper. Except for the apple juice, the pocket was empty.

"Oh damn," she said under her breath. She had forgotten to grab the diaper bag before she left the apartment.

Anna was in the mood to buy clothes; she did *not* relish taking the baby all the way home to change her diaper. The solution, she suddenly realized, was her parents' apartment, a few blocks away. Her mother had laid in a complete supply of baby paraphernalia.

No one would be there, but Anna had the key. Her mother spent summers in Southampton, and her father commuted back and forth for long weekends. He was probably on his way to the Island at this very minute.

Pushing the stroller through the steamy streets, Anna decided she needed to take a cool shower before heading back to the Madison Avenue boutiques. The elevator man in her parents' building was someone new, probably a summer fill-in. He kept the elevator door open, and Anna under a watchful eye, until she produced her key and unlocked the door. She carefully unstrapped Olivia, who had dozed off, and left the stroller in the hall.

"Pugh!" she whispered to the baby as they went up the carpeted stairs to Anna's old bedroom.

From down the hall she was temporarily startled to hear her father's voice, on the telephone, talking loud. She was surprised he hadn't already left for Southampton. Well, she'd talk to him after she'd taken care of Olivia.

Anna headed for her room, placed the baby on the middle of her bed, and cleaned and changed her. Olivia slept through it all.

Deciding she had better let her father know she was there before taking her shower, Anna headed down the hall to her parents' room. Her father was still on the phone. As she got closer, she began to make out his words.

"But darling, it's all set," Wyatt was saying. "We'll meet in Florence. We'll spend a few days there, then fly to Barcelona for my meetings . . ."

Anna stopped dead in her tracks. Her mother had not mentioned a trip to Europe. In fact, Anna distinctly remembered Elizabeth telling her that she was devoting the summer to growing orchids. But if not her mother, then who was *darling?*

"All right," she heard her father continue, "here's an alternate plan. I'll go to Barcelona first, then fly to Paris. You can meet me there. August isn't the best month, but it's still beautiful. I'll book a suite at the Ritz. All right, darling . . . I'll talk to you after the weekend. Yes, I'll call Monday evening . . . I love you."

Anna stood paralyzed. Her father? With a lover? She backed away, down the hall, feeling dizzy and nauseated.

And then she heard him say, "Wait! Are you still on? Madeleine? Yes, one last thing . . ."

Madeleine!

Anna turned and hurried back to her room. Yanking Olivia off the bed, she cradled the baby in her arms and raced down the stairs as fast as her legs could carry her. As she quietly closed the front door, she could still hear her father talking on the phone.

Out on the street, Anna frantically waved down a taxi, threw the folded stroller into the trunk, and headed uptown, home, the sleeping baby in her lap.

11

"I want to go on holiday with you. But it's impossible," Madeleine declared, finishing her Pepsi. She and her friends Christof and Katrina were enjoying their midday break in a beer garden near the institute. The summer term was nearly over, and there were two weeks of holiday coming up before the fall session began.

"But, Madeleine," Christof said, "you must come with us to the seashore. Summer will be over and you will never have gotten a tan."

"Yes, please. We will be lonely without you," Katrina added. The small Dutch girl put her hand over Christof's. They had fallen in love during the summer term at school and were talking of marriage. "We'll have such a fun time. Brigitte is coming, and Anton . . . perhaps Pieter."

"Believe me," Madeleine raised her hands in surrender, "I'd love to. But I can't get out of the trip to Paris."

"Oh, Madeleine," Katrina said, "when are you going to end this affair? This man Wyatt runs your life."

"No he doesn't!" Madeleine said defensively. "He's showing me Europe, first-class. He's terribly generous."

"But you don't love him," Katrina pointed out. "You can't spend your life with a man you don't love."

Madeleine shook her head. "I'm not going to spend my life. But for now, it's working out."

"Madeleine! Madeleine!" A woman's voice interrupted, calling out from down the street.

Madeleine turned to see Frau Fischer hurrying toward them. "I hoped I would find you here." The stout, middle-aged woman paused for breath. "You have a visitor . . . at the house. Come quickly!"

"Who is it?" Madeleine asked in German.

Frau Fischer shrugged. "A young lady. Rather stern. She would not give her name."

"Well . . . I'd better go see what this is all about," Madeleine said, puzzled, hastily giving Christof money to pay for her drink. "See you later, in class." She headed quickly down the street with Frau Fischer. At the corner, they parted company, and the older woman went into a market to shop for the evening's meal.

An odd premonition came over Madeleine as she let herself through the gate to the Fischers' house. Across the street, a black Mercedes with a driver was parked, waiting. She had no idea who her visitor could be, but her hunch told her that something was wrong.

The front door was wide open. Madeleine let the screen door slam shut as she rushed to the parlor where Frau Fischer had left the guest.

A plump young woman with curly red hair stood, her back to the door, looking at the books on the shelf by the mantel. She was wearing a loose-fitting silk chemise and high heels to accentuate her still-shapely legs. Hearing Madeleine enter, she wheeled around.

"Anna!" Madeleine said, breaking into a grin. She rushed across the room to hug her friend. It *was* a shock to see her so overweight. In recent photographs, Anna had been flatteringly arranged into more slimming poses. "Oh, what a wonderful surprise! I can't believe it! Why didn't you tell me you were coming? Did you bring Olivia?"

Anna McNeill Ferguson sidestepped Madeleine's outstretched arms, to avoid physical contact. "I came alone. And I'm leaving just as soon as I've said what I have to say."

Something was very wrong. All sorts of possibilities raced through Madeleine's head, but she had a very nasty suspicion just why Anna had come. Anna's expression, however, was impenetrable.

"Won't you sit down?" Madeleine nervously indicated the sofa. "Can I get you something cool to drink?"

"No. This won't take long."

"What's wrong, Anna? I've never seen you like this. What's happened?"

"You know damned well what's wrong." Anna's voice was flat,

controlled. "And I've come all this way to tell you that never in my life have I known anyone as totally amoral as you. I'd like to slap your face. I'd like to do *more* than that. But I wouldn't lower myself," she sneered.

The words struck Madeleine's body as if they were blows. She staggered back and stumbled against a chair. *Wyatt.* It finally hit her. *Anna must have found out.* Madeleine felt as if she were going to faint.

"I don't expect you to say anything in your defense," Anna went on. "You probably think you've done nothing wrong." She paused and dug into her handbag for a cigarette and her lighter.

"Anna," Madeleine began softly. "Please understand. It's very complicated. You can't begin to . . ."

"Oh shut up!" Anna lit the cigarette and exhaled a lungful of smoke impatiently. "Don't say a fucking word. I'm here to talk, and you're here to listen. I know about you and Daddy. *He* doesn't know I know, and I don't want him to. I've told Hadley, of course, and he agrees with me one hundred percent. Neither of us ever wants to see you again. *Ever!*"

"Please, Anna, let me try to explain . . ."

Anna strode across the room, her gray eyes full of loathing, and stood a foot in front of Madeleine. The excess flesh of her postpartum body twitched with emotion. "There's nothing you can say, you bitch! We took you into our family. We gave you everything. And *you,*" she sucked on her cigarette, *"you* fucked us all. Literally. Me, that night in Boulder. Then you fucked my brother. And now you're fucking my father! I hate you more than I thought it was possible to hate another person!"

Anna thrust out her arms and pushed Madeleine so hard she reeled back, losing her balance, sprawling to the floor.

"I'd like to kill you!" Anna shouted. "But since I can't do that, then, somehow, someday I'll make your life as miserable as you've made mine."

Madeleine sat, dazed, on the floor, watching Anna's puffy face distort with repulsion. Anna ranted on, barely pausing for breath. Madeleine could not absorb everything that was being said. Certain words and fragments of sentences penetrated her brain. Slowly it began to sink in.

". . . *never see him again,* do you hear me? You have to break it off *without* telling him that Hadley and I know. We have to protect Mother. Poor Mummie. She cared for you as a daughter. And *you . . .*"

It was what she had dreaded all along. Madeleine's head felt woozy. As she closed her eyes and struggled to catch her breath, Anna's vitriolic words faded into the distance.

Of course, Anna was right, up to a point. But Anna idolized her father: he could do no wrong as far as she was concerned. Of course Madeleine knew she shouldn't have become involved with him, but after all, Wyatt had instigated it. She had been lonely and he had been there, arms outstretched to her, offering *love*. Anna could never understand. She had never been abandoned as a child, forced to survive alone, hungry and cold. Anna had always had everything she ever wanted.

". . . the most thoroughly corrupt, *evil* person," Anna continued, her voice penetrating Madeleine's stupor. "If you ever come near me or my family again I'll see that you regret it, you scum!" Anna snapped open her handbag again. This time she pulled out some tissue paper and unwrapped the bracelet that Madeleine had made for Olivia, hurled it onto the floor.

"I hope I've made myself perfectly clear. If you break off with my father right away, then that's it. You'll never hear from me again. But if you *dare* continue the affair, I'll find a way to have you put behind bars for the rest of your life."

"Anna . . . please. Won't you even listen to my side?" Madeleine pleaded. "You don't understand. You're going too far."

"Too far! Look who's talking. You do what I say. And *think* about us. Think about what you've done. Poor Hadley broke down and *cried* when I told him . . ." Anna stuck out her foot and jabbed Madeleine in the ribs with a pointy toe of her designer shoes. "Get out of my way, you slut," she said with disgust. "You goddamned *slut!* I hope someday you get what you deserve."

With that, Anna left. Madeleine heard the screen door slam shut and Anna's angry footsteps retreating down the walkway. She heard the sound of the door of the Mercedes being opened and closed, the motor starting up, the car driving away. Then there were more footsteps on the walkway, and the screen door slammed again.

"Madeleine! What's wrong?" Frau Fischer asked, alarmed to see Madeleine sprawled on the floor.

"Everything," Madeleine said. She picked up the tiny, glittering bracelet she had made for Olivia.

Yes, everything was as wrong as it could ever be.

Less than an hour after Anna's dramatic visit, Madeleine heard the phone ring. Up in her room, curled in a ball on her lumpy bed with the curtains drawn shut, she calculated the time in New York. Before Frau Fischer even summoned her, she knew it would be Wyatt. It was Monday; he was due to call.

Madeleine took an aspirin for her aching head before she went downstairs. If only it would all go away. Well, of course, it would. In a few minutes it would all be over.

"Madeleine, darling," Wyatt said after she picked up. "How was your weekend?"

"Oh, it was . . . all right," Madeleine answered, trying to figure out how to tell him what she had to.

"That's good. I want to give you my flight number. Air France, number 534. Turns out I won't make it to Paris until an hour after you. So I thought you might as well wait at Orly . . . then we'll take a cab to the Ritz together."

"Wyatt, I won't be able to come to Paris," Madeleine said softly, trying to gather courage.

"What? What do you mean?"

"What I mean, Wyatt, is I can't come to Paris. I, er, can't see you anymore."

There was a momentary silence on Wyatt's end. "What? What do you mean, darling? What's this all about?"

"Us. Everything." She cleared her throat, stalling. "I've been thinking a lot about us. And it's just not working out. I feel too guilty . . ." Madeleine paused for breath, suffocating. "Oh, Wyatt, you know how much I care about you. But I can't come to Paris . . . I can't marry you. Besides, you know Anna and Hadley would never forgive us if we got married. You'd be estranged from them forever. I couldn't let that happen."

"It won't, darling. Trust me. It'll all be fine after the initial shock is over. They're adults, after all. And we have to think of ourselves."

"I am," Madeleine said sadly. She longed to tell him about Anna. That would make him understand. But she couldn't. "It's just not working. I can never marry you. We can't see each other anymore."

"Oh, Madeleine. Come to Paris. We'll talk about it. We can't break it off this way. We can't break it off. I love you."

"Wyatt, if I came to Paris it would be even harder than it is now. This isn't easy for me, you know. Please, try to understand."

"Understand? What? After all this time you've decided you feel too guilty about my children to go on? Madeleine, we've talked about this." He paused. "Look, just come to Paris. We have to discuss it in person."

"No. I told you, I can't."

"Okay, okay," Wyatt said angrily. "The bottom line is you don't love me. That's it. Isn't it?"

Madeleine paused, hating herself, hating him, most of all hating the moment. "Yes. I thought that I might . . ."

"Darling," he said, pleading now, "please. This too important to end over the phone . . . I won't let you. I have to see you again."

"No. We can't see each other anymore," Madeleine said, picturing the hatred in Anna's face to gather strength. "My mind is made up. I'm going to the Italian Riviera instead. With friends."

"Oh? Then there's someone else. That's it, isn't it?" Resentment seeped into his voice. "Someone from the institute, your own age? Tell me the truth!"

"No, there's no one else. Oh, Wyatt, I'm so sorry. I'm so grateful to you for everything. You've been wonderful."

"Please, spare me the crap."

"I can't help it, but I don't love you." God, the words kept coming out wrong. If only there had been more time to prepare for this, to rehearse what she was going to say.

"But someone twice your age doesn't quite cut it, eh?" Wyatt sneered.

"You know that's not it! Age has *nothing* to do with it. It's your *family*. I should never have let myself get involved in the first place."

"As it turns out, neither should I, Madeleine," he said. "I'm sorry you feel this way. I've been happier the past six months than I have in years. I thought you were too."

"I was happy . . . Oh, I'm *really* sorry, Wyatt. But there's no future to this."

"There was a future. Didn't you believe that I'd divorce Elizabeth? Is *that* what's bugging you?"

Madeleine sighed. "No. Oh, Wyatt, I don't want to hurt you. You've been so kind. Can't we be friends?"

"No," Wyatt said simply. "We can't. Under the circumstances, you'll understand if I don't continue to finance your education."

"But that was a loan!" Madeleine protested. "I'm going to pay back every cent."

"I doubt it. You enjoyed being kept too much for me to think that you'll ever settle down to a career," Wyatt pronounced coldly. "Or at least a career as a jewelry designer."

"That's a lie! That's a horrible thing to say."

"I don't think so. I've been a damned fool. Good-bye, Madeleine." Wyatt hung up. The sound of his voice was replaced by static.

Madeleine slowly set the phone on its cradle and drifted, trance-like, back to her room. The littlest Fischer child bounced into the hall.

"Madeleine!" she said. "Come see my new game."

Madeleine shook her head. "No, Ursula, I can't play now. I need to rest. I don't feel well." She spoke in English, not even realizing.

The little girl watched Madeleine as she went into her room and shut the door. Ursula didn't understand what Madeleine had said, but she could tell that something was very wrong with the pretty American.

12

The row of buildings on the north side of West Ninety-ninth Street between Broadway and West End Avenue was adorned with window boxes full of petunias and English ferns. Skinny, newly planted maple trees—staked with chicken wire to prevent dogs from taking advantage—gasped out of holes in the pavement, struggling to survive. Gentrification was starting to move into the neighborhood. What had, until recently, been dilapidated tenements were now being remodeled into spacious, one-family brownstones.

The south side of the street, in contrast, was still awaiting the fairy godmother's wand, remaining the *before* to the other side of the street's *after.* Madeleine checked the rentals section she had torn out of the New York *Times,* to see what number she was looking for. Three eighty . . . just as she had feared: even numbers were on the south side.

Walking past a group of Haitians sitting on the front steps of their building, listening to full-volume Island music, Madeleine still could not believe she was back in New York. Although she had liked New York in the past, choosing to return here to live had been mostly an economic decision. She did not want to spend what money she had left on the additional plane fare to California, her second choice. The idea of returning to Colorado was unthinkable.

Of course, Madeleine had considered staying in Europe, but after the confrontations with Anna and Wyatt she had been in a state of confusion. She had not been able to think clearly, especially after she had called her stockbroker, Gary Pollock—the whiz-kid son of Wyatt's broker—who was supposed to parlay her fifteen-thousand-dollar inheritance into a fertile nest egg.

"Well, babe," Gary had drawled on the overseas telephone line, "I knew you were hungry to see that little portfolio grow. So I've put you into two real jazzy stocks, Voisin Motors and Datatrax. You'll be rolling in clover in a few years."

"That's great," Madeleine had said, "but I need money now. To pay for school."

There had been a pause long enough for Madeleine to think they had been disconnected. Then Gary explained that he couldn't sell the stocks *now*. They were highly speculative. They wouldn't be worth anything until the companies really got their footing.

"What?" Madeleine had asked. "Are you telling me that you can't give me my money?"

"Babe, hey, don't get riled. It's cool. It's just that, er, you're in on the ground floor of Datatrax. I got you ten thousand shares, but that's to finance their expansion. Down the road a few years it'll be worth five hundred times what we paid. Right now, we can't sell."

"Well, what about the other one? Voisin Motors?"

"A little problem came up at Voisin. They're reorganizing. Just filed a Chapter Eleven. Nothing serious . . . they'll get it all together. But for *now* there's—"

"Are you trying to tell me that out of my fifteen thousand there's *nothing* you can sell for me to be able to stay in school?" Madeleine screamed, astonished.

"No, no. Let's see . . . there're a few shares of IBM here that Wyatt insisted I buy you." He paused. "According to today's market, they're worth about fifteen hundred. I can sell that. The others are going to have to wait a couple of years."

"Okay," Madeleine stammered, "sell the IBM and send me the fucking fifteen hundred." She hung up in tears. Wyatt and his damned financial advice. Fifteen hundred would not cover her tuition at the institute plus room and board for a year.

She had trusted Wyatt McNeill; he was so wealthy and successful. Wyatt had said, long before the affair, that he wanted to help her, hadn't he? A loan was always what she had considered the money he had given her. She planned to pay it back, and still would, damn him.

Back in her room at the Fischers', packing to leave, she had pondered the latest lesson learned: never trust *anyone*.

"Excuse me?" she said to a black man dressed in an Hawaiian-print shirt. "Number three eighty. Do you know . . . ?"

"Next block, miss," he said politely, pointing toward West End Avenue. " 'Tween West End an' Riverside."

It was a culture shock for Madeleine, coming to the Upper West Side. When she had spent time in New York before it had always been on the landscaped, well-groomed East Side, where the McNeills lived. This part of town, above Eighty-sixth Street, throbbed with the idiosyncracies that made New York so eclectic. Soloists from the Philharmonic lived side by side with cabdrivers from the Dominican Republic. Koreans manned fruit stores and East Indians ran stationery shops. A renovated art deco movie house that showed reruns of foreign films sat between a head shop and a thrift store that sold old, dirty shoes. Cuban and Szechuan restaurants sprang up next to odd little establishments that were rumored to be fronts for numbers racketeers. Jewish delicatessens, Irish bars, Mexican take-out places, Latin music stores—they all coexisted, in indifference if not harmony.

Coming from immaculate, rebuilt Pforzheim, Madeleine was not accustomed to the garbage that blew around in the breeze off the Hudson. Or the smell of it, emanating from huge plastic rubbish bags stacked by the hundreds in front of the service entrances of large apartment buildings.

She crossed West End and walked downhill toward Riverside Drive. This block was considerably worse than the previous one. The room she was going to look at was the cheapest she had seen advertised. A musician owned a floor through with three bedrooms and rented out two of them. Besides the bedroom, one was allowed one shelf of space in the refrigerator, and cooking and bathing facilities according to a prearranged schedule. One would not be allowed to use the living room, or entertain in the bedroom.

Stopping in front of 580, Madeleine debated whether to go in. Part of the building was being renovated and looked bombed out.

Oh well, what the hell, she decided. This was no time to get squeamish. She couldn't afford to keep her dingy room in the Chelsea Hotel for much longer.

In the foyer, Madeleine searched the mailboxes for the name of the man who had advertised. There it was . . . number 3B—Sandberg. Several names were jotted above his, in pencil. She pressed the doorbell and, a few moments later, was buzzed in. The dark lobby contained a threadbare sofa. A *Daily News* had been flung down in disarray on the dirty cushions. Next to the sofa was a fake-wood end table with a large plaster lamp with real seashells glued onto the base.

Madeleine walked to the rear and rang for the self-service elevator. At that instant, the door swung open, and she jumped back, startled. A young man balancing a stack of boxes, a blender, and a shopping bag stepped out.

"Sorry. Hold it, would you, love?" he said in a Southern accent. "I've got to get my suitcase and the palm tree." He was slight, with curly blond hair that frizzed around his shoulders.

Madeleine held the door. "Er, are you moving out of 3B, by any chance?"

"I sure am, honey. Couldn't take it any longer." He pulled his suitcase out of the elevator. "Is that why you're here? To look at it?"

Madeleine nodded. "Yes. Is it an okay place?"

"Well, let's just say you have to be *desperate* to live here. The landlord plays electronic music all night long. And then there're the bugs . . . roaches check in but they don't check out. They stay forever. It's like livin' in an Asian kitchen."

Madeleine's heart sank. "I am desperate . . . I've been looking all over town for two weeks."

"You don't want to live here; take my word for it. Okay, you look like a nice girl," he drawled, pausing to scrutinize her for a moment. "Come with me. I've got something better for you. Here, take the blender and the shopping bag."

"Well, I don't . . ."

"Do whatever you want. But you just hit the right place at the right time. I'm lookin' for a roommate. My new apartment has two bedrooms, and I haven't had time to put an ad in the *Voice.*" He smiled. In the process, his blue eyes crinkled up and disappeared behind heavy lids. His clothes were London trendy; he didn't *look* like a weirdo. Madeleine had an instant to make up her mind. She had to trust her intuition.

"Okay," she said. "I'd like to look at it. But I can't promise until . . ."

"Fair enough," he said. "Let's go find a taxi."

Once they were packed inside a cab and he had given the address to the driver—some place near Avenue A in downtown Manhattan—the young man extended his hand. "I'm Edward Randolph . . . pleased to meet you."

"I'm Madel— I mean, Jewel Dragoumis." It was the first time she had actually used the new name she had invented for herself. It seemed odd, calling herself something different. But she would get used to it. And the McNeills would never find her.

"Oh come off it, honey. We're goin' to be roommates. Let's get the name straight . . . the *real* name."

"I'm not sure we're going to be roommates. I haven't committed," Madeleine protested. "I mean, you're a complete stranger."

"I won't be by the time we get to the Lower East Side," he joked. "Come on . . . fess up."

"Well, er, I recently changed my name . . . for my career. I'm not quite used to it yet."

"Then you're an actress?"

"No . . ."

"You're not dealin' drugs, are you?" Edward interrupted. "Or hidin' from the cops? Tell me if you are. I don't need any more hassles in my life."

"No, it's nothing like that. It's very complicated. I just moved back here from Europe," Madeleine said, wiping her sweaty palms on the Zabar's bag in her lap. The cab was not air-conditioned, and New York was in the midst of a humid Indian summer. "There are some people here that I want to avoid. I don't want them to find me."

"Oh goody," Edward grinned with delight. He was smaller than Madeleine and had fresh-faced, boyish looks. "I love intrigue. So, what do you do . . . for a livin'?"

"I'm a jewelry designer," Madeleine held out her arm to exhibit several bracelets and a ring she had made at the institute.

"Oh, I get it. *Jewel*. Perfect."

"But I don't have a job. It's a long story . . . I suppose if we end up rooming together I'll tell you all about it."

"I have no doubts that we'll room together," Edward said simply.

"We're already roommates. Maybe soul mates. I feel like I've known you forever, Miss Jewel with secrets."

Madeleine cocked her head. "Soul mates? But I thought soul mates were lovers."

"Not necessarily. I mean, we might have been in another lifetime. I can guarantee we won't be this time around. I'm gay," he announced without fanfare.

"Oh?" Madeleine said, not exactly surprised. "That's fine with me. I've had it with men anyway." She hesitated. "Anyway, what's this about another lifetime? You believe in reincarnation?"

"Doesn't everybody?" Edward studied her expression and realized that she didn't. "No, I suppose not. I think we've all lived before and we'll live again. My current lover's very big on metaphysics. He's very big, period," Edward giggled. "A bodybuilder named Demetrius. Don't you love it? It's his *real* name, I swear to God."

The cab pulled up in front of a seedy building on Sixth Street between Avenues A and B. Madeleine had gotten her hopes up, but this place looked no better than the last. Edward paid the driver, and Madeleine helped him unload and carry his belongings up three steep flights of stairs. On the fourth floor, they paused in front of a graffiti-covered door, one of two on the hall.

"This is it. Home sweet home." Edward took four keys out of his pocket and unlocked the door from top to bottom.

Madeleine held her breath. The halls had an ammonia stench. Whether it was caused by urine or cleaning solvent she couldn't tell.

The door to the apartment swung open. "Voilà!" Edward stood aside for Madeleine to enter. The large room was a blast of white—even the floor had been painted. It was filled with high-tech furniture that could have come straight from a designer's workshop. Sunlight bathed the room from three windows and a skylight. Floor-to-ceiling steel bookshelves partitioned off the dining and cooking areas from the living room. The sectional, oversized sofa was covered with a fifties red-and-black floral pattern. It provided the only color in the room, except for a large canvas on the far wall that picked up the red and black in a free-form abstract.

Madeleine couldn't believe her eyes. "This is fabulous."

"I knew you'd love it. There are two teensy rooms off this one, so we can each have our privacy. They're big enough to hold a single bed and a dresser, or a double bed and no dresser. I measured. I'm optin' for a high double bed, with drawers built underneath."

"This is a great place," Madeleine said. "But I'm afraid I'm not going to be able to afford it."

"Don't forget we're talkin' Lower East Side. You still have to brave the streets to get here. I'll charge you one hundred until you get a job. Then one fifty. And we share the phone and utilities." Edward paused. "So . . . are you in?"

Madeleine grinned and shook his hand. "Absolutely. This is the first good thing that's happened to me since I came back to the States."

Edward Randolph, it turned out, was a designer too. After graduating from Parsons he had started out as a stock boy at Bloomingdale's and had worked his way up to assistant buyer before quitting to go to work on Seventh Avenue, as an apprentice to an Italian leather designer of belts and handbags. The job paid well but, at twenty-six, Edward was anxious to move up again. He was on the constant lookout for new opportunities.

Madeleine, who was now used to calling herself Jewel full time, enjoyed Edward. He was witty, with a soft-spoken Southern manner, very easy to live with. The evening he helped Jewel move her worldly possessions from the Chelsea Hotel, they stayed up over a bottle of Chianti, and Jewel, getting a little drunk, told Edward her life's story—the truthful, unabridged version—leading up to the unfolding events of the past month in Pforzheim.

"Why, you poor baby," Edward crooned sympathetically when Jewel finished, sobbing into a tissue. "You were caught up in something you merely lost control of. So you've learned a lesson. Now it's time to pick up the pieces and go forward."

Jewel blew her nose. "I'm only twenty-one . . . but already a handful of people would like to see me dead. Oh, Edward, I never set out to hurt *anyone*. Even Brady, in Boulder. I ended up hurting him because I was so dazzled by Anna, but that seems like an eternity ago. I feel like I'm twenty-one going on fifty."

"You've packed quite a few experiences into that small frame of yours," Edward agreed, "but that's what life's all about: livin' and learnin', and above all, havin' fun."

"What about you? I've been monopolizing the conversation for hours. I don't know much about you at all."

149

Edward smiled. "I was raised to be a real nice boy. And I am. That's all there is to tell."

"Oh no. You're not getting off that easy after I've told you everything. Let's have it. The behind-the-scenes, unexpurgated epic."

"You may regret this . . . or I may," Edward said, opening another bottle of wine. "I grew up on a farm in Gordonsville, Virginia. My daddy's reasonably well-to-do, raises Angus cattle. I went to a boy's prep school nearby. I have four sisters. I was the only boy. My mother adored me. My sisters would always be gettin' into hot water, but not me. In spite of it all, I'm still close to them. I had a girlfriend all through school, Mary Page Scott. Typical normal boyhood."

Jewel nodded. "How come I have the feeling you're leaving out something?"

"You're wonderin' how I ended up gay," he said. "I don't know, really. I sure didn't set out to be. But the guys used to go on about their girlfriends . . . how fabulous sex was. And, here I was, screwin' Mary Page during vacations and I wasn't *feelin'* anything. I mean, I liked her. But she kind of did everything. I didn't have to work very hard." He took off his sneakers and twisted his legs into a lotus position. "I always wanted to be a designer, much to everyone's disapproval. I was supposed to go to Princeton, like Daddy. But Mama pleaded my case, and I got to go to Parsons. It was there that I . . . there was a boy in one of my classes. He was great lookin' and he seemed to be real nice. One night we went out and it happened for the first time. It was like being hit by lightnin'."

He bit his lip with embarrassment. "But it scared the hell out of me. Where I come from, this was something you did not do. So I stayed away from this guy, Mark, and I went home and proposed to Mary Page. We got married that summer. One of those big Southern weddings at the country club . . . off to Bermuda for the honeymoon. Then Mary Page moved to New York with me. She went to NYU while I finished at Parsons. We got along fine, although we were both real busy studyin'. I thought everything was perfect until one day Mary Page comes home and tells me she's fallen in love with her psychology professor and they're havin' an affair. She also told me, rather gently, actually, that I wasn't really cuttin' the mustard in bed. Hell, I thought I was doin' fine. She *seemed* to like it.

"So we got a divorce. Real amicable. Mary Page and I still have lunch together every so often. She wound up marryin' an actor.

Then, after all this, I ran into Mark again. And, well, this time around I decided you have to live your life for yourself, not other people. I came out of the closet, as far as my sisters were concerned. But they won't let me tell my parents . . . they think it'll break their hearts. I took Demetrius home for Christmas, and everybody was cool about it. You know, he was introduced as a friend . . . we had separate rooms, that sort of thing. But I'm still not used to it. I was raised to be a mainstream person. And now I find that I'm not. Sometimes it really hurts, deep down. Acceptability is very ingrained in me."

"Well, I find you totally acceptable the way you are," Madeleine said, squeezing his hand.

Edward smiled. "That's only 'cause you're currently fed up with men." But his eyes were glistening, and he reached over and pulled Madeleine to him and hugged her tightly. "We *are* soul mates," he said. "Regardless of whether you believe it or not. We found each other for a reason."

13

To celebrate getting a new job—as a salesperson at the Golden Buddha, a jewelry shop on Bleeker Street—Jewel invited Edward and
Demetrius for dinner, her treat, at a Japanese restaurant on University Place. It had been two months since she had moved in with
Edward, and they all had become great pals. They went to movies
together in the evenings, and museums and galleries on the weekends.

For his part, Edward liked having Jewel accompany him and Demetrius when they went out. Having grown up with four sisters, he
was used to having women around. He felt comfortable with them, as
long as sex was not involved. Jewel, in turn, enjoyed the fun-loving
companionship of Edward and Demetrius. They kept her from sitting alone in the apartment, feeling sorry for herself.

To pay the rent when she first moved in with Edward, Jewel had
taken a waitressing job at Borscht, a dairy restaurant on Second
Avenue. She worked the breakfast and lunch shifts, having to be
there by six in the morning and not getting off until after three. Then
she would come home and, fighting exhaustion, try to sketch designs
for jewelry.

It was an exercise in frustration. Jewel did not yet have the equipment or raw materials—save the semiprecious stones from Wyatt
that she had not used to make her godchild's bracelet—to create the
jewelry she designed. But she was bursting with ideas for pieces that
she would craft when she could afford to. On her days off from the

restaurant, she combed the city to see what jewelry was out there and selling. She was confident she could hold her own against the top designers, that it was merely a matter of time. But biding it was hard.

Finding the job at the Golden Buddha had been a lucky fluke. Edward happened to be walking by the shop at the precise moment the owner had put a Help Wanted sign in the window. He rushed inside and told the owner—a thirtyish, blond Englishwoman named Betty Blessing—about Jewel, sweet-talking her into not hiring anyone until she had interviewed the fabulous Jewel Dragoumis.

At the interview, the next day, Betty had taken to Jewel at once, and vice versa. They had a great deal in common; Betty had studied at a different West German academy, in Hanau, but their experiences had been similar. After two cups of tea, Jewel not only had a job, she felt as if she had made a new friend as well.

To celebrate, Jewel put on the Saint Laurent gypsy dress that Wyatt had bought her in Baden-Baden. It was the first time she had worn any of those clothes since the affair ended. Enough time had passed, she thought, but wearing the dress brought it all back in a flood of sick-making memories. She was about to take it off when Edward knocked on her bedroom door.

"Are you decent? I want to show you my new jacket," he said, entering. "Oh my God, Jewel, you look super. A Saint Laurent? You've been holdin' out on me."

"Oh, this is something Wyatt bought me. I haven't wanted to wear any of the things. . . ." she trailed off.

"Well, it *is* time to start livin' again. And I forgot to tell you . . . we're all invited to a party after dinner. A friend from my Bloomie's days is celebratin' her anniversary. There'll be tons of interestin' people there. And Bambi asked me to bring you when she heard you were a jewelry designer. Lookin' like that, I just know you'll meet somebody tonight."

"I'm not ready to meet anybody," she sniffed. "But I guess if it looks that good I won't change."

"You look *that* good," Edward said.

After indulging themselves for several hours on sashimi, tempura, and sake, Jewel, Edward, and Demetrius left the restaurant and hailed a cab for the Upper East Side.

"Now, let me give you some background," Edward said once they were underway. "Bambi's a buyer in the Young East Sider shop. Her husband Leonard's a lawyer. Really loaded. Twenty years older than she is, and she's gaga over him. You know, it's really quite sweet . . ."

As the car sped up Park Avenue, Jewel could barely concentrate on Edward's convivial chatter. They were in McNeill territory. Ever since her return from Pforzheim it had made her uneasy to be in that part of town, and she avoided it. She lived in terror of running into any one of them.

Some days Jewel wished she had stayed in West Germany. Katrina and Christof had both offered to loan her money so she could continue studying at the institute. But she already owed Wyatt; she did not want to go further into debt.

It had been a sad parting, leaving Pforzheim, but, true to their word, all her friends at the institute had written, filling her in on gossip and news. Jewel wrote back to them faithfully, determined never to lose touch.

The cab stopped in front of a sterile high rise.

"Isn't this adorable?" Demetrius said. "A building without a wino sleeping in the doorway. They really know how to live up here."

"Admit it," Edward said, paying the taxi fare. "You'd die to have an apartment in a place like this."

"No, I grew up downtown. I *like* litter. It's part of my aesthetic sensibility."

"Well, your aesthetic sensibility is *garbage*," Edward laughed. "Come on, my dears. Time to party."

Edward's friends were celebrating their first anniversary. This was Leonard's third marriage, Bambi's second, Edward reported on the way up in the elevator to their penthouse apartment.

"Oh, Edward . . . and Demetrius!" Bambi gushed when she saw them. "I'm so glad you could make it. And"—she turned to Jewel— "you must be Edward's roommate," she said, kissing everyone's cheeks. "My heavens, Edward, living with such a beautiful woman, I'll bet you wind up going straight. Oh, don't worry, Demetrius, I'm only kidding," she added quickly.

Bambi grabbed Jewel's hand. "Come with me. There's someone you *must* meet. He's very shy . . . sitting by himself ever since the party started." Bambi and Jewel wove around the mass of bodies. The apartment, large as it was, was not meant to accommodate the number of people Bambi had invited.

On their way across the living room, Bambi stopped by the bar and stuck out her champagne glass for a refill. "Have some champagne, Jewel," she said. "I hope you don't mind helping me out. Sascha seems so sweet. He defected from the Soviet Union about six months ago. I'm afraid he doesn't speak much English." She put her hand on her throat to touch her necklace, a silver-and-topaz choker, of very contemporary design. "Lenny gave this to me on my birthday. Sascha designed it. That's how we met him. Now Bloomingdale's is handling some of his pieces."

They reached a sofa in the corner of the room by the fireplace. A large bearded man with wild, curly, black hair and blue eyes as pale as Paul Newman's sat, empty glass in hand, watching the party. His eyes lit up when he saw Bambi and Jewel coming toward him.

"Alexander—Sascha—Robinovsky . . ." Bambi said, speaking loudly and slowly, above the din of the party. "This is Jewel . . . er?"

"Jewel Dragoumis," Jewel said.

"I wanted you to meet her. She designs jewelry too."

Sascha stared, uncomprehending, then smiled as Jewel stuck out her hand to be shaken. He stood, awkwardly extending the hand that contained the empty glass. He switched it to his left hand.

"Good to meet you," he said, with a thick accent. "You sit."

Jewel smiled and complied. Bambi disappeared off into the maze of guests. "The necklace you designed, Bambi's necklace, it's really beautiful."

"Necklace? Yes . . . necklace," he nodded and smiled.

Jewel was struck by the sadness in the man's eyes. She considered how difficult it must be to defect to a new country, leaving friends and family behind forever. Adjusting to Pforzheim when she had first arrived, barely knowing the language, had been the loneliest time since her childhood.

"Er, instead of English, *sprechen Sie Deutsch?*" she asked, hoping that German would hurl them over the linguistic barrier.

He shook his head. "No German . . . *peut-être vous parlez français?*"

Jewel smiled ruefully. "No, I never learned any French at all."

There was something about Sascha, in ill-fitting clothes that were too snug in the shoulders, that touched Jewel deeply. It was an immediate reaction: she knew she liked this man. He was so out of place among the champagne-drinking, perfectly accessorized East Siders. In this setting, this Russian bear looked as if he had been caged in a zoo.

Jewel set her glass of champagne down on the coffee table. "Let's go someplace quieter and talk," she said, illustrating her words with pantomime. He seemed not to understand. She pointed toward the door. "Go."

"Ah, go. Yes," he stood and held out his hand to help her up. His eyes expressed gratitude. "We go."

Before they left, Jewel caught Edward's eye across the room, and waved good-bye, indicating Sascha with a quick nod of her head. Edward waved back, mouthing "Good work."

As they moved through the crush to the door, Sascha kept his hand firmly locked on Jewel's shoulder. The grasp of his large hand was so vigorous it almost hurt her. But his solidity also made her feel secure, grounded.

By the time they had reached the pavement in front of the building, Jewel suspected she could fall for Sascha Robinovsky.

"I live in Bronx," he said. "We go."

"No, no," Jewel said quickly. "I thought we'd go to a bar . . . for a drink." She pretended to hold a glass to her lips.

"Ah, I have vodka in Bronx."

"No . . . that's not what I want to do. Oh God, you think I'm picking you up, but really I'm not. I just wanted to talk." Jewel pointed to a bar across Third Avenue. "Let's go there and have a drink."

Sascha frowned. "No money. You come to my home. For vodka."

"Er, no. Not tonight." Jewel steered him uptown instead of crossing the street. "Look . . . I'll walk you to the subway," she said, frustrated. "How can you get work in this city if you don't speak English?"

"I speak."

"Oh God, Sascha, if you're going to live here you've got to take English lessons," she muttered.

"You teach? I want to learn." He nodded. "You teach."

She rummaged through her handbag for a pen and a piece of paper. Finding a sales slip for some toothpaste she had bought earlier, she turned it over and handed it to him.

"Write down your address . . . where you live," she said distinctly. "And the telephone."

"No telephone," he said, writing the address.

"Oh, great."

"You come home with me."

"No, Sascha. I told you, not tonight. We'll walk to the subway together. Then I'm going home. This is too difficult," she said impatiently. She jotted down her name and number on the inside of a book of matches from the Japanese restaurant where she had eaten dinner that evening.

"I have good vodka. We drink together."

"Maybe some other time," Jewel sighed.

"Time is good now," he said.

"I don't *want* to go to the Bronx. Thank you, but no."

By the time Jewel had walked Sascha to the Eighty-sixth Street subway station and explained that she was going home, downtown, *not* home with him, uptown, she had decided that he was too much trouble to bother with. Sascha Robinovsky would have to be one of the ones who got away.

14

"Jewel, get your ass over here right away," Edward Randolph insisted over the phone. "Sandro's decided to clean out his storeroom. Some of his most outrageous belts and handbags are going for way below wholesale. *Such* a deal," he laughed. "Bring Betty too."

"Sounds great." Jewel turned to Betty in the back of the Golden Buddha. "Betty . . . fabulous sale at Sandro's. Edward says we have to come right over."

Betty Blessing shook her head. "I'm too frantic. I'll have to check it out tomorrow. Some designer called me. He's coming round with his baubles for me to have a look."

"Well, do you mind if I run over there for half an hour?"

"Heavens, no. It's practically lunch hour anyway. Take your time," Betty said.

Jewel spoke again into the receiver. "Okay, Edward, I'm jumping in a cab. Want to have lunch after?"

"Sorry, darlin', can't do." He lowered his voice so as not to be overheard. "I'm breakin' bread with a guy who works for Anne Klein. He's thinkin' of goin' out on his own. There may be a job in it for me."

"Terrific. Okay, see you in a few minutes." Jewel put down the phone and grabbed her coat. "I'll bring a sandwich back here, Betty. You want something?"

"Yes . . . but no," Betty said. "I'm starving myself this week so I can fit into my red slinky for the opera gala Roland's taking me to."

"Okay . . . see you." Jewel was out the door.

"Wait! Jewel!" Betty called out. "I've changed my mind. Bring me some lean roast beef, a dill pickle, and maybe the tiniest bag of chips. Oh, and a Diet Pepsi."

Jewel laughed. "Okay, Betty. How about a teensy bag of Oreos, too?"

"Very funny, Jewel. Skip the chips."

They went through this nearly every day. Betty Blessing dieted and broke diets constantly, to keep her figure a consistent ten pounds over the proper weight for her height. She was always threatening to fire Jewel for eating everything in sight and staying rail thin.

It had been six months since Jewel had moved to New York, and now her life had settled into a comfortable routine, revolving around Edward and Betty, her two closest friends. Edward, of course, knew all the details of her past life, but although she adored him, Jewel regretted having spilled the unexpurgated contents of her twenty-one years to him. When someone knew everything about you, it left you extremely vulnerable, and Jewel hated feeling exposed. Edward had seen all her scars; now, as dear as he was to her, she wished desperately that he hadn't. But what was done was done. No more repeating one's mistakes. It was time to learn from them.

For that reason, when she and Betty Blessing became friends she made Edward swear to absolute secrecy.

"But why?" Edward had asked. "I don't understand."

"Because that's the way I want it," she said curtly. "I'll tell Betty what I want Betty to know. Nothing more, nothing less."

"God, what a mood you're in today, honey. Are you gettin' your period?"

"No, Edward!" she said, exasperated. "And even if I were, my life's my own business. Just because I broke down and told *you* everything in a particularly vulnerable moment doesn't mean I want anyone else to know. I have an intense need for privacy. What people know about you can be used *against* you. I don't want to leave myself open."

"But you and Betty are friends. If you can't trust your friends, who can you trust?"

"No one. I don't trust anyone!" she snapped.

"Well, excuse me! I'm sorry I know so much, since you don't have any faith that our friendship *means* something to me," he said, hurt.

"Honesty's real important to me, you know, and I *don't* gossip about my friends. I thought you knew me well enough . . ."

"You have to see my side of it!" Jewel pleaded; she did not want to quarrel with Edward. "There are so many things I'm ashamed of. I don't want to go airing them every time I meet somebody new. It leaves you so open. Please try to understand. I'm not sorry I told you, but you're the *only* one. Please promise me you'll *never* breathe a word of what you know to another living soul."

Edward came over and gave her a hug. "Of course I'll promise. You have my word as a Southern gentleman and a soul mate," he smiled. "Actually, I'm kind of honored to be your only confidante. It makes me feel important."

"You *are* important to me, Edward. You're my closest friend in the whole world. And . . . I guess I do trust you. You've been nothing but wonderful to me." She hugged him back tightly.

"I love you, Jewel. I really do." The corners of his mouth crinkled up into a smile. "As long as we don't sleep together."

"You're safe, darling," she smiled back, teasing. "I've decided to go in for women from now on."

When time came to let down her hair with Betty, Jewel gave a very abbreviated version of her life story, mixing truth and fiction. Betty sensed that Jewel was holding back, and it hurt her feelings. But she had her steady male companion, Roland Axelrod, to keep her from worrying very deeply over Jewel's reserve. And on a day-to-day basis, she and Jewel were really quite chummy.

There was still no man in Jewel's life. Betty often fixed her up with friends of Roland's. Roland was an ex-investment banker who had become a professional poker player. His friends were an odd assortment of mainstream and beyond-the-fringe types. Usually, they were fun for an evening or two, but Jewel had not taken to any of them enought to carry it further. Wyatt had been her latest sexual partner. Edward teased her that she was turning into an old maid. Sometimes Jewel was afraid that she actually was.

Every so often she thought about Sascha, the mad Russian, as Edward referred to him. He had not called her since the evening she had given him her number. And she hadn't been able to bring herself to visit him at his apartment in the Bronx. That was too much of a commitment for anyone who lived in Manhattan. For a few weeks after the party, she had hoped she would run into him somewhere, and she even contemplated taking a course in conversational Russian at Berlitz. But time passed and she neither ran into Sascha nor signed on at Berlitz. Thoughts of him gradually faded from her mind: he was not in the cards for her.

Jewel returned to the Golden Buddha barely able to carry the bags of bargains she'd picked up at Sandro's sale and lunch for her and Betty. Betty was at the front counter with a man who was showing her his work. Jewel staggered through with her packages and dumped them in the back room. After she had taken off her coat and opened up her container of coffee, she sauntered back out front. Betty was leaning intently over the man's shoulder, oohing and aahing.

"Come here, Jewel. You *must* see these pieces. They're absolutely super."

Betty moved to one side, and Jewel caught a glimpse of the designer. His eyes caught hers at the same moment.

"Jewel?" Sascha Robinovsky said, pronouncing her name *Jewwelll*. "Hello. I am Sascha. You remember?"

"You two *know* each other?" Betty said, astounded. "I don't believe it."

"Of course . . . Sascha." She extended her hand. "I remember I gave you my phone number . . . but you never called."

"Phone number?" He looked blank. "Oh, oh yes. I lose it. Give matches to someone. I want to meet you again. But you never come see me."

"Oh, er, no. The Bronx is a long way."

"I move," he said. "To Spring Street . . . only few blocks from here."

The doorbell rang and Betty buzzed in two women whom Jewel had waited on several days before. Jewel went over to help them. By the time she had sold them matching gold rings, Sascha had packed up his case and was preparing to leave. Betty had accepted several rings and bracelets on consignment. They were contemporary, bold pieces for women, fashioned out of beaten gold, with faceted yellow citrine quartz.

"I'd love to take more, but your prices are too high for my clientele, Sascha," Betty said. "You should be selling uptown."

"I am," Sascha said. "I sell everywhere I can. Need to make

161

money." He put on his gray tweed overcoat, vintage Good Will, and gathered his portfolio and leather sample case. "Jew-welll?" He came over to the cash register and waited for Jewel to give the women their change. Then: "You come and I fix dinner for you tonight."

Jewel hesitated, considering whether she should be unavailable on such short notice. But she *was* available, so why pretend?

"All right," she smiled. "Where?"

Sascha picked up her hand and pretended to write into her palm. "One Sixteen Spring Street. Third floor." He closed her fingers around her palm, raised her hand to his lips, and kissed her fingers gently. "Eight o'clock," he said as he went out the door.

"My God, Jewel . . . he's to die for!" Betty exclaimed after he left. "Is he not the most dynamic man you've ever met? And so talented! Aren't Russians divine? Where on earth did you meet him? Tell me every last thing!" she ran on without stopping for breath.

"I'll fill you in later," Jewel said, putting on her coat. "Right now I'm going to dash over to the Strand and pick up a Russian phrase book."

On the walk over to Sascha's that evening, Jewel stopped by a liquor store, to buy something to contribute toward dinner. She debated whether to bring a bottle of wine or vodka and settled finally on vodka. Then she could not decide whether to buy Russian vodka: she wasn't sure what his feelings were toward his native country. Finally, to be safe, she bought one from Sweden.

When she reached Sascha's building, she pressed the buzzer, stood on the street and waited, nervously telling herself not to be. Finally she heard his voice calling down from an open window. "Jewel! Here are keys." He tossed them out the window, and she let herself into the rundown building, an old plumbing-fixtures factory, she noticed from a faded sign in the entryway. Walking up the three steep flights of stairs Jewel breathed in a variety of aromatic cooking smells drifting down from Sascha's apartment.

"Welcome." He greeted her at the door, kissing both cheeks.

Jewel handed him the vodka. "For you," she smiled. "I hope it isn't too much of a cliché." It had been so long since she had had a date with someone she found attractive. And the way Sascha had of looking at her, as if he could penetrate her most intimate thoughts, totally unnerved her. It was silly, feeling like this, after all she had been through. Pretending to cough in order to take a deep breath, she looked toward the kitchen.

"Whatever you're cooking smells fabulous," she said casually, following Sascha into the loft. He did not offer to take her coat so she tossed it onto a lumpy, faded chair that looked like a thrift-store reject.

"I am great cook," he declared simply, shoving the vodka into the small, frosted-up freezer. The open kitchen, dining, and living areas filled one gigantic dingy-white room. There was a vast expanse of space, with very little furniture to fill it. The walls were hung with a few abstract paintings and some posters of the New York City Ballet. Several photographs of Sascha with another man were attached to the refrigerator door with masking tape.

An enormous gray cat with a tan diamond-shaped patch on its forehead appeared out of nowhere and began rubbing its back against Jewel's leg.

"Oh, hello," she said. "Who're you?"

"That is Lisa . . . cat of roommate, Zhenya. He find her before we move here. In Russia, is good luck for cat to be first to enter new home. Bad luck if any cat crosses your path, not only black."

"Really? Do you believe that?"

Sascha smiled. "Yes, I am superstitious about some things. Cat cross my path in Bronx. Next day my apartment was robbed. Lucky I had appointment with my jewelry. They steal only cheap radio and toaster. But they leave big mess."

"Burglars trash places when there isn't anything good to take," Jewel said. "But I wouldn't blame a New York robbery on a cat crossing your path. It was a coincidence." Jewel picked up the heavy cat. "God, she's big. Eating a lot of good Russian food, are you?" she said to the purring animal. "I love cats. I had one as a child. It was my best friend." She paused, thinking of Scrappy. "I think they're good luck."

"Me, I like dogs," Sascha said. "But too much trouble in city. Someday I live in country . . . with big family and big dogs." He laughed. "I dream American dream, no?"

Jewel laughed too. "Then you like it here? You don't regret . . ."

"There are regrets, of course. But now I have found you . . ." he trailed off. "I hope you have big appetite," he said, going over to the stove. "I make pirozhki, and cabbage stuffed with lamb, and good

163

black Russian bread with caviar made from eggplant. I am sad I cannot buy real caviar. But someday soon."

"No problem," Jewel smiled. "I don't like caviar."

"What? How come? We fix that . . . when I can afford."

"No rush. I really can't eat the stuff," Jewel insisted.

"You cannot be lover of Russian man and not like caviar," Sascha said.

Jewel started to object. She was *not* his lover. But she decided to say nothing and let the subject drop. Most likely, he did not mean to use the word. Sascha's English was considerably better than it had been, but she was aware of his struggle to find the right words to express himself.

"Can I do anything to help?" she offered, still feeling uneasy.

He pointed to a chair. "Sit. You drink vodka."

She wasn't sure whether it was a question or a statement. "Well, I never have actually."

"What? You are strange girl," he said, pouring vodka halfway up in two liqueur glasses. He handed her a glass and raised his to her. *"Na zdorovie!* To your health!" He tossed his back with one gulp, then popped a slice of pickled cucumber, from a small bowl on the kitchen counter, into his mouth.

Jewel took a dainty sip. In truth, she did not like the taste of spirits. Wine, she enjoyed, when it was part of a good meal, or beer, with pizza or Chinese food. Anything stronger went straight to her head.

"Drink!" Sascha ordered. "Do not sip. All of it . . . at once."

"No . . . I can't do that," Jewel balked.

He went to the oven and brought out a plate of little meat-filled pastries. "Here are pirozhki. Now, first you drink vodka. Breathe out . . . get rid of breath. Then you drink." He stood over Jewel and watched her. She exhaled, then brought the glass to her lips and let the clear liquid enter her mouth.

"Ugh!" she swallowed quickly, downing the vodka in one gulp. Then she launched into a spasm of coughing.

"Good," Sascha said, ignoring the coughing fit. "Now, follow with pirozhki." He picked one up and shoved it in her mouth the moment the coughing stopped. She took a bite, chewed and swallowed it, obeying. After the jolt of vodka the warm pastry was comforting, delicious.

"Good. Now you know Russian secret. Always breathe out before you drink vodka. Always eat after. Drink . . . eat. That is Russian way."

"That still doesn't keep you from getting drunk, does it?" Jewel asked, smiling. After the initial jolt, she felt a congenial warmth invade her body.

"No. But food and drink, they go together. Always remember. Never drink without food." Sascha refilled their glasses and handed her another pastry. "Never eat without vodka."

"You have to be patient with me," Jewel said, setting the second vodka on the kitchen counter. "If I drink too much it'll make me sick."

"You not used to vodka. You will get used."

"No . . . I don't think so." Jewel remembered that her friend Christof told her that Russians were rumored to coat their stomachs with olive oil so they could drink their comrades under the table. Perhaps she would try it before she saw Sascha again, if she saw him again. It was still too soon to tell what was going to happen, although she knew what *Sascha* thought was going to happen.

"Er, I brought some sketches of my work . . . my jewelry designs," she said. "I thought maybe you'd like to look at them."

Sascha set down his vodka and stared at her with interest. "You design jewelry?"

"Well, yes, of course." The night Jewel had met him, Bambi had introduced her as a fellow jewelry designer. But his English wasn't very good then. He probably hadn't understood. "I make gold rings for Betty's shop. Simple stuff, but there's a market for it."

"Well, where are they? The sketches," Sascha demanded. "Dinner ready soon."

"Oh, well, we don't have to look at them now."

"Yes. I want to see," Sascha said.

Jewel regretted having broached the subject. She had brought the sketches along as an icebreaker. Now too much importance had been attached to them. Sascha waited in silence while she went to get her portfolio.

"There really isn't much here. I only brought a few . . ."

"No apologize. Let me see." He took the portfolio from her and set it on the kitchen counter. Without comment he turned the pages, studying each drawing carefully before going on to the next one.

When he reached the end, he closed the book and handed it back to her.

"You show promise," he said finally. "Good, clean ideas. Perhaps when you study you will carry these ideas further."

"But I have studied!" Jewel flared. "At one of the best technical schools in West Germany. And at the University of Colorado. And with the top jewelry designer in Boulder."

Sascha shrugged. "Would be better if I saw actual pieces. Then I could advise . . ."

"Well, I haven't been able to make them. I haven't had time and I don't have the right equipment. I can't afford the materials yet."

"Then you cannot be serious about being designer," he said.

"I am! But it takes time. You know that."

He poured himself another vodka and downed it in one swallow, following it with another pirozhki. "Jewel, please understand. When I arrive in this country I have nothing. Forty dollars and address of Russian family who help other Russians. I come here and take job cleaning vegetables in kitchen of Chinese restaurant in Bronx. I walk around to stores and pawn shops. I walk and look and walk and look. I buy cheap . . . opals, amethyst, pearls, topaz, silver knives and forks. All real stuff nobody knows is real. I take home and melt down. I *make* my own tools and find cheap ones on Canal Street. Sleep only two, three hours a day. In four months I have small collection to show stores. I am good designer. I work hard. Every day I go to stores. Finally get appointments with buyers. They like. They buy. After six months in States, I quit vegetable job and work full time on what I love." He paused and looked into Jewel's eyes. "I do not mean to criticize. But you need to work. The *will* is everything. The will to succeed. You need more will, my Jewel. And more study. You have talent, that I can see. But you need to develop."

Jewel sighed and looked away. There was no way she could top Sascha on the subject of hardship.

And he was right. Ever since she had arrived back in New York she had made up excuses as to why she couldn't do what she wanted to do. She thought about her childhood, after her mother deserted her, when she had *really* been hungry. Life, on the whole, had been good to her since then. But all she had done the past six months was whine to herself, in secret, about how she had been mistreated by the McNeills.

"You're right, Sascha. I've been avoiding work. The rings I do for Betty I can make with my eyes closed. I guess when it comes down to it, I'm scared. Scared that I won't be good enough."

"But you will never know if you do not try. Stop taking vacation," he said.

Something about that made Jewel laugh. Here she had been grinding away, day after day, making ends meet in this expensive city. A vacation indeed! Still, she knew what Sascha meant. And he was right.

"Okay, I'll get off my ass," she said. "I promise."

"Good, Jewel. That I like to hear." He was back over by the stove, stirring something in a large kettle.

"It must have been very hard, leaving your country and coming here."

"Hard. Yes. But right choice for me as artist."

"Did you leave a lot behind? Family, I mean."

"Yes, of course. But I wait to leave until after my mother and father are dead. Now . . . no talk of past. No looking back, as they say."

"But how did you get out of the country?"

"Everybody think I go on holiday to seashore. I pack little. Leave everything in Moscow . . . tools, jewelry, sketches, photographs, books. No one suspicious. I have connections. Underground. I get to Turkey. Then work on freighter to States. After three months, I am here. Now, Jewel, no more questions. Past is past."

Jewel nodded, respecting Sascha's privacy, despite her curiosity. After all, she expected people to respect hers. He would tell her more when he wanted to, if he wanted to. That was the way it should be.

"Okay . . . is ready," Sascha said abruptly, scooping stuffed cabbages onto a serving plate. "We eat."

The dining table was a door propped up on two sawhorses. The chairs were stacked orange crates, painted purple. Sascha lit candles that had been stuck into Chianti bottles and prepared a plate for Jewel.

She sat in the chair he designated for her and placed her napkin in her lap. "After dinner, will you show me your work? I'm dying to see more," she said, searching for something new to talk about.

"Of course . . . but you must eat first. I cook a lot of food for you," Sascha said. "To give some fat for your bones."

Jewel laughed. "You think I'm too skinny? Haven't you heard, you can't be too rich or too thin?"

"I don't agree," he said. "You can be . . . both."

There was great seriousness in his eyes, and Jewel didn't pursue the subject. She felt off balance enough as it was.

"The cabbage is delicious. So is everything," she said to cover her embarrassment. "You must have spent all afternoon cooking."

"When I cook for you, Jewel, there is no time . . . only happiness. I will cook for you often," he said without fanfare.

Jewel decided to let the remark pass. "This is a nice loft. Where's your roommate?"

"Zhenya? He is dancer. On tour a lot. Is convenient."

"Hmmm," Jewel nodded. *I'll bet it is,* she thought. "Your English has certainly improved since I met you. You've been working hard."

"I meet Russian girl. She has lived in America five years. We spend much time together. She teach me."

"Oh. Are you . . . do you see her . . . a lot?" Jewel asked, immediately regretting it.

"We are friends," he grinned. "That is all."

Jewel swallowed. "I didn't mean to pry. Anyway, all I really meant is that your English is so much better."

God, why did this man make her feel so uncomfortable? Of course, she knew why. As tense as she was, the physical attraction was undeniable. Jewel wanted to have an affair with Sascha, except the negative angel sitting on her shoulder reminded her that she shouldn't take up with a struggling immigrant. She had her own career to think of. That hinged on good connections with the right people. What she needed was a well-heeled society boyfriend. Not Sascha. But, oh, those pale blue eyes. She could imagine making love to him, being swallowed up, engulfed by the largeness of him.

Suddenly, Jewel realized that Sascha was staring at her, as if reading her thoughts. She felt so embarrassed she almost blushed. He smiled at her, and she managed to grin back. There was no doubt that he wanted her too.

What the hell, she had not slept with a man in many months.

"You are very special woman, Jewel," Sascha said, giving her a look that took her appetite away completely.

She felt nervous anticipation in her stomach.

"I knew I would find you again," he said softly. He walked around the table and held his hand out to her. "This time I will not lose you. Come, my darling Jewel," he whispered. "Food will wait. We eat later . . . when we are more hungry."

Well, okay. She would sleep with him. But that didn't mean she had to become *involved*.

15

A taxi containing Jewel's worldly possessions waited patiently on the corner of Sixth Street and Avenue B. Edward helped Jewel rearrange suitcases and shopping bags so the trunk would close. "Where *is* Potemkin, anyway?" Edward asked. "I thought he was goin' to help you move."

"Saks called and he had to rush uptown. They're interested in his work for next Christmas's catalog. It'd be really fantastic," Jewel said. "His pieces would be in all their stores, all across the country."

"Good for him," Edward said unenthusiastically, but Jewel didn't notice.

"Here, be a love and take this back upstairs, would you? It's not going to make it." Jewel handed Edward her collapsible worktable. "I'll pick it up tomorrow."

Edward propped the table against a mailbox. "Well . . . I'm goin' to miss you, old girl. If things don't work out you come straight home, promise?" Edward held out his arms to her.

"Oh, Edward, what am I doing?" Jewel giggled happily, hugging her friend. "This is crazy. But Sascha's absolutely overwhelming. He's the most romantic man. Still, I know it's going against everything I've planned . . ."

"Excuse me, lady," the cabdriver interrupted, "but this is no time to have second thoughts. The meter's running."

"I know," Jewel said. "Just hold on a minute."

"Well, nobody said love was supposed to go accordin' to plan,"

Edward drawled. "And when all is said and done, love *is* everything
. . . almost. Sex alone has its moments." He grinned.

"Oh, Edward, you're terrible!"

He opened the cab door for Jewel. "Look, I mean it, if it doesn't
work out, don't be too proud to move back here. I'm not rentin' out
your room."

Edward's new job had come through, designing belts and handbags for Adrian Kelsy, one of Seventh Avenue's newest darlings.
Edward was now going places and clearing three times what he had
been making at Sandro's.

"I know how you feel about Sascha. I agree. There are a lot of
differences. But it'll work. We're mad about each other. And you'll
get to like him." Jewel kissed Edward's cheek and stepped into the
cab. "You'll come for dinner soon, for a relaxing evening. Sascha's
very sweet and caring. You'll see. It's just that he's had such a hard
life."

"I guess so. Defectin' and all." Edward sighed. "Look, for your
sake, I'll try to like him . . . I really will." He felt Jewel was making a
big mistake, but he knew better than to say anything. God knew he
had made a fool of himself over love often enough. He just hoped she
wouldn't be hurt.

"That's the spirit. I'll call tomorrow and check in," Jewel said. "And
thanks. You're a real friend."

"God, darlin', get the hell out of here before I burst into tears."
Edward turned away, picked up Jewel's worktable, and rushed back
into his building.

"Hey, lady, where are we going?" the driver said, putting down his
News.

"One Sixteen Spring Street," Jewel said, heading off to begin her
new life.

It *was* crazy, she knew, moving in with Sascha Robinovsky after
only being with him for a couple of weeks. But Sascha was irresistible,
and she was madly in love with him. He took up all of her and had
been able to banish the ghosts of Hadley and Wyatt McNeill. With
Sascha, there was no room for anyone else. And so, Jewel knew, her
plans would have to be revised accordingly.

She was unpacking her clothes, trying to find space to put them in
Sascha's disorderly closet, when the door to the Spring Street loft was

flung open and Sascha appeared. When he burst into a room it was always with great energy.

"Oh, my darling. You are here!" Sascha said, throwing his arms around her. "We celebrate tonight. You are living with me as my woman. And Saks is buying my jewelry!" He burst into a wide grin. "I think you bring me luck. No, I *know* it. My life will change with you."

"Oh, Sascha, with you my life has *already* changed. I'm happy. And it's so wonderful to feel happy again." She looked up into his shining eyes. "I love you so much. This is the real thing."

"Real thing for me too," he said. He took off his overcoat and opened his briefcase. "I make present for you. Here. To celebrate our being together."

He handed her a delicate, eighteen-karat-gold bracelet, engraved with flowers and set with pavé diamonds, sapphires, and aquamarines.

"Oh, Sascha. This is absolutely beautiful." She slipped it onto her wrist and held it up so the gemstones would catch the light.

"I pick blue stones in many different shades—to match your eyes. Color of your eyes changes often . . . many shades of blue."

"Oh, darling, thank you," Jewel said, glowing. "This is the most beautiful bracelet I've ever seen, much less owned."

"Saks want to buy it. I tell them, 'No . . . it is sold.' They want me to copy it. I tell them, 'No . . . it is one of a kind.' " He leaned down and kissed her tenderly. "Only for you, my Jewel."

He kissed her again, more passionately and she responded, ecstatic to be in love again after having been afraid she never would be.

"We make love now," he said. "And then go out to dinner for celebration."

He chased Jewel over to the bed and pulled off her clothes with lustful exuberance. Giggling, she undressed him, then she tried her new bracelet on his erection.

"Oh God, it won't fit," she exclaimed. "You're bigger than my arm!"

"I am big Russian bear," he laughed, letting his massive body engulf her tiny one.

"Yes, you are," she whispered. "And you're mine."

"I love you, my Jewel."

As it turned out, they celebrated by staying in bed for the entire weekend, ordering in Chinese food and pizza rather than dressing and going out. And when it was finally time for Sascha to get back to work, Jewel could barely walk.

But she was deliriously happy.

Early summer sun was deflected through the dirty windows of Sascha's loft. Although Jewel had not yet gotten around to cleaning the old, loose, glass panes, signs of her presence over the past months were in full evidence. Sascha cared nothing about decorating; he considered it woman's work. Jewel could do anything she wanted.

There was now a smattering of furniture, real pieces acquired from the Salvation Army and re-covered by Jewel with a bright Swedish fabric obtained below cost from a friend of Edward's. On the wall above the kitchen counter was a colorful display of inexpensive Chinese fans from Chinatown. Jewel's lifetime collection of costume jewelry from garage sales and thrift shops glittered from nails bored into the wall alongside the bed. There were some Indian dhurrie scatter rugs that Betty had lent her. Old movie posters, cut from a book and staple-gunned into place, papered the bathroom walls.

The dancer roommate, Zhenya, had moved out after the first month, much to Jewel's relief. Fortunately, he had not been around much. The loft was large, but divided in such a way that it really only suited two people if they were a couple, and no more than two.

So Jewel was unprepared, this beautiful summer day, for Sascha's announcement.

"Jewel, my darling?" Sascha said, looking up from his worktable where he was soldering stainless steel links into an intricate, geometric design for a bracelet and choker set. "My old friend Yuri comes to New York tomorrow from Paris. He will stay here. Go buy inflatable mattress from sports store. We put in corner."

Jewel stared at him through her dark glasses. She was standing in the doorway on her way to work, but stopped dead in her tracks. "Come again?"

"What? I do not understand, 'come again.' "

"You invited your friend Yuri to *stay* here without asking me? And now you expect *me* to go buy him a mattress and lug it back here myself? You must be out of your mind," she said indignantly.

"But I am busy. I promise this piece to Saks by end of week. And you will like Yuri. He is artist. With good humor."

"Maybe I will. But you could have at least *told* me."

"I did tell you," Sascha said. "Just now."

"But when did you hear from him? There were no letters in today's mail."

"I hear through network. Nikolai called."

"Well, why doesn't Yuri stay with Nikolai? He and Marfa have more room than we do."

"Yuri is old friend. Have not seen him in five years. Much to catch up on. He stays here," Sascha said, matter-of-factly.

"For how long?"

Sascha shrugged. Jewel knew by that shrug that Yuri would be there for anywhere from two days to two months, perhaps longer. "He arrives tomorrow afternoon. We fix big feast to celebrate. I will call Nikolai, Boris, Grigory, Sofia . . ."

"Wait a minute! Tomorrow's Friday. Betty's going away for the weekend. I have to work from noon till eight and all day Saturday. We can't have a party."

"Tell Betty you can't work."

"I *promised!* After all she's done for me, I can't very well flake out on her. Look, we'll have a party Sunday, my day off."

"Yuri comes tomorrow. We must welcome him."

"We can take him out to dinner, for Christ's sake. He'll probably be tired anyway, from jet lag."

"No, Jewel. We have friends over tomorrow night," Sascha got up from his workbench and came over to the door where Jewel stood. He closed it, leading her back into the room.

She knew that he was going to try to change her mood by making love to her. It had often worked in the past. But not this time.

Sascha gazed lovingly into her eyes, smiling. He leaned down and began brushing her face, all over, with tiny kisses. His giant bear paw of a hand strayed down her back and squeezed her buttocks. When he pulled her to him tightly, she could feel his hardness, and she shuddered with uncontrollable excitement. His lips found her mouth, and his tongue dug deeply down the tunnel of her throat.

Jewel was weakening. She knew Sascha could feel her arousal. "I have to get to work," she whispered hoarsely.

"Work can wait. Love comes first." He picked her up and carried her over to the bed, pulling her skirt up and her panties down, roughly. He unzipped his fly and entered her quickly, without further foreplay.

Jewel's anger melted into an emotion more urgent as she rocked and swayed, in a time warp—it could have been minutes or hours—until she screamed out, coming in waves, seconds before Sascha.

Afterward, he held her in his large arms, still kissing her face. Finally, she came back to reality, looked at her watch, and began to disengage herself. He whispered in her ear, "You buy food and vodka. I will cook. Party will start at nine."

Jewel sighed. "You know, sometimes you're fucking impossible."

"But you love me, my Jewel. Don't you love me?" He rubbed his soft, bearded cheek against hers.

"Yes, Sascha, I do. In spite of myself." And of course she did, passionately.

In spite of Jewel's love for Sascha, their relationship ran a bumpy course. She knew she was not the docile creature that he expected in a woman. She was always challenging him, endlessly provoking him into deep discussions on subjects ranging from Dostoyevski (whose complete works she had devoured since she met Sascha, in the hope of understanding the Russian temperament better) to Andy Warhol. Sascha was adamant when he argued. He maintained always that his point of view, whatever it happened to be, was the right one. If Jewel agreed with him about something, then she too was right. If she disagreed, she was wrong.

Jewel hated losing arguments. She liked to have the last word. But so did Sascha. Often they would come to an impasse. Then they would both fume silently until the phone rang or someone arrived to break the mood, or until Jewel stormed out to go to a movie with Edward. (Sascha, after working his twelve-hour days, was always too restless to sit through movies or plays, which irked Jewel no end.)

There was another area of discord. Sascha was extremely jealous of Jewel's friends. He hated Edward, but wouldn't say why. Jewel assumed it was because of their closeness, although she suspected it might also be because Edward was homosexual. Sascha found Betty Blessing rather brash and could not be in the same room with Roland, her gambler boyfriend, without sinking into a self-indulgent gloom that embarrassed Jewel while the others pretended not to notice. After several awkward attempts at entertaining, Jewel decided it best to see her friends on her own and not include Sascha. Everyone, it turned out, preferred it that way.

On the other hand, Jewel put up with Sascha's friends without complaining. Every Saturday night they would come over and drink and eat and scream over each other in Russian until they were too bleary to gesticulate and shout anymore. But they were a colorful, passionate bunch, and Jewel was intrigued by them. She studied them to find clues to Sascha's behavior. She was curious as to whether Sascha's assertiveness was a Russian trait, or merely Sascha's.

One of the women who came over, a Czech named Marfa who lived with Sascha's best friend, Nikolai, often took time to talk with Jewel while the two of them prepared zakuska, "small bites" or hors d'oeuvre, in the kitchen. Marfa was in her early forties, an actress, and dramatically beautiful, with high cheekbones and wide-set gray eyes. Jewel liked her.

"Well, my darling," Marfa said at their first meeting. "How are you handling living with a Russian? It's different, no?"

"It's wonderful," Jewel had replied.

"Yes? Well, you are still very much in love. When you have problems, you come and talk to me."

"Why should I have problems?" Jewel's differences with Sascha were just that to her, differences, not problems.

"Why should you not?" Marfa had said. "You are living with a Russian—the most passionate, and exasperating, men of all."

Since Sascha's friends drank and smoked to excess, Jewel generally excused herself after dinner and went to bed, curled up with a pillow over her head to block the light. Except for Marfa and Nikolai, she felt the others regarded her merely as Sascha's woman. She wondered if they arrived one Saturday and some other girl was there whether they would even notice.

But interacting with each other's friends was not what life with Sascha was all about. Life with Sascha meant being with him, encompassed by him, adored by him, lectured by him, and loved by him. He gave all of himself to Jewel, except for the Saturday nights with his friends from his homeland. He was devoted to her and loved her without reserve.

He still cooked for her, both because he wanted to fatten her up and because Jewel was not a good enough cook to suit him. Sascha did, however, consider it his duty to educate her in the kitchen. Jewel, always up to a challenge, proved to be an able student, which pleased him. He taught her how to make a proper borscht. ("There are as many recipes for borscht as there are grandmothers in Russia," he would say.) And he talked her through the proper making of dozens of recipes, including flattened chicken tabaka, and varenyky —dessert dumplings filled with cheese—the way his Ukrainian babushka, grandmother, had made them.

"In Ukraine," Sascha liked to tell her, "a baby girl must learn to sift flour before she can walk and knead bread before she can talk."

"Then how come *you* learned to cook, a man who grew up in Moscow?"

"My mother was ill for long time before she die. It was up to me to cook for her. She tell me her recipes, just like I am telling you."

"Well, one good thing about all this," Jewel joked, "if I don't make it as a jewelry designer I can always get a job at the Russian Tea Room."

They made love every night and often during the day. In bed, their compatibility astounded Jewel. She had only to think something and Sascha would do it. "Sexual telepathy," was how she once described the experience to Betty.

Not unlike Wyatt McNeill, Sascha had opinions on everything having to do with Jewel, from how he liked her to wear her hair (long and flowing) to how he wanted her to dress (jeans *only* when she was working at home, skirts when they went out). He made her eat three meals a day and take vitamins. If she put up a fuss over something he wanted her to do, he'd slump into a silent sulk.

Most of the time, though, Jewel did not complain. At this point in her life she didn't have strong feelings about how she wore her hair, and everyone said vitamins were good for you. Sometimes it was easier to give in than fight, since they still found plenty to argue over.

Most of all, with Sascha, Jewel felt utterly alive. Everything was magnified. Food tasted better when she ate with him, because he enjoyed it with such uninhibited gusto. The city, through his eyes when they went on daily walks together, was more beautiful than she had ever noticed before. Sascha took in everything and shared every insight with her.

Life, according to Sascha, was to be embraced with total exuberance. Even his sudden fits of depression, which struck sometimes without warning, seemed exaggerated. He lived in the moment, *for* the moment.

Sascha was the most mercurial man Jewel had ever encountered.

One minute he would be open and expansive, sharing everything with her. The next, something would set him off and he would close up like an oyster. Sometimes the mood passed quickly. Sometimes he seemed to bask in self-indulgence. During those times, Jewel would go visit Edward or Betty. It was more fun than sitting around, feeling his chilliness cool the loft like a Siberian winter.

Inevitably, if she did go out, Sascha would be in a rage when she got home, furious that she had deserted him. They'd shout it out and then fall into each other's arms, in bed. When Sascha's moods had passed, they were totally forgotten by him, and he expected Jewel to follow suit.

On a day-to-day basis, life with Sascha was never dull. Jewel was endlessly entertained by this incredible, impossible, lovable man.

On the day of Yuri's arrival, Sascha, as was his custom, rose at six and was already at work—making a wide silver bracelet inlaid with jade and lapis lazuli—by the time Jewel had brewed strong black tea, gone out to buy rolls for their mid-morning break, and settled in to work herself.

Jewel was going through a period of great insecurity over her designing. Sascha tried to help, but his enormous professional ego annoyed her. There was room only for one great designer in the family, *him*, as he let her know often.

She had cut down her hours at Betty Blessing's shop in order to get back seriously into making jewelry. Betty had suggested Jewel try working on a line of inexpensive copies of Victorian pieces they had discovered in an old book of Betty's from England. Betty felt there was a market for inexpensive elegant jewelry. Jewel had to come up with a way to make them look elegant while keeping the price down. Materials were not the problem; she used fake pearls, glass doublets, copper, and German silver—white metal that resembled the real thing. The problem was labor. Each piece took Jewel far too long for the price Betty wanted to pay, since there would be the usual triple keystone markup.

As she worked across the loft from Sascha, she muttered to herself with frustration. "This was really a rotten idea. There's no way I can put all the work that needs to go into these pieces and keep them inexpensive. I need better equipment. I need more space. I'm just so fucking out of practice! Everything I try to do is like starting out all over again. Shit, maybe I'll give up on trying to design," Jewel ranted on. "Maybe I should go back to working at the shop full time."

"No, no, my darling," Sascha said. "You are merely in a sour mood. Your fingers will behave. But you must direct them with your will. Perhaps you are beginning with designs that are too complicated. Start simple, then work up. Perfect your craft. Do it well . . . or not at all. Betty is *wrong,*" Sascha accused. "You should not be doing cheap copies. You should be working to find your own voice as designer. Then, only then, will I see if you have talent or not."

"What do you mean by that?" Jewel snapped. "I've shown you my work from the institute. You said it was good!"

"I said you have promise. And you do. But we will have to wait to see. In my family are jewelry-makers for three generations. It is bred in us. We work for nothing else all our life. It is all I was trained to do." Sascha's eyes glazed over, and Jewel saw a familiar melancholy expression take over his face before he shook his head to clear the memories. "You have American attitude that you can do anything"— he snapped his fingers—"fast . . . fast. You are all impatient. You want fantastic results without work. But, my dear, there are no shortcuts if you want to design good jewelry. *If* you want to—"

Jewel threw down her pliers, knocking a tray of imitation emeralds onto the floor. "I'm really not up for this lecture. And if you don't like the way Americans do things then why the hell did you come here? There were lots of other countries to choose from."

"Please . . . let us not go into that. I am fortunate to be here. I *had* to leave Soviet Union. There was no place for real creativity anymore." Sascha put down the soldering torch. "Jewel, my darling, you must learn to take criticism. I think you will be good. But you have not worked as long as I have. You must allow time." He got up, went across the room to Jewel's worktable and picked up the glass emerald necklace she was working on. He turned it over and over, examining it carefully. Jewel stood nearby, fuming.

"I see you are *attacking* the problem, Jewel. Is wrong. You must *caress* it first. Live with it. Don't—how is it you say?—don't lock horns. It will come."

"God, Sascha, I've been working on this for three days! Nothing is coming." She blew a piece of hair away from her eye. "I can't stand it!"

"You act like spoiled American debutante."

"Dilettante . . . I think that's the word you want."

Sascha shrugged. "Word not important. Attitude is. Your attitude is shit."

"Thank you very much for your constructive criticism. And now, if you don't mind, I'm going to work. Then I'm having dinner with Edward. I'll be home late. Start the party for Yuri without me."

Sascha turned abruptly to her and flung the back of his large hand across her cheek. "You are one hell of a difficult woman."

"You hit me!" Jewel shrieked. "That may be the way you do it in the Soviet Union, but you hit me again and I'm out of here forever!"

Furious, he slapped her again, same hand, same cheek. Jewel went berserk. She burrowed into him like a linebacker onto a quarterback, except with the bodies reversed. For one-hundred-pound Jewel it was like going up against one of the Caucasus. She stared at Sascha with hatred and began pounding his massive chest. "You are a barbarian, like your ancestors. You don't have the foggiest idea how to treat a woman. Fuck her . . . that's all you know how to do."

He grabbed her hands and held them still. "That is not so! You have never had complaints about the way I make love to you. You are mad because I criticize you."

"I'm mad because you *hit* me! Now, let go of my hands, I'm late for work. And I'm getting out of here for good! You and Yuri will have plenty of room. I'll get my stuff later. I'll call before . . . then I'd appreciate your not being here when I come to pick it up."

"Jewel, darling, this is not end of us."

"Oh, isn't it?"

"It is very deep . . . what we feel for each other. Will not go away so easy." He let go of Jewel's hands.

She strode across the room and grabbed her handbag and denim jacket. "That's what you think. Four months is enough. I've had it! You don't like my work . . . you put down my friends . . . what's the point?"

"The point is us," Sascha said. "You don't love my friends either. The point is us," he said again. "We love each other."

"Well, I don't think so. Not anymore! It's over. Good-bye, Sascha." And with that she slammed the door and headed out to work.

Jewel half-wanted him to open a window and call down an apology to her when she got down to the street. But she knew he'd never do that.

By the time she arrived at the Golden Buddha, Jewel did not know whether to be sad or relieved. Mostly she was still angry from replaying the scene in her head during the seven-block walk to work. Her relationship with Sascha was impossible. Marfa had known what she was talking about: there were *problems,* not differences. Sascha brought out the worst in her. So many things were not working out. But he was right about the sex.

And he was right that it was not over between them.

16

"Well, here we go again," Jewel said, across a table from Edward at Emilio's on Sixth Avenue. Her mussels marinara sat on her plate, untouched, but she was on her third glass of white wine.

"I don't believe you're goin' to leave him," Edward said. "It's a lovers' quarrel. You've had them before."

"Yeah," Jewel agreed, "I storm out and I go back. This time it's different. He fucking *hit* me! I'll tell you, he's got to come *begging*. Oh please, can I stay at your place?"

Edward grinned. "I put clean sheets on your bed after you called. Just in case."

"You know me so well, Edward," Jewel laughed. "What *would* I do without you?"

"Get a room at the Y, I suppose," Edward smiled. "Anyway, stay with me until you've calmed down. Then reevaluate. But don't ask me to help. You know I think you're better off without him." The waiter poured the rest of the wine from the bottle into their glasses, and Edward ordered zabaglione for himself for dessert.

Jewel nodded. "I know . . . and you're probably right. But Sascha's so totally *consuming*. I've never known anyone like him. Oh, I don't know what to do."

"Don't do anything right away. Relax. Come to the ballet with Demetrius and me tomorrow night. Just have fun."

"You're right. A break is what I need. Then I can think clearly."

Two weeks later Jewel was still living at Edward's, her thinking completely clear. Sascha had not called, nor had he stopped by the Golden Buddha. It was over. He did not care about her. That was that.

Then she noticed that her period, which had always been so irregular that she had stopped bothering with birth control, had not come for two months. She began to feel nauseated every morning and could not seem to drink wine any longer without feeling ill after a few sips.

A visit to Betty's gynecologist confirmed the suspicion. Jewel was pregnant. As if she wasn't upset enough by the fight and estrangement with Sascha, now there was this to contend with.

Jewel longed to talk with Marfa—she definitely had problems *now* —but her friend was acting in a repertory company in Wisconsin for the summer. She thought about Anna and what she went through with Randy, and that made her sadder. She missed Anna. It hurt to have a whole chunk of your life that was out-of-bounds, a best friend to whom you could no longer speak.

The McNeills had crept into Jewel's mind often over the past year; she had even come upon Wyatt's picture in the business section of *Newsweek* once. He looked handsome, successful, unchanged. She wondered what was happening in their lives now. Once she thought she saw Hadley getting onto a bus on Fifth Avenue and Fifty-sixth Street. She had raced to catch the same bus and squeezed through the crowd to the back, only to discover that it wasn't Hadley at all, only a vague look-alike.

Anna was her only friend who had had a baby, and Jewel needed knowledgeable advice. Would she be making a lifelong mistake if she had an abortion? Would she be making a lifelong mistake if she had the baby? And how would Sascha feel, if they ever did get back together, if she told him about the abortion?

"Do me a favor and stop mopin'," Edward said, looking down from a rickety, wooden ladder. He was in the process of painting the kitchen a glossy black. "You haven't left the apartment all weekend. Something's gotta give. Either have the abortion . . . or go tell Sascha and get his input. And I hate to say it, but I think that's the only fair thing to do."

"No! If he can stay away from me, I can stay away from him. He knows where to find me. He obviously doesn't care."

"And you're obviously miserable. God, the two of you both have so much pride. I think *you* were Russian in a former life."

"I can't believe you, of all people, are counseling me to get back together with Sascha," Jewel said, carefully edging around the ladder to get a yogurt from the refrigerator.

"I'm merely saying you should *talk* to him. You're in limbo, kid. You're stuck. The only way you're going to be able to get on with your life is to discuss this with the man involved. I wouldn't say this if I thought you didn't still love him. But he'll listen. He's sure not goin' to throw you out the door and down the stairs. Look, I'll even call him, if you want."

"No!"

"Well then, get your act together. Get on with your life," Edward urged.

At work the next day Betty told her basically the same thing. And so that evening Jewel swallowed her pride, realizing she was too miserable to do anything else. She washed and blew dry her hair, put on her favorite skirt and sexiest blouse, and took a cab to Spring Street. She still had her keys, and she let herself in the street entrance. After the two straight flights up to Sascha's, she stopped to catch her breath before knocking.

She tapped on the door, then prayed that Sascha wouldn't be home, so she could leave a note for him to call her, but no such luck. She heard footsteps, and the door opened.

There, standing before her, was a tall, gaunt man whom she had never seen before.

"Er, is Sascha here?"

"No . . . he come back soon. You wait?"

"Oh, no. Just tell him Jewel was here."

"Jewel!" The man smiled and opened the door wider. "I am Yuri. You come in. Wait, please. Sascha, he want to see you. He very sad that you leave him."

And then the downstairs door was flung open and Sascha's voice boomed up the stairs. "Jewel? My darling, is it you?" He came racing up the steps, two at a time, until he was in front of her. His arms went around her, and his mouth found hers without hesitation or further words.

"I think I go out for a walk," Yuri said, skirting around the embracing couple and down the stairs.

Later, after they had made very passionate love, Jewel confronted Sascha on his silence of the past weeks.

"You're obviously happy to see me again . . . why didn't you call? Is it because you can't ever bring yourself to apologize?" she demanded to know.

"Nothing to apologize for. You get mad, you leave. Is out of my hands," he explained, not to her satisfaction. "You must do what you must do. I cannot change. I must suffer consequences, but suffering is part of life. To suffer is good for soul, good for art. Creativity comes out of suffering. I work very hard while you were gone."

"But you didn't *have* to suffer," Jewel said. "You could have called me. We could have talked it over."

Sascha shrugged. "I hate you for leaving. I did not want to call you."

"But now I'm back you say you *love* me . . ."

"Yes, my darling, I do," he interrupted. "Is possible to love and hate same person at different times. You must understand. We are capable of anything at any time. When we are together I am faithful to you. I love you. But when you leave, I sleep with another woman."

"What?" Jewel asked, shocked. "Hold on a second. *What* other woman?"

"Her name is Rachel. I will not see her again now that you are back. It was not important."

"It's important to me! We have a fight and the next thing you do is find someone else? Poof! Jewel is gone," she said in a fake Russian accent. "Must find replacement . . . need new woman. Jesus, you're impossible. You know, I really hate you for that. *How could you?*"

"You see," Sascha said, pleased, "it *is* possible to hate someone and love them at same time."

"Ahhhhhh!" Jewel screamed in exasperation.

"My darling, Jewel," Sascha said, grabbing her and pulling her to him. "Come here. I will show you again how much I love you. I miss you so much. We will not hate each other anymore."

"Oh, Sascha . . . I do love you. But you're difficult. I mean, the reason I walked out is that you *hit* me. If I move back in with you, I'm not going to put up with that. You hit me again, and I leave. Forever. Amen."

Sascha made a circle of tiny kisses on her cheek. "I understand. And I promise, no matter how angry you make me, I promise never again. You have my word. I never hit a woman before. It make me feel bad."

Jewel smiled. "All right. And I promise never to hit you."

In early August 1972, with Edward, Betty, Yuri, and Nikolai standing by, Jewel and Sascha were married quietly by the priest at the Ukrainian Orthodox Church on East Eleventh Street. Jewel had never been particularly aware that Sascha was religious, but he insisted that a priest marry them instead of some clerk at city hall. It made no difference to her. She was still in shock from the speed at which the events had taken place.

Sascha, his suffering over, was euphoric to have Jewel back. He would not hear of her getting rid of the baby.

"Abortion is for unwanted child," he told her. "Not for us. We love each other. You are my woman. You have my babies."

He adored children, he assured her, and promised that he'd make a wonderful father. Marriage was important to him, and he insisted that they make it legal as soon as possible.

"But Jewel Dragoumis Robinovsky?" she shook her head, and patted her belly. "How the hell am I going to get through life with a name like that?"

"You will be happy with my name," Sascha said. "You will be happy with me, my darling."

Jewel looked at him and smiled. "Yes . . . I will be. I adore you, Sascha. Even if you are the most impossible person in the world."

"No, no, you got it wrong. *You* are most impossible. I am merely second," he grinned. "And we will not argue about it."

"Just this once, we won't argue about it," she replied.

And so Jewel and Sascha embarked on the adventure of married life together. Sascha made Jewel a wedding band, a thick braided ring of red, yellow, and white gold. To match it, he wove her a delicate choker.

"A fine necklace . . . for a fine neck," he said, tenderly clasping it around her throat.

"And for you," Jewel said, presenting him with an ornate antique brass samovar that she had found in a Ukrainian shop on East Seventh Street, "a fine samovar for a fine Russian."

As wedding gifts, Edward gave them a week's car rental, and Betty obtained a friend's cabin in the Adirondacks for them. Nikolai sent them off with champagne and caviar from Balducci's, and Yuri offered to take care of Lisa, the cat that Zhenya had left behind when he moved out. Yuri also promised—his greatest gift to them—to find another place to live as soon as they returned to the city.

The week of their honeymoon was perhaps the most carefree that Jewel had ever spent. It had been a long time since either of them had communed with nature, and the cabin was set at the edge of a large woods. A long expanse of lawn, filled with field grasses, daisies, dandelions, and black-eyed Susans, wound down to a small, private lake.

The cabin itself was rustically charming, filled with functional antiques and copper pots in the kitchen. There was an herb garden outside the back door, and a large screened-in sitting and eating porch overlooked the lake, where Sascha fished for the trout they grilled for dinner every night.

During the day, while Sascha read or fished, Jewel lay out in the sun or went on foraging walks, returning with blackberries and raspberries that she made into tarts and jam, or fresh corn and tomatoes that she bought from a roadside stand about half a mile away. She felt alive, carrying the baby within her, and healthy. The morning sickness had stopped, and she began having an appetite again. The reality that she would be giving birth in six months began to sink in. She began to sort through names.

"What do you think about Jasmine?" she said in bed one night, after they had made love.

"Is good, strong fragrance. I like," Sascha replied.

"No, no, I mean for a name. For the baby, if it's a girl."

Sascha shook his head. "Is bad luck to name baby before it comes. Same as I told you . . . is bad luck to say *when* baby will come."

"Yeah, but what am I supposed to answer when someone asks me when the baby's due? I can't look blank and say, 'I don't know.' God, you and your superstitions!"

"Many people believe what I do. Is best when someone asks, you say, 'sometime during winter.' "

Jewel sighed. "And now we can't even talk about names until after the baby is born? This is ridiculous."

"You can think about names in your head. But don't discuss with me out loud."

"What exactly do you think is going to happen if we talk about it out loud?" Jewel wanted to know.

"Baby can be born dead . . . or sick. Is best not to take chances, you understand, my darling?" He leaned over and kissed her.

"Not really," she said. "But it's not worth fighting about."

"You know, this is first time I relax since I was teenager," Sascha said. "I forget what it feels like for your mind to take a holiday. No working, no deadlines. Ideas can flow. I am having great ideas for new jewelry. Very romantic jewelry. Contemporary, but fitting as if it should be part of the body . . ." He grabbed a pad from the table beside the bed and began sketching with quick, sure lines. "You see, something like this. Perhaps I use amber, with silver. Before I leave Moscow, I do many beautiful pieces in Russian amber. You like?"

"Yes!" Jewel said, before she even looked at the sketches. "Amber! I love it."

It would be a perfect name for a girl.

Summer ended, and autumn flew by. Sascha had more work than he had time for, doing pieces now exclusively for Saks Fifth Avenue. With mixed feelings, Jewel quit her job with Betty so she could stay home and help Sascha.

Working for him was not always easy. Jewel had to do Sascha's pieces *his* way, and she was not allowed to finish anything, only to work on them up to a certain point. Sascha made it clear that he wasn't interested in her suggestions or ideas.

Jewel put up with it. She was learning advanced techniques, finishing her schooling at home while apprenticing under a master craftsman. What more could she want? Besides, since she had become pregnant she felt all her creativity went to her belly.

Jewel's days began and ended at the loft on Spring Street, and most evenings were spent there as well. Except to buy groceries, Jewel seldom went out. She glowed with health, but thought she looked fat and unattractive. Her ankles were bloated, and she felt like a gigantic marshmallow in the white down jacket that Sascha gave her for Christmas.

Every so often, she lunched with Edward or Betty, but she began to feel, as the months of her marriage accumulated, that she had less and less in common with her old friends. She was too busy to dwell on it though. Working for Sascha, cooking for him, entertaining his friends who had become almost a family to her now—that took up all of her time.

Since she considered herself back in the apprentice phase of her life, Jewel decided one day that it would aid her future career as a jewelry designer if she understood more about gemstones. She wanted to know what to look for, how to recognize good stones versus flawed ones without having to rely on experts to tell her, when she was finally in business for herself. So she enrolled in an intensive home-study course that the Gemological Institute of America offered on the identification and evaluation of diamonds and colored gemstones.

Her energy returned, in spite of the large belly and nearly forty pounds of extra weight she was carrying. In the eighth month of her pregnancy, Jewel trudged through snow-slushy streets, rushing here and there, taking out books on precious and semiprecious stones from the library, and going on expeditions to the Museum of Natural History to study their gem and mineral collection. She bought herself a ten-power jeweler's magnifying loupe and began haunting pawn shops and thrift stores, as Sascha had in the old days, for real gems that might not have been recognized.

One day, at a store on Second Avenue, her sleuthing finally scored her a prize. It was a ruby, she was positive, over a carat in size, set into a ring with pearls. It had been tossed into a bargain bin in the back of an old, dusty shop that had been around for decades. Casually, she bargained with the elderly shop owner, getting the price cut in half, from a dollar to fifty cents. Then, feeling smug as hell, she flagged down a cab, just as snowflakes were beginning to fall, and raced across town to show off her treasure to Sascha.

"You won't believe it!" she gushed as she came into the loft, panting from running up the stairs. "I found a ruby!"

"You are right," Sascha said. "I don't believe. Bring it here."

"I looked through my loupe. I thought I saw silky lines. Isn't that what you're supposed to see in Burmese rubies? Silklike inclusions? Oh, Sascha, I know it's absolutely, definitely not glass. Here." She handed it to him, anxious as a schoolgirl to impress her teacher.

"Is very dirty . . . hard to tell anything."

He soaked the ring quickly in cleaning solution, then looked at it through his magnifying loupe. "Hmmm," he said. "Interesting."

"Yes?" Jewel said excitedly. "It's real, isn't it?"

"I clean again," he said. "Need better look."

"Oh, you're driving me crazy! Tell me it's real."

Sascha dried the ring with a piece of soft leather and peered again through his glass. "Yes, just as I thought," he looked up. "It is balas ruby . . . a spinel."

"Shit!" Jewel cursed. "A spinel? Are you sure?"

"Am positive. But it is *real* spinel . . . not synthetic. How much you pay for this?"

"Fifty cents."

"You do good, my Jewel," Sascha smiled. "You know story of Black Prince's Ruby?"

"No," Jewel said, still disappointed.

"It is huge stone, two inches across. Was given to Black Prince of England in fourteenth century, by Spanish king. Later part of Crown Jewels, worn by many kings. Finally it was set into crown for Queen Victoria. Then in this century they discover that famous ruby is not ruby at all. It is magnesium aluminate—spinel. So you see, my darling, spinel fool kings for centuries. And you find good spinel. Worth few hundred dollars. I will make it into special ring for you."

By then Jewel was no longer concentrating on what Sascha was saying. A pain that had begun knifing up between her legs was peaking to a crescendo. She felt weak and dizzy—and scared, if this meant the beginning of labor. Her pregnancy was supposed to have three weeks to go.

"Sascha! I think it's happening . . . call Dr. Abrams," she said.

The next morning, the third of February 1973, after fifteen hours of labor that ended in a cesarian, Jewel woke to find Sascha sitting by her, stroking her hand. Outside, large flakes of snow were tumbling down, the end of a snowfall that had dumped over a foot of snow on the city.

"The baby?" she whispered with a dry mouth.

"Good morning, my darling," he said quickly. "You now have wonderful baby girl, weighing eight pounds. She is healthy. Big like me." He slipped a ring onto her finger.

Jewel shakily held up her hand to look at it. "It's my spinel," she smiled. The stone had been set into a wide gold band that had been engraved with a delicate leaf design. "It's beautiful. But when did you . . . ?"

"I come home from hospital and stay up all night. Working with great energy . . . joyful energy. Oh, my Jewel, we have a baby. Are you happy, my darling?"

At that moment, a nurse rolled a crib into the room, and Jewel saw her daughter for the first time.

"Oh," she said, as the smiling nurse handed her the baby. "She's beautiful." She counted the fingers and toes, ten of each. "I don't believe it. Me—us—with a baby. It's really happened."

"Yes, and now we can think of name."

"I have a name," Jewel smiled. "Amber."

Sascha thought for a moment, then nodded. "Is good. I like. Baby will be named Amber Anna Robinovsky."

"Anna?" Jewel asked.

"After my *mamitchka*, my mother," Sascha said.

It occurred to Jewel at that moment that she had never before heard the name of Sascha's mother, or father. In fact, he had never talked about his life in Russia, except to impart offhand information, such as how he used to love to hunt wild mushrooms in the country every fall. Whenever she asked direct questions, he always managed to evade them by changing the subject.

But Jewel had never told Sascha anything about her past either. In fact, he had never asked.

"Sascha," Jewel said, polishing to a final luster the engraved silver baby bracelet she had made for Amber, "I'm going out for groceries now. Marfa and Nikolai are coming for dinner, remember?"

Jewel put on her raincoat, tied a scarf over her hair, and braced herself for the cold, wet, early May afternoon. It had been an unusually rainy spring. She had not even been able to take Amber to Washington Square Park, her favorite place to show off the baby, more than twice a week because of the weather.

The dreariness had had its effect on Jewel's mood as well. The obstetrician called it postpartum depression, but what was there to be depressed about, Jewel quizzed him, except the incessant rain? It was true that the baby was a bit colicky. It was true that Jewel was lucky to get two uninterrupted hours of sleep a night. And she did have a cold that had hung on for weeks. But depression because one has given birth to a miraculous creature? Jewel would hear none of it.

"If Amber wakes up," Jewel continued, "please change her diaper and give her a little bottle of juice. I'll nurse her when I get back."

"No, no, no, my darling," Sascha said from his worktable. "I mean it when I tell you I never change baby's diapers. I will give her bottle."

"God, Sascha," Jewel snapped. "Can't you do it just this once? She'll be soaking when she wakes up, and I've got to go to the drugstore, the bakery, the greengrocer's, the butcher's, and the supermarket. Jesus, I do *everything* around here. You've turned me into a fucking slave."

"No!" Sascha said adamantly. "Not true. I *make* you do nothing except change diapers. You do because you want to. You want to learn to cook. You want to become apprentice to me, to know proper jewelry skill. You are happy to be wife with me taking care of you. If you are slave—if that is what you choose to call it—it is because you want to be."

"Oh, spare me," Jewel sneezed. And then sneezed again.

"Darling Jewel, you know we are happy," Sascha said. "You are in bad mood because of your cold. Look, I will call Nikolai and tell them not to come. Then I will ask Yuri to watch Amber. I will take you out for dinner, to the new French restaurant on Prince Street." He smiled, and blew her a kiss. "Okay?"

Jewel nodded, melting. "Okay."

Whenever she convinced herself that things were terrible, they turned out not to be. Marfa had told her once, "To understand a Russian, you must be Russian," and Jewel supposed it was true. She would never understand Sascha completely. He was full of surprises, but life was never dull.

One day, mostly for fun, Jewel began making whimsical paste-and-plaster figures that she baked in the oven, painted and glazed, and turned into earrings and pins. Street People, she called them, and when Betty Blessing saw Jewel wearing a pair of the earrings, she immediately ordered some for the shop. After two days, they had sold out, and Betty wanted more. Several weeks after that, the owner of a shop on Madison Avenue called Jewel and placed an order, having seen Street People in Betty's window. Soon other stores around town were calling, and Jewel was in full production, selling the pieces as fast as she could make them.

It was a great morale booster for her. The small brightly-colored figures were easy to produce in the midst of tending to Amber. And she could take Amber with her around town when she made her deliveries. Although the jewelry was inexpensive and Jewel wasn't hauling in a tremendous profit, she enjoyed getting out, meeting new people, and having them ooh and ah over both her baby and her designs.

Sascha, however, was critical and condescending. "It is not really jewelry," he told her. "It is fad. It will not last."

"That's fine with me," Jewel said. "I don't want to make Street

People for the rest of my life. It's something fun to do now. And I like meeting new people. I've been in such a rut."

"Oh? So sorry," he said coldly.

"No, it doesn't have anything to do with you. It's me. I realize that I've been in a self-imposed isolation. I mean, when was the last time I had lunch with Edward? It was months ago. He's upset with me, and I can't blame him."

Sascha shrugged. "So call him. Have lunch. I am sorry you feel so isolated with me."

"No! Look, I don't want to turn this into a fight. But you have to understand that I need my life with you, *and* apart from you. I feel good about the success of my Street People. It's been so long since I've done anything on my own, except those rings for Betty that I can do with my eyes closed."

"Okay. Do what you like. I am not jealous."

Of course, Sascha *was* jealous, she was sure. But, as much as she loved him, she had to think of herself too.

In mid-July however, Jewel discovered that there was going to be another person to think of besides her and Sascha and Amber. She began to experience the familiar queasiness of morning sickness, except this time it lasted all day. At first she thought it was flu, but soon realized that flu was wishful thinking.

"This is impossible," she told the doctor when the pregnancy test came back positive.

"What do you mean? Have you been abstaining from sex?" Dr. Abrams joked.

"I didn't think you could get pregnant again so fast."

"You can if you don't use birth control, Jewel. Diaphragms don't work sitting in the medicine cabinet."

"I use my diaphragm!"

"Obviously you don't use it regularly. Let's see, according to the calendar we're talking sometime around February fifteenth. *If* you want to have the baby."

Jewel sighed. "My husband wouldn't think of my *not* having it."

"What about you? It's your body."

"Oh, I'd like Amber to have a brother or sister. It's a little sooner than I'd planned, but what the hell."

As Jewel anticipated, Sascha was delighted with the news. But, as she had not anticipated, this was a far different pregnancy than the first.

"Your blood pressure is abnormally high," Dr. Abrams told her when she went for her fifth-month checkup. "And your edema—the swelling—is worse than last time. To make a long story short, you have a condition called preeclampsia. It's a form of toxemia. I don't want to get you upset, but from now on you're going to have to alter your life-style, as they say."

"What do you mean? Am I in danger of losing the baby?" Jewel asked, alarmed.

"Not if you do what I say." The doctor smiled heartily. "But you *have* to do it . . . otherwise there are risks for both the fetus . . . and you."

"What do I have to do?" Jewel was beginning to be scared.

"Basically you're going to have to take to your bed and stay there. I'll give you a prescription for diuretics. And no salt, absolutely none. Have lots of milk and milk products. But the main thing is rest. We have to keep your blood pressure down."

"Oh boy," Jewel said, thinking about how she was going to take care of Amber from bed, and how Sascha was going to react to the news.

"Have your husband call me," Dr. Abrams said before Jewel left the office. "I want to make sure he understands the seriousness of your condition. I don't want you attempting to do anything strenuous. I don't even want you to cook. And absolutely no sex."

Jewel went home and climbed into bed, more depressed than she had ever been in her life. Sascha could see that she was terrified and called the doctor right away, to get the firsthand report.

When he hung up, he went over to the bed and held her in his arms, crying. "I will take care of you, my darling. You will be fine. You will not lose baby. You will not die."

Die? Was her condition that serious? Or was Sascha merely overreacting in his usual passionate way?

"Look, darlin'," Edward said over the phone, after she had told him the news. "I was going to give you a nanny for a few months after the baby was born, as my baby present. Now I'll just give you one sooner."

"But, Edward, I can't accept a gift like that. You know what nan-

nies cost? I know you're making a lot of money, but I don't want you
to spend it on me."

"I insist, darlin'. Look, it doesn't have to cost a fortune. You need
someone to come in, do a little housework and cookin', take Amber
out for walks. Maybe Sascha can find a Russian grandmother type
who'll work part time. But, listen, it's a gift. I don't ever want to be
reimbursed."

"God, Edward, you take better care of me than my husband."

"Don't ever let *him* hear that! He hates me enough as it is," Edward laughed. "But put Sascha on the case, to try to find someone. I'll
stop by after work to see you."

"Wonderful. Sascha's having dinner with the buyers from Saks."

"Okay . . . I'll cook. Vegetables and brown rice. A nice, healthy,
nonsodium, macrobiotic meal."

"Ugh!" Jewel laughed. "How the hell am I going to make it through
the next four months? Do you realize without salt I can't even eat
Chinese food . . . or french fries . . . or street pretzels . . .
or . . . ?"

"It'll do you good to lose some weight, darlin'," Edward teased.
"You were gettin' thick around the middle anyway."

"Very funny, Edward! See you later."

That was how Nushka Krupa came to be part of the family. She was
Polish, not Russian, and Marfa found her, not Sascha. Nushka was not
a grandmother. She was in her forties, widowed, with children old
enough to be gone from the house all day. Nushka had an imposing
girth that was full of muscle, stringy grayish-brown hair and moles all
over her face. She smelled of garlic and cloves and could have been a
Slavic witch, but one who practiced white magic. Even Sascha took
to her, after having sworn that he didn't want another person hanging around the loft during the day. Nine-month-old Amber adored
her and loved cuddling up in her immense lap. For Jewel, it was like
having a mother again.

Nushka kept a pot of unsalted soup going on the stove at all times.
She made her own yogurt. She baked custards and concocted fruit
milk shakes, fussing over Jewel in broken English liberally laced with
malapropisms. The lady of boundless energy ran errands for Sascha,
without complaining as Jewel had. When she went home at night, she
made clothes for Amber, and she never failed to drop by on Sundays,

her day off, to see if Jewel needed anything, or to bring a freshly baked pie or loaf of bread. In short, the woman was perfect.

Jewel spent her bedridden days still helping Sascha, working on her home-study gemology course, or listening to language tapes, trying to learn French. Her friends Katrina and Christof had married each other and had left their families' businesses to start their own, somewhere on the Left Bank in Paris. As soon as the children were old enough, Jewel wanted to go there and visit her friends. Sascha was agreeable, since Yuri had recently returned to Paris to live, and there was a large Russian community there.

The months passed. Jewel's condition stabilized, and the doctor was pleased that she was following his advice so conscientiously. Not to have done so would have been even more dangerous than he had let either Jewel or Sascha know. Had the preeclampsia become severe, the fetus would certainly have been lost, and Jewel herself might not have pulled through.

In early January, however, Jewel began suffering headaches, and her edema worsened. Her hands and face swelled up, and the doctor decided immediately upon seeing her, during a regular office visit, that he had better induce premature labor.

Nushka rushed home from the doctor's office, where she had accompanied Jewel.

"Mister Sascha!" she called out with alarm, as she opened the front door. "Miss Jewel need suitcase. Doctor take her to hospital now, in ambulance. Deliver baby now!"

Sascha stopped soldering the bracelet he was working on. "Oh no. And I have deadline for this order . . . no matter. This is very bad?"

Nushka shrugged. "Miss Jewel—she look very worried when she tell me to prepare to spend night with Amber." She located Jewel's already packed suitcase, and added Jewel's toothbrush, hairbrush, and makeup from the bathroom.

She handed the suitcase to Sascha. "Here, you take. You go now. Don't worry, I take care of things here." She picked up Amber, who had begun crying in her playpen. "Not to worry, baby. Everything fine. We change diaper, then we go for walk and buy flour to make cookies. Everything fine, baby." She hugged Amber tightly, and it dawned on Sascha how scared Nushka was.

His own fear began to set in as he got into his overcoat, put the suitcase under his arm, and headed over to St. Vincent's Hospital. For what seemed like an eternity, he paced up and down the hall outside the delivery room. The cesarian was difficult because Jewel's condition had to be monitored carefully. There was danger of convulsions or coma.

When the doctor emerged, finally, from the delivery room, Sascha could not tell from his exhausted face whether everything was all right or not.

"Mr. Robinovsky, your wife has given birth to a girl, but the baby weighs only five pounds. There's reduced circulation that we're working to combat. The next twenty-four hours will be crucial."

Sascha's face went white. "And Jewel?"

"She's weak, but stable. We'll want to keep her here for a while. But since she wasn't suffering from hypertension before the pregnancy there's no indication that the condition will continue. She's been through a lot, though. I would seriously advise against her having more children. In fact, I'm going to recommend sterilization, tying the tubes. Another pregnancy could kill her."

Sascha nodded, the words barely sinking in. "When can I see her?"

"She's still under sedation. You can go in, if you like. But she won't be fully conscious for some time."

Sascha spent the next hours sitting by Jewel's bed, stroking her hand over and over again. She appeared more frail than ever before, thinner, more childlike. When Jewel awoke, around six, Sascha told her what had happened and prepared her for the fact that the baby might not survive.

"Oh no," Jewel cried. "No . . . I have to see her!"

"You can't, my darling. Not now. For now, I get nurse. You rest."

"But we have to decide on a name! She has to have a name," Jewel insisted.

Sascha sighed and smiled. "Yes, if you wish."

"Well, I've been thinking," Jewel said. "I made lists and lists but . . . continuing our gem theme . . . what do you think about Beryl?"

"Yes, it is fine name," he said, not really wanting to think about it until he knew whether or not the child would live. "I go get nurse now."

Jewel knew from Sascha's tone that he did *not* expect Beryl to live. But he was wrong. She had had a dream, two weeks before, that she hadn't told anyone about. In it, Amber was about five and she was playing with a slightly smaller girl named Beryl. Jewel was there too, laughing. They were in the country, having a picnic by a lake. They were all fine and healthy. The only odd thing about the dream was that there was a man there too. And the man was not Sascha.

Five weeks later, three weeks after Jewel herself was released, tiny baby Beryl was allowed to leave the hospital. By then she had gained over a pound and was pronounced completely healthy. Amber, now over a year old, was very excited to have a sister, and Nushka might as well have been their biological grandmother, the way she loved them both.

"I am so proud to have such beautiful babies to take care of," she told Jewel. "I am full of luck."

"Me too," Jewel agreed. "Even if I can't have more, I think I've done damned well."

Jewel had heeded Dr. Abrams's advice and had had her tubes tied. She didn't want to have any more children with the risks involved. She had done it, spent four months in bed, but she could never do it again. Besides, she had two beautiful daughters. What more could she want?

As she still had to take it easy, Jewel put all her energy into finishing her gemology course. On Beryl's third-month birthday, Jewel passed her final exams and graduated as a certified gemologist. She was full of ideas for jewelry she wanted to make. For the time being, though, she went back to helping Sascha fill his orders. With the hefty hospital bills to pay, he was working longer hours than ever, cramped into the loft with a wife, two babies, and a housekeeper.

"Tonight I go out to meet Boris," Sascha said one evening, stretching as he quit work for the day.

"But I made jellied veal and potato pudding," Jewel said. "You'll eat first, won't you?"

Sascha shook his head. "No . . . I tell Boris I meet him at eight. Is nearly that now."

"Oh well," Jewel sighed. "I'll save it till tomorrow. I think I'll make a sandwich and get in bed. Beryl will be awake again at eleven."

"Okay," Sascha said, kissing her on the cheek. "I see you later." Within seconds he was out the door.

"But, no, I don't think I can join you tonight," Jewel said out loud, as the sound of his footsteps disappeared down the stairs. "Thank you for asking though."

Jewel, for the most part, did not complain when Sascha announced he was going out with his friends, which was more frequent than in the past. She was still too tired to join him. Besides, watching Sascha and his friends enjoy their orgy of eating and drinking wasn't much fun for her. Whenever a bottle of vodka was opened, she had noticed over the years, it was always finished before the evening was over. The Russians loved their drink, but Jewel still could not tolerate spirits.

On the nights when Sascha went out drinking, he came home and woke her up, to make love before falling asleep. On a day-to-day basis, however, Jewel was aware that Sascha was no longer as passionate as he had been.

Of course, she was always tired; that was part of the problem. She had cut back on Nushka's hours, to economize. When Beryl was three months old, Jewel had insisted to Edward that his gift had expired. She could not expect him to subsidize Nushka forever, although it was tempting, since Edward enjoyed being her and the girls' fairy godfather, as he jokingly called himself.

And so she was back to cooking full time, carting laundry out to the laundromat, and doing most of the shopping, in between taking care of the babies and working for Sascha. Her life was hectic, but she knew this phase of it wouldn't last forever. She worried a bit about Sascha's drinking, but mostly she was too exhausted to dwell on anything very long. Winter melted into spring, into summer, into fall.

She realized one day just after Thanksgiving that, although she talked to Edward and Betty often, it had been months since she had actually seen them. They would have dropped by the loft, but Sascha always made them feel unwelcome, and that made Jewel ill at ease. So she called them and arranged a Saturday lunch, while Nushka took the children to the park.

"Well, here's to us," Jewel giggled, toasting Edward and Betty with her first glass of wine in months. They were having an uptown splurge, lunch at the Four Seasons, by the pool. "And to our debts that are no more. We finally got the hospital paid off. Just as well we're not going to have any more children. We couldn't afford it."

"This is just like old times," Betty said, sipping her kir. This was her first drink in months too, because she had joined Weight Watchers. Fifteen pounds thinner, she looked dazzling in a slinky Betsey Johnson dress. "Except now you're the most married lady I know."

"Well, *you* might as well be. You and Roland have been together for five years now."

"*Eight* years," Betty corrected. "Not five. Time marches on. But I've given him an ultimatum. Either we get married . . . or it's over."

"What did he say?" Jewel asked.

Betty laughed. "He said he'd marry me if I'd move to Lake Tahoe with him. Really shrewd of him. He knows I can't leave New York. But I'm thinking about calling his bluff. I mean, I could sell the shop; I could *try* Tahoe for a while." She signaled the waiter for another kir. "I really want to get married. Perhaps have a baby."

"Why doesn't Jewel take over the shop?" Edward suggested. "You know, seriously, it'd be a great idea. You could get out on your own, Jewel, and make enough money to hire Nushka full time again. I think it's hard on all of you, livin' in basically one room day in and day out. No wonder Sascha's out carousin'."

"He's not carousing! He's merely seeing friends. Anyway, I can't go out on my own yet. I mean, Sascha needs me to help him. He's so busy."

"That I know. After that piece in *Vogue,* he's on his way to the Really Big Time," Edward said, referring to a short article the magazine had done the month before. In the text, the writer had mentioned Jewel merely as Sascha's "appropriately nicknamed wife."

"Actually, Jewel," Betty said, beginning to pick up on the idea, "I think Edward's suggestion is splendid. You've got to get out from under a bit more. Fight for your own identity as an artist. It's wonderful that you're helping Sascha, but you do have to consider *yourself.* If you took over the shop, it would be a nice income. You'd be independent as an artist. And I could marry Roland and try Tahoe. It'd be perfect!"

"All well and good," Jewel said. "But Sascha's and my relationship isn't based on my being independent. I've gotten myself into this position, and I must admit it hasn't been bad. Working for Sascha keeps me from facing my own insecurities."

"Workin' for Sascha has *given* you insecurities. You've lost your balls, darlin'," Edward said firmly. "I know I sound like a broken record, but you're talented. It's just that you've changed, you've become complacent. Too goody-goody and long-suffering. I mean, when was the last time you *laughed?*" Edward paused, realizing he was letting her hear everything he'd been thinking for the past couple of years. "I'm sorry, but you can't spend your whole life in Sascha's shadow. *You* wanted to be famous, didn't you? And you were goin' to pay back that McNeill guy the money you borrowed. What have you done about it lately?"

Jewel blinked her eyes. "God, what is this? Pick on Jewel day? I thought I was very happy."

Betty patted her hand. "Don't get upset, dear. We're merely kicking this around. No one's *forcing* you into anything."

"I know," Jewel sighed. "You're both friends who care about me. All right. I'll think about the shop."

"Good. I mean, I haven't made up my mind yet either," Betty said. "Maybe I'd hate Tahoe."

"Well, girls," Edward said, picking up his menu, "now that nothing's settled, why don't we order lunch? I'm starved."

"Good idea," Betty said. "You know I always am." She looked at Jewel. "I shouldn't say this, but quite frankly, you're looking far too thin. Now you may think it's sour grapes, coming from me, but there's no meat on you anywhere." She turned to Edward. "Don't you think she's too thin?"

Edward nodded. "I'm afraid I agree. I won't make the obvious analogy, but you'd be fabulous in about twenty pounds. And your hair—why did you cut it all off?"

Jewel shrugged. "It's been coming out ever since I had Beryl. It's getting really thin. Cutting it is supposed to thicken it up, so I went over to that barbershop on Astor Place and had them chop it all off. Only cost me three bucks."

"What a bargain," Edward said, rolling his eyes. "Look, after lunch, we're hittin' a health food store and gettin' you some vitamins." He paused. "I thought you took vitamins."

"I haven't bothered for months. There's too much else to do."

The waiter appeared. After Betty ordered her salad, Edward said, "I'll have the lamb chops, and this lady here . . ." he indicated Jewel "will start with the pasta primavera, a large portion, then she'll go on to the roast prime ribs, the squab stuffed with apricots, a cheese-burger, some grilled fish with beurre blanc, the Caesar's salad . . ."

"Edward!" Jewel laughed. "You're insane." She looked up at the waiter, still giggling. "Just the pasta primavera, please. A half portion."

Edward turned to Betty. "What are we going to do with her?"

After lunch and a shopping spree to buy vitamins, Edward dropped Jewel off at Nushka's apartment on East Fourth Street, to pick up the children. Walking home, with Amber in her stroller and Beryl tucked into the Snuggli, Jewel felt happier than she had in months. Perhaps it was the wine—she was still a bit tipsy—or perhaps it was the carefree afternoon with Edward and Betty.

Over the past hours, Jewel had become more than a little excited about the suggestion of taking over Betty's shop. As she strolled across town, her mind raced with thoughts of how she would change things around and redecorate. Of course, it would all take money, a commodity of which she was very short these days.

Then a thought popped out of nowhere, one that had been buried for years. Although she hadn't heard from him, she suddenly remembered Gary Pollock, her stockbroker. Hadn't he said that those stocks would be worth something if she waited? Well, time had certainly passed. She would call him on Monday and find out if she had any money at all. Funny, after that last conversation with him, she had put him completely out of her mind.

She unlocked the street door and took Amber out of her stroller.

"Okay, sweetie . . . time for you to walk. That's right. That's a good girl. Up the stairs."

There had been talk among the tenants of fixing the building's dilapidated elevator. It had been broken for years. Jewel smiled to herself as she contemplated the luxury of an elevator, something that most New Yorkers took for granted.

As they slowly made their way up the two flights, Jewel suddenly remembered that she had meant to pick up milk and bread. Well, she would park the kids with Sascha and let him deal with naptime.

Unlocking the door, she let Amber into the loft and headed directly to put the sleeping Beryl into her crib. "Sascha," she called out, "I'm nipping right out again. I forgot the . . ."

Jewel stopped in midsentence. There, on the sofa, was Sascha, with his arms around another woman. Sitting on the floor were three dark-haired children, two boys and a girl. They looked to be between seven and twelve.

"Come in, my Jewel," he said. "You better sit down. We got to talk."

Jewel took off her coat and hung it on the rack by the door. It fell to the floor, but she didn't bother picking it up.

The other woman, large like Sascha, but with a sensual, dark-eyed beauty, stared at her. With fear? Or hostility? Jewel could not tell.

Sascha leaned forward and filled his glass from an open bottle of Stolichnaya that sat on the coffee table. "You want a drink?" he asked Jewel.

"I have a feeling I'd better say 'yes,'" she said. He handed her a glass, and she sat down in a chair, across from them.

"This woman here is Aïna. She has come from Soviet Union, after many months of travel. She does not speak English."

Jewel did not say a word, but waited.

Sascha took a drink and avoided her eyes. "Aïna is . . . my wife, Jewel. From Moscow," he said, after a while.

"And these here are my children . . . Yuri, Alexei, Tanya."

Jewel was silent. Amber toddled over and climbed onto her lap. She hugged her curly-haired daughter tightly, as a numbness began to invade her body. Was this really happening?

Sascha continued talking, sadly, quietly, but Jewel seemed unable to decipher the words. Perhaps he was speaking in Russian. She wasn't sure.

He talked for a long time. Some of it finally sunk in. Jewel began to realize that she and Sascha weren't really married at all. That it was over, although he didn't want it to be. Somehow he wanted to keep both of them, her and Aïna. He was sure he could make it work.

Jewel glanced at Aïna from time to time. The woman did not understand what was happening. It was obvious that she had not known about Jewel and the babies. She seemed to be as much in shock as Jewel.

"I love you, my darling. I never think this would happen. When Aïna and I say good-bye, it is with understanding that she will stay in Russia. She do not want to leave there, and I do. We part for good, I think. But a part of me has always missed her and children. I am happy they come here. We will work it out. I do not want to lose you, my Jewel. Say something," he pleaded. "Say you do not hate me."

Jewel took a sip of vodka. "I don't know whether I hate you or not, Sascha. But it's over."

"No, Jewel. We work it out," he insisted.

Jewel shook her head. "No, Sascha. No way. The girls and I are moving out."

"Please, my darling . . . we *will* work it out."

"No," Jewel said again. "No." And she took the children and left.

In a dramatically rash gesture that would have been appreciated by Sascha, had he known about it, Jewel walked thirteen blocks over to the Hudson River, and hurled the gold wedding band that he had made for her into the cold, choppy water.

After three years and two babies, Jewel knew everything about Sascha . . . and nothing.

One thing she did know: it was over.

Jewel was in shock. Three years with a stranger. She had cooked for him, knowing nothing of the man who ate her food. She had lain beside him and worked beside him—lain under him and worked under him was perhaps more accurate. She had learned a great deal about his craft, but very little, she reflected bitterly, about his heart. And nothing about his past.

She had loved a man who wasn't there. Now she hated the man who was.

These were phrases, she knew. As she stood above the Hudson and watched its gray shiny surface slide sluggishly beneath her, she made these phrases in her head to test their power to hurt, and knew that they were short on substance. They were not the whole truth, not yet.

Jewel still loved Sascha; or rather, she could not completely believe that she did not. But it was like the shock at the death of a loved one, like losing her mother, Jane. One knew the person was gone but did not believe it. One kept waiting for the loved face to appear at the next corner, to come through the doorway, to call on the telephone, to smile again from the end of the kitchen table.

Love itself was like that too. But the fact that Jewel could not yet fully believe it was gone did not make it any the less dead.

And if every death is a birth somewhere else, the birth of her hatred for Sascha Robinovsky would not be far behind.

18

Edward popped the cork off a bottle of Veuve Clicquot, and poured champagne into Jewel's waiting glass.

"To us," he said. "Together again. Honestly, darlin', if I were *that way* I'd marry you in a second."

"Well, it seems to be your lot in life to take care of me nevertheless," Jewel said, helping herself to some pâté that Nushka had made.

"At least you had the good sense to change your life around *after* I found a bigger apartment."

The new place was a three-bedroom duplex, half of a brownstone in Chelsea, that Edward had bought. He had moved up again, changing jobs to work for Harry Harper, a hot designer of women's wear who had recently licensed his name for everything from men's sweaters to sheets and chocolates.

"This place is great. It's a real house . . . I feel like a grown-up!" Jewel giggled. "And I promise not to be the woman who came to dinner . . . with her children. As soon as I get it together, I'll be out of here."

"Don't rush," Edward said seriously. "I enjoy havin' my little family. It makes me feel . . . well, let's just say it's fun playin' Daddy. You should have heard the tongues wag when you and the girls stopped by the office today. Nobody knows *what* my story is anymore, and I'm not tellin'."

Jewel laughed. "What's Harry Harper really like? I saw him on TV. They were interviewing him at his farm in upstate New York. He's good looking. His wife's gorgeous. The kids were galloping around on horseback. All too perfect."

Edward shrugged. "That's how he likes to come across. Yeah, he's a nice guy . . . straight *most* of the time. I hear every once in a while he likes to splurge. A cock in the ass to him's the equivalent of whipped cream and nuts on a chocolate sundae to an overweight, middle-aged woman. He strays occasionally, then goes back to his wife."

"You know," Jewel said, helping herself to more champagne, "I read somewhere that some psychiatrists now say there's no such thing as a bisexual person. You're either one thing or the other."

"I wouldn't know," Edward said. "I mean, when I was straight it was just 'cause I was afraid to be anything else. Look . . ."—he leaned forward—"we're talkin' around the real subject that's on both our minds."

"Sascha?"

"Who else? How *are* you? What are you feeling?"

"I'm numb, mostly," Jewel said. "How can you live with someone for so long and know so little about them? Oh shit!" Jewel started crying. "I don't want to do this. He isn't worth it. I *hate* the bastard!" she sobbed. "And I don't want anything from him. No money, nothing. I just want him out of my life forever. Boy, do I have shitty luck with men! Next time, I'm walking into it with my eyes open . . . and they're going to *stay* open."

"Well, at least you're lucid enough to admit that there'll be a next time."

"Yeah," Jewel laughed bitterly, holding out her glass for more champagne. "Men! Can't live with 'em, can't live without 'em. Except for you, Edward. You're the exception."

Edward nodded. "Yes, well, you can live here as long as you want. And we're goin' to get you famous. I've got some ideas."

"Yeah? Well, I want to be *really* famous . . . not just sort of. I haven't been subscribing to *Town and Country* and memorizing all those names for nothing," Jewel said. "Besides, before Jane came on the scene, I had a lousy childhood. I *know* what it's like not to know where your next meal is coming from. Now I'm on my own again . . . but my kids will never have a life like that. I'm going to work my ass off. Amber and Beryl are never going to want for *anything*."

"I'll help you," Edward said, "in any way I can. And don't worry. Everything's goin' to be all right."

They stayed up talking for hours. By bedtime it seemed that Jewel's entire future had been mapped out for her. It was wonderful to have a friend like Edward, a man who wanted absolutely nothing from her, except companionship.

"Good lord," Gary Pollock said over the phone, "Madeleine Lathem? I thought you'd been abducted by a spaceship. You disappeared totally. I didn't know how to get in touch with you."

"Have you wanted to get in touch with me?"

"Sure . . . things are looking up. Datatrax was bought by GE, and Voisin Motors reorganized under new management. Let's see . . . I'll just punch it up on my computer here. Yeah, you're doing okay, babe."

Jewel couldn't believe it. "I am? How okay? If I were to sell . . ."

"Don't sell! The market's going up."

"Gary, I need money. That's why I called you."

"Okay . . . right now they're worth something in the neighborhood of thirty-five grand."

"*What?*" Jewel laughed, stunned. "Thirty-five thousand dollars?"

"You heard me, babe."

"Oh my God, I don't believe it. Wyatt McNeill was right. You *are* a whiz kid."

"No longer, babe. I turned thirty last week. You seen McNeill lately?" Pollock asked.

"Oh no. Not for years," she said quietly.

"Well, I ran into him a while back. He asked me about you, matter of fact. Wanted to know if I'd heard from you."

"Listen, Gary, I want you to do me a favor. I owe him some money. I figure it comes to about eight thousand dollars, including interest. Could you send him a check for that, out of the money from the stocks? And don't give him my address. Just write a note telling him that I appreciated his financial support when I needed it and that, as promised, I'm paying him back."

"You sure you don't want to give it to him yourself? I got the feeling he wanted to see you again."

"Sell all the stocks," Jewel said, ignoring what Gary had said, "and after you've taken out Wyatt's money and your commission, send me a check for the balance. To P.O. Box 2337, zip code 10011. And thanks. When I get rich, I'll look you up and open a new account."

"You're on, babe," Pollock said. "Good luck."

Edward took Jewel and her daughters to spend Christmas with his family in Virginia. His parents and sisters were exuberant to see Edward with a woman. They treated Jewel as family, hoping that Edward was about to finally settle down. Amber and Beryl were showered with toys from Santa, and Christmas morning under the thirty-foot tree made Jewel wonder whether she and Edward really should get married. She couldn't imagine winding up with anyone nicer, but sex was the problem.

Sex was always the problem. With Sascha she had tossed all her plans in the air because he was so good in bed. With Wyatt she had lost her best friend because she was so flattered that he wanted her. Jewel decided it was time to stop thinking with her vagina and give her brain a shot.

"You know, I've finally figured it out," Jewel told Edward, after they had returned to New York. "A good sexual relationship has to be an affair. A good marriage has to be a financial arrangement. If I ever fall in love again, I'm *not* going to marry the guy! What I want for a husband is a rich, straight, best friend."

"Which leaves me out," Edward said.

"I've thought a lot about us," Jewel said, pouring herself a glass of milk to go with the bag of chocolate chip cookies she was devouring. "But if we were married I'd be jealous of your lovers. I might not know who they were, but I'd know they existed."

"But you could have lovers too," Edward said. "Maybe we *should* get married. There are worse ideas."

"No, Edward. I love you too much to marry you," Jewel said. "You're on to all my flaws. We know each other too well."

Edward wiped away the milk mustache from Jewel's upper lip. "Yes, that we do."

"You know," Jewel went on, "talking to my stockbroker about Wyatt McNeill made me think of Hadley. We were really happy together, except it didn't last very long."

"What do you suppose happened to him?"

"Hadley? Probably married a preppie and works on Wall Street."

Jewel shrugged. "I have no way of finding out. Can you imagine if I called the McNeills and said, 'Hi, this is Madeleine Lathem . . .'"

"Good God," Edward interrupted. "Madeleine Lathem! Do you realize that this is the first time I've heard your real name?"

"Well, Dragoumis is my real name. Jane Lathem was my adopted mother."

"I can call."

"What?"

"I can call the McNeills," Edward said. "Say I'm an old college buddy. Where'd he go?"

"Yale."

"It figures. What's the number?"

"KL5-1332, unless it's changed."

Edward dialed. "Is this the McNeill residence? Yes, this is Edward . . . Bentley. I'm a friend of Hadley's from Yale. I'm in town from L.A. and I wanted to look him up. Oh? Really? My goodness . . . yes, well, I'm not surprised. Is there an address?" Edward signaled Jewel to hand him a pencil and he jotted down an address on the pad by the phone. "Oh yes . . . Bentley . . . Edward. Well, thank you. Take care."

"What?" Jewel asked, excited. "Where is he?"

"Kashmir. Working for CARE."

"Is he married?"

Edward shrugged. "Don't know. I didn't want to be too quizzy."

Jewel smiled. "So he really did it after all. Broke away from his background to go out and help the world. Good for you, Hadley. Good for you."

She wondered if she would ever see him again. Then dismissed the thought. Even if she did run into Hadley McNeill somewhere, he probably wouldn't bother to speak to her.

Betty Blessing's lease on the Golden Buddha was about to expire: the rent was going to double. She and Jewel spent weeks looking and finally found a tiny shop on West Broadway, in Soho, for a fraction of the rent the old place commanded.

"It *is* tiny," Betty said.

"But it's a great location. And if I cover the walls with mirrors, it'll look bigger."

"Hmmm . . . yes, and with marvelous lighting . . . I think it'd make it."

Jewel threw her arms around Betty. "Is this really happening? I'm so excited."

"You bet it is, baby. We're really doing it!"

Betty had agreed to sell her business—inventory and suppliers—to Jewel, on a time arrangement. Jewel would pay installments for two years. If Betty hated Lake Tahoe and wanted to return to New York within that time, Jewel would take her back in as a partner.

"Only one thing," Jewel said over coffee, after signing the lease. "And I don't want to hurt your feelings. But I was thinking I might change the name of the store."

Betty laughed. "God, I don't blame you. The Golden Buddha's a name whose time has come and gone. What do you have in mind?"

"I was thinking of Glitter, or Sparkles, or Bijoux . . ."

"Bijoux," Betty repeated. "I like that. It's marvelous, actually." She looked at her watch. "God, I've got to go pack. Can you believe after all these years Roland's taking me to meet his mother in Florida? I'm beginning to feel so legitimate. I think marriage is going to be tons of fun."

"It can be," Jewel said, hugging her friend good-bye. "As long as you don't pick a bigamist."

"I think you should send the bastard to jail," Betty said, "instead of getting an annulment."

"Much as I hate Sascha, I wouldn't want to be responsible for putting him behind bars. I owe him something. Without him I wouldn't have Amber and Beryl. They're my life now . . . I'm so happy to have them."

"Well, entre nous," Betty said. "I think I may be pregnant."

"That's great!" Jewel bubbled. "You know, I think you'll go to Tahoe and it'll be the last we'll ever see of you. You'll really be happy there."

"I think so too. Things are picking up for all of us," Betty said, hailing a cab. "Talk to you soon. I know Bijoux is going to be an enormous success."

Jewel spent the next two weeks working nonstop, moving Betty's stock from Bleeker Street and making the most of the space in her hole-in-the-wall shop. Edward helped her build shelves, and Demetrius, no longer Edward's lover but still a friend, came by and consulted on the lighting. It was his suggestion to illuminate the wall niches and glass cases with tiny, white Christmas tree lights that they found, off season, at a factory in Chinatown. Demetrius did up an alarm system for Jewel for half what her other estimates had been.

Finally, on Valentine's Day 1975—just after Beryl's first birthday and Amber's second—Jewel opened Bijoux. To celebrate the day, she displayed the jewelry among little chocolate hearts and red tea roses.

"What a year this has been," Jewel said, ringing up a sale, after a remarkably active first day. "Do you think my life's going to settle down now?" she asked Edward, who had taken off from work early to come by the shop.

"I wouldn't bet on it," he said. "Now you're goin' to have to work your little tush off."

"Thank heavens for Nushka. I've been so busy I think the kids are beginning to think she's their mother."

"I have an openin'-day present for you," Edward said when the shop had emptied out and they were alone. "I called a friend at *New York* magazine and told him about the shop. He's interested . . . and promised to stop by. If he likes it, there's a good chance of gettin' it into Best Bets. I also called *Glamour, Vogue, Cosmo, Harper's Bazaar, Mademoiselle . . .*"

"That's fabulous!" Jewel cried. "Thank you! Oh, Edward, I can't believe it's happening."

She had read somewhere that when you're ready for a big opportunity you always attract an obstacle first, and that you must get over the obstacle before you can move ahead. Jewel coldly viewed her years with Sascha as having been her obstacle. And now she was over him. She did not give him credit for having helped her finish her jewelry education and perfect her craft. She only allowed him an offhand role in the creation of Amber and Beryl, and now, as time went on, his importance in that feat began to diminish in her mind. *She* was the one who had suffered their births, after all; Sascha had only participated in the fun part.

But some nights she dreamed of him, dreamed they were back together as a happy, loving family. On those nights she would wake up from the dream and cry. When she wasn't busy hating him, she still missed him.

Before closing up for the day, Jewel slipped her arm through Edward's and paused to study her glittering, precious shop. It was perfect, as she had imagined it would be. Success was around the corner, and Bijoux in Soho was merely the beginning.

"But you have to start somewhere," she told Edward. "And of all the places in the world, West Broadway in Soho in New York City ain't bad. It ain't bad at all," she laughed giddily.

Jewel was finally on her way.

19

Wedged into a minuscule space on West Broadway, hardly bigger than a refrigerator, we unearthed Bijoux beyond our wildest dreams. There are stunning displays of delicious mostly costume trinkets, gleaming among tiny Christmas lights. Jewel Dragoumis, the shop's owner and chief designer, had us salivating over her nonpareils—enamel rings inlaid in motifs patterned after Oriental rugs ($175–$450, depending on width of the band). Mark our words, Jewel—she swears it's her real name—has created a gem of a shop. Bijoux, 435½ West Broadway. Hours: 12:00–8:00, Tuesday–Sunday.

Jewel smiled as she reread the piece in *New York,* slipping it into an art deco frame to hang in the shop. Ever since the article appeared, three weeks earlier, dedicated shoppers had been flocking downtown to check her out. It was madness. In less than six months, she was a success, mostly thanks to Edward's tireless propagandizing to People Who Matter at the magazines.

But success had its price. Jewel hadn't seen a movie or play since the shop opened, and the idea of a summer weekend in the Hamptons with Edward was as farfetched as a trip to Mars. Every night, after she put the girls to bed, she made the enameled, Oriental-rug-patterned rings that were the current rage. She worked mornings before the shop opened and on Mondays, her day off.

It was exhilarating, and frustrating. There weren't enough hours in the day to make jewelry, tend the shop, and be a decent mother.

Nushka, of course, kept Amber and Beryl happy and occupied. And although part of Jewel knew she was missing out on precious hours of their childhood, she rationalized her absence. Her ambition and struggle for success, she told Edward, was every bit as much for Amber and Beryl as it was for herself. They would have the best childhood possible. Once she had it made, she would have plenty of time for her daughters.

Jewel was already contemplating expansion, which, of course, to do right would take time and a lot more money than she could put her hands on. So expansion could wait. For now, there were only two things missing from her life: a man to do things with and the time to do them.

Edward's new boyfriend, Peter, who had recently graduated from a course of Silva Mind Control, told Jewel that the powers of positive thinking and creative imagery were the key to getting what you wanted in life. If you concentrated, meditated, and were *very* specific about what you wanted, it would come. Peter said he got cabs in rush hour all the time that way. He had also landed a great new job. So Jewel visualized and created images every night as she drifted off to sleep. What the hell, it didn't cost anything.

And, within a week, along came Cathalene Columbier, tiny with large doe eyes and a short, boyish haircut. She looked no more than twelve, but swore she was twenty-one. She was French but spoke practically accent-free English.

"Hello? Are you Jewel? I am Cathalene . . . from Paris," she said, walking into the shop one day. She was wearing an oversized Grand Canyon T-shirt, khaki shorts, and sneakers without socks. "I'm a friend of Katrina . . ."

"And Christof! They wrote me ages ago that you were in the States and might show up," Jewel smiled. "But I'd forgotten. You design jewelry for their shop."

"Yes, I do wire work. Very delicate. I have samples with me. Would you like to see them?"

"Of course. Here." She set an empty black velvet tray on top of a glass case.

"These I did in Santa Fe—silver wire with turquoise chunks stuck in," Cathalene said, taking a leather box out of her large canvas handbag. "They'll go over well in Paris, perhaps not in New York."

"Hmmm, you're right. Indian jewelry's had a big revival here, and now it's pretty much done. But your workmanship's excellent. I adore the ring you're wearing."

Cathalene held out her finger to display a ring fashioned out of intricately-woven gold and silver wire, with a one-carat chunk of amethyst crystal in the middle. "Yes . . . it's one of my favorites. I had a bracelet to match that I traded to a friend in L.A. for room and board."

"If you want to make some of those for me, I'd be interested. In fact," she said, reaching under the counter and bringing out a leather pouch, "I bought some Brazilian topaz crystals from a guy who stopped by here the other day. See . . . orange, gold, yellow, pink, blue. I hadn't figured out what to do with them. But if you want to use them we could work out a deal. And I'll buy your pieces outright, rather than do consignment."

Cathalene picked up the small crystal chunks and looked at them. "Yes, they'd do very well. The only problem is, I'm living with a guy in a studio apartment, and he works at home. He's a writer. Do you have a place I could work?"

Jewel laughed. "I use my bedroom. I turned it into a workshop and sleep on a pull-out sofa that I usually don't bother pulling out." She paused. "Here, well . . . what you see is what you see. There's no back room."

"This is okay. If I sat behind the counter I could work there," Cathalene suggested. "I don't need much space. I could even handle sales when you want to go out. I'm good at talking to people."

Jewel couldn't believe her luck. If Cathalene worked in the shop it would free up Jewel's time considerably. And Cathalene's wire work was technically flawless; Jewel knew it would sell.

"Okay," Jewel shook hands with the small French girl. "We're on. When do you want to start?"

"How about tomorrow?" Cathalene said.

Cathalene was the perfect solution to Jewel's problems. She was happy to weave her rings while tending the shop, and the arrangement gave Jewel more time to stay home with the children and make her own pieces. It was a profitable arrangement too. Cathalene's rings and bracelets began to sell as fast as she could make them.

As for her own work, Jewel was flying high. Edward introduced her to his boss, Harry Harper, and he liked the new pieces she was working on. They were influenced by art deco, employing elements of stainless steel with faceted smoky quartz and cubic zirconium. Harper commissioned her to do the jewelry for his next spring's womenwear show.

"Edward's been raving about you for some time now," Harry said. Traces of a New Jersey accent outlined his words. "I'm glad we could finally get together, Jewel. You don't mind if I call you by your first name? Women are so uptight about that these days."

Jewel shook her head. "I don't mind. As long as I can call you Harry."

Harper laughed, displaying the whitest teeth Jewel had ever seen in her life. "Look, my wife and I are having a party on Saturday, just a cocktail thing, for Genevieve Davis, who's in town for a few days. Edward's coming . . . why don't you drop by too? Bring a date, if you want. There'll be people there you should meet. And . . ." he quickly picked through her jewelry samples on his desk, "wear this . . . and this, and this. With a black dress. You're thin enough to wear one of the models' samples. Ask Emma, my secretary, to find you one before you leave."

"Well, thank you but . . ."

"You suspect I'm putting the make on you?" Harry asked bluntly. "Believe me, as attractive as you are, I'm not. You have a lot of talent. It's time you started working the main rooms. And I'm going to help you." With that, he stood abruptly. "I have a lunch date." He headed for the door, then paused. "Be there Saturday."

Jewel did not know what to make of Harry Harper. All his money and power, yet he seemed genuine in his praise of her work. Maybe he liked her too, and this was the way he operated, but she knew she could deal with that. After gathering up her jewelry, she headed down the hall to Edward's office, to report on the meeting.

"Fantastic, darlin'," he responded. "You never can tell with Harry. I thought he'd like your work, but everything depends on the mood of the day. He got praised in *WWD* this mornin', so this was good timin'."

"And he asked me to his party Saturday. Some shindig for Genevieve Davis, whoever she is."

"She's London society. Owns a club there. Mistress of one of the world's financial leaders, Sir Charles Harding, who happens to be one of Harry's backers for the new menswear division. Harry's out to give

Pierre Cardin a run for his money." Edward glanced at his watch. "Oh, late for lunch. Sorry I can't take you, but it's business."

"That's okay," Jewel said. "I'm going to wander around the Museum of Modern Art for a little inspiration. Cathalene's minding the store till four."

"Jewel," Edward said before he left, "it's terrific that Harry likes you. He's a powerful man these days. But as a word of friendly advice, I'd try not to . . ."

"Step on his balls?" Jewel said. "And act like a good little girl? I liked him. He wasn't what I was expecting."

"Good. Just remember, he's mercurial. You have to watch yourself, but he can take you places."

"Okay, Daddy." Jewel smiled, as they walked to the elevator together. "I'll be nice to the boss. At this point, I'm willing to do anything to get ahead."

"You don't have to go *that* far. Just be reasonable." The elevator appeared, and Edward stepped on. Jewel stayed back. "Aren't you comin'?"

"No, I have to pick out a dress for Saturday night."

Edward smiled and made a victory sign with his fingers as the elevator door swung shut.

After about forty-five minutes of wandering around the Museum of Modern Art, jotting down notes, feeling totally exhilarated from the morning's meeting with Harry Harper, Jewel stopped in front of one of her favorite objets, a box made by Joseph Cornell in 1940, titled Taglioni's Jewel Casket. The brown hinged case contained a necklace of glass stones, jewelry fragments of red, blue, and clear glass chips, and twelve ice cubes made of clear glass. The interior of the lid was covered with brown velvet, framing Cornell's inscription.

Jewel turned the page in her notebook, and began jotting down the story: "On a moonlight night in the winter of 1835 the carriage of Marie TAGLIONI was halted by a Russian highwayman, and that enchanting creature commanded to dance for this audience of one upon a panther's skin spread over the snow beneath the stars. From this actuality arose the legend that to keep alive the memory of this adventure so precious to her, TAGLIONI . . ."

Jewel was suddenly aware of a man standing next to her, watching her write. She glanced up, and he smiled.

"I'll dictate, if you like," he said, and started reading slowly from the file card. ". . . 'TAGLIONI formed the habit of placing a piece of artificial ice in her jewelry casket or dressing table, where, melting among the sparkling stones, there was evoked a hint of the atmosphere of the starlit heavens over the ice-covered landscape.' That's it," the stranger said. "A very romantic legend."

Jewel slipped her pad and pen back into her handbag. "Yes, isn't it? Thanks for dictating." She took a good look at the man and made a quick appraisal: not bad. Attractive in a young bankerish sort of way, wearing a conservative gray suit, with well-shaped light brown hair. His eyes were light brown too, behind round wire-rimmed glasses. He was about six feet tall, and his body was slim and long waisted.

"I've been following you," he said. "Watching you write secret thoughts in your little notebook."

"Oh you have, have you?" Jewel smiled. "I'm casing the place, getting ready for the big heist."

He nodded. "I won't tell, but I think that guard who just passed behind you pricked up his ears. They may not let you leave without intense questioning."

"Why were you watching me?" Jewel asked.

"I like to pick up women in museums."

"Oh? Well, you're direct. I like that."

He shook his head. "Actually, I don't. Pick up women in museums. I've never done it before . . . but I was struck with you. Extremely curious about what you were writing."

"Well, I'm sorry to disappoint you, but it's just random thoughts. Ideas, catch phrases, anything that might inspire me later."

"Then you're a painter?" he said.

Jewel shook her head. "I design jewelry." She looked at her watch. "And I have to go."

"Don't," he said, following her out of the gallery. "Come downstairs and have some coffee with me. Or lunch. You look as if you could stand a meal."

Jewel hesitated for an instant, and he picked up on it. "Aha!" he smiled. "You don't want to . . . but you can't think of a good excuse."

"I have to get downtown."

"Right this minute?"

"Okay," Jewel relented. A cup of coffee. A little flirtation. MOMA was a safe enough place to talk to strangers. And this stranger seemed rather nice.

"I'm Allen Prescott," he said as they walked downstairs.

"Jewel Dragoumis."

"What a great name," he said. "Is Dragoumis Greek?"

Jewel shrugged. "I guess. Actually, I don't really know."

"Oh? Most people have some idea of what their heritage is."

"Most of the people *you* know, maybe. But Dragoumis took off when I was a couple of weeks old. We haven't kept in touch."

That silenced him. But after they had sat down with coffee and pie, Jewel decided to make an effort. Allen Prescott was nice-looking, well dressed, perhaps someone she would like. "So, here we are."

"Having coffee and apple pie." Allen smiled. "And trying to decide whether this is a pickup that's going to lead somewhere. Or whether we'll shake hands in fifteen minutes and head back off to our lives . . . never knowing what might have happened if we'd given it a chance."

"Are you a writer? You have a great imagination."

"I'm working on a play. But then I've been working on it ever since I graduated from college."

"Where was that?"

"Brown. I majored in art history and minored in creative writing."

"Then you must be well off," Jewel said.

"What makes you think that? I could have gotten a scholarship."

"Your major. People who have to make money usually wind up with something more . . . business oriented. I don't mean to be nosey. It's just something I've observed."

Allen laughed. "Well, I work. I have an office downtown."

"Where you write your play?"

"My play's recreation, actually. Day to day, I manage money."

"Oh?" Jewel smiled. A financier. A wonderful contact for when she was ready to expand Bijoux. "Then why aren't you downtown managing money now? Instead of wandering around the museum."

Allen shrugged, grinning. "You think I'm lying. That I'm some ne'er-do-well who hangs around this place picking up women. Actually, I wanted to see the Matisse show again before it closes."

"Yeah," Jewel nodded, "it's a great show. Someday I want to be rich enough to collect art. Just think about it. Back then, some of those paintings were bought for next to nothing. I mean, can you imagine owning a Matisse?"

"I do some collecting," Allen said.

"You do? That's fantastic." She was impressed, if he was telling the truth.

"Well, at one point I wanted to be a painter," Allen said. "But fortunately I discovered early on that I have no talent."

"Why do you say fortunately?" Jewel asked.

"Because if you don't have talent and you *know* it, you save yourself years of frustration and rejection. Then I discovered I do have *one* aptitude when it comes to art. I recognize talent. I have a sixth sense for it. Every painting I've bought has at least doubled in value," he said casually.

"That's great. But it's an expensive hobby." She still didn't believe him, this stranger telling her he collected art, insinuating that he was rich as Croesus.

"Oh, I had a little family money . . . a bit of an inheritance that I decided to gamble on the art market," he said.

Jewel nodded, not wanting to pry, but wanting very much to believe him.

"I grew up in Oklahoma. A very normal boyhood. Except I had this one aunt . . . my father's oldest sister. The renegade of the family. She used to take me antique hunting with her, and to furniture auctions. She loved furniture. I got interested in the paintings. She's the one who left me the money. I think she would have been pleased if she knew I was spending it that way. My parents never approved of her, or of art. To this day the only pictures hanging in their house are of me and my sister as children, painted by Tulsa's leading—and only—portrait painter."

Jewel laughed, then suddenly caught sight of the clock on the wall. Four o'clock. "Oh my God, I'm late!"

"But I don't know anything about *you*. What if I want to see you again?"

Jewel fished in her purse and pulled out a business card. "This is my shop. Look, thanks for the coffee. I have to run."

Allen Prescott picked up the card and stuck it in his pocket. "I'll guard it with my life," he called out.

Jewel was halfway across the cafeteria, but she turned and smiled. " 'Bye." She waved and dashed out.

She wondered if Allen Prescott was telling the truth. If he wasn't handing her a line, he was obviously well off. Of course, there was every chance that he was handing her a line.

Still, there was something about him that she liked. He was the first man to interest her since Sascha. Not that it was anything resembling love at first sight, but he appeared to be an attractive, amusing man who could afford dinner and a couple of theater tickets.

At the very least, he could provide a pleasant diversion in her life. She hoped he would call.

20

"Ah, so tonight is the fancy party with Harry Harper?" Cathalene Columbier said. She had brought a bright green feather duster to the shop and was dusting the jewelry displays that were inset into deep wall niches.

"Yeah, at seven. Look, if you can't stay till eight you can close up. Just put a sign on the door: 'Emergency—had to leave early. Come back tomorrow,' " Jewel said, getting ready to run home and dress.

"Oh, that's okay. I don't mind staying. Jimmy's got some big deadline . . . an article for *Rolling Stone.* He's working all weekend. I'd just as soon be someplace else," she sighed.

For an instant, Jewel considered asking Cathalene to go to the party with her. But as much as she appreciated Cathalene, over the past weeks Jewel could not help noticing how ambitious the French woman was. Her wire rings were selling as fast as she could make them, and Jewel suspected that Cathalene hawked them shamelessly to customers when Jewel wasn't around.

So she wasn't about to share Harry Harper, or provide Cathalene with an opportunity to dazzle him with her European charm. Jewel wanted to be the jewelry designer of Harper's eye. After months of Edward's working behind the scenes, Jewel finally had Harper's attention. She wasn't about to let Cathalene try to steal the show.

"Well, see you tomorrow then. Have a nice evening," Jewel said.

"Yes . . . you too," Cathalene sighed again.

Jewel had wanted to invite Allen Prescott to the party. He would have fit in well with the society crowd that would undoubtedly be at the Harpers'. And, she thought, it would have impressed Allen that Jewel knew these people. But Allen hadn't called her or come by the shop. So much for him and the pickup at MOMA.

"Oh, I forgot to tell you," Cathalene said as Jewel was heading out the door. "You know that guy I mentioned to you, the one named Jeb who went crazy over your work?"

"The man who bought my anodized-silver-and-lapis necklace?"

"Yeah, well, we started flirting, and he said he'd come back in a few days to see me. And, er, I thought I'd better let you know . . . I sort of let him think that I own the shop. And, er, that I designed the necklace."

"Oh?"

"Yes. I know I shouldn't have," Cathalene gushed innocently. "But he really liked me, and he liked the necklace. Then he said that if I'd designed it he'd feel obligated to buy it. So I said I had. I mean, it was only to make the sale. I'm not one to take credit for someone else's work."

"Yes, I see," Jewel said coolly, knowing for sure that she had made the right decision in not inviting Cathalene to the party. She wouldn't put it past Cathalene to tell Harry that *she'd* designed all of Jewel's art deco pieces. "Well, in the future . . . and even to make a sale . . ."

"I know. I understand completely," Cathalene said. "But if this guy Jeb comes in, I'd appreciate it if you'd kind of act like you work for me, rather than the other way around. I really like him."

Jewel stared at her, amazed by her chutzpah, and let a stony expression convey her reaction to the matter.

"I'm sorry, Jewel," Cathalene said, now fully aware that she had stepped on Jewel's toes. "It won't happen again."

"Good," Jewel said.

Harry and Vivian Harper's penthouse on Fifth Avenue overlooking Central Park was impressive but spare, done in grays and blacks. There was nothing ostentatious about the furniture, and there was very little to-die-for art on the walls, save a large Jackson Pollock that dominated one end of the living room. There was a lot of heavy-duty jewelry though, around the slim necks and arms and fingers of the women, most of whom Jewel recognized from the pages of *Women's Wear Daily.*

"God, Edward," Jewel said, as they made their entrance. "Why am I so nervous? It's just a party, but I feel as if this is my society debut. Well, actually it is the first party like this I've been to in years—since the days when I hung around with the McNeills."

"Darlin', all those years with Sascha got you out of touch. Until you get used to this crowd you've got a right to be nervous. This room is full of people who'd as soon step on you as not. Remember what I said about puttin' on your best behavior."

"I'll be charm itself," Jewel smiled, as Vivian Harper came over and Edward made the introductions.

"Oh, I'm so pleased to meet you," Vivian said. She was blond, with a cultivated Eastern-boarding-school accent. Jewel knew, by way of Edward's gossip, that she was the daughter of a wealthy Las Vegas hotel owner and had been an aspiring model when Harry Harper married her ten years before, crowning her queen of his expanding empire. This evening, she looked the part, lovely, appealing, gem studded. "Harry's excited about your work. In fact I thought I might run by your shop next week."

"I'd love it," Jewel said, and then had an inspiration. "I also do custom work. If you have any old jewels you want redesigned . . ."

"How fabulous. What timing! My mother gave me a diamond ring of hers. It's a pretty stone, about three carats, but it's *so* boring. You know, a six-prong platinum Tiffany setting," she said. "I'll never wear it the way it is. I'd love to turn it into something fun."

"Call me," Jewel said, "and we'll get together. I'll be happy to look at it and make some suggestions."

"Wonderful!" Vivian crooned. "You're every bit as terrific as Harry said. Get a drink, Jewel, and then I'll put you into circulation. I want to introduce you to some friends."

As Vivian drifted off to greet new arrivals, Jewel whispered to Edward, "I'm doing good, eh?"

"Home run on the first ball. Since when do you do custom work?"

"The idea suddenly came to me. I want to work with precious stones, but I can't afford them. This is the ideal way."

"You're quick, darlin'. Let's get that drink and start introducin' you around."

An hour later, after two glasses of champagne and much admiration, Jewel was high on success, that of those around her as well as her own at capturing the attention of the elegant elite she was meeting.

"You're sparkling tonight," Harry said, coming over and brushing her cheek with a kiss. "I feel like a proud father. Vivian can be a tough nut to crack, and you have her eating out of your hand."

Jewel smiled. "I'm overwhelmed. I'm having such a good time. This is the first party I've been to in years."

"What? You have to be kidding," Harry said, obviously not believing her.

"I've been leading a very sheltered life. Work and motherhood."

"We have to do something about that. I want you to start getting exposure. Have you talked to Marilyn Cunningham over there?" He indicated a tall, blond, horsey-looking woman wearing extremely thick glasses. "She wants to interview you for *WWD*. You're on your way, and I think we're going to be a great team." His eyes drifted down over her body and back up to her face, holding it in his glance. He grinned, giving her a full dose of the Harry Harper charisma that had hypnotized the press over the past ten years. "Your jewels, my clothes . . . they're made for each other. Look, let's have dinner next week."

Jewel hesitated.

"It's okay. All you have to do is say 'yes.' "

"You're married. Don't you usually have dinner with your family?" Jewel asked.

"Vivian's bored by business stuff. And it *is* business between you and me. I want you to know that from the start."

Jewel smiled, relieved. "Then I'd love to have dinner with you."

"Good," he said, giving her a little squeeze around the waist. "I'll call you the first of the week."

"Well, what do you think?" Jewel asked Edward when they got home that evening. "Is he coming on to me, or not? I can't tell. I mean, he's married . . . and you told me he's gay."

"I didn't exactly say that. I heard a rumor that *occasionally* he likes to grab a fruit off the forbidden tree. But he has more than a few notches in his heterosexual belt too. My advice, if you want it, is stay cool. Be the lady he doesn't get. That way he won't tire of you."

Jewel nodded. "I'm inclined to agree. Harry and I are going to be strictly business, just like he said." She giggled. "He is attractive though. In the way that money and power make a man."

"No, darlin', I know what I'm talkin' about."

"Okay, Edward . . . but we have to make a pact. If I don't get him, neither do you."

"You're safe," Edward sighed. "Unfortunately, I'm not his type."

The next Tuesday afternoon, Jewel was alone in the shop. Cathalene was home with a devastating case of cramps.

It was a slow day, and Jewel was rearranging the displays when the doorbell buzzed. She turned to see Allen Prescott standing outside, smiling and carrying a single red rose in his hand.

She rang him in. "Well, hi. I didn't expect to see you again."

"Didn't you?" He handed her the rose. "I would have called sooner, but I've been in Tulsa. My father died. The night I met you, as a matter of fact."

"Oh, I'm sorry," she said. "Are you okay? Were you very close?"

Allen shrugged. "I loved him . . . but he never approved of me. Wanted me to become the family lawyer. I actually went to the University of Virginia law school for a year. But I couldn't hack it. Anyway, Dad had a heart condition and he smoked like a chimney. This wasn't totally unexpected."

"Even so, it's still hard. My mother died when I was a freshman in college," Jewel said. Jane popped into her mind often these days. It still hurt when she thought about Jane dying so young, without ever knowing her grandchildren.

"Yeah, you're right. It's harder than you think it'll be. In subtle ways," Allen swallowed. He looked younger today and was more casually dressed, in slacks and a tweed sports jacket. "Anyway, I wondered if you'd have dinner with me tonight?"

"I'm afraid I can't. My roommate Edward's having a dinner party, and I'm cooking. He's been letting me live with him, rent free, for ages. So I cater his parties." She deliberated a moment. "Well, actually, you could come. I mean, if you don't mind a bunch of strangers."

"With you there, I wouldn't mind at all. But would it bother Edward?" He paused. "What exactly is your relationship with this man?"

"Friends. Absolutely nothing else. And I may as well tell you right off in case you want to change your mind: I have two little girls. I'm . . . widowed."

"Hell, I can hold my own with kids. My sister has four, and I'm devoted to them. Oh, that's the other reason I'm here. It's my sister's birthday. I wanted to get something."

"Well, everything you see is for sale," she grinned.

Allen looked around for a while, praising Jewel's work. "You're really good, you know that?"

"Yes, but it's nice to have it reaffirmed every once in a while. What does your sister like? Maybe I can suggest something."

"Here . . . I'll show you a picture," he opened his wallet. Something about the fact that he carried a photograph of his sister struck Jewel as charming. And when she saw that he carried photographs of her children as well, she was struck by the sweetness of it. The sister was very attractive. Wealthy looking, well dressed.

"How much do you want to spend?"

"Doesn't matter," he said offhandedly.

Jewel started to steer him to her most expensive necklace—a highly-polished silver choker embedded with bottle green tourmalines of varying sizes—but decided not to take advantage of him.

"Do you want something for day or evening?"

"Hell, you tell me. I don't know much about that sort of thing."

"Basically, you're saying whatever I pick out's fine with you, regardless of price," Jewel said. "Aren't you afraid I'll suggest the most expensive thing?"

"You're trying to make a living—and when it comes to my sister, cost is no object."

"Most men say that about their girlfriends," Jewel teased.

"Isabel's been very supportive," Allen said seriously. "She stood up for me against Dad, kept me from getting disinherited. So I owe her a lot. We're best friends."

"That's nice," Jewel said, wondering even as she said it how she and sister Isabel would get along. "What about this engraved gold-plated bracelet? It's simple, elegant."

"That's fine. How much?"

"One fifty."

"Is that all? I told you I'd buy anything."

"But I don't *want* to take advantage of you." Jewel smiled. "And your sister looks as if she'd prefer something on the classical side, nothing too innovative."

Allen nodded. "You're a good judge of character, Jewel. I think you're right." He reached for his wallet again and put two hundred-dollar bills on the counter. "Can you gift wrap it and send it for me?"

"Of course."

"Hey, look, how much is this one?" He pointed to the tourmaline-studded choker.

"The most expensive thing I have in the shop. There's a total of fifteen carats of verdelite tourmalines in this piece. It's twenty-five hundred."

Allen took back the two hundred. "Sold. If you'll trust me enough to take a check."

"I trust you. But don't you think it's too avant-garde for your sister?"

"It is, and she'll love me for picking it out. Underneath her conservative exterior there lurks a bohemian. She thinks I'm the only one who understands her." He wrote the check and handed it to Jewel. Her eyes nearly popped out when she saw the Sutton Place address. This guy was unattached, she knew that, wealthy—the Sutton Place address proved that he had not been handing her a line—and he liked her. He was a catch she was not going to let slip through her fingers.

"Thanks, Allen. You didn't have to buy my most expensive piece. I'd have liked you anyway."

"God, Jewel, you're refreshing," Allen said earnestly. "Not like most of the women I've met since I moved here. What time do you want me tonight?"

"Eight. I'll have the girls in bed by then."

"Then I'll come at seven-thirty. I want to meet them," he said, smiling. "See you then."

Jewel caught herself smiling all the rest of the day. To have met the eligible Allen Prescott as a random pickup? It was unbelievable. And he liked kids. Even more unbelievable.

Her luck, she decided, was definitely changing.

21

Harry Harper was deliberately soft-spoken—part of his image—and the din of Pearl's Chinese restaurant on West Forty-eighth practically drowned him out. Jewel was forced to lean forward and lip-read to catch what he was saying. So far it had been all business, as promised, and Jewel was beginning to relax.

After cracking up at one of his Seventh Avenue jokes, Jewel said, "I enjoy you, Harry. You're very funny."

Noting that she had let down her guard, he pounced. "Vivian's at our house on Martinique for a couple of weeks, with the kids. Why don't you come out to the place on Montauk this weekend? We can get a lot of work done . . . without interruption." He dipped his chopsticks into the serving platter of lemon chicken, eating directly from it rather than dishing the food onto his own plate.

"You forget . . . my shop's open on weekends. I can't get away."

"Sure you can," Harper announced.

"Well, it's not a good idea," Jewel said, back on guard. "I want to keep our relationship strictly business."

"Hey," Harper grinned, "that's what I've been saying all along."

"That's what you've been *vocalizing*. The look in your eyes says something else."

"I'm a natural flirt," he said. "I can't help it. Put me in a room with a beautiful woman and I'm going to be charming. But that doesn't necessarily mean I'm trying to get in her pants."

Jewel smiled, disarmed. "Look, you're very attractive . . . and I like you. It's very tempting, Harry. But every time I go the route of my emotions I crash into a wall." She took a sip of her TsingTao beer. "And I may as well be honest. I've recently met the man I'm going to marry."

"Oh? He's proposed?"

"Not yet, but I think he will."

"So you love him and you don't want to get involved in something that might mess it up," Harry said.

"That's it. Except I don't love him. I'm never going to be taken advantage of by a man again. From now on, I'm calling the shots." She paused. "That's why you're out of the question. You wouldn't let me call the shots, Harry."

Harry laughed. "God, Jewel, you're wrapping me around your finger."

"With Allen," she continued, "I think it'll work out. And he adores my kids. I'm not going to cloud it up by sneaking out to see you. And if you want me to design a collection for you because you want *me*, then let's call it quits now . . . before I daydream any more about how famous I'll get by being associated with you."

"You know I can have any woman I want," he said. "And you're right, I want you. But I can handle rejection. Don't worry. I want you to design jewelry for my spring collection because you're talented. In spite of what you may think, I don't make decisions with my cock."

Jewel smiled, relieved. "I'm glad. I'd like us to be friends. That's what I need in my life, not lovers."

"Okay, you're on. But you have a rain check."

"I won't use it, Harry."

He clamped a spicy shrimp from another platter between his chopsticks and fed it to her. "Maybe you won't. Maybe you will. I'll be around. But I won't bring it up again. Next time, you make the pass."

"Fair enough," Jewel said, smiling.

As the weeks went by, her relationship with Allen Prescott grew stronger, although what she had told Harry—that Allen would propose—was still wishful thinking. Allen never brought up the subject of marriage even though he and Jewel spent almost every evening together.

Allen adored Amber and Beryl, and they adored the attention he lavished on them. Jewel could read a bedtime story to the kids, and

Allen would sit on the end of the bed, listening with rapt attention. Always, he arrived with some sort of toy for the children, and some nights he suggested that they stay home with the kids rather than go out. He knew Jewel worried about not spending enough time with them.

Allen and Edward got along well too. Edward wholeheartedly approved, which set Jewel's mind at ease even more. She valued Edward's opinion and was glad her old and new best friends liked each other.

That's how she had come to regard Allen, as her new best friend. He was comfortable to be with, funny, chatty, intelligent, caring, everything that one looked for in a friend. He wasn't much as a lover, Jewel found out after their sixth date, when she went back to his apartment for the first time. It wasn't that he was inexperienced, but she guessed that sex ranked about fourth on his list, after acquiring art, eating in top restaurants, and running his daily five miles. Sex, she could tell, wasn't a passion of his like the others. So sleeping with Allen wasn't waves crashing against cliffs, but that was fine with her. She equated love and passion with the two men in her life who had ignited those feelings in her: Hadley McNeill, and Sascha. But after what had happened with those relationships, Jewel was happy to settle for friendship with Allen. Passion left one emotionally vulnerable, and she had vowed never to allow herself to be hurt again.

Jewel knew she was on Allen's list somewhere. Allen said she was at the top of it, but she wasn't sure whether, if he had to choose between her and a Rembrandt sketch, he would choose her. It didn't matter. He definitely liked her, but Jewel fretted over whether the relationship was leading anywhere, namely to marriage.

Then one day he announced, "My sister Isabel's flying in tonight."

"Oh? Do you want to cancel with me so you can take her out, just the two of you? I don't mind," Jewel said.

"No," Allen said. "She adored the necklace. She's dying to meet you."

"Oh no. I guess I'll have to be on my best behavior," Jewel said.

"Not at all," Allen assured her. "Just be yourself. Isabel's down to earth, even if she did marry the richest man in Oklahoma. Anyway, I know you two will get along. You're a lot alike."

"Except I'm a lot poorer," Jewel quipped, dreading the meeting.

She knew exactly the purpose of it, without having to be told by Allen.

His sister was coming to check her out. This was when she would make the club or be sent back to the minor leagues. God, she hated Big Occasions like this. Allen had made a dinner reservation at Le Cirque, but Jewel was to meet them at his apartment for a drink first.

If ever making a good impression was important, this was it. After she got off the phone with Allen, she dialed Harry Harper and was delighted when she got straight through to him.

"Hi, doll. What's on your mind? Montauk?"

"I thought you said *I'd* get to make the next pass."

"That's right, I forgot. Is that why you're calling?"

"Nope. I need a favor. I need a to-die-for Harry Harper to wear tonight. Dinner at Le Cirque with my future sister-in-law . . . *if* I succeed in impressing her."

"Okay. The sooner I get you married off, the sooner you'll be ready to stray. Come by this afternoon and pick out anything you want."

"Oh, Harry, I love you!"

"Would that you did, Jewel," he said.

Jewel arrived at Allen's promptly at seven, wearing a drapey thirties-style red skirt with a long, drapey top to match—Harry Harper at his most expensively understated.

Isabel Prescott Farraday was examining Allen's newest acquisition, a Carol Mothner still life, when Allen led Jewel into the living room to make the introductions. Isabel was several inches taller than Jewel, tanned, and athletically muscular. She shook Jewel's hand firmly and looked her straight in the eye. "I can't tell you how many compliments I've received on that necklace you made. Wore it to the big thirtieth-birthday bash that Floyd threw for me." She turned to Allen. "You know, I'm real sorry you couldn't make it, sweetie. All your old girlfriends were there . . . and they *all* asked about you."

Oh dear, Jewel thought to herself. *I'm in for it.*

Isabel turned back to Jewel, smiling. "Now don't you worry. Allen's old girlfriends are all married. They tried their best, but Allen was holding out. And now I understand why." She winked at Allen. "Jewel's as gorgeous as she is talented, sweetie. For once you weren't exaggerating."

Allen beamed. "I told you she was special."

"Tell me something," Isabel said to Jewel. Allen's sister now seemed less forbidding than Jewel had anticipated, with dark brown hair, pale skin, and startlingly blue eyes. "How old are you?"

Jewel paused, off guard. "Twenty-five."

"And are you ambitious . . . or is this jewelry business a hobby?"

"Anything but. I want to be the best. With a store on Fifth Avenue, then Paris, London, all over the place." She stopped, afraid that her ambition might be a turnoff.

Isabel nodded. "Well, Allen was right about you. You let it all hang out. I actually like that. But my brother wants to marry you."

So he *did* love her!

Jewel smiled and looked at Allen, and he smiled back.

"I told him," Isabel continued, "that he was crazy to pick a woman who had two children and couldn't have more. How's he going to carry on the family line?"

"I know . . ." Jewel said. "It's a real problem. Even if he adopted my daughters it wouldn't help the situation. If we married, we'd have to adopt or choose not to have more children. But, of course, we're getting way ahead of ourselves. Allen hasn't proposed to me."

"Jewel, I want to . . ." Allen said.

"Interesting," his sister interrupted. "You've got a straightforward view of life."

"Well, really I'm quite old-fashioned. I want all the creature comforts. A nice place to live, good clothes. I'm not out to raise eyebrows . . . except with my jewelry. *That* I want people to notice."

"So you'd keep working if you married Allen?"

"Of course. I've barely gotten started."

"Allen," Isabel said suddenly. "Go get me another drink, would you, sweetie?" she held out her glass.

When Allen was out of earshot, Isabel asked Jewel the question she'd been dreading all evening. "So, Jewel, do you love my brother?"

Jewel swallowed. To lie, or not to lie? "Yes . . . I absolutely adore him."

"You're hedging," Isabel said, her eyes riveted on Jewel.

"I love him very much," Jewel amended. "But I'm not *in love* with him, if that's what you mean. I love everything about him. I love being with him. Allen's one of the most wonderful men I've ever known. He's taught me so much about art, he's so enthusiastic about everything." She smiled, thinking about the day he had danced into her shop after he had bought a small Caravaggio drawing at auction. "And my girls are crazy about him."

"Well, I'd prefer you to be madly in love," Isabel said. "Allen's very special to me—he's my baby brother, after all." Allen was three years younger than Isabel. "But I've never seen him like this over anyone before. He certainly loves *you*."

Jewel sighed. "I understand how you feel. But I don't think you'd want me to lie about it."

"No," she said quietly.

"I really believe I'd make Allen a good wife. We're very compatible," Jewel said in her favor.

Allen appeared at the door. "Is the coast clear? I have your drink, Izzy."

"Dump it out," Isabel said. "And bring out that Dom Pérignon I saw sitting in the refrigerator. I want to propose a toast . . . to you and Jewel." She smiled. "I like her, Allen. She's the best woman you ever brought home, by far."

Jewel felt dizzy. She had won the big round.

"Well, Isabel, first I have to propose," Allen said. "You've taken away all of my thunder, you know."

"Then ask her, for heaven's sake! *I'll* get the champagne and leave you two alone," Isabel said, heading off to the kitchen.

Allen took Jewel's hand. "This isn't quite what I'd planned. I was going to take you for the weekend to some cozy little inn in Connecticut. And over a candlelit dinner, I was going to drop one of the family jewels into your wine and tell you to redesign it into an engagement ring. I was going to tell you how happy I've been since I met you, and how good you are for me. I love your energy, and your drive. I love you, Jewel. So how about it? Your girls need a father . . . and I'd like to adopt them." He smiled sweetly. "Will you marry me."

Jewel was surprised to feel her eyes filling with tears; maybe she loved Allen more than she thought. He was a dream come true, after all.

"Yes . . . oh, yes!" she exclaimed, melting into his embrace.

"Oh, splendid!" Isabel Farraday came in carrying a silver tray with champagne and crystal tulip glasses. "Now that the formalities are over, let's drink to it."

"To you, Jewel," Allen said, handing her a glass. "To us."

"To us," Jewel replied, exuberant that her future was no longer in limbo. She would never have to worry about money again.

"To you both!" Isabel toasted. "And to the happiest of futures together."

Jewel Dragoumis. Soon-to-be Jewel Prescott . . . a *much* classier name. A name that would enhance her career.

And Allen had confided to her, later that night, that he was worth close to fifty million. That wouldn't hurt her career either.

22

If Jewel managed to pull it off with Isabel Farraday, she did not fare as well with Allen's mother, the formidable LaDonna Prescott.

Heeding Isabel's advice, Jewel and Allen agreed to be married in an informal ceremony at the rambling Prescott residence outside Tulsa. On New Year's Day 1976, family and close friends, including Edward, Nushka, and a pregnant Betty Blessing Axelrod, clustered around as Allen and Jewel said their wedding vows. The officiate, an aged Episcopalian named Dr. Donavan, kept losing his place in the ceremony and, until quietly prodded by Allen, Father Donavan forgot entirely to pronounce them man and wife. Jewel looked understatedly elegant in a beige crepe de chine wedding suit designed especially for her by Harry Harper. She wore a single gardenia tucked into her upswept hair.

When the ceremony was finally over and Allen had kissed his bride and two new daughters, the flower girls, everyone huddled around to wish them well. Everyone except LaDonna Prescott, who stood looking on from the back of the living room in stony silence.

"My mother leaves something to be desired in terms of wit and tact," Allen had warned Jewel before they arrived. "But don't worry, Isabel's gathered the rest of the relatives into our corner."

"In other words, you don't think your mother's going to like me?"

"I *know* my mother. She was from Maud, Oklahoma. Her family was large and poor. When Dad struck oil and they made it big, she quickly forgot her past. She didn't want any relatives showing up for handouts, so she simply cut them dead. Told them to get lost and stay lost. She thinks everybody in the world is after her money—and mine."

"So she's sure I'm *only* marrying you for your money," Jewel said.

"Of course. She knows you have none of your own."

"Well, how does she know that? I mean, couldn't we invent some kind of classy background for me?" Jewel suggested.

The irony was that she had already invented a new background for herself for Allen's benefit. He knew her father had deserted her at birth; she had unwisely blurted that out when they first met. To rectify the situation, she made Jane Latham her real mother, then told him Jane had been from a wealthy steel family. But poor Jane had been disinherited, at the age of eighteen, when she ran off with the glamorous, handsome Dragoumis. Jewel spoke of growing up in various hotels in Europe (under the charitable auspices of a Great Aunt Greta, who had taken pity on Jane), while her mother resumed a promising career as a cellist. She buried Jane in Munich, not Pine Ridge, dead of consumption, not cancer, then buried Great Aunt Greta as well.

"What's the point? Mother would only hire detectives to check your credentials," Allen said. "Better to come across with none at all than go through that kind of scrutiny."

"Tell me something, darling. How come you turned out so nice, with a mother like that?"

"I'm convinced she found me under a cabbage leaf." Allen grinned. "I was always different. I read a lot, kept to myself. Got myself away from Tulsa at the earliest opportunity. Oh, I'd better prepare you for something else: Mother's bound to make a case for us moving back here to live. But don't worry. I'd never do it."

Jewel *thought* she was combat ready, but one look at the buxom, black-haired, sixty-year-old LaDonna Prescott, her countenance set in impenetrable blankness, and Jewel knew that she and "Mother" Prescott were never going to be chums.

"So you work in a jewelry store," she had said at dinner the first evening.

"I'm a jewelry designer . . . I own my own business," Jewel replied.

"Yes, that's right—I remember something about that. How much money'd you make last year?"

"Mrs. Prescott, I thought money was a forbidden subject among the rich," Jewel countered glibly. She had Allen; she didn't give a damn what his mother thought of her.

"So you're not making any?" LaDonna rejoined.

"I opened the shop eleven months ago, and I'm already turning a profit. Most stores can't even hope to break even inside the first three years."

"Isabel says you're ambitious. Are you going to spend my son's money to get ahead?" LaDonna asked, helping herself to a large slab of the roast beef that the black servant was passing around.

"Allen and I haven't talked about it, but I'm doing fine on my own. I've been making a lot of contacts lately. *Harper's Bazaar* is featuring four of my pieces in their February issue. I've done the jewelry for Harry Harper's spring collection. I don't *need* Allen's money," Jewel said self-righteously. Not that she hadn't considered that his vast fortune would propel her farther, faster, but she'd never admit it. Nor would she *ask* Allen for money.

"Allen . . ." LaDonna Prescott turned abruptly to her son. "Is there anything in the world I can say to make you change your mind about marrying this woman? Jewel . . . what kind of a name is that?" she muttered as an afterthought.

"I told you, Mother . . . I love Jewel. And if you keep acting this way," Allen flared, to Jewel's surprise, "we'll take the next plane back to New York and get married there."

"Do what you want . . . but Isabel took care of all the wedding arrangements. You don't want to hurt *her* feelings, do you?" she said.

"I don't want to hurt anyone's feelings, Mother. Not Jewel's, not Isabel's, not yours. Why can't we call a truce and make the best of a situation that you're not going to change?"

"You're a fool, Allen. You always were. All right, you're making your own bed . . ."

"Whew!" Jewel said after dinner. Mrs. Prescott had retired to watch her favorite show on television, and Jewel and Allen were having coffee in the library. "That was intense. She doesn't let up, does she?"

"Nope," Allen said, putting his arm around her. "And your back was up too. Well, thank God we don't have any more meals alone with her. Tomorrow night's Isabel's party, then the wedding, then we can get the hell out of here."

"I'm sorry, darling. I'll try to be nicer. After all, she is your mother."

"It's okay. I never got along with her myself. Isabel kept me alive in this family . . . that's why we're so close."

"Well, thank God *we* get along. I really like your sister."

"She likes you too," Allen said. "But even if she hadn't, I'd still have proposed." He kissed her. "You know that, don't you?"

Jewel nodded. "You're the sweetest man in the world. I absolutely adore you."

"Let's go up to your bedroom," he suggested. They had, of course, been given separate rooms, at opposite ends of the hall.

"Hmmm," Jewel purred, letting her hand slip down into his crotch, "excellent idea."

Over the past months, Allen had moved sex up on his list. As a lover, he didn't compare with Sascha. But he had it over Sascha in every other way. Life was getting better. And Jewel was immensely relieved that Allen was not going to let "Mother" Prescott interfere in their lives.

Allen insisted they take Amber and Beryl, along with Nushka, on their honeymoon trip to Europe aboard the *QE2.*

When he heard the plan, Edward pouted, "What about me? I'm part of the family too."

"You want to come? Allen will buy you a ticket," Jewel said seriously. "He knows how much you've helped me . . . and he really likes you."

"You're sweet, Jewel. But I think your honeymoon party's big enough as it is," Edward said. "God, everything's turnin' out so well. A year ago you'd hit the rocks. Now you're married to a guy who idolizes you. You're movin' into an enormous pad on Park Avenue. And your collection for Harry is the talk of New York."

"Yeah," Jewel said, "this is a hell of a time to go away. Somebody told me once, 'when you're hot, it's no time to take a vacation.' "

"Jewel," Edward corrected, "we all know you're a workaholic . . . but this isn't a vacation. It's your honeymoon. You owe it to Allen *and* yourself. Besides, you're going to come back from Europe with all sorts of new ideas. Getting away is good for creativity as well as the soul."

"You're right, of course," Jewel conceded. "It'll be a fabulous trip."

And it was. Traveling with Allen was first-class, but more than that. Knowledgeable and enthusiastic about everything, Allen wanted to see and do it all, from shopping and sightseeing to eating in starred restaurants. Every day was chock-full of activities, both planned and spontaneous.

After a week in London, the honeymoon party arrived in Paris and checked into a set of adjoining suites at the magnificent Bristol, on rue du Faubourg St.-Honoré. Jewel was aghast to discover that the sumptuous rooms were costing over a thousand dollars a day; she had to keep reminding herself that Allen could easily afford it. Every so often she pinched her arm hard, to make sure it wasn't a dream.

The second day they were in Paris, Jewel took Allen to a store at 40, rue St.-Sulpice. They entered and Jewel headed straight for the counter farthest back.

"Bonjour, madame," the sales clerk said, without looking at her, *"est-ce que vous voudriez quelque . . ."* Then the young woman glanced up. *"C'est incroyable!* Jewel! Is it really you? I can't believe it! Christof!" Katrina Von Berlichingen called out to the back room. "Come here . . . there is a surprise."

The reunion was everything Jewel had hoped it would be. Katrina and Christof were overjoyed to see Jewel and meet Allen. Jewel loved their shop. It resembled the inside of Taglioni's jewel box, all polished mahogany and velvet, with eye-catching, innovative jewelry.

Over lunch at Le Palanquin, a nearby Vietnamese restaurant, Jewel said, "The photos you sent me of your work don't do it justice. It's absolutely unique. Katrina, I love those necklaces you're doing in silver with the dyed emu feathers. And Christof, your geometric gold pendants are incredible. When I get a larger space, will you let me be your exclusive New York outlet?"

"Of course, with delight," Christof said. "But we did not know you were moving. We had a letter from Cathalene. She mentioned nothing."

"I'm not anytime soon. But . . ."

"Jewel's moving when we get home," Allen interrupted, to Jewel's surprise. "It's my real wedding gift to her. I found a great space on Fifth Avenue."

Jewel dropped her chopsticks. "What? What are you talking about?"

"It's my surprise. You want to be a star . . . so we're going to make it happen," Allen said, beaming. "You know that fur store between Fifty-third and -fourth? They're going out of business. I have my lawyer negotiating the lease, even as we speak."

Jewel leaned across the table and kissed her husband. "I can't believe it! But that's the best location in New York! Oh, Allen, is this really true? You're not putting me on?"

"I wouldn't kid you about something this important to you," he replied. "Forty-five hundred feet of floor space."

Christof whistled. "This is fantastic. You've hit the big time, Jewel."

"Want to hear my plan?" Jewel smiled, still dazed. "I've been fantasizing about this for years—a shop filled with little boutiques, each featuring a different designer . . . with, of course, the biggest space devoted to my pieces," she said immodestly. "There'll be the thickest carpeting, huge bouquets of fresh flowers, displays of raw gems and rock crystals, and music . . . different music to match the mood of each designer's work. And there'll be a little bar where we'll serve espresso, and Perrier—and champagne to the best custom-ers . . ." She paused, to envision all the wealthy buyers drinking champagne.

"I'm going to have one room lit by candlelight," she continued, "to show off my most romantic pieces. And a niche for antique and estate jewelry. Oh, and a pearl room . . . with a waterfall and the sound of ocean waves. The furniture will be bamboo and shell. There'll be a cage of birds. Jasmine and bougainvillea will be growing up the walls." She paused to catch her breath.

"*C'est formidable.* How long have you been planning this?" Katrina asked, amazed.

"Ever since I decided to be a jewelry designer," Jewel said. "I want a store like no other. I want to be the P. T. Barnum of the jewelry business. With a place that people will love to visit. A mixture of elegance and fun. People will *love* spending their money at Bijoux." She grabbed Katrina's hand. "We're going to make so much fucking money!" she squealed, and the others laughed with her.

"You never told me about being the P. T. Barnum of jewelry," Allen said, reaching over to pick up Jewel's uneaten rouleau de printemps.

"Well, I had no idea it was going to happen so soon," Jewel replied. "The last thing I want is a stuffy, snooty little shop where everybody tiptoes around and you can't talk louder than a whisper," Jewel said. "I've been jotting down ideas for *years*. This is only the tip of the iceberg."

"I'll bet it is," Christof said. "Knowing your energy and drive. And I think we will come to New York for the grand opening. It sounds as if it will be quite an occasion."

"It will be," Jewel promised. "It definitely will be."

The rest of Jewel and Allen's honeymoon was spent taking the children around to museums, the zoo, and the bird market, seeing as much as their limited attention span would allow. They bought wonderful clothes for them at Baby-Dior, and toys to fill their new rooms at home. Jewel couldn't stop Allen from spoiling his new daughters. He insisted on buying them antique mechanical toys and parlor games, a theatrical set with hand-painted marionettes clothed in silks and fur, and antique dolls, born before 1914, complete with furniture, dishware, and accessories such as satin gowns, feathered hats, and lacy parasols.

In the afternoons, after lunch, when Nushka took two-year-old Beryl and Amber, now three, back to the hotel to nap, Jewel and Allen checked out the auctions at the Hôtel Drouot, the famous auction house founded in nineteenth century. Often they strolled around the sixth and seventh arrondissements, on the Rive Gauche, looking for Renaissance jewel boxes for Jewel, and objets from the art nouveau and art deco periods for Allen. On weekends, they plowed through flea markets, especially the Serpette and Marché Biron, which focused on furniture.

"You get to do your store any way you want it," Allen told her. "But I want to decorate the apartment."

"Okay, that's fair," Jewel said, for she had little interest in creating the perfect nest for Allen. He was a perfectionist, she had come to realize, and had far better taste than she when it came to art and interior decoration. Whatever he did to the apartment would be eclectically elegant and creative. Best of all, she would be able to devote all *her* time to launching the new Bijoux.

Jewel was impressed with Allen's ability to bargain and get the best prices on things. He would visit a gallery that interested him many times, subtly courting the owner, and in the end, he always wound up with a large discount, sometimes as much as thirty percent. But after the painful poverty of her childhood and years of living on a shoestring with Sascha, Jewel still couldn't get used to the amount of money Allen was spending without batting an eyelash. It was hard to keep track of it all, and after a while she stopped bothering to translate the francs into dollars.

"I can't stand those people who redecorate every couple of years to show off," Allen said. "What we start off with is what we'll end up with. Of course," he grinned, "I can't promise not to *add* to it from time to time."

"It's your money," Jewel heard herself say often.

Before they left Paris, not only had they dined at all the great restaurants, but Allen had bought himself a priceless stash of art deco treasure: vases by Daum and Gallé and Maurice Marinot; a set of white porcelain plates painted in silver and gold by Jean Luce, and silver cutlery and a silver-and-jade soup tureen by Jean Puiforcat; an Albert Cheuret metal clock; Süe and Mare gilt-bronzed door handles for the new apartment; champlevé-enameled candlesticks by Jean Goulden; a Lalique chandelier and lighting fixtures by Rateau and Brandt and Perzel; a Benedictus knotted carpet in a triangular pattern; a wall hanging by Raoul Dufy; ornately leather-bound books by Creuzevault, Bonfils, and Pierre Legrain; and a six-leaved Jean Dunand screen with a geometric design in red and gold lacquer on a black lacquer base.

And that didn't even include the furniture that took Allen's fancy: a Pierre Chareau sofa, upholstered in a Jean Lurçat tapestry; a cubist bedroom set by Marcel Coard, in macassar ebony veneer with ivory and lapis lazuli inlay; a Eugene Printz palmwood bookcase with carved doors; an Eileen Gray carved red lacquer-and-leather chair with arms in the shape of snakes; a slinky Armand-Albert Rateau chaise longue; an alcove sofa by Pierre Lehalle; a pair of André Groult beech gondola chairs; a Paul Follot amboyna chest of drawers with the inlaid motif of a nude girl. And more, even more. Jewel could not keep track of the money he spent.

But the items that pleased Allen most of all were two he had gotten at auction for a fraction of their worth: a small Bugatti art deco bronze of a nude woman, and a painting by one of the symbolists, Levy-Dhurmier. Allen practically floated back to the hotel after those bargains had been knocked down.

On their last night in Paris, Allen and Jewel returned to Taillevent for a romantic meal à deux. Jewel had had a wonderful trip. As Edward predicted, her head was brimming with ideas. But she was anxious to get home, to start redesigning the space on Fifth Avenue that would soon be hers.

"Darling, this has been a wonderful trip," Jewel said, ebullient to be leaving for New York the next morning. "What a way to start off our life together."

"I'll drink to that," Allen said, raising his wine glass, "and to future adventures. I'm really happy, Jewel. I'm glad it's working out."

"What?" she said, alarmed. "Didn't you think it would?"

"Well, you know what they say," Allen joked, "a man tends to marry someone like his mother."

"Oh . . . you!" Jewel exclaimed. "Well, I think you lucked out . . . at least for now. I can't promise what I'll be like by the time I'm her age." She crossed her eyes and puffed out her cheeks just as the waiter appeared to take their dinner order.

Allen burst out laughing; so did Jewel. The waiter stood by, appropriately aloof, waiting for the silly Americans to come to their senses.

23

1976

Limousines jammed the block of Fifth Avenue between Fifty-third and Fifty-fourth streets. On this crisp October evening, spectators crushed against wooden police barricades, excitedly watching fur-draped celebrities—famous names of the Manhattan night scene as well as lower-profile magnates of the international money market—stream through the shimmering crystal-imbedded facade into Bijoux on Fifth. It was the store's opening night, and the show was playing to a packed house.

"So what is it?" A mink-coated lady from New Jersey asked her companion. "Some kinda new nightclub?"

"Beats me," the companion said. "Maybe they're shooting a movie."

"It's a new store," a young man in the crowd offered. "Bijoux . . . sells jewelry."

"What? All this fuss over a *store?*" an elderly woman remarked to her twin as they passed by. "I wonder what Tiffany thinks about this."

Inside the new Bijoux, models, social dowagers, and celebrities smiled glitteringly at newspaper and magazine photographers, attempting to upstage the merchandise that nestled on silk and velvet in carved wood and beveled glass cases. The young designers Jewel had chosen to feature in her store nervously gave impromptu interviews and patiently answered the questions of the purchasing public.

246

They were Cathalene Columbier, and Katrina and Christof Von Berlichingen, of course, as well as three designers Jewel had combed the
country to find: Rody Abrams, Tom Tinker, and a talented Hawaiian
known only as Leilani. Those, besides Jewel, were the stars of the
show. Jewel had hired six additional behind-the-scenes craftspeople.
They were in charge of producing classics, such as wedding bands
and chain necklaces, as well as making the nonsigned but limited-
edition pieces that she and her stars designed for the nonpareils
section of the store.

"Now, admit it, it's a *fun* party," Isabel Prescott Farraday said to
Jewel, after they had posed for a barrage of photographs for the news
media.

"I wouldn't know," Jewel answered. "I'm too wound up. After the
past nine months of twenty-hour workdays to get this place ready, I
don't remember the concept of fun anymore." Jewel was decked out
in a simple red taffeta Harry Harper, with ruby and amethyst Jewel
Prescott jewelry adorning her neck, wrists, and hair. On her fingers
she wore rings that had been made by each of her designers.

"That's a lie," Allen said, squeezing through the mob with glasses
of champagne for his sister and Jewel. Although there was plenty of
champagne and hors d'oeuvre, the waiters seemed unable to replen-
ish their trays fast enough. There were hundreds of people crushed
into the moss green carpeted store.

"For you, my darling," Allen continued, "*work* is more fun than
fun." He kissed his wife, then put his arm affectionately around
Isabel's waist. "If my sister didn't come to town every month and let
me squire her around I'd probably be a social outcast by now."

"Poor baby," Jewel said to Allen. "I promise you things will change
from now on. Now that Bijoux's actually open, I can become a real
human being again."

"Jewel, love!" Bijoux's preopening public relations expert, rich,
blond Camy Pratt, came squeezing through the crowd to give Jewel's
cheek a kiss. "Isn't this wild? I mean, it's the most successful opening
I've ever choreographed. This gang absolutely adores jewelry. And
all the comments I've overheard have been raves."

"I know you say that to all your clients, Camy," Jewel replied. "But
God, the place is packed. How'd you do it?"

"Six months of hard labor . . . that's what it's all about. The cover
article on you and Allen in *New York* didn't hurt, plus the piece in the

Times Magazine. People have been chomping at the bit for Bijoux to open. Remember, that's what I promised . . . six months of steady build, then poof! here it is. I'm delivering."

"Allen says you cost a fortune . . . but I suppose it's worth it," Isabel said coolly. "Mother, of course, believes press agents—"

"Isabel, I'm a public relations expert," Camy corrected.

"Sorry," Isabel said. She had known Camy Pratt as a teenager at boarding school and had never liked her. "Mother believes that *public relations experts* were put on earth by the devil. But, I must admit, you do know your stuff."

"Where *is* your mother anyway?" Jewel asked Allen. LaDonna Prescott had grudgingly agreed to come to New York for the opening. Isabel felt that seeing the store in person would pave the way for improved relations between her and Jewel.

"Mother's back in the pearl room, talking to the parrot," Allen said. "She seems to like it there, although she's complaining that the waves sound too loud."

"Well, let's face it, sweetheart," Jewel said. "When it comes to your mother I'll never be able to do anything right. If I'm a failure, she'll hate me. If I'm a success, she'll hate me more."

"Then she's going to hate you more. Who are we talking about?" Harry Harper asked, joining them with his wife, Vivian, who was wearing the diamond ring Jewel had redesigned for her, as well as two other rings, a necklace, and earrings, all made by Jewel. Harry, Jewel could not help noticing, had been eyeing her all evening. She hoped his lust for her was not as obvious to his wife.

"This is definitely a smash," Vivian said, kissing Jewel on both cheeks. "But I have to warn you. Harry's angry with you."

"Oh dear, what have I done?" she asked casually, keeping her eyes on Vivian.

"Nothing yet," Harry said. "But I've heard a rumor . . . that you're going to steal Edward away from me."

"I would never *steal* him," Jewel smiled. She *had* offered Edward a job, but he had declined. "Anyway, he's very loyal to you, Harry."

"I'd better give him a raise then," Harry said. "Will you excuse us a moment? There's someone I want Jewel to meet."

He guided Jewel through the crowd to meet one of his European associates. That done, he said, "I have to talk to you alone."

"No, Harry. Not now. I still have about two hundred people to dazzle." She gave him a friendly pat on the cheek, smiled, and slipped away from him through the crowd.

"Oh, Jewel, darling!" Camy Pratt called out. "Come over here. I want you to meet . . ."

For the next hour or so Jewel spoke to so many people that she began to get hoarse. She snatched a glass of champagne from the tray of one of the circulating waiters, but the champagne bubbles made her throat tickle, and she began to cough. She excused herself from the society matrons to whom she was talking and made her way to the back of the room and out to the foyer that led to the second floor. She knew there was a water cooler there.

As she leaned over to drink, she was suddenly aware of the door opening behind her. Just as she turned to see Harry Harper, his hands brushed against her hips.

"Jewel, darling. You've been avoiding me all evening. That's not very nice. If it weren't for me, you wouldn't be here now."

"Oh? I thought I was here because of my talent. And Allen's loan."

"Ah, how quickly they forget."

"Oh, Harry, I haven't forgotten. You gave me my big break. I'll always be grateful."

"But not grateful enough."

"Harry, darling," Jewel smiled, slightly annoyed, "let's not get into that. I thought we had both agreed that our relationship is business and friendship, nothing more."

"We did agree. Once. But now I want to change the rules. You're on your own now . . . and you're more exciting to me than ever," he said, moving so close to her that she could feel his breath on her cheek. "Come on, Jewel. How about one nice, passionate kiss . . . to tide me over?"

Jewel sidestepped away from him and over to the door. "To tide you over till when?" she said, putting her hand on the knob.

"Until you come around. God, I'm mad about you, Jewel. Your success, my success. We go so well together."

"No, Harry. I've told you . . . I'm not interested," Jewel said, pulling the door open. "Come back to the party. We'll be missed."

With one hand, Harry pushed the door shut again. With the other, he pulled her to him and planted his mouth firmly over hers. Against her better judgment, Jewel gave in to the moment, too exhausted to fight it. The intensity of Harry's passion stirred something deep within her, something she did not want to acknowledge. But she pushed Harry away when his hands began to squeeze her body more urgently.

"Please, Harry. Just give up. I know you thrive on dangerous situations. But if anyone saw us . . ."

"Who the hell cares?"

"I do! You're flattering to say I'm a success . . . but this is only the beginning. I can't make mistakes now. I don't want to hurt Vivian. She's been one of my greatest supporters. And in spite of what you think, Harry, I love my husband."

"Oh? Since when?" Harry said. "One look at the two of you together and I know. Something's missing."

"Nothing's missing, Harry! Now leave it alone. I don't want to have to get mad at you." Jewel flung open the door that led back to the party. "I've told you. I'm not available."

"Want to make a bet?" Harry said, patting Jewel's buttock as he followed her through the door.

"Oh, Jewel!" Cathalene said, rushing over. "There you are. Your friend Edward is looking all over for you. His parents are here, in the cave room." She flashed Harry Harper a dazzling smile. "Oh, Mr. Harper, I am Cathalene Columbier. I have wanted to be introduced to you, but now I will do it myself. You are my favorite designer. Have you seen the kiosk with my jewelry? Would you like me to show it to you?"

Harper's eyes had been following Jewel's lithe body as she made her way through the crowd to find Edward. Now he looked at the attractive French girl, dressed tonight in emerald green silk with black feathers. "Sure . . . I'll look at your work. Who did this dress?"

"I did," Cathalene laughed modestly. "I cannot afford your clothes, so I make my own when I need them."

"Oh? You seem to be multitalented," Harper said.

"Oh yes . . . I am," she said seductively. "Perhaps we could have lunch together and talk about it."

Harry Harper smiled. "Yes, the three of us—you and me and Jewel."

"Oh, of course. Jewel," she said.

"You owe her a hell of a lot, you know. The designers she picked for this store have it made. She's already spent a fortune publicizing the lot of you. You have no idea how lucky you are," Harry said.

Cathalene lowered her eyes, "Oh, but of course I do," she said humbly.

But her mind was traveling a different circuit, making connections. The flushed look on Jewel's face and the leer on Harry Harper's as they emerged from the staircase door. Was something going on between her boss and this man?

What interesting information. It might, at some point, come in handy.

"Come on, let's get dressed, girls," Jewel said one Sunday, shortly before Christmas. "We're going for brunch with Uncle Edward. Then I'll take you to the store so you can play in the big window."

The Bijoux Christmas window display featured a Scotch pine decked out in gold bracelets with bezeled red gemstones (rubies, spinels, and garnets) or green (emeralds, tsavorites, and verdelite tourmalines). Gathered around the tree was a large family of bears, elegantly dressed and bejeweled, singing Christmas carols. The music was piped out onto the street so that passersby could hear it.

"Oh goody!" Amber exclaimed. "Will you turn on the waterfall in the pearl room?"

"Of course, darling," Jewel said as she helped her daughters into Laura Ashley dresses and black patent Mary Janes, and fixed bows in their long, dark hair. "You can play anywhere you want."

The girls loved to visit the store on Sundays, when they could have it all to themselves. And Jewel loved it too, because she could work and be a good mother at the same time.

She grabbed the silver fox that Allen had given her for Bijoux's opening and threw it over black pants and sweater.

"Isn't Daddy coming?"

"Daddy got up early to go to an estate sale in Connecticut," Jewel said, carrying her daughter over to look in the closet. "He's buying some jewelry for the store." Allen had become so knowledgeable on the subject of antique jewelry that Jewel had enlisted him as Bijoux's official buyer of estate jewels. She had also made Allen president of the company, although he insisted that he wanted nothing to do with the day-to-day running of it.

"Oh, I wish Daddy was coming with us," Amber said.

"Well, he'll be back in time for dinner, lambie."

Since Amber and Beryl were still babies when Jewel left Sascha, they did not remember him at all. Jewel kept all the photographs of Sascha with the children locked away in a safe deposit box. She did not want them to see the album, yet couldn't bring herself to destroy it. It was more convenient to let Amber and Beryl think that Allen was their real father; she had sworn Nushka to secrecy on the subject. When they were old enough to understand, Jewel supposed she would tell them the truth. But that had always been a relative commodity for Jewel. She hadn't yet decided whether the truth would be *the* truth, or whether she'd merely say that their father had been a Russian who was now dead.

Sascha was as good as dead to Jewel. In the beginning, after she left him, he had tried repeatedly to call, but she'd refused to speak to him. He sent presents to the children that she returned unopened. Finally, he stopped trying.

He did not disappear, however. Sascha had become very successful. Tiffany had recently hired him as one of their exclusive designers, much to Jewel's displeasure. She hated Sascha and was jealous of his talent as well.

Jewel and the girls were meeting Edward at Maxwell's Plum. It was the children's favorite, because of its wonderful Hollywood set decor that included stained glass, Tiffany lamps, and several hundred giraffes, lions, zebras, hippopotamuses, and rhinoceroses, and because the waiter always gave them balloons when they left.

Edward, as always, was on time and waiting for them at the giant horseshoe bar when they arrived. On the floor next to his stool was an oversized shopping bag full of Christmas presents.

"No . . . you can't open them now, girls," he said, as they pounced on the bag with squeals of delight. "They're for under the tree."

"My, you're organized," Jewel said. "Christmas is still ten days away. I've barely done a thing."

"Well, I leave for Hawaii on Tuesday. I had to get it all done early."

"Hawaii?" Jewel asked. "I didn't know . . ."

"Yes you did. Remember the long conversation we had when I was tryin' to decide between Maui and the Big Island? And you asked Leilani, and she said definitely the Big Island?"

Jewel nodded. "It's coming back to me. There's so much stuff going on all the time, it's hard to keep track."

"Mummie?" Beryl said. "Can I have two desserts? Instead of anything else?"

"No, sweetheart. You have to have something healthy. Then you can have *one* dessert," Jewel said. "Anyway, Edward . . . I know it's not the time and place to talk about it . . ."

"But I have the feelin' we *are* going to talk about it. Whatever *it* is."

Jewel laughed. "You know I have a one-track mind: business, and then there's business. I promised Allen he'd see more of me after the store opened. But now I'm working harder than ever."

"I don't want anything else. I'm not hungry," Beryl complained. "I want dessert."

"Me too," Amber said.

Jewel rolled her eyes at Edward. "How'd you like to talk some sense into them?"

"I have an idea," Edward said to the children. "Why don't you and Amber split a hamburger or a salad . . . and then you can each have dessert."

"Okay," Amber nodded agreeably. "You want to, Beryl?" The younger child nodded.

"What a good father you'd make. Anyway, where were we?" Jewel asked.

"You and Allen never see each other."

"Well, we go out together for all the parties and charity things. But that's business, really, for both of us. I have to chat it up with the ladies because they're the ones who keep Bijoux going . . . and Allen's always off talking art and auctions. The only time we see each other is in the car going to and from." Jewel opened her handbag, took out a pack of cigarettes, and lit one.

"When did you start on those?" Edward asked.

Jewel shrugged. "Oh, ever since Bijoux opened I've been crazed. They calm me down. I only smoke five or six a day. Anyway, what I have to talk to you about . . ."

The waiter appeared to take their orders. After much going back and forth, Amber and Beryl settled on pasta. Jewel ordered chicken salad, and Edward, grilled sole sans sauce, as he was dieting to get in shape for the beach.

"What I have to talk to you about . . ." Jewel said.

"Mummie, Amber pinched me! I don't want ska-betti," Beryl whined. "I just want cheesecake."

Jewel laughed. "Amber! No pinching, and Beryl, sweetie, try to eat what you can. You *like* spaghetti." She reached into her handbag. "Here . . . a pad and two pens. Why don't you draw until the food comes?" She turned back to Edward. *"Anyway,* I told you this wasn't the time or place to talk."

"I'm still waitin' to hear what you have to say," Edward said, leaning over to tear a page out of the pad for each girl. "I'm all ears."

"I *need* you, Edward," Jewel said. "I'm completely overwhelmed. There's a part of me that wants to do everything myself. And another part of me, a new part . . . that's beginning to realize that I can't. *Please* come to work for me . . . as executive vice president and design director? I'll pay you a third again what you're getting from Harry. And raise that as soon as I can. I know you turned me down before, but please, Edward," she said, "please, please, *please.*"

Edward smiled. "I said no before because I owe a lot to Harry, and I like my job there. I also said no because we're such good friends, Jewel. If I worked for you I'm not sure what that'd do to our friendship."

"Then be my partner," Jewel said with sudden inspiration. "I'll call my lawyer tomorrow and get it all worked out. That way you wouldn't be working for me."

"You forget—first and foremost I'm a designer."

"I know. You have fabulous ideas. You can design jewelry, and work with the craftspeople to make it up. But Harry told me you manage the menswear line. He said you're in charge of practically every detail," Jewel said.

"Yes, well, I guess I am."

"You're so smart, Edward. You can do anything you set your mind to. I need someone to oversee the store. Nudge the designers. Change the look of the place from time to time to keep it fresh," she said, talking faster. "Look, the guy I hired, David Drake? He's not working out. The chemistry isn't right. I want him out before he gets entrenched.

"Oh, Edward, don't you see how perfect it would be?" Jewel continued breathlessly. "Working together. Seeing each other every day. The store's doing gangbusters business. And Allen will lend me expansion money when I need it." Jewel lit another cigarette. "I want to manufacture an inexpensive line called Bijoux Too that'll sell in department stores, then open *our* stores in all the biggest cities. And then start a direct-mail business, with a classy annual catalog and smaller monthly bulletins. Eventually, a Bijoux fragrance. And, on top of all that, I want to make real knock-'em-dead, one-of-a-kind pieces that'll be like nobody else's. But I need *time* to design, and that's what I'm lacking. I need *you*, darling. Please say yes."

"Stop! Take a deep breath. You're goin' to start hyperventilatin' any second now. You have to remember to breathe every once in a while." Edward squeezed her hand. "Look, it's very temptin', and your enthusiasm is contagious. But, Jewel, we're good friends. I'm not sure what this would do to our friendship. And I'm very happy where I am."

"But you promise you'll think about it?" Jewel urged. "This isn't a brush-off, is it? Level with me."

Edward laughed. "Calm down, darlin'. Look, I'll have to think long and hard about it. I can't give you an answer anytime soon."

"But you *will* think about it."

"Yes," he sighed. "I promise."

"Hurray," Amber, almost four, said, as the waiter appeared with their plates. "The food's here."

"What color would you like your office painted?" Jewel grinned, stamping out her cigarette.

"Jewel," Edward laughed, exasperated. "You're really too much. I don't know how Allen puts up with you these days."

"Neither do I."

In truth, Jewel *didn't* know how Allen put up with her; their life was so hectic. But she was going to change. If Edward came to Bijoux, she would have more time. She knew she was doing too much—not that she didn't enjoy every minute of it.

But Allen had made it all possible, had made it all happen so fast. She owed him everything. For his sake, she would try to tame her ferocious ambition and become a more conventional wife. Of course, that would have to be down the road a bit. First, Jewel had to make Bijoux a raging success, to repay Allen every penny he had given her to open the Fifth Avenue store.

Jewel hated being in debt to anyone, even her husband.

24

1978

When Edward finally came to work for Jewel, a full two years later, Harry Harper called her to have lunch.

They met at La Côte Basque, a block away from Bijoux.

Harry stood up as Jewel approached the table. He was dressed dashingly as always, in a charcoal gray pinstripe of his own design, with a purple silk scarf tucked casually into his breast pocket. Jewel smiled, expecting the usual suave seduction.

He surprised her. "What will you have for lunch, Jewel?" he said, coldly ignoring the cheek she presented for a kiss. "A hand? That's what you do, isn't it, bite the hand that feeds you?"

"Harry, what is it? If it's about Edward . . ."

" 'If it's about Edward,' " he mocked, resuming his seat. "Good God, Jewel, what do you think? That I can take this with a smile? It's not merely losing Edward," he said. "It's the way you did it. Buying him off."

"I did not!" Jewel snapped. "I needed a partner. Someone I could trust."

"Yes, well I thought I could trust him. And you." Harry looked at his watch. "Let's order. I have to be back at the office in forty-five minutes."

"Oh, Harry, don't be angry. You knew this would happen sooner or later. And the bottom line is, you don't need Edward as much as I do."

"I don't believe you're handing me this shit," he said. "Who says I don't need him?" He paused. "In my menswear division, Edward had carte blanche to make decisions. I wonder, at Bijoux, is he willing to let you run the whole show?"

"What makes you think I'd do that?"

"Because that's the way you are, Jewel. That's the way you have been and always will be," Harry said.

Jewel shrugged. "Well, of course, Edward understands that I'm the motivating force behind Bijoux. He understands that, from the word go. But we both know Edward's creative and professional enough to carve out his own special niche within the company. I'm not going to step on his toes."

"Well, tell him for me that we'll keep his chair warm. You'll drive him crazy. You drive everybody else crazy."

"Yes? And what's that supposed to mean? Who have you been talking to?"

Harry shrugged and remained silent.

"Oh, Harry, you knew it was only a matter of time before Edward joined me. It was a hard decision for him. And, I'll admit, I did press a bit," Jewel said. "Really, I had no idea you'd take it so hard. You're in Fortune 500 now. You have tons of people working for you." She lit a cigarette. "Look, darling, I owe you a favor. I won't forget it."

"As I see it, you owe me more than one favor. You were scrounging around Soho when you met me. Designing the jewelry for my collection was your springboard into the big time. I introduced you to everyone. I got Vivian to jump on your bandwagon."

Jewel was becoming annoyed. She had looked forward to a flirtatious lunch, and now it turned out Harry wanted her to kiss ass. "Of course I owe you a lot. Don't I give Vivian discounts? Don't I bring your daughters nonpareils every time we come for dinner? Don't I buy your clothes exclusively?" She glanced down at what she was wearing, a Mary McFadden, and laughed. "Oh come on, darling, is it Edward that's really bothering you? Or is it something else? Let's get it out in the open."

"It's you, Jewel. You're what's bothering me," Harry said, digging a fork into the lobster that the waiter had set in front of him. "Sometimes I think I know you, but other times I realize I don't have the first clue of what goes on deep down inside you. You can be candid and fair on the surface, but I never know what's lurking underneath. You're such an enigma that I can't let you go. Yes, I'm pissed that you took Edward away from me. And Cathalene tells me you're a tyrant to work for."

"Cathalene?" Jewel interrupted. "Where the hell does she come in?"

"She's a sweet girl. I buy her lunch every once in a while."

Jewel took a sip of her Perrier and pushed her plate of uneaten scallop salad to the middle of the table. "Cathalene's as sweet as deadly nightshade. You should recognize that, Harry. I keep her on because she's talented. But I know where she's coming from. She's jealous of me. Possibly she hates me. Mostly, I think, she wants to *be* me. I see Cathalene with my eyes wide open. She's as ambitious as I am. As far as the future of Bijoux is concerned, *she* is a limited edition."

"You're booting her out?" Harry asked.

"No, not at all. I'm waiting for her to go out on her own. Which she'll do sooner or later. I'm sure of it. Anything I can do she'd like to do better. And she'd absolutely jump at the chance to go to bed with you. But I'll warn you . . . she won't stop at that."

"I don't believe I'm hearing this. Why are you bad-mouthing Cathalene? She's damned loyal to you."

"How do you know that? Have you already tried to get her away from Bijoux in retaliation for Edward?"

Harry shrugged. "I'm above retaliation. You say you see Cathalene with your eyes open? Then see how much she idolizes you. She'd never stab you in the back."

"Hmmm, she's already got you in her pocket, Harry. Watch out for . . ."

"Harry! This saves me the trip down to Thirty-seventh Street." A trim, fiftyish man with thick, froggy features, well turned out in a gray Armani suit, stopped at the table. He smiled at Jewel. "Sorry, didn't mean to interrupt what you were saying."

"You two know each other?" Harry said without enthusiasm. "Jewel Prescott—Neil Tavlos."

"How do you do?" Jewel said. "You own the Pierre Chance boutiques."

He nodded. "And you are Madame Bijoux. I've wanted to meet

you." He turned to Harper. "Tell me if I'm interrupting. May I join you?"

"Have a seat," Harry said. He and Neil Tavlos were friendly rivals. They each wanted to buy out the other, but neither was budging.

"I hear you're launching a Pierre Chance fragrance," Jewel said. "Tell me, did you license out the name?"

"Nope. Started a whole new division to manufacture and market the stuff. Bigger profits."

Jewel perked up. Somewhere down the line she wanted a Bijoux fragrance. "Oh? I'd love to hear more about it."

"Yes, well," Tavlos reached into his wallet and handed her a business card, "call me. I'll be more than happy to tell you about it. In fact, let me take you to lunch."

"I'd love it." Jewel dropped the card in her handbag. "I'd better be going. Thanks for lunch, Harry. And don't be mad, darling. I'll pick up the check next time and we'll finish our chat." She smiled. "Nice to meet you, Mr. Tavlos."

"Neil," he corrected. "The pleasure was certainly mine."

"See you, Jewel," Harry said. "And relax. You're paranoid about Cathalene."

Paranoid, indeed! Jewel thought, as she walked back to Bijoux. The sophisticated Harry Harper was as naive as a horny teenager when it came to women like Cathalene Columbier.

But maybe he deserved her, if indeed he had offered her a job. Cathalene as a direct rival might be better than Cathalene underfoot, always trying to see what Jewel was up to, always playing up to her.

On the other hand, Harry Harper was *her* ally. Why not make Cathalene come up with someone on her own?

"Jewel, darling," Allen handed her a cup of black filtered coffee, waking her out of a deep sleep. "Room service."

"God, what time is it?" Jewel said, disoriented. Outside, it was dark; the streetlights were still on.

"Five-fifteen. But I needed to talk to you before I take off . . . since we missed each other last night." He was heading to Tulsa to visit his mother, taking Nushka and the girls with him. For some reason, unfathomed by Jewel, Amber and Beryl, now nearly six and five, liked LaDonna Prescott, and the old crone seemed to enjoy them too. Besides, Jewel didn't mind these forays home that Allen took every few months. They gave her more time to work without feeling guilty.

"When I get back," Allen continued, "I want us to get away for a holiday. We haven't had a real one since our honeymoon. And this time I want it to be just the two of us. I spoke to Nushka. She'll handle things while we're away." Allen pulled down the lace-trimmed sheet and began to fondle Jewel's breasts through her satin gown. "Christie's is having a major sale of early-twentieth-century paintings next week. I thought we could go over and play in London for a few days while I do the auction. Then we'll head to Wales or Scotland and relax." He leaned over and kissed her forehead. "And get to know each other again. We've both been running overtime."

"Sounds good," Jewel said sleepily. "But next week? I couldn't possibly . . ."

"That's what you say every time I suggest we get away," Allen snapped. "The children and I will be out of your hair for seven days. You can work the entire fucking time. But *next* week, you're going to London with me. No buts . . . just clear your schedule and do it."

"Oh God," Jewel said, "it seems like everybody's mad at me these days. I'm only trying to make a living."

"You don't *have* to make a living. You married me," Allen said. "And if you want to stay married, I suggest you try harder to be a wife. Oh shit, Jewel . . ." He put his arms around her. "I love you. But I want to see you more often. Once a week, from now on, I want us to set aside an evening to go out, just the two of us. If this marriage is going to survive, you've got to put some effort into it." He glanced at the metal art deco clock on the night table. "Okay, I have to go. I'll make all the arrangements for the trip. Figure we'll be gone two weeks."

Jewel started to protest but sighed instead. "Okay, darling, whatever you say." She raised her hand and gently stroked Allen's cheek. "You're right, we haven't spent much time together lately." Allen smiled back. "I'm glad you approve. I'd better be going. The car's waiting."

"Have a good trip," Jewel said, grabbing her silk kimono. "Wait . . . I want to kiss the girls good-bye. And Allen . . ." she said, flipping rapidly through the calendar that was implanted in her brain, "could we make it ten days instead? The catalog's due to go to the printer's on the twenty-first. I have to check—"

"Okay . . . okay," Allen said, "ten days is better than nothing."

It was a typical morning at Bijoux. After Jewel arrived at the office she spent forty-five minutes with a Texan discussing the resetting of her twelve-carat canary diamond ring into a necklace, conducted a meeting of the staff and resident designers, returned calls, and consulted with her gemologist, Erik Sanders, about his upcoming buying trip to Brazil. Then she headed over to "21" to meet Neil Tavlos for lunch.

"Jewel," Neil Tavlos said, rising from the table to greet her. "I'm so glad you called. I've been looking forward to this. You have quite a knack for what you do. I should know. The soon-to-be-*ex* Mrs. Tavlos has spent quite a bundle of my money in your store."

"Really? I keep close track of our customers. I don't remember . . ."

"She's an actress. Goes under the name of Leslie Scott."

"Oh, of course. Yes, she's mad about my collector's pieces. Oh dear. Do give her a generous settlement or I'll lose one of my best customers," Jewel said.

"Ah, for you, anything," Neil laughed. "This is the first time I've laughed over this divorce. It's been a hell of a mess. No kids—you'd think it'd be simple."

"I guess it never is."

"You been divorced?"

"Widowed. My current husband adopted my two children. I'm very lucky. Oh, by the way," she said, getting to the point, "did you bring a sample of your new fragrance? I'm dying to try it."

Neil reached into his breast pocket and brought out a small tester bottle, plain with no label. Jewel stretched out her wrist for Neil to squirt it with perfume. Then, rubbing her wrists together, she sniffed and closed her eyes to let the aroma surround her.

"Hmmm, it reminds me of early spring . . . daffodils, hyacinths, lily of the valley, and field grasses. Oh, Neil, it's delicious. I like it!"

Neil Tavlos beamed. "You've got a damned good nose, Jewel. That's exactly what we wanted, spring. We have a youthful audience for our clothes, so we wanted a young scent. In the perfume circles, they call it a 'green' fragrance."

"Yes," Jewel nodded, "I know. I've been reading up on it . . . doing my preliminary research. I already know what I want Bijoux to smell like. Rubies. The most expensive gems in the world. Rich, refined, sensual, full of history and romance." She stopped. "Oh goodness, I tend to go on and on about my ideas. You must forgive me."

"There's nothing to forgive. You're a bright woman, Jewel," Neil smiled.

Over steak tartare, they chatted lightly—mostly about the current theatrical season, as Tavlos, it turned out, dabbled in backing plays.

And later, over coffee, Neil said, "Listen, Jewel . . . I have an idea. I told you I started my own company to market our fragrance. Why don't we do yours? It'll save you a hell of a lot of money, and we're set up with distribution. You're not going to be a mass-market fragrance, neither are we. We're distributing in our shops and only the top department stores. It's all there for you, including the manufacturing."

"Sounds interesting," Jewel said casually. It was what she'd had in mind all along, but she wasn't going to be the one to bring it up. "Of course, I'd have to toss the idea around a bit with my partner, Edward Randolph. Look at the figures."

Neil handed the waiter his American Express Gold Card. "Take your time. Sit with it. It's merely an idea—one that could be lucrative for both of us."

"I will think about it, Neil. And thanks for lunch."

He took her hand, raised it to his lips and kissed it. "Jewel, you are well named. We'll do this again soon."

When Jewel arrived back at the office, she dropped in on Edward to report on her conversation with Neil Tavlos.

"We may not want to do this," she said excitedly, "but it's an option. It's fantastic, really, the way it's fallen into our laps. Bijoux, the fragrance . . . in all the top stores. What great advertising!"

Edward leaned back in his chair, shaking his head doubtfully. "How do you suppose Harper'll take it? He and Neil are rivals, even if they are cordial. And he feels territorial when it comes to you."

"Harry doesn't figure into it at all," Jewel said offhandedly. "What the hell do I care what he thinks? Business is business. That's what he always tells me."

"Okay, do what you want about the fragrance. But tell Harry yourself. Don't let him hear gossip. He's still pretty touchy because of my defection," Edward counseled.

"All right. I promise. I'll let Harry know after I've made up my mind."

"Good. When are you takin' off for London?"

Jewel looked puzzled. "How'd you know about that?"

"Had lunch with Allen yesterday. He told me he planned to lure you away on a holiday. Wanted to know if this place would survive without you. I assured him it would . . . if he didn't keep you away too long."

"We compromised on ten days. It's really a shitty time for me, but . . ."

Edward went over and closed his door. "Allen adores you, Jewel. You have to be more considerate of his feelings . . . and his needs."

"I am! Didn't you see the watch I designed and had made for his birthday? Eat your heart out, Rolex. And besides . . ."

"Look, honey," Edward broke in. "I'm not accusin' you of anything. I'm merely sayin' that the guy loves you. Maybe you love him too, but you don't show it."

"Did he come crying on your shoulder? Is that what your lunch was all about?" Jewel said, annoyed.

"No. You know Allen wouldn't do that. I'm givin' you the benefit of my observations as a longtime friend. Take it or leave it. I happen to like Allen a hell of a lot. He's a decent guy and he deserves . . ."

"Someone nicer and *more* decent than me?" Jewel snapped. "God, I *am* nice, but I'm busy. You know that; you work as hard as I do. We're building an empire here, and that takes a hell of a lot of work," Jewel said breathlessly. "Allen can't understand because he *doesn't* work. He spends all his time going to auctions and art galleries. God, we're running out of wall space. But he's not making money . . . he *fritters* it away! He tells me I don't have to work, but if you knew what he goes through in a year—well, thank God I *do* work. One of these days I'll be supporting him."

"Remember to *breathe* when you talk, Jewel. And you can lower your voice," Edward said. "I'm not attackin' you. I was merely givin' you some advice. I understand you, darlin'. And it doesn't upset *me* that you work so hard." He smiled. "Look, since Allen's away, why don't we have a drink after work? We haven't done that for ages."

"After work? You must be joking. If I'm going to let Allen cart me off for ten days I have to bust my ass this week. No time to relax."

"Calm down, darlin'. You're pushin' yourself too hard. It isn't necessary."

"Oh isn't it? Edward, I'd have thought you would understand," Jewel fumed. "I've still got a lot to prove. And I will."

Edward leaned back in his chair and expelled a deep breath. "Jewel, you're a success now. What more do you want?"

"To be a *bigger* success."

Jewel and Allen went on vacation as scheduled. They spent the first part in London, which Jewel enjoyed. She visited museums and checked out the jewelry competition while Allen enriched his art collection with three prewar Russian canvases bought at auction, and a Roger de la Fresnaye and a very good Kokoschka that he acquired from an alcoholic, down-at-the-heels nobleman who was selling the family heirlooms.

Then they took a slow train through the English countryside to Wales, for a week of idyllic idling. Jewel found it enchanting—for about two days. After that the strain of relaxation began to tell on her. Allen's driving terrified her. He could not seem to get used to driving on the left-hand side of the road, and Jewel spent most of the tour oblivious to the gorgeous Welsh scenery, screaming "Watch out!" and slamming her foot onto phantom brakes, until Allen finally pulled over alongside a rolling green meadow where several dozen sheep grazed.

"Here," he said, *"you* do it."

"No, I just meant . . ."

"No," Allen insisted. "I'm sure you'd do a much better job."

So Jewel slid over behind the wheel (it *did* seem peculiar, having it on the wrong side of the car), and Allen settled happily into her former role; for the rest of the day it was he who got to scream Watch out!

They stayed in a beautiful old manor house in Llandudno, on the Creuddyn peninsula in North Wales, and made their daily forays from there. The place was called Bodysgallen Hall. It was an imposing historical mansion, a huge building with stone cottages around it that were adorned with ivy and exotic names (the Prescotts were in one called Pineapple Cottage).

From there each morning, after a hearty Welsh breakfast for Allen and toast and coffee for Jewel, they would collect a lavish picnic prepared in the kitchens—roast pheasant, hare pâté, marinated vegetables, freshly baked bread and pastries, all fitted into a wicker hamper—and roam the lush, hilly, sheep-dotted countryside. They visited woolen mills, and inspected magnificent crumbling old castles, such as Caernarfon in Gwynedd, built by Edward I in the thirteenth century to defend the outposts of his realm. They sat in colorful country pubs, drinking stout or brandy and listening to the people around them speaking the Welsh language, totally foreign from English, musical and fascinating.

When it rained, they stayed inside, bathed together in the large tub and then fell back into bed to make leisurely love. When the rain stopped they strolled out through the vast formal gardens and intricate shrub maze that were the pride of Bodysgallen Hall.

Still, Jewel was bored. She wanted to return to London for some city action.

"But sweetheart," Allen pleaded, exasperated, "the point of a vacation is to relax. To not *have* to do anything."

"Maybe you don't, but *I* do. Sitting around counting sheep is amusing for a bit . . . and it is bucolic and all that. But we've *done* it. If we went back to London we could catch some more shows."

Allen frowned. "I'd hoped that spending some *quiet* time together would get us back on track. We were very much in touch in the beginning, but it's been a long time now. Oh hell, maybe it's not worth it." Allen sat down sulkily on a stone wall. "You know I'm proud of you, Jewel," he sighed, "and of your success. But you're so busy dealing with the world at large there's no time left for anything personal. You never touch me anymore."

"What?" Jewel snapped. "We've made love every day since we left New York."

"That's not what I mean. You never take time to kiss me on the cheek anymore. Or put your hand on my shoulder. Or look up and smile at me. You treat me like a business colleague, just another person on your daily agenda. We can't go on like this," he said seriously. "At least *I* can't."

Jewel took a deep breath and sat down next to him on the garden wall. "Well, darling, let's face it. Running a marriage is a lot like running a corporation. I mean, there're so many details to be dealt with every day . . . the children, the help, money, entertaining, keeping it all going smoothly. And then there's Bijoux. I'm sorry I don't touch you enough. But I'm busy. And you're busy too. *I'm* not the only one," she sniffed indignantly. "You're always off in search of another *acquisition.*"

"So that's how you think of us? As business partners who happen to fuck from time to time?"

"No. I'm not that cold-blooded. But I do feel we're partners . . . in the best possible way. We make a good team, Allen. I don't see why you can't appreciate it and be grateful for what we have. We're a hell of a lot happier than most of our friends who flit around from lover to lover," she said. (Not that she hadn't *considered* taking a lover. But there wasn't enough time in the day as it was. How could she ever fit illicit sex into the schedule?)

Allen shrugged. "I suppose you have a point. Oh, Jewel, I'm not saying I'm not happy. I only want you not to be preoccupied about work during the time we spend together."

Jewel smiled and kissed Allen's cheek. The crisis was passing, she could tell; they had been having variations of this conversation for years now. And she knew everything would be fine if she could be more politic; she did not give in to Allen often enough.

"All right," she said, "I can handle it. From now on I'll make a real effort to leave the office at the office."

"Good, that's a start," Allen nodded. "Now what about London? Do you still want to head back?"

"No. I'm sorry, I guess the weather's been getting me down. Actually, it's quite pleasant here." Jewel slipped on her dark glasses as the sun broke suddenly through the leaden bank of clouds. "You were right to drag me away. It clears the head. And," she added, squeezing her husband's balls coquettishly, "the body too."

Allen grinned, his anger faded. "I'm sorry about the weather. Next time we'll go someplace sunny. Will you promise we'll do this more often? Or do I have to get it in writing?"

"You won't have to have your lawyer draw it up, I promise," Jewel said, in a conscious attempt to lighten her mood. "I mean . . . *look* at these roses," directing his attention toward a cul-de-sac garden of tree roses bearing a plethora of fragrant white flowers. "You know, it might be fun to have a house in the country someday. With a wonderful garden that I'll tend myself. Maybe that's what I'll do in my old age."

Allen put his arm around Jewel and pulled her close to him. "I can see us having a house in the country. I can see us having ye olde English garden. But in a million years I can't see you putting trowel to dirt."

"But I'd be a *fabulous* gardener. If I had time."

"That's what I mean. How am I going to drag you off to the country house when it's taken all this time to get you to take a vacation?"

"Well, a country house would be easier to get to."

"What? You mean you're really serious about this?"

"Yes, I mean, we could start *looking.* You know, it'd be wonderful for the children and Nushka to spend the summers in the country. Now that they're getting bigger, the girls need that balance in their life. And we'd go for weekends. Of course, that means we'll have to teach Nushka to drive." The idea of Nushka driving a car, with her squat body and short fat legs, made Jewel laugh. "Do you think she could master it at her age?"

Allen laughed. "It's not her age I'm worried about, it's whether she could see over the steering wheel. I think I'd feel safer giving them a car and driver."

They strolled around the gardens, sparkling in the late sunshine after the rain, and talked about where they would buy their country house. Allen was partial to Connecticut. Jewel favored the eastern end of Long Island. She remembered the week in Southampton before Anna was married and how much she had loved the wide, white-sand beaches along the Atlantic. She knew she was secure enough within herself and her own success to handle running into the McNeills, if that ever happened. But she was beginning to think it wouldn't. New York was a bigger city than she had given it credit for in the beginning.

"Up around Roxbury . . . over toward the western part of the state . . . is really quite nice," Allen said, reopening his campaign for Connecticut. "It's under two hours from the city, and the traffic's nothing like the Long Island Expressway. You know, I think a country house is a great idea, Jewel. More wall space to fill," he chuckled.

Then a thought came to her. "You know, darling, it really doesn't matter to me where we buy a house." It really didn't, and if she could please Allen by letting *him* make the choice it would make him happy. After all, he'd be much more docile about being left alone for a weekend in a place of his own choosing. And there was no way that she'd have time to spend *every* weekend in the country. "I think I *love* the idea of Connecticut. And the children have plenty of friends to visit at the beach. We don't need to live there."

Allen smiled. "Sometimes you amaze me, Jewel. I was digging in my heels for a fight, and you've surrendered before the first battle."

"It's the new relaxed, easygoing me," Jewel said. "Get used to it."

"I think I could," Allen laughed. "Come on. It's teatime."

They headed back to Pineapple Cottage, holding hands and discussing what their perfect country place would be like.

Book Two

1979 — Present

25

Of course there was nothing for Allen to get used to: the new relaxed, easygoing Jewel did not happen. He began to fear it never would.

It was not until 1981, three years after their holiday in Wales, that they found the perfect country place in Connecticut—a hundred-acre farm, with sheep, weathered-wood barns, stone outbuildings that would be transformed into guest cottages, and a rambling, two-storied frame house, part of which dated to 1790. It needed massive renovation, and Allen decided to design and oversee the work himself, while Jewel continued to dig her heels into expanding Bijoux.

Jewel loved having Allen so totally occupied with his renovating and art collecting. He was as busy as she; she didn't have to feel guilty.

She entered into a deal with Neil Tavlos for the development and manufacture of her fragrance, to Harry Harper's displeasure. However, Jewel followed Edward's advice and told Harry about it ahead of time, so as not to ruffle his feathers more than necessary. Then, making Katrina and Christof partner-managers, she opened a chic Bijoux-Paris on the Boulevard St.-Germain. After that, she launched Bijoux-Honolulu with her designer Leilani, and Bijoux-Beverly Hills on Rodeo Drive with an old friend of Allen's. Plans were underway for Bijoux stores in London, Dallas, Houston, Chicago, Atlanta, and San Francisco.

Although Jewel took on limited partners for each of the stores, she still retained controlling interest. Each Bijoux had to conform to a certain look. Each had to chip in to the national advertising budget. Only the best-quality gems and raw materials were to be used, and Jewel and Edward devised strict controls. Her gemologists—there were now three—traveled the North and South American continents, as well as Africa and Asia, to buy gemstones for the Bijoux designers.

Jewel licensed a manufacturing company in New Jersey to produce her line of inexpensive designs—executed in gold and silver alloys, with synthetic stones—to be called Bijoux Too.

The catalog business took off, and Jewel expanded her office space into two more floors above the original Bijoux offices. She and Edward hired more people—to run the marketing and direct-mail divisions and to produce their own in-house advertising.

When that was all running smoothly, Jewel talked Edward into overseeing an atelier of apprentices. They worked out a program with the country's top universities and design schools to bring in the most promising students (a limit of three each year) to create jewelry in the Bijoux workshops for a summer. At the end of their stint, in late August before the students returned to school, Bijoux threw an elegant "summershow" party to display the students' work. The most talented were promised jobs at Bijoux when they graduated. Bijoux —and Jewel—received a great deal of favorable press for the program.

After that, Jewel researched and wrote a book on the folklore and reputed healing qualities of gemstones. When it was completed, her publisher sent her on a lecture tour around the country: more publicity for Jewel and Bijoux.

Finally in the fall of 1985, after several setbacks, the perfume Bijoux was finally launched, at a gala party in the gem and mineral hall of the Museum of Natural History. Sales for the fragrance exceeded Jewel's and Neil Tavlos's wildest projections. The direct-mail business quadrupled, and plans were underway for issuing monthly, rather than quarterly, mail-order catalogs. Jewel looked ahead and saw a tranquil sea. All was going so smoothly.

Except there wasn't enough time in any given day to get everything done. On the home front, Nushka continued to manage things under Jewel's erratically watchful eye. But the girls were growing up mostly without her. Amber was now twelve and Beryl, eleven. They had nearly reached their full height, did reasonably well in school, and were quite accustomed to the luxury of their lives. If Jewel failed to give them a great deal of her time, she never went back on her promise that her daughters would have everything she herself lacked in her own childhood.

Yes, the girls were given everything they wanted. But what they wanted most was a mother to be there when they needed her. Amber, especially, was beginning to resent Jewel's ambition.

One evening in year 1986, Jewel rushed home, late as usual. She and Allen were expected at a dinner party at Harry and Vivian Harper's. Before going upstairs to dress, she poked her head into the library where Amber and Beryl were doing their homework.

"Oh, hi, Mummie!" Beryl said, getting up to give her a hug. "Daddy's already dressed. He's watching the news. I wish you didn't have to go out tonight."

"Oh, I know," Jewel said, kissing her younger daughter. "Me too. But we'll have the weekend together."

"Don't you remember? I'm going to Quoque with Emily and her parents."

"Oh, that's right. Well," she said to Amber, who was still hunched over her schoolwork, "we'll do something fun, just the two of us, on Saturday."

"I have a basketball game," Amber said, without looking up, "and then the coach is taking the team back to her place for a pizza party."

"Oh? But I'd left the weekend open, to spend time with you."

"You should've checked with us first. We have lives too," Amber snapped.

"Amber Prescott! Just what do you mean by that?"

"That you never *think* to find out what we're doing. And remember? The school craft show was this afternoon. You didn't show up."

"Oh God. Oh, sweetie, I'm sorry. The day just got away from me," Jewel said. "Was it fun? Did you buy anything?"

"Yeah," Amber said. "We bought some cooking stuff for Nushka."

"Jewel?" Allen called from the stairs. "Are you going dressed like that?"

"No. It'll just take me a minute to change."

"Well, hurry it up. We're due five minutes ago."

Jewel looked back at her daughters. "Come on up and chat while I get dressed."

"Sure," Beryl said.

"I have too much homework," Amber said, turning away.

And so it went.

Edward came into Jewel's office, as was his morning custom, to have a cup of espresso and go over the day's events.

"You know," he said to her, when they had finished discussing business, "it's so ironic. Here we are, makin' money like crazy and there's no time to spend it."

"Well, you're exactly like me," Jewel said. "We both love to work. We hate the idea of vacations, and yet when Peter drags you off or Allen makes me go somewhere, it's okay. I can adjust. It's the *idea* of leaving that I hate. There never seems to be a perfect time." She went over to the wall calendar. "But you're well overdue. Set aside some time and just go. We can manage."

"Well, Peter's been talkin' a lot about Greece."

"Then do it."

"Okay," Edward nodded. "I will. Peter will be delighted. Think the place can last three weeks without me?"

"No, but we'll try. You need a rest."

Edward paused. "There's something I have to talk to you about. The time never seems right, but . . ."

"Okay," Jewel glanced at her watch. "I have a couple of minutes. Is this something serious?"

"Well, sort of," Edward said, heading over to close the door.

"Oh God, I feel a lecture coming on." Jewel buzzed Meg Higdon, her secretary, and told her to hold the calls. Then she walked around and sat on the edge of her desk, opposite Edward. "All right . . . what's wrong? Which one of the staff have I insulted this time?"

"It's not anything you've done."

"Well, that's a relief. But what is it? Why the closed door?"

"I, er, I saw Sascha the other day," Edward began, testing the waters.

"Oh? Where?" Jewel's voice turned icy.

"We had lunch, actually."

"What!" she shrieked.

"He called me."

"Sascha called *you?* Why on earth? The bastard certainly doesn't need a job." Sascha had joined Tiffany & Co. in the early eighties, as one of their chief designers. Jewel's hatred had mushroomed since then, as he became more famous. She had been known to go through fashion magazines, tearing into shreds the pages that featured his jewelry.

"No, he's doin' great at Tiffany. Actually, he's called me a number of times over the past few years. I always put him off out of loyalty to you. But I couldn't any longer."

Edward took a deep breath. "Jewel, Sascha wants to see the girls. He wants 'em to know he's their father. He wants . . ."

"Hell, he wants to walk back into my life and mess it up!" Jewel said. "You know the girls think Allen's their father. And that's how it should be. He's the one who's been a father to them."

"They love Allen," Edward said. "They'd love him just as much if they *knew* he'd adopted them. But, honey, I think they have a right to know who their real father is. It isn't as if he's down-and-out somewhere. He's successful . . . wealthy. He and Aïna own a house in Westchester."

"How lovely for them. And thank you for sharing all this with me, Edward," Jewel said crossly. "But you can tell your friend that I don't want my daughters finding out that they're illegitimate. Sascha lied to me. He has no rights whatever, legal or moral."

"Look, don't jump down *my* throat," Edward said, getting angry. "After all this time you should be able to let go of this bitterness. Sascha loved you. He just made a mistake. We all make mistakes."

"You call lying to me, marrying me when he already had a wife, fathering two illegitimate children, a fucking *mistake?* He's lucky I didn't send him to jail for bigamy. He's lucky I didn't have him deported. I owe Sascha *nothing*, absolutely nothing. And he's not getting his hands on my children!" Jewel paused, breathing heavily. "God, I can't believe he came to you. He couldn't *stand* you. You should've heard the things he used to say . . ."

Edward stood and headed for the door. "Okay, Jewel, that's enough. Subject closed, for the time bein'. I just wish you'd think about it."

"Tell Sascha for me," Jewel seethed, "that if he ever tries to see Amber or Beryl I'll have him before a judge as fast as you can say 'double agent.'"

"Oh come on, Jewel. Be reasonable. Sascha's no spy."

"If he comes near the kids I'll say *anything* to have him thrown out of this country! You tell him that. And who do you think they'll believe, him or me?"

"You're making a big mistake, Jewel. Where's your compassion?"

"I have no compassion!" Jewel screamed. "Not when it comes to Sascha."

"You're wrong, Jewel. You've come far enough to be able to forgive him. Look at all you have now."

"If you bring the subject up again, Edward, I'll fire you," she said hatefully. "I mean, I'll buy out your share of Bijoux."

"God, you're fuckin' impossible!" Edward walked out, slamming the door behind him.

Jewel reached for a cigarette and lit it, her hand shaking with emotion.

It was the first serious fight she had ever had with Edward, but she was livid that he'd try to butt into her private affairs. She leaned back in her chair and sucked angrily on the cigarette, replaying the scene. Of course she realized that there was no rationale for her being so angry with Sascha Robinovsky after all these years. Yet the idea of his seeing Amber and Beryl, of *them* knowing the truth, caused a rage to well up within her that was totally unreasonable.

Her head throbbed with a pain that started at the base of her skull and shot hot darts up behind her eyes. Jewel leaned her elbows on her desk and cradled her head in her hands, waiting for the worst of it to pass. Then she buzzed Meg.

"Aspirin, Meg. And telephone my husband. Tell him I can't make the fund raiser for the public library tonight. I have to put the finishing touches on the spring catalog."

"Okay, Ms. Prescott. Your ten o'clock is waiting. Rita Roberts."

"What? Who's that?"

"Mr. Randolph wanted you to see her."

"Oh shit. That daughter of some friend of his. Okay Meg, you sit in on this too. But first, call and get two first-class tickets to Athens. Have them delivered to Mr. Randolph with a red rose and a note. No. Skip the note. He'll know what it's about. Okay . . . send in what's-her-name. I want to get this over fast."

Rita Roberts appeared in Jewel's office several moments later. She was startlingly tiny, yet not a midget. Her hair, obviously inspired by Cyndi Lauper, was crew cut on one side, shoulder length on the other, in shades of red and purple, and partially covered by a gray fedora. The outfit—a leopard-print leotard, several ruffled blue pet-ticoats, zebra-striped tights, and a black coat that reached the ground —combined with her smallness to give her a comical appearance: something like Toulouse-Lautrec crossed with Jane Avril. Her makeup was a tribute to Technicolor movies of the fifties, primary colors with a bit too much yellow washed over them. Her black portfolio was plastered with stickers of Disney characters. Under her arm was a large brown Dewar's scotch box tied with string.

"Okay, come over here. I'm Jewel Prescott. Spread everything on this table. We have to make it quick."

Meg entered the room. Jewel's eyes met Meg's, high above Rita, and they exchanged a "has-Edward-gone-bananas?" glance.

"This is sure some office," Rita said as she unpacked the jewelry she had carefully wrapped in purple tissue paper. Her voice was South-ern, gentle and melodic. It clashed with the fashion statement she projected. "I really appreciate your takin' the time to see me, Ms. Prescott. This is the most excitin' day of my life. I met Edward because my mother went to Mary Baldwin with his sister. That's a college in Virginia."

"Hmmm . . . yes, that's nice," Jewel acknowledged impatiently. "Please understand, I have only a minute."

"I work in reactive materials . . . titanium, tantalum, niobium." Rita explained, then apologized. "I'm sorry. I don't need to explain it to you. You mixed niobium with iolite and garnets in your 1983 collection . . ."

"It was 1984," Jewel corrected, picking up a necklace that seemed to pop out at her. The pieces—geometric shapes strung together with crystal beads—were brilliant examples of what could be achieved when certain metals were exposed to intense heat or charged with electrical current. In Rita's work, the metal's dull gray surface had been transformed into hues that glowed almost neon, yet with a subtle, ethereal beauty.

"How did you get this luster?" Jewel asked. "It's quite unusual."

Rita smiled, almost sheepishly. "Well, I tried somethin' one night. Just to be silly. I put a scrap of titanium under a pyramid that a friend had made out of toothpicks . . ."

"Toothpicks!" Meg said, scrutinizing some earrings, obviously taken with Rita's collection.

"Yeah, as long as it has the proper angles it doesn't much matter what you make a pyramid out of . . ."

"Are you trying to tell me," Jewel interrupted, "that a *pyramid* did this?"

Rita nodded. "Well, yes. I mean, I still expose the metals to heat. But first they spend a day in the pyramid. Don't ask me to explain. The pyramid just does somethin' different to them."

"Well, remind me to send you all my dull razor blades," Jewel said, flipping through Rita's portfolio. The girl had talent; Edward was right, as usual. "Okay. Your work shows real promise. If Edward can find room, you might as well try it here for a while. We'll touch base in a few months and see how it's working out." Jewel extended her hand. "And now I have to go."

Rita shook Jewel's hand, flabbergasted. "Er, thank you. Does that mean I actually have a job at Bijoux?"

"If Edward can find a nook. He'll discuss salary. It won't be much to start."

"I'd work for free! I mean it."

"That won't be necessary," Jewel said.

As Meg steered Rita to the door, Jewel called out. "Rita dear . . . do us all a favor and try dressing a bit more monochromatically. And . . . get rid of the hat."

Jewel returned to her day. She hoped Allen wouldn't be too furious about the public library benefit.

There was a quick rap on her door. "Come in," she called out, wondering where Meg was.

Mike Marshall, Jewel's newest in-house advertising director, entered, closing the door behind him. He walked over to her and planted a kiss on her cheek. "Hello, darling," he said. "I just stopped by to remind you we have to work late tonight."

"I haven't forgotten. I had to cancel a benefit with Allen."

"Oh darn. Too bad. I thought maybe we'd better work at my place again, seeing as how we'll be up so late," he said, grinning.

Jewel grinned back and stood to let him kiss her, this time on the lips, passionately. God, the guy had it. He made her springs springy again.

"I'd better tell Allen not to wait up," she whispered.

"I wish you'd tell him you won't be home at all," Mike said, running his hands down her back.

"You know I can't do that. Anyway, at the end of the month, the San Francisco store's opening. Allen's too busy to come, and Edward will be in Greece. We'll have five days together . . . more or less away from watchful eyes."

There was a knock on the door. Quickly, she pulled away from Mike, and he scooted around the desk and dropped into a chair. "Come in," she said, in her most businesslike voice.

Meg entered. "Oh, hi, Mr. Marshall. Sorry to bother you, but I have some stuff for you to sign, Ms. Prescott. The Federal Express man is waiting for it."

"Well, I have to get back to my office anyway," Mike said, standing. "You won't forget tonight, will you? Putting the spring catalog to bed?" he said, smiling behind Meg's back as he exited.

Jewel smiled back. "I won't. But let's try to make it an early evening," she said, for Meg's benefit.

No one knew it, but she had finally allotted time in her schedule for a lover. Not that she loved Mike Marshall, but there was a passionate chemistry between them. And it was so convenient, working under the same roof, traveling together.

There was excitement in the danger involved, in keeping it a secret.

There was excitement in the sex.

And there was plenty of it.

26

1987

As the years flew by, the Connecticut house had been added onto
several times by Allen and had been featured in *Architectural Digest*.
He and Jewel had recently remodeled and moved into a new Manhattan apartment, a penthouse-triplex on Fifth, that Allen desperately coveted because it provided much more wall space than the
apartment on Park. Allen had a knack for renovation and decoration.
At the weekly dinner parties they gave, guests could not stop raving
about Allen's talent. He lapped up the praise, and Jewel admitted
that he deserved it. Besides, she was getting her share of praise. She
had won two Coty awards for her jewelry design, and the Bijoux print
ads had garnered advertising honors for their originality.

As the girls continued to grow, Amber continued to grow away
from Jewel. Having moved from kindergarten at the Park Avenue
Christian Day School to elementary school at Dalton, they were now
boarding at the Sheldon Arms School in Connecticut. There, Amber
—now fourteen—and Beryl, a year younger, were near the Prescott
country home for weekend visits, and far from the Manhattan high-
pressured academic fast lane, of which Allen did not approve.

Allen made most of the girls' educational decisions, and Jewel was
grateful that he cared so much. Every year for their birthdays he
gave Amber and Beryl each a contemporary work of art that he
assured them would be worth a fortune when they came of age. The

girls were usually less than thrilled. When they were younger, their hearts were always set on a new bicycle or Madame Alexander doll; now, it was clothes. Therefore, it was Jewel who won kudos at birthdays or Christmas, by producing whatever it was that the girls really desired. (Even Amber could still be bought off occasionally.)

"The art will be their dowry," Allen told Jewel when she suggested that he wait a few years before giving them such grown-up gifts.

"But their rooms aren't suitable for kids their age . . ." Jewel complained. "Here I go out and buy them lace-canopied beds . . . and you give them sculptures of mashed-up cars and paintings of vulvas."

"Well," Allen was always quick to note, "according to the current art market, Amber's and Beryl's walls already contain hundreds of thousands of dollars' worth of pictures that I bought for only a few grand each. They'll thank me someday, when they've outgrown all the presents you've bought them."

Jewel had to admit he had a point but she just wished he would *sell* some things rather than buy new houses and apartments to provide additional wall space. But she did not lose much sleep over it. It took all of her energy to manage her flourishing jewelry empire.

One day, shortly after Jewel had returned from a business lunch with Edward at the Café des Artistes, he called her on her extension.

"Got a minute? I need you in my office."

"What? I thought we just covered everything in the world."

"Well, we missed this. Something's come up."

When Jewel entered Edward's dark wood-paneled office, she found Cathalene Columbier sitting across from his desk.

"Oh, hello, Cathalene. Am I interrupting?" Jewel asked. "I'll come back."

"No," Edward said, "Cathalene wants to talk to us both. She has some news."

"Oh?" Jewel came in and sat casually on the corner of Edward's desk. "What's up?"

"I was just telling Edward," Cathalene said, "that I'm afraid, after all these years, I must leave Bijoux." She was wearing a black dress with a long white aviator's scarf wrapped around her neck. Jewel realized that she could not remember having seen Cathalene wear anything but black and white for years, not since the early days.

"Oh?" Jewel said, not surprised. Cathalene had always been ambitious. What amazed Jewel was that it had taken Cathalene so long to make her move. "What are you going to do?"

"I have found myself a backer. A very rich person who believes in my talent as much as I do. My backer feels that my creativity is not being showcased enough at Bijoux . . . that it is time for me to open my own shop."

"Really? I'm sorry we've mistreated you so badly," Jewel said coldly.

"Jewel," Edward broke in, "I don't think Cathalene means we've treated her badly."

"Well, she just said that we haven't been showcasing her creativity enough. Who else, I ask you, besides Tiffany, which makes umpteen millions more than we do per year, who *else* advertises their designers like we do?" Jewel said bitterly. "When is all this going to happen?"

"I've already signed a lease for a glorious space on Columbus Avenue," Cathalene said. "I will open in a few months, as soon as we can renovate the interior."

"Columbus Avenue's prime rental these days," Jewel said. "Your sugar daddy must be very well-heeled. Who is he?"

"It's a secret. My backer wants it that way."

"Oh come on, you can tell us," Jewel said.

Cathalene lowered her large doe eyes. "No, I'm afraid not."

"It's Harry Harper, isn't it?" Jewel guessed Harry might savor stirring up trouble at Bijoux, to get back at her for never going to bed with him. After all these years, he still wanted her, and she still resisted.

Cathalene smiled. "I wish I could let you think that. But no, it's not him." She stood. "Anyway, this is my formal notice. And Edward, I want to tell you that I've enjoyed the years we have worked together. You have always been a gentleman to deal with."

Edward stood and bowed. "Why, thank you, Cathalene. Good luck. I know you'll do well. You have a lot of talent. We're sorry to lose you."

Cathalene picked up her handbag, then paused in front of Jewel. "Now that I am leaving, I can't resist telling you what a bitch you are," she said. "You've only got where you are because you married Allen Prescott. But you're selfish, Jewel. You ignore the needs of other people. You have taken advantage of me, ever since the beginning. I worked hard for you, but never once did you appreciate it. Well, now I'm going to be a big success, bigger than Bijoux, and everybody will appreciate me. Just you wait and see. Someday, Jewel *dear*, you may have to come begging to *me* for a job. And now, it gives me great pleasure to tell you good-bye . . . and fuck you."

After Cathalene had exited, Edward sat, holding his breath against the inevitable tirade that he was sure Jewel was preparing to spit out.

"God, what an ungrateful bitch! Riding my heels to success and then biting them. I *never* trusted her," Jewel said on cue. "Boy, I'd like to know who her backer is. I'll bet it *is* Harry."

Edward shook his head. "No. I'm sure it isn't. Harry's smart enough not to pit Cathalene against Bijoux. Hell, it doesn't matter who it is. She's leavin' and that's that. Cathalene Columbier with one shop is not goin' to put much of a dent in *our* market. Just wish her well and be done with it."

"Okay, Edward. You're right. I wish Cathalene every success in the world." Jewel smiled.

He looked at her skeptically.

"I *do*, darling. Believe me."

Jewel knew Edward was right; Cathalene's shop wouldn't hurt Bijoux's business particularly.

But when Cathalene had her grand opening several months later, Jewel made a point of being out of town.

Naked in bed, Mike Marshall opened a bottle of Puligny-Montrachet, to accompany the cheese and French bread that Jewel had picked up for them to nibble on. As had become their routine over the past couple of years, the lovers were grabbing an illicit hour or so at a loft on Twentieth Street that belonged to a trusted friend of Mike's.

"Ten to two," Mike said, glancing at his watch. He set the tray of food and wine on the floor and slid over closer to her. "We have time for another."

"Well, actually, no. I need to talk to you."

Mike put a finger over Jewel's lips. "Not now," he said, climbing on top of her.

Jewel was pleased that her affair with Mike had been conducted with such discretion, on both their parts. Aside from Edward, who had guessed she was having one, but not with whom, she was sure no one knew about them. At the office, it was business as usual. Jewel saw Mike alone only on evenings when Allen was in Connecticut or when they traveled together on business.

Mike had been an ultrasatisfactory lover. He was as hungry as she for money and power, and their sex—it had always been ravenous, fantastic sex—had been intensified by the heady mutual turn-on of their unabashed ambition.

But Jewel had become bored with the situation. Being with Mike was becoming more tedious than exciting for her. They had had a lot of fun, but passionate sex without love, Jewel had concluded, was beginning to pall.

Mike kept saying he wanted to marry her, but what was the point? She didn't love him and she didn't think he really loved her. Why upset the status quo with Allen and her daughters? Besides, Mike was seven years younger than she; sooner or later Jewel knew that would become an issue.

So it was time, Jewel had decided, to shed Mike the lover. But not at the expense of losing Mike the hotshot art director; he was the best.

After they had finished making love, she rolled over and lit a cigarette.

"God, I wish you'd quit," Mike said. "How many packs a day are you up to anyway?"

"Just a couple," Jewel murmured, exhaling a long trail of smoke. "I know. It's a nasty habit. I smell bad. I'll die of cancer. Honestly, I *do* plan to quit soon. Just as soon as I've finished researching and writing my new book."

"Book? What book?" he asked.

"Darling, I *told* you about it. It's called *The Power and Romance of Gems,* about all the famous gemstones that people have fought and died for over the centuries—the Kohinoor diamond, the Black Prince's ruby, the La Peregrina pearl. It's quite fascinating. Did you know—"

"Yeah, you did tell me all about it," Mike interrupted, not particularly interested. "Hey, there's somebody I've been meaning to ask you about. My sister, Laura, in Greenwich keeps running into her. They play tennis sometimes."

Jewel took her makeup case out of her handbag. "Who? One of my customers?"

"I doubt it. She seems to hate your guts."

Jewel froze, peach lipstick poised against her mouth. "I can't imagine who you're talking about," she said, guessing what was about to come next. It was finally going to happen. The collision with the past.

"Her name's Anna Ferguson. She told Laura you two were college roommates. That you were called Madeleine Lathem then."

"Yes, it's true," she shrugged. "Madeleine's my real name. Jewel became my nickname when I was studying in Germany."

Mike nodded. "Anyway, tell me more about this Anna Ferguson. Laura says she practically has a spasm every time she sees your jewelry. I love the idea of you with enemies," he said, kissing her shoulder. "It's a real turn-on."

"Oh, it's a long story," Jewel said casually, although her heart was beginning to pound. "And terribly boring. Anna had a bad case of jealousy. Obviously she must still. We were rivals over the same boy in college, and I won. She married Randy Ferguson out of spite. She's probably been miserably unhappy ever since."

"What happened to the guy? Was it Allen?" Mike asked.

"No. Just someone I was mad about. Then I went off to Europe. When I got back we'd outgrown each other. Anyway, Mike, I don't want to talk about Anna. It's not worth the time of day." She crushed out a cigarette and lit another. "I want to talk about us."

"What about us?" Mike asked. "Are you leaving Allen?"

"No, I told you, I can't. It's too complicated. My daughters . . ." She paused. "I just think it's time for us to ease out of this. We barely have time for each other anymore, and when we do, it's so rushed."

Mike stared at her. "I thought you were happy with this arrangement. I am, except that I'd like to have you all to myself, all the time."

"Of course I've been happy. But we've been going on for a long time. And if you want to know the truth, I'm tired of sneaking around."

Mike came over to her, put his hands on her slim shoulders, and kissed her forehead. "Hey, what's this all about? I thought you loved me. I love you. I don't want it to end."

Jewel sighed. She had misjudged Mike, thinking he wanted her because of *who* she was, the wildly successful creator of Bijoux. It never occurred to her that he had been serious all those times he said he loved her. Now she had to change her tack before she made him mad.

"Well, you may as well know. Allen suspects something. And Edward insinuated the other day . . . Oh, darling, we have to lay low for a while. We can't afford for this to get around the office."

"I see," he said, hurt.

Jewel took Mike's hand in hers. "I'd feel safer if we put it on the back burner for now. Besides, I need time away from us. To sort it all out," she lied.

"I'm crazy about you, Jewel. What a team we make."

"Oh, darling, we can't think about that now."

"Okay, okay," Mike said, miffed. "I get the point. We'll cool it, if that's what you want."

"It's not what I want; we *have* to."

They finished dressing silently, Mike sulking, and headed out to catch a taxi uptown. Jewel was sure that when Mike allowed it to sink in he'd realize it was all for the best. At least she hoped so.

When they reached the street, Mike walked on ahead of her and signaled for a cab.

All of a sudden, from behind, Jewel felt a hand clamp down on her shoulder. "Madeleine?" a man's voice said.

Startled, Jewel turned to see the smiling face of Wyatt McNeill. His hair was more silver than before. A few additional lines crinkled around his mouth and eyes, but he had changed far less than Jewel would have imagined.

"Wyatt!" she managed to smile back. "What a surprise."

A taxi pulled up to the curb. Mike Marshall opened the door and called back to Jewel impatiently, "You coming?"

"No, Mike," she said. "We'll talk later."

Mike got into the taxi without saying good-bye and sped off.

"I'm rushing," Wyatt said. "Or I'd offer to buy you a cup of coffee."

"That's okay. I have a meeting."

"Are you headed uptown?" Wyatt asked.

Jewel nodded. "Back to the office. Fifth and Fifty-third."

"Then we'll share a cab. I got rid of my car and driver. I'm not in town enough to make it cost-effective."

Something about the way Wyatt said it made Jewel relax a bit. She laughed. "God, Wyatt . . . it's actually good to see you again."

Wyatt flagged down a taxi and they climbed in.

"What do you mean? Actually good to see me," Wyatt said, carrying the thread.

"Well, after all that's happened. There was a time when I prayed that I'd never see you again as long as I lived."

"I understand," Wyatt said. "I was angry. Oh, by the way, thank you for returning the money," he added. "I must admit, I never expected to see it. But then I was more than angry. You really hurt me when you left."

"I know." Jewel lapsed into silence for the next few blocks, thinking about how young and naive she had been. "I suppose the truth can come out now," she said finally. "It would never have worked out, you and I. I felt so guilty about your family. But the real reason I broke it off when I did . . ."—she paused, playing it for all it was worth—"is that Anna found out. She flew over to Pforzheim and confronted me, just before I was supposed to meet you in Paris. She tore in, shouting, screaming . . . threatening me with everything you can imagine—"

"What?" Wyatt's face went pale. "Why didn't you tell me?"

"Anna *threatened* me, Wyatt! She made me promise to break up with you and never let on she knew. She told Hadley too, but wanted to spare Elizabeth. I'm telling you now because it's been so long. It really doesn't matter anymore."

"This explains it all," Wyatt said. "I always wondered why your and Anna's friendship ended so suddenly. Why didn't I figure it out myself? I should have guessed." Wyatt took her hand and held it. "God, what you went through. And the way I reacted . . . I wish there was some way I could make it up to you."

"Not necessary." Jewel smiled, loving every minute of the confession. "We learn from our mistakes. I was wrong to get involved with you, because of who you were. But I was so insecure then, so anxious to be taken care of. You were wonderful and loving. I couldn't help myself."

Wyatt shook his head slowly. "I wonder how Anna found out."

"I don't know."

"Anna's a complex woman—spoiled, I guess. First by me, then by Randy."

"Then they're still married?" Jewel asked, curious.

"Yes. I don't know if they're happy. They have three kids, and Anna's very much the suburban mother. Randy travels a lot. Anna doesn't have enough to do. Plays a lot of tennis. Looks good, lost all that weight. It's too bad, all this. You two were such great friends."

The taxi turned the corner onto Fifty-third. "Right up there, driver," Jewel said. "Well, here I am. It was good to run into you, Wyatt."

"You too, Madeleine. You're quite a success. I'm proud of you."

"Thanks. Stop by the store sometime and spend some money."

Wyatt grinned. "Will do. I'd like to continue our conversation. There's a lot to talk about. What about lunch next week?"

"Oh, I can't. I'm off to Paris on business, then California," Jewel said, grabbing her briefcase and brushing Wyatt's cheek with a quick kiss.

"Yes, well, I'll call you sometime," he said, realizing that she did not want him to.

Jewel looked back at Wyatt and gave him a quick wave as she headed into Bijoux. How ironic it was. After so many years Anna and Wyatt McNeill had both merged back on the perimeters of her life.

Damn! she thought, as she climbed the private back stairs to her office. She had meant to ask Wyatt about Hadley. He was the only one of the McNeills that she really wanted to hear about.

Meg Higdon, who had been promoted from Jewel's secretary to her personal assistant, handed her a stack of messages. "You look wonderful, Jewel. And you're smiling. You hardly ever smile at this time of day," she said matter-of-factly. Her boss was a hard woman to work for, but Meg had learned that the more candid you were with Jewel, the more she respected you.

"I ran into an old friend," Jewel said. "Someone I haven't seen in ages. And it went well. I vindicated myself on a certain point."

Jewel headed into her spacious office-workroom and sat down to return phone calls.

It felt good to have Wyatt back in her corner, sympathetic to what she had gone through. *Serves you right, Anna,* she thought to herself.

Jewel wondered whether Anna would forgive her someday, then decided that she really didn't give a damn.

27

1988

"I'm leaving now," Meg Higdon said. She stood in the doorway of Jewel's office, tall and leggy, with unfortunate buck teeth that kept her face from being more than pleasingly pretty. "Unless you need something?"

"No . . . no. Run along. What time is it, anyway?" Jewel asked. She was sitting at her worktable, examining a thirty-five carat pink morganite through her microscope.

"Just past six," Meg said. "I'm going to the theater tonight with Mike Marshall. I had tickets, asked him, and he accepted. I can't even believe it!"

"Hmmm, that's nice," Jewel said. She and Mike had cooled down their affair, but she had found it impossible to ditch him completely without his quitting Bijoux. Now, here was a possible solution: maybe Mike would like Meg. In fact, he and Meg were probably well suited to each other. They both put up with her mercurial temperament so well. "Have fun."

"Oh, Jewel, I'm really nervous. Mike makes me so tongue-tied. We're going to have dinner after . . . at a new French place. I'm terrified I won't be able to think of anything to say," Meg admitted.

"You? Tongue-tied?" Jewel laughed. Meg's nonstop chatter was a running joke around the office. "You'll be fine."

"Oh, I hope so!" she gushed. "Well, see you tomorrow."

Jewel turned off the light of her gemscope and took the large morganite out of the pliers. It was a nearly flawless stone that her chief gem buyer, Erik Sanders, had brought back from California. Next year's big promotional push for the Bijoux stores was to feature an all-American collection. All the gemstones used by the designers had to be mined in the United States. They would be featuring rubies, emeralds, and hiddenite from North Carolina; sapphires from the Yogo Gulch and along the Missouri River in Montana; opals from Nevada and Idaho; pearls from the Mississippi River area; morganite, kunzite, tourmalines, and benitoite from California; Arizona peridot; Texas and Colorado topaz; Southwestern turquoise; Wyoming jade; red beryl from Utah; aquamarines from Maine; Arkansas diamonds and quartz; and garnets and amethysts from all around the country.

Jewel set the pink gemstone on a black velvet tray, under the glow of the Tiffany table lamp that Allen had given for her thirtieth birthday, an eon ago, it seemed to her now that she was thirty-eight. She went over to the safe and took out some eighteen-karat gold bracelets and chokers that her craftspeople had made up for her.

Back at her desk, she sat and stared at the antique-cut morganite sitting next to the shimmering gold. Her eyes began to hurt, and she cupped her hands over them. Yes, the headache was back too. She had finally gone to an eye doctor. He had given her both glasses and contact lenses, but, so far, neither had made a noticeable difference.

It was nearly six-thirty. Jewel and Allen were having people for dinner at eight. Allen's sister, Isabel, was in town, and they had put together a small party for her, with Harry and Vivian Harper, and a bunch of Allen's friends—some art dealers and several trendy artists, including one particularly obnoxious young stud from Oklahoma, Billy Cales, whom Allen had taken under his wing.

Jewel sighed. She wished she could skip the party and get some work done, but what was the point? Allen would be furious if she missed dinner, and what to do with this stone was totally eluding her. She hadn't been able to complete a piece of jewelry in weeks, or was it months? She sighed again and stuck the tray back in the safe.

The motivating force in Jewel's life, what had kept her going all these years, was her work. When the children were babies and needed her, that had been important to her. But with Nushka and Allen around full time, the girls, now teenagers, had grown away from her. Oh, she could still talk and gossip with them about superficial things. Or, at least, she and Beryl did. Communication with Amber seemed to have closed down completely when her elder daughter became a teenager. Now that the girls had started boarding school, Jewel wrote them once a week and sent them cartoons she had clipped out of *The New Yorker* or amusing headlines from the *Daily News*. But, other than that, her daughters did not occupy a great deal of her thought.

All of her adult life, regardless of what was going on *in* her life, Jewel had always been able to turn to her designing to find fulfillment and a sense of inner peace. Working with precious metals and price-less gemstones brought her life a beauty and balance that otherwise escaped her. Creating her jewelry—not the sketches she gave to her craftspeople, but the signed, one-of-a-kind pieces that were the cor-nerstone of her business—centered Jewel in a way that nothing else did. Selecting a new stone, handling it, meditating on it, deciding how to use it, was the closest thing to a religious or spiritual experi-ence in Jewel's life. Becoming one with the gem, *feeling* the purest way to display it in a new design, that was what Jewel really lived for. That artistic process was what kept her going. She derived her en-ergy from it. When she was not creating she felt hollow inside.

And that was how Jewel felt now; as if she were one of the walking dead. Her creativity had vanished. One day she woke up and it wasn't there. She hadn't panicked at first, figuring she was merely tired. She even gave in to one of Allen's vacation requests and went sailing around the British Virgin Islands with him.

But when she returned, after a week of seasickness and sunburn, she still had not been able to communicate with the stones and turn them into the unique gold-and-jeweled compositions that were her trademark. The predicament put her in a worse mood than usual at work. Her colleagues tiptoed around, trying not to upset her. Every-one was aware that something was wrong. No one, with the excep-tion of Edward, Allen, and Mike Marshall, knew *what*. The dizzy atmosphere of the spiraling early days of Bijoux was gone. There were no more peaks to scale. The designers and staff all speculated that Jewel was bored.

And she was. Not only that, everyone around her was annoying her more and more. It seemed as if her employees came to her only to whine or complain these days. They needed more money, more time off, more recognition, more you-name-it.

Jewel was also seething with jealousy over Cathalene Columbier's success. Her former designer had become *Women's Wear Daily's* newest darling. Whoever he was, Cathalene's sugar daddy had come through in a big way for her: there were rumors that Cathalene was going to open stores nationwide, trying to copy Bijoux's success.

Jewel was dying to know who the mysterious backer was. She had accused Neil Tavlos, but he firmly denied it, and she believed him. He had no reason to sabotage Bijoux. From recent conversations with Harry Harper, she suspected that he knew who it was but was refusing to talk.

There was so much on her mind these days. At home, Allen was beginning to grumble even more than usual about her work schedule. He had even brought up the subject of adopting a child several times, but Jewel had quickly discouraged such thoughts. Nushka, still the housekeeper, pined away because the children were no longer underfoot on a day-to-day basis.

On Allen's birthday, Jewel had given him a dog, a King Charles spaniel, hoping it would please him and Nushka and give them something to lavish affection on. It worked, for a while. Then the puppy wriggled out of its collar one day during an outing in Central Park and ran out into rush-hour traffic on Fifth where its short life came to an end beneath the heavy wheels of a Checker cab. After that, the atmosphere at home went from bad to worse.

"Look, Allen," Jewel had suggested one night as they arrived back from a Costume Institute gala at the Metropolitan Museum, "why don't we take the girls out of boarding school? Bring them back here? Millions of children have been educated in the city and lived to tell the tale."

"No," Allen sighed. "The pressure's too intense. Especially for Amber. And I don't want to separate them. They need each other. I think the solution would be to spend more time in Connecticut, let them become day students."

"Jesus," Jewel snarled, "they're *my* children. I think I have some sort of say in the situation."

"You're the reason Amber is going through this angry phase. You've never spent enough time with them," Allen accused. "Her awe of you has turned into hostility."

"Yes, yes, blame me," Jewel said, hanging her Russian sable in the hall closet. "I've always spent quality time with them, but no one ever gives me credit. I'm the one who's been out there in the real world slugging it out, making money, creating something. Paying for your excesses."

"Oh, please, let's not go into that again," Allen said. "You're *not* supporting me, in spite of what you think. I can sell some paintings any time I need to raise cash. Look, you've proven your point. Bijoux is a success . . . you're a success. Why can't you sit back and *enjoy* it? Relax. Let go of the reins. Give Edward more power."

"I'm going to bed," Jewel said, huffing upstairs. "I have a breakfast meeting tomorrow."

"When do you not?" Allen had muttered, heading into the library to pour himself a cognac and watch a videotape.

And so it went, life with Allen, life with everyone, these days.

Jewel replaced the painting over the wall safe and gathered up her things with a sigh.

The last thing she felt like tonight was being charming to a lot of guests.

One of Allen's friends, Tony Firstein, sat at the baby grand and launched into a Cole Porter song as the party adjourned to the two-storied Prescott living room for espresso and cognac. Jewel, in spite of her exhaustion, had gamely kept up her part of the conversation during dinner. It was a witty, congenial group, with the exception of the cocky Billy Cales. Allen seemed in especially ebullient spirits and was over by the Barnett Newman, talking animatedly with Sara Richards, an art registrar whom he sometimes used.

Isabel Farraday, who had been seated at the other end of the dinner table, on Allen's right, came over and put an arm lightly around Jewel's waist. "Let's steal away and have a little chat, just the two of us," Isabel whispered. "They won't miss us for a few minutes, and my plane's leaving early in the morning."

Jewel led her sister-in-law into the forest green library, and they settled themselves on a rose suede sofa, under a Matisse that Allen had bought at auction. Jewel lit a cigarette, earning Isabel's disapproving glance.

"Yes, I'm quitting soon. I promise." She smiled, anticipating Isabel's unspoken comment.

"What I want to talk to you about is rather delicate," Isabel said.

293

"And you may feel that I'm butting in where it's none of my business. But we've always been frank with one another."

What a day, Jewel thought to herself. "Of course. What's up?"

"Well," Isabel began, "for the past six months or so I've been noticing that Allen's seemed rather depressed—nothing specific, just a general mood."

"Hmmm," Jewel noted. Why was everyone always fawning over Allen? *She* was the one who'd been depressed, with her designing going so badly. But too many people depended on her; she had to exhibit strength at all times. She couldn't lapse into self-indulgence as Allen was apt to do, especially around his sympathetic sister.

"And then," Isabel continued, "he suddenly snapped out of it . . . he stopped wanting to talk to me. You know he *always* tells me everything. He became so evasive I decided to do a little sleuthing, quietly, on my own. Oh, Jewel, I'm sorry to have to tell you this, but I think you should know." She took Jewel's hand and squeezed it. "Allen's seeing someone. I'm telling you only because I'd hate to see the two of you break up. Oh, Jewel darling, I know you work damned hard. And I'm terribly proud of you, but you leave Allen with a lot of time to kill."

Allen? Playing around? Jewel couldn't have been more surprised. "Who is it? Do you know?" Jewel asked, cutting through to the essence.

"I don't know," Isabel hesitated.

"It's amazing how one learns new things about friends, the longer you know them." Jewel crushed out her cigarette, and reached into a silver case for another. "I just discovered you don't know how to lie."

"Oh, I don't know for sure. I have no solid proof. It's more intu- ition."

"Who?" Jewel pressed.

"What are you going to do about this?" Isabel asked nervously. "I shouldn't have told you. Allen will be furious."

"Your name won't come into it . . . *if* we have a showdown," Jewel assured Isabel. "But I think for now it's better to leave well enough alone . . . let it run its course." After all, she had been having the affair with Mike; how could she begrudge Allen? "Now tell me . . . who do you *think* it is?"

"Well, you think about it. Who would *you* guess?"

Jewel hadn't a clue. Allen saw many people without her, in his art-buying rounds. It could be anyone. No. That was wrong. There was his friend Sara Richards, who advised collectors on what to buy. Weren't they out there in the living room chatting at this very moment? Jewel looked toward the door. "I think I know. She's in there, isn't she." How could he fall in love with her, she wondered? Sara was pretty enough, in a wholesome, milkmaidish sort of way, hardly Allen's type.

Isabel nodded. "I could be wrong. It may be merely a flirtation. I don't actually know how serious . . ."

"Oh, it doesn't matter," Jewel said, getting up. "I'll never give Allen up without a fight. We complement each other too well."

Isabel smiled. "I'm glad you feel that way. I certainly think my brother's worth fighting for. But perhaps you should let *him* know you feel that way," she suggested tactfully, as she followed Jewel back to the party.

"Yes, I will," Jewel mumbled distractedly, as her eyes sought out Allen and Sara. To her surprise they were no longer talking. Sara was sitting on the piano bench next to Tony Firstein, and Allen was hunkered down over a sculpture—two heavy boxes by Donald Judd —with Brad Tobias, a painter of large, ominous abstracts that Jewel found oppressive.

As Jewel paused, looking for Harry Harper, Billy Cales came strolling over to her, wearing his inevitable paint-stained jeans with cowboy boots, a rather foppish silk buccaneer's shirt, and a Southwestern bolo tie.

"Yo, Jewel, how's it going?"

"Fine, Billy, just fine," she said, heading for the piano.

"Hey," he blocked her, taking her by the elbow and guiding her over to the floor-to-ceiling windows overlooking Central Park, "you don't like me much, do you? You're always trying to avoid me."

"Let's just say we don't have much in common," Jewel answered wearily.

"I think we do," Cales smiled seductively. "I think you're just playing hard to get."

"Believe me, with you I'm not *playing,*" she said, walking back toward the gathering. His hand reached out and grabbed hers roughly. He pulled her close to him. "Please, Billy," she sighed. "I'm not interested."

"That's not what I hear."

"And what do *you* hear?"

"That you and Allen haven't done it for years. That you race around pretty good."

"Oh?" Jewel said coolly. "Well, your information source is unreliable."

"Look, Allen's going to London this weekend. I'd like to see you," Billy said, rather boyishly. "I mean, I'm going to be working here anyway."

"Working *here?*"

"Yeah. Allen's commissioned me to do trompe l'oeil on the guestroom walls. It'll take a couple of weeks. He said I could stay here while I work. And," he smiled, satisfied, "they're going to be gone at least a week."

"They?"

"He and Sara Richards. She's going with him to the auctions."

Was that true? Jewel thought Allen was going to London only for a long weekend . . . and alone. Were Allen and Sara really *serious* about each other? Impossible.

"Come on," Billy urged, taking advantage of her hesitation. "You know it'd be real good. *I'm* real good," he bragged.

"Billy, I've never liked you and now I know why. Allen's been opening doors for you all over town. You've gotten where you are because of him. And is that how you *thank* him? By trying to screw his wife?" Jewel hissed. "Listen to me. I'll *never* give you the time of day. And I'm telling Allen what a little shit you really are. So don't count on moving in here anytime soon. Go *trompe* on somebody else. I adore my husband and I turn fierce whenever I think he's being taken advantage of." She paused, relishing every moment of telling off the young brat. "Billy, you've overstayed your welcome. Now get the hell out of here!"

"Oh, Jewel, I love it when you get mad. It really turns me on," Billy leered.

"Get the fuck out!" Jewel said loud enough so that the rest of the party stopped dead in its tracks and turned its attention to her.

Billy gave a cool but rather nervous smile, mumbled a general good-night, and headed for the door.

"Sorry, everybody." Jewel smiled. "Just a not-so-friendly misunderstanding. We were having a disagreement over cubism."

Allen came over and put his arm around her, concerned by her outburst. "Are you okay?" he said quietly. "You look upset."

"Oh, I'm okay. What a prick that guy is. Trying to stab you in the back. He thought it'd be great fun to share my bed while you're away. I sent him packing. I'm afraid you'll have to find somebody else to paint the guest room."

"Jewel," Allen said, looking at her with an odd smile, "I didn't know you were that loyal to me."

"What the hell did you think? What's going on here?"

"Oh, nothing."

"Look, my head's splitting. I'm going to say a quick good-bye to everyone and then slip upstairs to bed. I need a good night's sleep."

"Okay. But we have to talk," Allen said, looking at her seriously.

"Oh, we will. When you and Sara get back from London," she said pointedly.

Allen crossed his arms and watched Jewel as she circulated around the room, leaving a trail of smiles and kisses and good-nights. She even kissed Sara Richards on her rosy cheek.

Jewel glanced back at Allen before she left the room and was surprised to see him still standing there, studying her with an enigmatic look on his face. She blew him a kiss as she headed through the wide archway into the hall.

"Wait!" Harry Harper said, catching up with her, looking handsome in a dinner jacket of his own design. "You'll be there tomorrow, won't you?"

"What? Oh, your *show*. Of course I'll be there," Jewel said. "I wouldn't miss it; you know that."

There was a gleam in his eye. "Good. I'm glad."

She aimed a kiss in the direction of his cheek. "Well, good night, Harry. It's been a long day."

"It'll be a good show, maybe my best," Harry said, giving her a sly smile.

"I don't doubt it, darling. I can't wait."

"Me either," he said.

As she headed upstairs, Jewel tried to interpret the expression on Harry Harper's face as they parted. He looked like a cat that had just cornered a fat mouse and was waiting for the precise moment to pounce. She had no idea what it meant, but Harry was not always as subtle as he thought he was. He was definitely up to something. But what?

She supposed she would find out tomorrow.

For now, she had to take a couple of Advil and think about Allen and Sara Richards. She wondered if they were actually having an affair, or if it was merely a crush on Allen's part. As for Sara, well, *any* single woman would obviously love to nab Allen away from her. And this was definitely making her jealous. Perhaps that meant she loved Allen more than she thought.

Jewel slipped out of her clothes quickly and into a hot shower. She knew she had to completely reevaluate her life with Allen, the pros, the cons. Was it time to end the marriage? Or was she going to fight?

New York's fashion conscious—society doyennes, successful women executives, movie stars, and women's page reporters—were seated on gold chairs, slim knee to slim knee, sipping rum punch out of ceramic coconut shells. Harry Harper's fashion show was the hot ticket in town, and the newspaper photographers and television video crews were loving it.

Jewel and Edward arrived late, about ten minutes after the packed show had gotten underway. Harry's favorite model, a stunning six-feet-two black woman known as Saman, was strutting down the mauve-carpeted runway in a sassy, tangerine-dyed chamois strapless sundress, its cinched waist accentuated by a green snakeskin belt. Jewel and Edward quickly dashed to their reserved seats, applauding Saman as the colored spotlights switched to shades of yellow and magenta and three blond models bopped onstage in whimsical tie-dyed satin halter gowns with short, hooped skirts.

"Harry's in an outrageous mood this season," Edward whispered, checking his program to see if they had missed much.

"He's been in an outrageous mood for quite some time now," Jewel said, referring not merely to his clothes. She guessed that Harry harbored quiet resentment over the fact that she'd never fallen into bed with him. "I think I'd better order a lot today, to appease him."

Another model pranced down the runway, wearing black taffeta with a red-feathered overskirt and hat to match.

"What about that one?" Jewel asked Edward. "Do you think it's a bit too young for me?"

Edward rolled his eyes. "Don't be ridiculous. Harry probably designed it with you in mind. You're one of the few people here who could actually carry it off." As he spoke his eyes darted around the room, taking in friends and waving to them.

"Don't look now," he went on, "but Cathalene's over there."

"So what's new?" Jewel said. "She's had a crush on Harry for years."

Model after model sashayed down the runway to Latin American samba music, acting out the playful mood that Harry wanted to evoke with this season's collection. The audience adored it. With each new outfit, the crowd cooed and aah-ed and applauded feverishly. One of the movie stars, perhaps on drugs, or crystals, perhaps merely moved by the music, got up and danced in the aisle to the beat of the fiesta music.

At the end, all the models danced down the runway, and Saman appeared as an updated flamenco dancer, doing a cha-cha with Harry, sporting tight-fitting red Spanish dancer's pants, black snakeskin boots, and a bolero jacket. The audience whistled, clapped, and shouted spirited "bravos" for Harry's new collection. Harry took several deep bows, then broke into a Spanish dance with Saman that brought the house down.

"Well, Harry's done it this time," Jewel said approvingly. "Just when *W* insinuated that he had no new tricks up his sleeve. Boy, will they eat crow. Look, I've marked the numbers of *eight* outfits I'm going to order."

"Good. You'll have Harry eatin' out of your hand. Come on, let's make our way over to congratulate him."

As they wove their way through the crush of elegantly costumed and jeweled bodies, dodging flashbulbs while greeting friends and many of Jewel's loyal Bijoux customers, Jewel suddenly found herself eyeball to eyeball with Cathalene Columbier.

"Oh, hello," Jewel said indifferently, as she squeezed by her.

Cathalene returned an equally icy smile and put her hand on Jewel's shoulder. "Jewel, I'd like you to meet a good friend of mine, Anna Ferguson."

Jewel froze and turned to face Anna, the person she had dreaded seeing for seventeen years. "Hello, Anna."

Anna looked considerably different from the last time Jewel had seen her. She was X-ray thin, dressed in black to accentuate her pale skin. There was a sharpness to her gaunt face that aged her, although there were no visible wrinkles. Jewel searched Anna's eyes for traces of the girl with whom she had once been friends. But she saw nothing except coldness staring back at her.

Anna offered no greeting. "Jewel and I have met," she said to Cathalene, "when she was known as Madeleine Lathem."

"That was a long time ago," Jewel said, regaining her composure. "A lot has happened since then. As far as I'm concerned, Anna, the past is dead."

"Oh? Perhaps for you, Madeleine," Anna said. "I *use* the past, to remind me of mistakes I never wish to repeat."

"Oh, Anna, it's been years. What's the point?" Jewel said, wishing that Anna would let go of the hostility.

"The point is *never* to forget who's stabbed you in the back, and always to keep your back to the wall when you're around that person."

"But, Anna . . . we were so young. *Nothing's* the same now. Don't you suppose it's time to forgive and forget?" Jewel said coolly.

"Do you think I could *ever* forgive you after what you did? Do you think I could *ever* forget?" Anna hissed. "You're scum, Madeleine—Jewel—whatever the hell your name is." Anna's dark eyes flashed with the same hatred Madeleine had seen that day in Pforzheim. "Come on, Cathalene, my driver's waiting."

Anna turned abruptly and pushed her way through the crowd, with Cathalene tagging behind. Jewel took a deep breath and looked around, trying to locate Edward. Instead, her eyes met Harry's. He was standing a few feet away and had obviously witnessed the scene. He flashed Jewel a grin of delicious enjoyment.

So *that* was what he had insinuated the night before. Harry must have known Anna would be at the show and obviously had been looking forward to the fireworks.

Jewel decided not to allow him the pleasure of her anger. She lit up with a sparkling smile and ran over to him, kissing both his cheeks.

"You did it, darling! The most exciting clothes I've seen in years." She showed him her order card. "Look, I went absolutely berserk."

"I'm glad you liked the show, Jewel," Harry said. And then he put his arm around her shoulders. "You're a good sport, kid. I thought you'd be mad."

"Oh, Harry, I had to run into her sooner or later. Now it's done. She hates me and there's nothing I can do about it. But how the hell did she get to be friends with Cathalene?"

Harry shrugged. "I guess she likes Cathalene's jewelry," he said simply. "And now, if you'll excuse me, I have to go bask in the glory."

"Well, you did good, Harry," she said with forced perkiness. "I'm proud of you."

Jewel's smile vanished the moment she turned away from Harry. Her eyes frantically searched the room for Edward, then spotted him over in the corner. She quickly made her way over to him, avoiding everyone who might engage her in conversation.

"Let's get out of here," she seethed, grabbing Edward away from the young man with whom he was chatting. "Fast!"

After dropping Edward off at the office, Jewel picked up her car at the garage and headed for Connecticut. This weekend, of all times, was the one that the Sheldon Arms School had designated for parents, and Jewel had promised Amber and Beryl that she'd be there.

It was the last thing in the world she wanted to do now. She was livid, all the way up the Taconic Parkway, as she replayed the confrontation with Anna. The nerve of Anna, acting like that after all this time. God, the woman behaved as if Jewel had committed murder. It was so ridiculous to harbor such a deep grudge for so long, Jewel stewed, conveniently forgetting about Sascha and the hatred for him that she still carried with her.

By the time Jewel turned into the oak-lined driveway of the Sheldon Arms School, her head had begun to ache again, badly. What a week it had been. Finding out Allen had a lover, seeing Anna. And now she had to smile and play at being a good mother for the entire weekend.

Sometimes she wished it would all go away. Especially the headaches.

28

The room was blindingly bright, as if illuminated by mammoth movie strobes. Yet the intensity was comforting. Jewel did not feel the need to reach for her sunglasses. But what was she doing there, all alone? And where exactly was she? She couldn't remember.

But she knew she wasn't afraid. She was certain it was a place she had been before . . . there was a slip of memory just eluding her. It would come if she relaxed and thought of something else.

Jewel turned around slowly, but saw nothing except the light, so brilliant, so overwhelming. There was a spot near the center of the room, if indeed this was a room, that began to attract her attention, and she fixed her stare on it. Slowly the color changed, from bright orange to a pale lemon. Then green. Blue. Violet. There it stayed, and the violet light began to bathe more of the room.

Jewel had the feeling that she'd moved, but wasn't aware of moving; she was closer to the center now, the rich purple. She took a deep breath and inhaled the color deeply. Such peace, such exhilaration. The place was *so* familiar. Why couldn't she remember where she was?

She stood transfixed, waiting. For what, she did not know. But some voice, deep from within her, told her she *was* waiting. The violet light covered all now, became more luminous. She stretched out her hands and looked down at her arms. They shimmered with the same color as the room.

A bed appeared. Or had it been there all along? It was not actually a bed, but a rectangular slab that resembled marble, yet gave way to pressure when she touched it. She sat on it, sank into it, and breathed deeply again, beginning to feel sleepy. She lay back on the bed and rested her body. Oh, it felt so good to lie down.

Someone came and put a cover over her. It was not until then that Jewel realized she had been naked. The cover was light, silky. She could see the outline of her body underneath it. The color of the silk seemed to change every time she looked down at it, but that did not concern her.

Now she began to notice that the purple mist was clearing. The light changed suddenly to a warm amber-brown, as if the room had been lighted by invisible candles.

Jewel began to hear voices, although she couldn't distinguish what they were saying. Presently, shapes surrounded the bed. People. She was no longer alone and realized that she never had been, that they had been there all along, but she had chosen not to see them.

Jewel closed her eyes and inhaled deeply, letting the air sink all the way down to her solar plexus. With her eyes closed, she could still see them, feel their soothing presence.

She opened her eyes. They smiled at her, then busied themselves, bathing her with what looked like sponges of bright green light. Sparks, like static electricity, darted out from her skin. Were her eyes open now, or closed? She was not sure.

Jewel moved her mouth to speak, or tried to. No sound came. Then somehow she understood that she could *think* the question and they would understand. At least, it was worth a try.

Where am I? she asked with closed lips.

Forms parted, drifted away. New forms, no, people, drifted in. The room was crowded now. There was warmth from the energy of all the bodies.

You are all right, they all seemed to say at once, many voices melded into one, creating an echo. *You are with us.*

Jewel found the explanation satisfactory. Now she knew where she was. She *had* been there before, perhaps many times. And she felt good, so good, as if her body were being massaged by a thousand hands. *Relax, relax,* they seemed to say. *It is time to rest.*

Jewel sank into the bed, felt her body fall deep inside it, marveling at how she seemed to be able to move into and out of it.

Rest now, the voices said lovingly. *We will stay with you.*

303

Jewel, still not knowing whether her eyes were open or shut, sank into a deep sleep.

There was a dream, or several. She walked along a green meadow dotted with wild flowers, over to the edge of a hill, and looked down. There was a sandy beach below, and a tranquil, aquamarine sea, with huge crystalline boulders rising out of the water. It was so beautiful she took off her sandals and scampered, barefoot, down a sandy dune, across the hot beach, to the cool water. She was completely alone; but perhaps not. In the distance she could hear chanting, many voices joining into one pure note at a time. She sat down in the clear, sunlit water.

And found herself in a garden, the most ornamental she had ever seen. And odoriferous. Thousands of flowers in a palette of colors emitted their individual scents, then joined together into a chorus of fragrance. Jewel ran her hands along the soft green grass, feeling content.

You are very happy? a cheerful voice asked her, out of nowhere.

"Yes, very," she said, this time moving her lips, talking for real.

A man appeared before her. Or was it a woman? She could not distinguish the features. The body was covered by a hooded gray velvet cloak.

It occurred to Jewel to be scared, and she tested herself for fear, but found none. She felt as if she were confronting an old friend.

It is time to talk, the figure said, smiling. *Drink this.* He/she handed her a golden goblet containing a liquid that shimmered with prisms of glittery light.

Jewel accepted the goblet and drank all of the liquid, very thirsty all of a sudden. Refreshed, she sat, waiting. She could not think of questions to ask. There were no questions.

You can't stay here, you know.

"Why not?" Yes, *there* was a question. "I don't want to leave."

I know. But you must go back. You have not finished your stint. He/she laughed. *It won't be so bad. Once you're back, you'll be glad to have the chance to work things out.*

"No. I don't *need* to," Jewel said, amazed by the strength in her voice. "I don't want to."

He/she nodded, understanding. *Of course. But it has been decided. You cannot stay here, dear one, not this time. You are needed back home.*

"No . . . I *am* home," she insisted.

He/she smiled with affection, handing her a jug filled with the sparkling liquid she had drunk from the goblet. *Go and rest now . . . and drink all of this.* He/she handed her a large green emerald, unfaceted, the size of an egg. *Carry this with you. You must heal yourself quickly and get on with it.*

"With what?" Jewel asked. "What do I need to get on with?"

Your life. Your children.

"My children?" Jewel said, suddenly remembering Amber and Beryl. "Oh, yes, I forgot. You're right . . . I must go."

That is what I have been telling you. The being's face glowed radiantly, and he/she hugged her tightly. *Now, be gone with you, dear one.*

Jewel found herself back in the amber-brown room, back among the crowd. This time, though, she noticed that the bed was gone. She was standing amid a sea of smiling faces, being patted on the back, lovingly, as if she had accomplished a good deed or won a race. No one spoke, but she felt the communication of good wishes they were bestowing upon her.

Then she was back in the dazzling yellow light. It was whirling around her. In the distance she heard her friends chanting. She closed her eyes, breathed deeply, and walked into the vortex. *Maddie . . . Madeleine . . . Jewel,* she heard the chorus of voices say, *good luck . . .*

"Jewel?"

"Mummie?"

"Oh, please speak to us! Please get well."

She came out on the other side of the light. There was darkness, a long tunnel of it, then the cold fluorescence of a hospital room which Jewel viewed from above.

There were Allen, Amber and Beryl, Edward, Nushka, all looking terribly grave, all standing around a bed. Her bed. Jewel hovered above them, watching with fascination. Amber moved slightly, and Jewel was startled to see herself, lying there, head bandaged, tubes connected to her arms and throat.

"No!" she called back, changing her mind. "I can't do it. I don't want to!"

But she felt a gentle push from behind.

And then Jewel was immersed in the pain, the shrieking inside her head. The dry mouth. The numbness of her body.

No! she said to herself. *I'm a vegetable. I can't move.*

A distant voice reminded her to drink all the liquid from the jug. She realized that she still had the container and drank from it thirstily, greedily, until the pain disappeared and she could move her limbs again. She clutched the emerald in her left hand.

"Look, Daddy! Her hand moved!" Beryl said excitedly.

Jewel blinked open her eyes. Everything was blurry, but with concentration, she willed her vision to clear.

"Get the doctor, Edward," Allen said.

Jewel saw Amber first. Her oldest daughter's face was streaked with tears, full of love and caring. It had been many years since she had seen such compassion in Amber's face.

Jewel opened her mouth, and again, with great effort, she began to speak.

"I'm here," she croaked hoarsely. "I'm all right . . ."

By then the doctor had arrived and was standing by the bed. He shined a light into each of her eyes, then flicked it off and looked into her face.

"Mrs. Prescott, you scared the hell out of us," he said, smiling. He reached out his hand. "Here, take hold of my hand."

Jewel reached out and grasped the doctor's hand, not as tightly as she had meant to, but slowly her fingers wound around his, and he smiled again.

"Yes," he said, "you're going to be fine."

Jewel lapsed in and out of sleep over the next few days, awakening intermittently, able to engage in limited conversation with Allen, her daughters, and the doctors.

Nushka had been responsible for getting her to the hospital in Waterbury, it turned out, after Jewel's dinner with her daughters during the Sheldon Arms parents' weekend. After Jewel had dropped the girls off at Sheldon Arms and returned home, complaining of a headache, the housekeeper had made Jewel some tea. When she brought it up, she had discovered Jewel collapsed, unconscious, in the bathroom. Without waiting for doctors or an ambulance, the woman summoned the caretaker and they took Jewel, wrapped in blankets, by car to the hospital.

Jewel regained consciousness almost two days after her collapse. Allen had rushed home from London on the Concorde, and Edward had come up from the city to keep vigil at the hospital with Nushka, Beryl, and Amber. What had happened to her, she learned, was a cerebral hemorrhage, resulting from the rupture of an arteriosclerotic vessel. It was a fluke. The headaches she had been suffering stemmed from another cause: hypoglycemia, low blood sugar, that had never been previously diagnosed. One had had nothing to do with the other.

"You're lucky, Mrs. Prescott," the doctor said. "Only a small vessel was involved. Your prognosis is gradual but steady improvement . . . although the permanence and extent of the neurological damage can't be completely predicted for six months."

"But my whole left side is weak," Jewel said raspily. In order to maintain an airway during her coma, they had performed a tracheostomy. Although the tube had now been removed, her throat was still sore.

"It's normal for one side of the body to be affected. To me, it's remarkable that you can move your left side as well as you can. The usual course in your case is severe hemiplegia—paralysis of one side of the body. Your left side is merely weak. With physical therapy, massage, and exercise you'll be back to normal in the optimum time. Another thing to be thankful for, your speech hasn't been affected. A common side effect of a stroke like yours is motor aphasia, which is the inability to speak, or sensory aphasia, an inability to understand words."

"I have a bit of that," Jewel smiled. "But then I always did."

"You sound just fine." The doctor smiled. "Your recovery is nothing short of miraculous. I've never seen anyone heal so fast. You'll be out of here and back home to recuperate in another week. Really, it's quite amazing," he said, heading for the door. "I'll check back in on you later. In the meantime, try to get some exercise. Have your daughters race you up and down the halls a little bit." He laughed, patting Beryl on the shoulder.

The doctor thought Jewel was doing well. She wondered if he'd pronounce her crazy if she told him about the magic healing water and the large green emerald that were still given to her whenever she drifted off into a dream state.

When he was sure she was going to recover, Allen told her that she had been clinically dead for several minutes. Jewel wondered if that was when she had dreamed about the place of blinding light. The dream still seemed so vivid to her; Jewel was beginning to think it hadn't been a dream at all. She *had* gone somewhere. Wherever it was, she knew that the beings there had helped her get home, and they were helping her heal.

But why? That was always the question. Why was she, Jewel Madeleine Dragoumis Prescott, being given a second chance? Why hadn't she died and stayed dead?

In the past she might not have dwelled on the fine existential points of her rapid comeback from death. But Jewel knew, deep inside of her, that the Jewel who awoke from the coma was a far different person from the one who had lapsed into it. She was not sure how she had changed or how the change would manifest itself, but she was positive that some sort of transformation, no matter how subtle, *had* occurred.

"Here, Mummie," Beryl said, coming into Jewel's all-white bedroom with a tray, "Amber and I made you breakfast all by ourselves. Nushka's downstairs baking a pumpkin pie."

Jewel was home at the house in Connecticut the next week, as the doctor promised. Allen had arranged to let the girls stay with her and attend the school as day students, at least until Jewel had recovered enough to return to the city and work.

"Oh my, this looks scrumptious." Jewel smiled, propping herself up in bed to receive the white wicker tray. "And I'm starving. Aren't you going to eat anything?"

"We had breakfast already," Amber said. "We got up early."

Jewel laughed. "Why is it you two bound out of bed on the weekends, and on school days it's all Nushka can do to get you to school before the warning bell?"

"Weekends are more fun," Beryl giggled. "Besides we have a project."

"Shut up!" Amber warned her sister. "It's a secret."

"Aha! Keeping secrets from your old, sick mother. Shame on you."

"You'll know soon enough," Beryl said, as Amber jabbed her in the ribs.

Jewel ate her breakfast slowly. Her left hand and arm were still weak. The fingers worked well enough, but it took great effort for her to raise her left arm even half as high as her right arm. Her left leg was the same. She could walk, using a cane, but the leg dragged a bit. It was difficult for her left side to keep up with the right. The doctor assured her that once physical therapy had begun she would be set to rights within a few months. But Jewel wanted to be well now, not sometime off in the distance.

As she ate her scrambled eggs and butter-drenched English muffin, she chatted with the girls about their studies at school. With her second cup of herbal tea, she felt the need for a cigarette, but they had all been removed. No more smoking, ever. Well, it was a drastic way to quit, having a cerebral hemorrhage, but it achieved the desired effect.

There was a quick rap on the door, and Allen entered, carrying his New York *Times* and a mug of strong black coffee. He went over to the bed and kissed Jewel on the cheek.

"Good morning," he said pleasantly. "I see you're surrounded by your trusty nursing staff."

"I am," she smiled. "They cooked me breakfast and *look* at my plate. I haven't eaten so much in the morning for years. It was delicious, darlings," she said to her daughters, as Amber picked up the tray.

"We have to go now," Beryl said. "We have things to do."

The children retreated, and Allen settled himself in a chair by the window to read his newspaper.

Jewel watched him read, oblivious to her. It was hard to believe they had been married for so many years. Looking at him now, Jewel had the sudden impression that she barely knew him. The people they had been were gone. Who was left now, she wondered?

"Allen," Jewel said after a while, "I think it's time to talk."

Allen looked up from the *Times*. "No, just take it easy. There's nothing that can't wait."

"Yes, there is. I'm feeling much stronger, and there's a lot that needs to be talked about."

Allen folded his paper, looking grave. There were dark circles under his eyes, and Jewel noticed for the first time that he had lost weight. "Okay."

"I want to know about Sara Richards. There's no point in skirting the issue. Are you having an affair with her?" Jewel asked. "Are you in love with her?"

Allen looked away guiltily, then sighed. "Oh shit, Jewel. Yes, we've been seeing each other. And yes, I thought I was in love with her. Then you got sick, and things have changed. I don't know what's going on anymore."

"But you *do* love her?" Jewel pressed.

Allen shook his head. "God, Jewel, I don't know. It's so complicated. Part of me still loves you. But so much has gone out of our marriage. Or maybe I kid myself by pretending things were once there that never were at all." He came over and sat on the bed, then leaned down and buried his head in Jewel's bony chest. "I'm so confused. I don't know what I want. And Sara understands the situation. She's not pressing. She was terribly upset when she heard about you. She insisted we not see each other until . . ."

"Until I'm well?" Jewel snapped. "That's damned nice of her."

"Sara *is* nice, Jewel. She's sweet, and she's easy to be with. We have a lot in common. She's one of the most informed people I've ever known—about art, about many things. But I don't want to throw our twelve years out the window. We have those *years* in common. And I admire you so much, Jewel. You continue to dazzle me with your energy, even now. The doctor told me again how amazed he is by your fast recovery. You *are* a remarkable person."

Allen paused, and Jewel could see the anguish in his face. He was clearly miserable. Jewel released some of the jealousy she harbored and tried to empathize with him.

"Allen, I know I've been hard to live with . . . my obsessive work schedule and everything. But I'm going to try and change that. I know why you fell in love with Sara. I haven't been around for you to share things with, and Sara has. I suppose it was inevitable. If it hadn't been her it would have been someone else." She sighed. "I'm going through a period of self-evaluation. I don't know if I'm going to change drastically. But I know I have to switch around my priorities. I told Isabel once that I'd fight like hell to keep you. But that's changed too. I'm not going to fight. If you stay, it's because you want to stay and I want you to stay. And that . . . we've got to figure out for ourselves."

"I've never heard you talk like this." Allen took Jewel's hand and held it tightly. "What about Mike Marshall? Do you love him?"

Jewel was caught off guard. How had Allen found out about Mike? "No," Jewel said. "We had fun for a while. It was a diversion. He *wanted* me so much. It was flattering . . . and, let's face it, you and I have never burned down buildings with our lovemaking. It's been comfortable, but you're often preoccupied."

"I'm not the only one," Allen bristled.

"I know, I know. And it's probably what happens in all marriages. There's no way to sustain the passion. That's why it's best to marry a friend . . . because when all's said and done you still have a friend," Jewel said. "What we have to decide, the two of us, is if our friendship's strong enough to keep us going."

They sat in silence for a few minutes, listening to the sounds of chickadees chirping at the bird feeder outside the window. "I don't know what to think anymore," Allen said finally.

"Neither do I," she sighed. "And there's something else that's been on my mind . . . on a different subject. Oh hell, I want a cigarette," she complained.

Allen picked up her smoking hand and kissed it. "Would you like me to get you some candy? Some sort of oral substitute?"

"If I reached for a bonbon every time I wanted a cigarette I'd weigh three hundred and fifty by the end of the year," she laughed bitterly. "No, it's going to be cold turkey for me—hold the bread and mayo." She reached over and ran the fingers of her right hand, her good hand, through his hair. "The other thing we need to talk about is . . . Sascha."

"Sascha?"

Jewel nodded. "He's popped into my mind a lot lately. I've begun to feel guilty that the girls don't know. I've been thinking about telling them. But I want to know how you feel about it, as their legal father."

"I can tell you right away. I think the girls should be told; I always have. Edward and I have discussed it at length. We even thought about telling them behind your back, but we couldn't. It's always been up to you, and you've been so adamantly against it. Tell me, what made you change your mind?"

Jewel shook her head. "I don't know really. Yesterday I was flipping though *Vogue,* and there was a Tiffany ad for one of Sascha's necklaces. It was really beautiful—chunky gold with black baroque pearls. It flashed me back to when we were together, back on Spring Street. I started thinking about him, about us, about how it ended. Hell, I started crying," she said, tears welling up again. "I don't know. Coming so close to death, you look at life differently. Maybe I just stopped hating him, all of a sudden, after all these years."

"Maybe so," Allen said. "And I'm glad. The girls need to know the truth. It'll be hard at first, but they'll adjust. We'll all adjust. When do you want to tell them?"

"Sometime after you've retrieved a photo album from the safe deposit box for me. It has pictures of them with him. That way they'll believe me."

"Would you like me to help you?"

"No thanks," Jewel said, "this is something I need to do on my own."

"I'm proud of you, darling," he said. "Really proud. And Edward will be happy. He and Sascha have become quite friendly over the past few years."

"Yes, I guessed as much." Jewel yawned. "Oh my, I think it's time for my mid-morning nap. I'm reeling from all this . . . I need my strength back."

"I'll do anything I can to help. I still care about you, darling. Enormously."

Jewel took his hand. "Thank you, Allen. I care about you too. I really do."

"Oh, Jewel. It's been years since we've talked like this. What happened to us?"

Jewel shrugged. "I guess it's the pitfall of a long marriage. We went our separate ways, then came home, slept in the same bed and called it a compatible life. It's been compatible. The question is, has it been a life?"

"Yes . . . it has." He leaned over and kissed her. "Okay, take your nap." He headed for the door, then stopped. "You never cease to amaze me. As infuriating as you've sometimes been over the years, you've never been dull."

Jewel smiled. "Thank you—if you meant it as a compliment."

"I did," Allen said, "I did."

29

Edward drove up to Connecticut in his new BMW, to spend Sunday with Jewel and his second family. After picking apples in the orchard with Beryl and Amber, they all sat down to an old-fashioned, middle-of-the-day Sunday meal that Nushka had prepared—roast chicken with gravy, mashed potatoes, corn, and salad, followed by apple crisp with vanilla ice cream.

"That was delicious," Edward said afterward. "But we should have waited to take our walk *after* lunch. Now we really need the exercise."

"I'm all for taking a little stroll," Jewel said. "If you don't mind a slow one."

Allen leaned back in his chair and stretched his arms up over his head. "Not me. The only walk I'm taking is into the library to turn on the TV. The Giants are playing Dallas today." He was a big Giants fan.

"What about you, girls? Did you finish your homework?" Jewel asked.

"No," Amber said sullenly, huffing off from the table. At fifteen, she was still going through the hormonal changes of adolescence. Now that Jewel was out of danger and recovering, Amber had, for the most part, reverted back to her old sulkiness.

"I did," Beryl said. At fourteen, she was having an easy adolescence. "But I have something else to do."

Jewel smiled. "Then it looks as if it's just us."

Jewel bundled up in a red-dyed beaver and wound a large scarf around her head and neck. They headed in the direction of a newly cleared field over to the right of the house.

"There was a plan," Jewel said quietly. "Allen was going to plant seven-year-old grapevines, right over there, in the spring. To try his luck starting a vineyard. But now, I don't know. I try to gaze into the crystal ball and it's totally clouded over." She grabbed Edward's hand, for balance. "Shit, Allen's in love with that art groupie, Sara Richards."

Edward nodded. "I didn't know for sure, but . . ." he trailed off. "How do *you* feel about it, darlin'? I mean, you and Allen have been goin' your own ways for years . . . but underneath it all I always thought you were a good couple. Allen really loves you."

"I'm not so sure, although I could probably get him to again if I really wanted," Jewel said. "I *know* how to play the game right. Trouble is, I don't know *what* I want anymore. I don't know whether I've ever loved Allen, but I like him. And we *have* built a rather impressive life together."

Jewel took a deep breath and expelled it slowly into the icy air. "Oh, Edward, there's this pressure on me. It's something new. But I feel that I've survived this damned stroke for a reason, and what the hell it is, I can't figure out." She reached out and put her arms around him. "Oh, give me a hug," and after he did, she said, "do you ever feel like you're just walking through it all, observing the goings on, but never participating? That's how I've felt for years now . . . and I let my impatient, driven, perfectionist, bitchy side take over, because at least getting angry at people made me *feel* something. Now I don't feel anger anymore . . . but I don't know what's going to take its place."

"Jewel," Edward sighed, "I think the best thing for you to do now is get well. Get your strength back. Then it'll start sortin' itself out— what you want, what Allen wants."

"Yes, I suppose."

Edward gazed out at the field, then looked back at her. "Jewel, darlin', there's somethin' we have to talk about . . . and unfortunately it can't wait." He guided her over to a fallen tree stump. "Let's sit down here."

"Oh no. What's wrong now?" she asked, looking at his grim face.

"Look," Edward sighed, "I wish it could wait till you're stronger."

"I'm strong as a racehorse already. One that's gone a little lame, I'll admit. But I'm starting physical therapy next week, and I plan to hit the office again as soon as possible."

"Well," Edward started, looking ill at ease. His cheeks and nose had turned red in the bracing November cold. "A lot has been goin' on the past few months. Behind your back. I've only recently been brought into it myself. Then everything came to a head after you got sick. People were speculatin' that you wouldn't pull through and, if you did, that you wouldn't be well enough to run Bijoux."

"I see," Jewel said, feeling a chill run down her back, a chill not brought on by the November day.

"Cathalene's brought Neil Tavlos over to her camp, offered him a chunk of the business for some major-growth financin'. She and Anna have decided it'd be easier to deplete our operation, rather than havin' Cathalene start from scratch in her expansion plans."

"Wait. What do you mean?" Jewel interrupted. "She and *Anna?*"

"That's the other thing I found out," Edward said. "Anna Ferguson's the secret partner who came up with the money for Cathalene to go out on her own."

Jewel listened, stunned. But of course it made sense. Anna and Cathalene had been together at Harry's show. And Anna would go to *any* length to ruin her, she now realized.

"Why the hell didn't I figure it out before?" Jewel said. "Now Anna must be rubbing her hands with glee at the idea of getting back at me."

Edward nodded. "And they're workin' fast, now that you're benched on the sidelines. Cathalene's been wooin' Rody and Tom, Leilani, Rita, Erik Sanders, Mike Marshall—hell, she's offerin' them anything they want to defect. She's even tryin' to raid Tiffany—Sascha especially, because she knows how much you detest him."

"How the hell did Cathalene find *that* out?" Jewel asked. "I *never* told her about Sascha. God, that bitch!"

Edward bit his lip nervously. "I'm afraid she found out about Sascha from me."

"What? I *swore* you to secrecy!"

"I know. And I'm sorry. But, as you admitted, you've been pretty much of a bitch these last few years. There've been times when I've been completely fed up with you. Cathalene always seemed to sniff out those moments. We'd go out to lunch, and she'd be so sympa-

315

thetic, so easy to talk to. We'd have a few glasses of wine . . . I didn't tell her on purpose. It just sort of slipped out. Really, darlin', I'm so sorry."

"Oh, it's okay," Jewel said, miffed, but trying not to get upset. "Let's not dwell on it. I want to hear more about the mutiny. What about *you?* Has Cathalene . . . ?"

Edward nodded. "Of course. And I must admit I was tempted, for about fifteen minutes. But when you got sick I had a lot of time to think about it all, sittin' in the hospital. About you. About us. I've been harborin' a lot of resentment. You've been difficult and aloof, these last few years. You think if you pay people enough you can treat them like shit. But you can't, Jewel. People will take *less* to be treated decently. With politeness and courtesy."

"I never treated anyone differently from myself. I work hard . . . I expect others to," Jewel said, slipping her left hand up into the right sleeve of her coat, to alleviate the numbness.

"Yes, that's the point, darlin'. You *are* driven. I know you brought this all on yourself . . . the hemorrhage. After years of bein' so hard on others, so hard on yourself, even *you* couldn't take it anymore."

"The doctor said the hemorrhage had nothing to do with *any-thing,*" Jewel sniffed.

"Maybe not," Edward shrugged. "Anyway . . . I'm sorry to have to lay this all on you now. But we have a major problem here that won't go away."

"Until Cathalene has destroyed Bijoux? Well, over my dead body! I'd rather have another hemorrhage and die than let her and Anna walk in and take over everything I've worked so hard for."

Edward put his arm around his friend. "Calm down. I didn't want to upset you. I just thought you had to know what's goin' on."

"Oh, Edward, what have I done?" Jewel began to cry softly. "Shit, I've ruined everything. *I* did it. I created it and I ruined it! There's going to be nothing left. And there's no point in even trying to blame Cathalene and Anna . . ."

"Now, now, darlin', you don't have to go *that* far. Your crime is bein' hard on yourself and the people around you. But Cathalene *uses* people: me, Harry . . ."

"Harry?" Jewel interrupted, wiping her eyes with Edward's hand-kerchief. "What do you mean?"

"Well, I've gone this far, I may as well give you the rest. Cathalene thought that you and Harry were havin' an affair. She used to have lunch with him too, from time to time. I think she wanted him, but he wanted you. He couldn't admit to her that you wouldn't go to bed with him, so he lied. Told her you two *were* havin' an affair. That made her even madder. I mean, darlin', Cathalene has a real love-hate relationship goin' with you. She's jealous of you, of your life. In her eyes, you have everything: all the glory, all the men, all the money. And you took her for granted."

"No, I *never* took her for granted!" Jewel snapped. "I always knew where she was coming from . . . she isn't very subtle. My real mistake was not firing her years before she left with all my secrets," Jewel said breathlessly. "But back to Harry . . . how did she use *him?*"

"He was how she got to Anna," Edward explained, putting an arm around Jewel. "It seems that Anna and Vivian got sort of friendly after Harry bought the big estate in Greenwich. They ran into Harry and Cathalene, all havin' lunch at Mortimer's one day. Vivian and Anna went to their own table . . . and Harry mentioned that Anna had it in for you. Well, that's all Cathalene needed. The rest is history."

Jewel shook her head. "God, you try so hard to bury your past and it all comes bubbling up from the ground like toxic waste . . . when you're least prepared. Hell, it would've been so much easier if I'd died. Then I wouldn't have to deal with all this shit," she uttered a wry laugh. "Amber has a T-shirt that says, 'Life's a bitch and then you die.' I'd like one that says, 'Life's a bitch, but it won't go away.' "

Edward smiled. "Come on . . . it's not so terrible. I'm not goin' to desert you. We'll win. If you're willin' to loosen up."

"Oh, I'm willing, I guess. But you can't change lifetime habits overnight."

"They're not lifetime habits," Edward said. "You were sweet and vulnerable when I met you. You've toughened up, but underneath the old Jewel's still there. I know . . . I've seen her from time to time. I mean, you haven't been *relentlessly* bitchy."

"Well, that's *something,* I suppose. Look, darling, thank you for leveling with me, and for hanging in there, even when it's been hard to be my friend. You may be out of a job by siding with me and not Cathalene."

"There never was a choice really. As angry as you've made me from time to time, I could never defect. We're a team. We always have been, always will be."

Allen spent the next week in the city, leaving Jewel time alone to think. The following Saturday she arose early, after a fitful night's sleep. She showered and dressed as quickly as she could with her weak left arm. She had put off telling the girls about Sascha. Now it had to be done. Jewel was dreading it more than she thought possible.

After a short walk outside, to clear her head in the freezing dawn air, she made herself a cup of peppermint tea and took it into the library. Shivering, she turned up the thermostat, went to the desk drawer and got out the photo album of Sascha with the girls that Allen had sent up from the safe deposit box in New York. She settled herself on the sofa, with the brown leather album in her lap.

Jewel had not looked at it for fourteen years. She wished she didn't have to now, but it was too late to chicken out.

Slowly, Jewel's right hand opened the leather album and, with all the trepidation of a gladiator preparing to face a pack of lions, she looked down at the page. The first picture, an eight-by-ten blow-up, had been taken with Sascha's camera by a nurse at the hospital. There she was, with Sascha, and twelve-hour-old Amber.

She didn't know what Sascha looked like these days, but Jewel was struck by how young she appeared. Her hair color had changed with such regularity over the past decade, after the first strand of gray appeared, that Jewel had practically forgotten what shade it had been. But there she was, with long, flowing brown hair, quite pretty actually. Maybe Edward was right. Maybe she had been sweet then.

Amber was so tiny, so angelic. It brought tears to Jewel's eyes as she remembered that day, the day of her elder daughter's birth, so many years ago. And then she allowed her gaze to wander over to Sascha's face. There he was, her burly, bearded Russian bear, with those pale eyes that had caught her in the beginning. In the picture, those eyes were focused on her. And there was such love in them.

The door suddenly burst open, and Amber and Beryl bounced into the library, wearing nightshirts and knee socks and fuzzy bear slippers. "Oh, here you are! We looked in your room but you were already up. We'd planned to make you breakfast in bed. We have a surprise for you."

Jewel closed the album quickly and smiled. "Good morning. You're both up early."

"What's that?" Beryl asked, pointing to the album.

"Oh, I'll show you in a bit."

"Can we give you your surprise now? Before breakfast?"

"Of course," Jewel said. Anything to put off telling them.

The girls rushed off and were back within minutes, carrying a large tray with a towel draped over something about a foot high and even wider.

"Close your eyes," Beryl ordered.

Jewel obliged.

"Okay, you can open now," Amber said.

Jewel opened her eyes to see, sitting on the coffee table before her, a gingerbread house, done as a replica of the very house they were living in, adorned with fantasy touches, of course, such as candy and feathers and miniature silk flowers.

"Oh my! This is fabulous! Is this what all the secretiveness has been about the past couple of weeks?" She held out her good arm, and the girls sat beside her. "I love it . . . thank you. You did such a great job."

"We showed it to Edward last week. And he said it'd be perfect for Bijoux's side-window Christmas decoration."

"Oh, it would. With jewelry draped all around it. I'll take it into the city tomorrow."

Beryl sighed. "I wish you wouldn't go so soon. Do you really think you're well enough?"

"I've got to work at getting better . . . start that physical therapy so I won't keep tripping every time I walk across a room."

"Do you really like the gingerbread house?" Amber asked.

"Oh, yes. I can't imagine how you did it. Look at all the detail."

"It took a long time," Beryl said, "but we had fun."

"Well, it's just perfect. Thank you again." Jewel took a deep breath. "Look, I have to talk to you two. About something serious that I've never told you before."

"What?" the girls both said, puzzled by the grave expression on Jewel's face.

"Well," Jewel bit the bullet, "it's . . . about your father."

"Oh no," Beryl cried. "Is something wrong?"

Jewel shook her head. "No. Allen's fine. I mean your *real* father.

You see, Allen adopted you when you were babies . . ." She opened the photo album. "Your real father is this man, Sascha Robinovsky."

Jewel heard her voice recounting the story, the story she had pushed to the back of her mind all these years. The girls sat still, listening, as she told them how she had met Sascha and fallen in love with him and, finally, how his real wife from Russia had appeared one day, with three other children. And how she had hated Sascha since then.

"I know it was a mistake not to tell you sooner," she said. "Sometimes I'd think about it and decide you were still too young to know. Then, later, it was easier not to tell you. Allen's been as much of a father as any man could be. He loves you, he's supported you."

"Where is Sascha now?" Beryl asked softly, obviously in shock.

"In New York. He designs for Tiffany . . ."

"Sascha Robinovsky!" Amber said, making a connection. "I know his work. I saw an article recently that the *Times* did on all the Tiffany designers. I can't believe it," she said, the news beginning to sink in. "All these years we've had another father—a *real* father—and *you* didn't tell us."

"Allen's been like a real father! Look, I know I was wrong. But Sascha hurt me more than you can imagine. I know I made a bad decision. But you spend your life making decisions. Some turn out good, some don't. But you live with them."

"But you *lied* to us!" Amber cried.

"I told you, I had my reasons. *Please* try and understand," Jewel pleaded. "I was very bitter . . . and hurt."

"Well, you hurt us!" Amber said. "How *could* you? No matter how you felt . . . we had a *right* to know. My God, I'm almost sixteen years old!" She flung out her leg and kicked the gingerbread house off the low table, then she stood up and crushed it under her foot.

"No!" Beryl screamed. "No, Amber! Don't ruin it! Please, *please* . . ." She burst into tears.

It was too late. The gingerbread, candy, feathers, icing, and tiny flowers collapsed into mounds of crumbs and debris on the Oriental carpet. Amber gave the tray a swift kick across the room, and it landed in the fireplace.

"I hate you, Mother!" she said. "I hate you as much as you hated Sascha! And if he's my father, then I'm going to live with him! I *never* want to see you again!" She stormed out of the room.

Beryl's sobs were reaching hysteria, and she flung herself into her mother's arms, spilling out an indistinguishable barrage of words.

Jewel hugged her younger daughter and tried to soothe her, in shock herself from the vehemence of Amber's reaction. She had known this would be hard for them to take, but she never imagined it would be this bad.

Nushka appeared in the doorway in her robe, awakened by the noise. "Oh dear, what's wrong?" she asked.

"You name it," Jewel said. "And it's all Sascha's fault." She sighed, patting Beryl's head. "No. Cancel that. It's all my fault. I've made a fucking mess out of everything."

30

Jewel returned to New York to begin her therapy, and Allen announced that any major decision concerning their marriage would
not be made in haste. He and Jewel, for now, would continue living
together. He would not see Sara, nor would she see Mike Marshall,
which suited her fine.

Allen hired a chauffeur to take Jewel around town. In the past, she
had preferred taking cabs or, on sunny days, walking down Fifth
Avenue to the office. But until she improved, walking to Bijoux was
out of the question.

"At my speed," she told Allen, "I'll get there just as everyone else is
leaving for the day."

Jewel was conscientious about her physical therapy, and even
bought two portable running tracks, one for the bedroom at home
and one to be delivered to her office. She could not yet run, but after
a week of therapy, she was walking with less of a shuffle. She was
determined to get as strong as possible before she returned to work.

If she hadn't heard from Edward about the rumblings of mass
defection at Bijoux she'd have had no inkling at all. The apartment
was filled with flowers and well-wishing notes from her employees.
She spoke with Meg every day, and her assistant gave no hint of
unrest. Perhaps Edward had been exaggerating. Or perhaps they
had merely decided not to kick her while she was down.

She would find out the truth soon enough.

The car pulled around the corner onto Sixty-eighth Street, and the chauffeur stopped in front of the therapists' offices. He came around and opened the door for Jewel.

"I can take it from here, John. Pick me up at one-thirty, please."

"Yes, ma'am," the chauffeur replied.

Jewel walked slowly to the doorway, with her cane hooked jauntily over her arm, and headed in.

"Oh, hello, Mrs. Prescott," the receptionist said. "We're running a few minutes late. Take a seat. Can I get you anything—a cup of coffee?"

"No, thanks. I think I'll get changed and do some walking around the track."

Jewel's hand was on the door that led to the gym and changing rooms when she heard a man's voice, behind her.

"Madeleine?"

It was Wyatt's voice. She turned, saying, "We keep running into each . . ." But she trailed off. It was not Wyatt McNeill.

It was Hadley.

He looked older, handsomer. Same dark brown hair, cut a bit shorter. Same dark eyes, a bit more intense. Same cheekbones, more chiseled than ever. He was dressed in faded jeans, a black turtleneck, and a down parka, looking as if he'd walked straight in from a ski slope. A pair of crutches were propped on the armrest beside him.

Jewel stared at him, stunned. "Hadley! I can't believe it. How did you recognize me? I look completely different."

"I recognized your voice first, but you haven't changed so much. Different color hair. But you're still recognizable—and beautiful."

"Except for this," she said, indicating her cane. "But what happened to you? A skiing accident?"

He shook his head. "I was riding a bus around some back roads of India. Up in the mountains near Bhutan. Hairpin turns and all that. Another bus rounded a corner into us. We went over a cliff and landed in a deep ravine. A lot of us—those who lived—were thrown from the bus. A lot of *them* walked away from the accident. But my legs got pinned under. That was two years ago. I've been in hospitals in Darjeeling and London since then. They told me I'd never walk again, but I've gotten this far . . ." he trailed off. "God, it's good to see you again. What happened to you?"

"A cerebral hemorrhage . . . stroke."

"Good Lord," Hadley said. "When?"

"Six weeks ago."

"Madeleine, I'm sorry." He shook his head with disbelief. "But you look as if you're coming along fine."

"Not as fast as I'd like," she said.

He nodded, understanding. "I take it you're married. I heard the Mrs. Prescott."

Jewel was amazed that Hadley knew nothing about her life now. Hadn't Wyatt or Anna told him *anything?* "Yes, for years now. I have two teenage daughters. What about you?"

Hadley shrugged. "Remember I told you I'd never get married. I haven't, although I lived with a woman for nine years. She worked for CARE, same as me."

"What are you doing now?"

"Healing," Hadley said with a wry grin. "That's been taking up all of my time."

"I'm really sorry, Hadley. What an awful thing to happen."

"Oh, things haven't been bad, at least not until the accident. I was really happy in India—doing something that was making a difference. You know me," he grinned.

They hadn't seen each other for so many years, yet it was almost as if they hadn't missed a beat. "Oh, Hadley, I'd love to talk to you."

"Jewel?" Linda, the therapist, appeared in the doorway. "I'm ready for you now."

"Jewel?" Hadley repeated.

"Yes, that's my name now. It's, er, a long story."

"Look, I'm leaving for Honolulu tonight. I'm going to see a kahuna . . . a healer. When I get back, I'll call you. I'd like to get together with you, catch up. There's a lot to talk about."

"Yes, there is." Jewel reached into her purse for a business card and handed it to him. "Well, so long. It's been . . ."

" . . . wonderful to see you again," he said, picking up her sentence.

Jewel replayed the coincidental meeting with Hadley in her mind for the next few days, but there was little time to focus on the possibility of their next encounter, if there was ever going to be one. Although he had seemed pleased to see her, there was a good chance, after what had happened in the past, that he would want to leave it at that.

After six weeks of convalescense it was time to return to work, and most of Jewel's time was now spent fretting over what was going to happen at Bijoux International. Jewel thought endlessly about each of her employees, analyzing their strengths and weaknesses. She considered the pros and cons of what would happen to Bijoux if, as Edward expected, many of them jumped ship to work for Cathalene.

Of course, there were many talented people out there in the marketplace. She and Edward could rebuild Bijoux, and it would not be starting from scratch. The reputation they had earned over the years would not disappear—after all, *she* was Bijoux. But it would hurt; it would be a major setback. A lot of momentum would be lost, not to mention money.

Sometimes Jewel looked around her incredibly beautiful penthouse and thought, why *not* enjoy it? She didn't have to work anymore. She could pack it in and devote herself to charity.

A few weeks earlier, when Edward had first warned her about the possible mass defection, she had—momentarily, at least—considered giving up. But that wasn't why she had returned from the grave, as she now jokingly liked to put it. She was going to fight. She—meaning the *new* Jewel—wasn't going to sit back and watch it happen.

And the old Jewel, the survivor, wasn't either.

The Sunday night before Jewel was to return to Bijoux, she telephoned Edward.

"Well, darlin', tomorrow's the big day. Are you excited?" Edward asked.

"No, nervous as hell. I can almost hear people whispering behind my back. I'm so paranoid I can even imagine Cathalene sticking pins in a voodoo doll shaped like me."

"Ah, the old Jewel returns," Edward laughed.

"No, not completely," she said seriously. "You don't go through something like this and come out the same. I'm really trying to change. You know, new approaches to old problems—and God, I have a lot of them. Anyway, I know we have to have a meeting with everyone, get it all out in the open. But I'd like to ease back in for a few days. Do you think you can stall them off from the big showdown . . . at least till the end of the week?"

"It won't be easy. But I'll manage it."

"Thanks, love. And now the real reason I called. Did Sascha go to Connecticut to see the kids today?" Jewel asked. "Have you spoken with him?"

"Yes. He just called. They had a nice enough time. It was awkward, as you might imagine. They have to get to know each other."

"Did Amber ask to live with him? Did he say she could?"

"I doubt it," Edward said. "Sascha didn't mention it."

"Well, I'll quiz Beryl when I call. At least *she's* still speaking to me."

"Amber will come around," Edward assured her. "She's stubborn, like you. And fifteen's a difficult age. Give her time. She loves you very much. You should have seen her in the hospital when you were still unconscious. I think she took it harder than any of us."

"Well, I wish there was something I could say to her. But she won't get on the phone when I call. And all last weekend she stayed in her room to avoid me."

"Maybe Sascha could help," Edward suggested. "Look, he really wants to talk to you . . . to *see* you."

"No! I told you . . ."

"Jewel," Edward said firmly, "you've come this far. Why don't you take the extra step? Clear out the cobwebs once and for all. I think you both need it."

"Oh hell, Edward, I don't want to."

"You have to. For more reasons than one," Edward said simply.

"Oh shit. All right. Tell him he can come see me at the office. He can call Meg for an appointment."

"I think you should call him."

"No! Don't push me, Edward."

"Okay," Edward sighed. "I'll set it up."

Jewel's return to Bijoux was more emotional than she had expected. Everyone gathered in her office when she arrived, and there were vases of coral roses, her favorite shade, on every table. On her desk was a long, slender, rectangular box, gift wrapped and accompanied by a card signed by everyone.

"A present? You didn't have to. What is it?" Jewel picked up the box and shook it.

"Why is it," Mike Marshall asked, "that people always do that instead of opening it?"

"Oh, I'll open it, don't worry," Jewel smiled. Over the past weeks of convalescence, she had managed to gain five pounds. Although she was still very thin, the extra weight had softened her face, taking away the sharpness of the angles. There was a softness around the eyes too, and in the way she looked at people—as if she were seeing them directly now, and not through the prism of work. Everyone remarked later that Jewel looked more beautiful than ever. No one could pinpoint why.

Jewel tore the wrapping paper off her gift and found an antique black ebony walking stick with a scrolled, sterling silver head. "This is beautiful," Jewel said, tears in her eyes. "Really, I can't thank you enough. When I've finished needing it, I'll hang it on the wall above the desk. So I can beat people when I need to," she joked, hoping they would take it as such.

The impromptu party ended with individual hugs and "welcome backs" for Jewel. But she could feel eyes avoiding hers, and she knew that, despite the show of affection, this was merely the still before the tornado.

Mike Marshall lingered behind, looking as nervous as the others. "Can we talk, Jewel?"

"Yes," she smiled. "We need to. Have a seat. First, thanks again for the baskets of flowers you kept sending. They were lovely. And Edward brought over the mock-up for the spring catalog. It's fabulous. I love the idea of covering the models with muslin so you can't quite see their features, only the jewelry against the outline of their bodies. It's absolutely inspired."

"Really? I was afraid you'd hate it. It's very surreal," Mike said.

"Well, I love it. I don't think I've let you use your own vision enough in the past. I've had a hard time letting go of all the details. But that's going to change."

"Look, Jewel—"

"I don't want to talk about Cathalene and all that . . . not yet," she said. "I do want to talk about us."

Mike crossed his legs, then uncrossed them, obviously uncomfortable. "You know I'm happy to see you again. You look really wonderful."

"Thanks, Mike." Jewel picked up a glass paperweight that Beryl had made, a collage of bird pictures, and toyed with it while she talked. "Mike, I told you I couldn't see you for a while, because of Allen. Well, it's more than that. We've been, *I've* been going through the motions for a long time. You liked me so much that I was afraid you'd quit Bijoux if we ended the affair. Oh, Mike, we had some wonderful times. But there's no future in it. You know that."

"I finally figured it out," he said. "You stopped having time for me. Is there someone else?"

"No." She went over and gently closed the door to her office. "I know you've been seeing Meg. She told me she's crazy about you, and I think you're perfectly matched. But I want to know if you're serious, or—"

"I, er, may be serious," Mike said. "Does that upset you? That I was seeing her?"

Jewel shook her head. "On the contrary. I want you to be happy." She glanced at the clock on her wall. "Oh dear, I have an appointment with Erik. He wants to show me the hiddenite that the gem cutters have just finished faceting."

Mike rose and came over behind Jewel's desk and kissed the top of her head. "Welcome back," he said. "We missed you."

The rest of Jewel's day flew by, with a succession of meetings. In each one, she tried to make contact, not gloss over what the person was saying, but listen and consider. It wasn't as hard as she had imagined it would be, quite relaxing actually. Jewel realized what a good job she and Edward had done in assembling their staff.

Edward had told her, in a brief huddle that afternoon, that Cathalene was pressing people for answers. She wanted to get everyone out before Jewel could change their minds. Not that she was entirely certain, Jewel admitted to herself, that she *could* change their minds. But Cathalene Columbier would get them over her dead body.

31

There were major fish to fry. Major fish; and Jewel had dressed for the occasion.

Even though the first fish was to be handled over the telephone, Jewel understood as well as anybody the importance of the right look to complement the frame of mind. And so she had selected, with the precision of a surgeon choosing her scalpels, a short black skirt and sweater, with a fitted deep pink jacket on top. Harry Harper, of course. The first fish demanded it.

"Morning, Jewel," Meg Higdon smiled as Jewel came in. "You're looking great."

"Thanks," Jewel said. "Get me Harry Harper on the phone, will you?"

"Sure thing," Meg said brightly.

In her office, Jewel put down her briefcase on her desk and opened the lock. She took out her appointment calendar and ran over the day. If she could get through this one, she was on her way, no doubt about it. She turned and checked her appearance in the mirror in the corner.

Meg buzzed. "I've got Harry Harper on line one."

"Put him through."

"Hi, love! Welcome back to the arena," Harry said, his voice full of enthusiasm. "Are you calling to take me to lunch?"

"Hardly," Jewel said coolly. "I'm calling to give you a piece of my mind."

"Oh? What have I done now?"

"Anna Ferguson, Harry. Ring a bell? Anna and Cathalene. Danger-ous elements to mix. Especially dangerous for an old friend. Jesus, how *could* you? The two people in the world who have it most in for me and you put them together! Smart, Harry. Thank you very much."

There was split-second silence on Harry's end. "Look, this is *old* news. All right, I'm sorry. Why get so pissy about it now?"

"It may be old news to you . . . Oh, look, I'll admit I *should* have figured it out for myself. I assumed Anna and Cathalene had met each other in some random way. I forgot we had Machiavelli Harper looming around on the sidelines, looking for trouble to stir up."

"Oh hell, Jewel, it just happened. Okay, I shouldn't have. But damnit, you don't appreciate me anymore. I thought you needed a little comeuppance."

"A little *comeuppance!?* That's what you call trying to ruin every-thing I've worked for all these years?" Jewel shrieked into the re-ceiver. "Don't you know what they're trying to *do* to me?"

"Look, baby," Harry sighed, "it all got out of hand. I had no idea it'd get this far. But then I didn't know how disgruntled your people over there were either, till I talked to Edward. I'll do what I can. But look to yourself a bit too, Jewel. You know the old saying, you can't break up a happy marriage."

"Oh, great," Jewel seethed; not least because the arrow had hit home. "A lecture. From Harry Harper."

"Dammit, Jewel," Harry snapped, "don't forget I've done a hell of a lot for you over the years. All right, this was a mistake, but—"

"*Mistake?* If I go down the tubes, Harry, that's some mistake! You've done a lot for me? *I've* done a lot for you too, you bastard! I've returned plenty of favors over the years. Jesus, I thought that was what friends were for!"

There was a long silence, and for a moment Jewel thought he might have hung up on her. Then his voice came back over the wire. "Look, Jewel, it was a rotten thing to do. Believe me when I say I didn't mean any real harm. You're right, I wanted to stir things up. I thought it'd be amusing to watch you gals pulling each other's hair a bit. What can I say? When I fuck up, I fuck up. I want to try to make it up to you. I'll do what I can."

"I think you're too late with too little," Jewel said sarcastically.

"Look, I'm heading out to Wyoming tomorrow. Let me take you to lunch when I get back. Thursday okay?"

"Hell, Harry . . ."

"Say yes. Come on, Jewel. I'll grovel."

Jewel found herself smiling, in spite of herself. "Oh, all right. If you promise to grovel a lot."

"I'll prostrate myself." A note of cheer came back into Harry's voice. "Hey, you're going to pull through, love. I'm not worried a bit."

"Thanks, Harry," she relented. "I certainly am."

That fish taken care of, Jewel glanced at her watch. It was shortly before eleven. She could feel her stomach muscles tightening as the clock hummed on.

Edward had not shown up. He had promised to be in her office by quarter to. She rang his private extension; he was not there. She paced, tried again. Finally she buzzed Meg.

"Where's Edward? He was supposed to be here by now."

"He's out at a meeting, I think. I'll check."

"Oh God, he's *supposed* to be here. What time do you have?"

"Eleven," Meg said. "And your eleven o'clock has just arrived. Mr. Robinovsky. Shall I send him in?"

Sascha. Right on the other side of that door. Suddenly Jewel didn't think she could do it. Where the hell was Edward?

Then she realized that Edward must have planned it this way. She was going to have to deal with Sascha on her own.

"All right, Meg," Jewel said, making her voice sound as steady as she could manage. "Send him in."

The door swung open and fifteen years vanished, melted away, in a split second. Sascha had changed, but he didn't look a day older. The largeness of him, which could have gone to fat, was all muscle now. His bushy hair was still shoulder-length, but the beard was gone. The face was more defined. And there were those eyes, the paleness now shining out from behind tortoiseshell-rimmed glasses.

For an instant neither spoke as they took each other in. Sascha strode midway into the room and stopped, awkwardly. Jewel got up from her desk and walked over to him carefully, so as not to let her weak leg betray her. She extended her hand to shake his, but instead of offering his hand in return, Sascha lunged forward, flinging his arms around her and kissing her hard on both cheeks.

"My Jewel," he said, his eyes scanning every part of her. "Since when did you get such bright red hair?"

That broke the ice. Jewel couldn't help but smile. If she were still with Sascha, he never would have let her do it. He would have insisted she grow old gracefully. But maybe not; he certainly had not aged. "Since about four months ago. Before that I was blond."

"You look different, so beautiful."

"You look good too, Sascha. You're all toned and fit." She showed him to a plush sofa by the corner windows and sat down next to him.

"I work out," he said. "Run five, eight miles every day. I was getting fat." Sascha smiled and put out his arms to indicate an enormous belly. "All day, I sit and work, sit and work. And Aïna only knows how to raise children and cook. Too much heavy food. Finally, I sent her to Weight Watchers and I joined a gym. I work out instead of eating a big lunch. I look better than when we were together, don't I?"

Jewel grinned, relaxing more. Although Sascha's English was perfect now, he still had the old accent, and she remembered how much she loved it. "You look great—but not better. You looked pretty good then too," Jewel said. All the former hatred, the reserve, the anxiety over seeing him again dissipated. Here he was, willing to meet her in friendship. Here she was, finally agreeing to meet him. Jewel had never imagined this day would come. Before her illness, she would have laughed at the idea.

All of a sudden, a wave of nervousness came over her. There was much to talk about, she was sure, but she couldn't for the life of her think what. She kept staring into Sascha's smiling face. He was obviously so happy to see her again. She could not quite decipher what *she* was feeling.

"So you've seen the girls. What did you think?" Jewel finally managed to ask.

"Nice young ladies. You have done a good job. They are both pretty."

"Well, Beryl's pretty. Amber, I'm afraid, is going through a rather awkward adolescence. But she'll come out of it soon, I hope. She's not speaking to me, because of . . . you know."

Sascha nodded. "She is a deep girl. Complex. Like you. Beryl *looks* much like you. Amber, she looks like me, but she *is* you. In her soul she is much like you. Loving, giving, but always afraid to love, to give."

"I wasn't afraid to love you," Jewel said softly.

He nodded. "Yes, that's true. But then I hurt you. I caused you a lot of pain. For that you'll never know how sad I am. It was something I would never have wished."

"Well, it's all yesterday's news, as they say. I'm making an effort now to face the past and come to grips with it. And it hasn't been easy, let me tell you." She tried to say it lightly.

"I know, my Jewel, I understand that it's not easy to see me after so many years. But I'm grateful you've forgiven me. You *do* forgive me, don't you?"

"Yes, I forgive you, Sascha." Jewel took a deep breath and expelled it loudly. "I never thought I'd hear myself say that." She glanced away self-consciously for a moment, then looked back. "But back to the girls. Is Amber going to move in with you?"

Sascha shook his head. "I think it's best for her to stay at school with Beryl. They are close. They need each other. Amber wouldn't be happy with me and Aïna. We lead a different life. Aïna's a very simple woman. Amber is used to much more. But she's welcome to visit. They both are. I would like that."

Jewel smiled. "That puts my mind to rest. I knew Beryl would be devastated without Amber. Then I was afraid they'd *both* go live with you and I'd never see them again."

"That would never happen, my dear. They love you." He got up and walked over to Jewel's worktable where she had been sketching designs to be worked up by her craftspeople, for next year's nonpareils collection. He picked up a sketch and looked at it. "Very nice," he said. "You're an excellent jewelry-maker now. You learned well."

Jewel smiled. "I apprenticed with the best. You are the best, you know."

"You have built a big business on great talent. If you didn't have the talent, you wouldn't be the success you are." He turned and looked at her. "I've heard rumors that Bijoux is in trouble. But I don't believe it. Bijoux can be greater than ever before."

"Yes," Jewel said, leaning back against the sofa, "that's what I keep telling myself. Except I haven't quite figured out how it's going to happen. I'll know after tomorrow's meeting who's staying and who's leaving. Then we'll go from there."

"I have proposal to make," Sascha said, coming back to sit by her. "I'll come to work for Bijoux."

"What?" Jewel sat up, astonished. "You? But you're locked into Tiffany."

Sascha shrugged. "Not locked in. I want more freedom. At Tiffany, only Elsa Peretti is allowed to work in silver. I am constrained."

Jewel sat staring at Sascha. "You'd leave Tiffany and come to work for me?" Sascha nodded. "But as big as Bijoux's become, we could never do the volume of business that Tiffany does. I couldn't pay you enough."

"I would not work *for* you, my Jewel," Sascha laughed. "That would never do. But I would work *with* you. As partner to you and Edward."

Jewel bit her lip, considering the proposition. If Sascha came to Bijoux it would be a coup that would turn Cathalene and Anna green. In fact, it just might tip the scales in the big battle that was looming.

But would it work? She and Sascha, together again? Well, Amber and Beryl might be pleased. Edward certainly wouldn't object. She didn't know what Allen would think. But . . . there was a big "but."

"I don't know," Jewel said. "I mean, in the past you always tried to overpower me with your will. I'm not the same girl, Sascha. Do you think we'd end up fighting all the time?"

"Who knows?" Sascha said frankly. "But I've changed too, over the years. I'm not as much of a bully as you remember. We could try it. If it does not work . . ." He trailed off into an expressive Russian shrug. "I know a little of the problems you're facing, my dear," he said. "And I want to help you. To make up for the past."

Jewel got up and began to pace, slowly. "Does Edward know about all this?"

"I have discussed the possibility with him. He likes the idea. But we decided nothing. The decision is yours to make."

"You'd really do this for me, Sascha?" Jewel said. "Why?"

Sascha came over and took her hands in his. "There will always be a bond between us," he said. "It is very deep." He wheeled away suddenly and walked over to the window that looked out over Fifth. She heard him clear his throat. "I think I'd like working at Bijoux," he said, turning to face her again. "I think we will work well together. I won't try to make big corporate decisions that are yours and Edward's to make. Nor will I dictate what you design. But you will not tell *me* what to design. Of that I must have complete control."

Jewel nodded. "I think I could live with that."

There was a knock on the door, and Edward entered, a bit hesitantly. He looked at Jewel, then at Sascha, trying to gauge the temperature of the room.

"Where've you been?" Jewel asked. "You were supposed to get here half an hour ago."

"I had a meetin' down in the Thirties. Got stuck in traffic comin' back," he said.

"Yeah, uh-huh. Well, come on in, Benedict Arnold."

Grinning uncertainly, Edward closed the door and dropped into the stuffed white leather chair. "So," he said, "how's it goin'?"

"Sascha told me the plan the two of you have cooked up."

"You make it sound like we were schemin' behind your back," Edward protested. "We weren't. We only barely discussed it. And it all hinges on you, darlin'."

"I know," Jewel said. "I thank both of you. But I still have to think about it. I can't commit right now, on the spur of the moment."

Edward nodded. "I understand. But don't forget the big powwow's at ten tomorrow. Be a good idea to make up your mind by then. If Sascha's joinin' us, I think people have a right to know before they make their final decisions. It might sway them."

"It might," Jewel said. "But this is a major decision for me. I need time."

"That's fair, my Jewel. I agree to that." Sascha got up. "And now I must be going." He shook Edward's hand and gave Jewel two more hard kisses on both her cheeks. "You call me when you decide." He looked down at Jewel again, then kissed her on the lips, more tenderly. "You don't know how happy I am to see you again. No matter what happens, I want us to be friends." Then he lumbered out of the room.

"Why do you have to think about it?" Edward asked, when Sascha was out of sight. "Why the hell couldn't you have accepted his offer right off?"

"You forget, Edward, I lived with the man for three years. He made me his fucking apprentice. How do I know he's not going to come in and start trying to tell me what to do? It *could* happen, you know."

Edward sighed. "It could. But Sascha only wants to design jewelry. Honestly, I don't think he gives a damn what you do . . . as long as he has complete artistic freedom to do his own thing. I think Sascha's askin' very little, considerin' what we'll get in return."

"Yeah, I know," Jewel said. "But I need to sort this out for myself. There's so much baggage . . . professional, personal. I just don't know." She looked at him, and for the first time that day her eyes glistened with tears. "This isn't just a partner decision, Edward. It's a personal one for me. And I've got to live with the one I make."

"Yes, darlin'," Edward said. He knew that pressing her at this point was the worst thing he could do. "You do what you gotta do." He hugged her and left the office.

Edward hoped she would make the right choice, for herself and for Bijoux. But he couldn't count on it.

Jewel was drained. She couldn't stay at the office any longer. Buzzing Meg to cancel the rest of her appointments, she shoved some papers into her briefcase and fled.

It felt strange to be going home in the middle of the day. But no stranger than a lot of things lately. She forced herself to walk all the way, through the lunchtime crowds, up Fifth Avenue to Eighty-first Street. It took enormous effort and nearly two hours. But Jewel needed to find out how strong she was.

She was in training for the big fight.

By the time Jewel reached her apartment, her left side was quivering, and she could hardly stand. She did not even have the strength to search for her keys. She rang. Shoki, the Japanese houseboy, let her in.

"Good afternoon, Miss Jewel," Shoki said, unable to conceal his astonishment. "You home early."

"I'm tired. I'm going up to rest. Is my husband here?"

"No. He out. He taking a meeting somewhere."

"Could you send up a glass of mineral water . . . and something to eat? I just realized I'm starving."

Shoki nodded. "I fix Mr. Allen good lobster salad for lunch. You want some?"

"That sounds wonderful."

She took the elevator to the third floor bedroom suite. For half an hour, she soaked in a bath as hot as she could take it. When she came out, wrapping herself in an antique chinchilla robe that had been a gift from Allen years before, she found the lunch Shoki had left in the bedroom and devoured it hungrily.

She picked up a book and settled into the pillows on the chaise longue to read. The chaise was an art deco piece by Rateau that Allen had purchased in Paris on their honeymoon, and she found her mind drifting back to that trip. How long ago it seemed; how young the children were then. How young they *all* were then.

Jewel put on her glasses and picked up the biography of Edith Wharton she was reading. Lately, during her convalescence, she had begun saturating herself in the fin de siècle period. And, wonder of wonders, she could feel her creative impulse opening up again in the warm light of that elegant era. She had been sketching new pieces that were wildly romantic and extravagant.

She began to read, but the words would not string together and make sense for more than a sentence or two at a time. Her eyelids drifted shut, opened, drifted shut again. A carriage rolled by, drawn by a team of handsome bays. A man in a top hat and tails came down the steps of a magnificent brownstone, escorting a lady dressed in a sumptuous evening gown of midnight blue satin. Around her throat was a fabulous necklace of gold filigree . . . with aquamarines and sapphires and diamonds pavé . . .

She opened her eyes, and Allen was there. He was standing in the doorway looking at her, a glass in his hand and a worried expression on his face.

"Hi," he said. "I didn't mean to wake you. Shoki said you were here. Are you all right? Do you want me to call the doctor?"

"Everything's fine," Jewel smiled. "I decided to knock off work early."

"You sure you don't have a fever?" Allen asked, coming over to feel her forehead.

"I just needed to relax," she insisted. "A tough morning. What about you?" She nodded at the scotch on the rocks he was holding. "Drinking before six?"

"What?" He gazed distractedly at the glass as if he had forgotten it, and took a sip. Then he went over and sat down on the edge of the bed. "As a matter of fact," he said, "it's been a hell of a day."

"What's the matter?"

"Oh, Mother's worse. Isabel called. They've had to hire round-the-clock nurses."

"Oh, Allen, I'm sorry," Jewel said, not particularly sorry except for Allen and Isabel. Jewel had never achieved more than a cool truce with LaDonna Prescott.

"Yeah, well . . ." There was a flutter of strain in his voice.

"Look," Jewel said, "why don't you take a bath and relax? Then maybe we could go out for a bite and a movie later. Just the two of us."

"Yeah, sure," Allen said.

She flashed him a smile, then picked up her book again. But after a paragraph she realized that he had not moved. Curious, she took off her glasses and found that he was looking at her with an anguished expression.

"Jewel," Allen said, "we have to talk."

She laid down her book. "Okay."

Allen gulped the rest of his scotch. "I saw Sara today," he told her.

"Oh?" She must be slipping. She had not seen this coming. "Does that mean I'm recovered?" she said nastily.

"It's the first time I've seen her since—" he said, ignoring the dig.

"Well, that must have been exciting. How is dear Sara?"

"She's pregnant."

Jewel exhaled deeply. For a moment she could not respond. "Oh?" she said finally. "And do we know who the father is?"

"Sara's willing to have an abortion," Allen said quickly. "But she felt she had an obligation to tell me first."

"How moral of her." Suddenly Jewel understood. She stared at Allen, letting it sink in. She saw the streaks of gray that had appeared at his temples, and the hint of jowl that had begun to pad his once-lean chin.

"You want the baby, don't you?" she said softly. "You want a child of your own."

"Oh, Jewel, I don't know *what* I want," Allen said miserably. "I feel like a lawn mower has plowed through my brains. Yes, I would like to have a child of my own. I never thought . . ." He plunged his face into his hands with a moan. "I'm confused as hell."

Jewel got up and went over to sit beside him. She thought she should feel angrier, sadder, than she did. But the feeling that floated to the top was relief, a sort of lightness.

She put her arm around his heaving shoulders. "But you do want the baby, don't you?"

Allen did not answer. She could feel him sobbing softly.

"If you love her that much, Allen, I think you should marry her."

"But Jewel, I love *you* . . . Oh Jesus, Jewel, I never thought . . ."

"Oh, Allen, I'm not happy about this, but maybe it's the sign we needed. Maybe this is the right time to make the break—friendly, no court battles, no alimony, no bitterness. I don't want much . . . a few of the paintings . . ." Jewel paused, then added, "And I'd like the house in Connecticut. I need to spend more time there."

Allen looked up at her. His face was pale, and there were red rims around his eyes. "But it would mean we wouldn't be married any-more." He shook his head. "Somehow I thought we'd always be married."

She hugged him tightly. "Allen, you can't have us both. And she's got your baby."

"Don't think badly of Sara," he pleaded. "She never meant for this to happen. She thinks the world of you, Jewel."

Jewel smiled wryly. "I do think she could've been more conscientious about birth control."

"It was an accident. She had an IUD. Apparently it came out without her knowing it."

"Oh, Allen," Jewel said. She kissed him on the forehead. *How gullible men are,* she thought.

Allen sighed again. "God, Jewel, I feel awful. And it's not just us. There's Amber and Beryl. They've gone through so much these past weeks. I can't do this to them. Look, I'm going to end it with Sara," he said with conviction. "It won't work."

"Darling," Jewel said, "you've been a wonderful father to my chil-dren. And you'll continue to be. They *love* you. And yes, it *is* going to be hard on them. But it's life . . . and life is full of change." She picked up his hand and put it in hers, examining his long, slim fingers. "I always felt bad that we couldn't have a child together, that you were being cheated. Well, now's your chance. It'll be hard, but we'll all survive."

"Will we?" Allen asked miserably.

"Look at the bright side. With Amber and Beryl around, think how much you'll save on baby-sitters."

Allen tried to smile. "Are you trying to get rid of me?"

Jewel nodded. "Yes, I think I am. Circumstances have merely brought it to a head sooner."

"And you mean it? We'll be friends?"

"Yes, darling. We'll always be friends."

Later that evening they went out to see the new Spielberg film and stopped afterward at the Ideal Luncheonette, a favorite of Allen's where Jewel usually refused to go. They ate meat loaf and potato pancakes, then walked home slowly, arm in arm, stopping to look in Madison Avenue shop windows along the way.

At home, they drank hot chocolate to warm up and then fell into bed together and made love, sharing the nostalgic sex of longtime lovers who would soon never be lovers again.

Her life with Allen was over, Jewel realized, as she lay with her hand on his naked hip and listened to his breathing settle into the steady rhythm of sleep. She was going to be on her own again, for the first time in many years. To her surprise, it wasn't painful. Allen would be okay; he had Sara and the baby. Amber and Beryl would adjust, after the shock; the poor girls were used to shock by now. She would survive too. Everyone knew Jewel Prescott was a survivor.

Long after Allen had drifted off to sleep, Jewel lay awake on her side of the bed. Tomorrow was crowding in on her. The first day, as the hoary cliché had it, of the rest of her life. The last of her professional life, if she did not handle the meeting perfectly.

Edward was probably right. Sascha might well be the key. But could she work beside Sascha, day after day, just to save her corporate skin?

A day ago, had anyone asked her, she would have said Arafat and Sharon were a more likely partnership. But Jewel had been amazed by her reaction to seeing Sascha this morning. All that hatred, all that energy wasted in bitterness since she had last set eyes on him! It gave her a feeling of peace to know that she could cut that loose at last, to know that she and Sascha could be friends again.

But friends were not the same as partners. Could she work with him again? Would the old patterns reemerge? And could she risk that chance? She would have to make her decision before the meeting tomorrow.

And Jewel still had no idea what that would be.

32

Jewel arose at six, having slept fitfully for only a couple of hours. But she was too keyed up to be tired. She showered, washed and dried her hair, and then spent half an hour in front of her closet, deliberating on what to wear; finally she chose a short, fitted, navy blue pinstripe suit that she had bought from Harry's fall collection. On the lapel, she pinned the heart made of opals—the one Jane had given her for high school graduation—for luck. Then she went to her wall safe and selected pieces of jewelry made by each of her designers, also for luck.

Allen was at the breakfast table when she came down. "You look smashing," he said, getting up to pour her a cup of coffee. "Dressed for total success."

"Oh, Allen, I'm a basket case. How I'm going to get through the next few hours I haven't the vaguest idea."

"No matter what happens today, you'll come out on top. One thing you'll never be is a loser," he said, taking her hand.

"Thanks, darling." She took a few sips of her black coffee and toyed with a croissant but decided she wasn't hungry. "Allen, I'm going to call a broker today. And look for apartments over the weekend."

"Oh, Jewel, please. Not so fast. Let's not do anything until after the first of the year."

Jewel shook her head. "The girls have to be told sooner or later. I'd rather get it over with sooner. I couldn't bear having us all spend

342

Christmas together, pretending we're one big, happy family when we aren't."

"But we will be. One big, happy family. Won't we? You said we'd always be friends."

"And we will," Jewel said. "You and I. I make *no* promises about Sara. Look, I'm being mature as hell about all this. Don't expect miracles. I'm not a hundred-percent pleased this is all happening, you know. My ego is more than a little bruised."

Allen sighed. "Oh, Jewel, I keep thinking I may be making the biggest mistake of my life."

"Maybe you are," Jewel shrugged, "but that's *part* of life. Making mistakes. God knows I've made a bundle."

"I guess you're right," Allen said. "But this morning the whole thought of losing you and marrying Sara really terrifies the shit out of me."

"Well, I'd certainly be terrified at the thought of marrying Sara Richards," Jewel said. "No, sorry, darling. I made myself promise not to be snide . . . for the girls' sake. That's the last bitchy thing I'll say about what's-her-name." She looked at her watch. "Oh dear, I'd better go. Wish me luck."

Allen got up and kissed her good-bye, tenderly. "Good luck. I love you. No matter what happens at Bijoux, I'll be here for you. I mean it. Our relationship isn't going to end just because we're getting a divorce."

"I know, Allen. I love you too," she said, grabbing her briefcase quickly. The reality, the finality, of it all was beginning to hit her. She had to get out of there.

"Maybe after you've married Sara *we* could have an affair," she quipped, to keep from crying.

John, the chauffeur, dropped Jewel off in front of Bijoux at 9:30 A.M., but she wasn't ready to take the elevator up to her office. Instead she headed back out onto Fifth Avenue and strolled down to Rockefeller Center to see the giant Christmas tree and watch the skaters. Along the way, she stopped at a pay phone and called Sascha. He was not at work yet, so she left a message.

The morning was the coldest, so far, of the season. Jewel held the collar of her sable closed with her gloved hand and adjusted the scarf around her throat, which still bore a pinkish scar from the tracheostomy. Fifth Avenue was bustling, as always, with tourists, shoppers, and workers rushing to the office or meetings. Christmas, still several weeks away, was in the air, and Jewel tried to make herself think about what she should get for people. But her mind kept flipping back to the meeting. It was time to go back, to face everybody.

The silence was palpable as she stepped out of the elevator.

Everyone was assembled in the conference room, of course, waiting for her. She went to her office, tossed her fur on one of the sofas, opened her briefcase, and took out the papers she needed. Then she went over to the mirror to check her hair and makeup. The clock on the wall said ten o'clock, exactly. Picking up the cane her employees had given her as a welcome-back present, she walked slowly to the conference room.

They were all seated, expectantly. Edward got up and came over to greet her.

"Jesus, Jewel," he whispered as he kissed her cheek. "I thought we were gettin' together *before* the meetin'."

"I'm sorry, Edward," Jewel said. "I ran late."

Jewel studied the assembled faces: Mike Marshall and Meg, sitting next to each other; Erik Sanders, Bijoux's chief gemologist; Jill Cross, the marketing manager; Charles Feldman, the display director; and the designers—Rody Abrams, Tom Tinker, Rita Roberts, Leilani, and Katrina and Christof Von Berlichingen, who had just arrived from Paris. *All* these people Cathalene was trying to steal away from her.

"Are you as nervous as I am?" Jewel asked with a smile.

A polite titter of laughter rippled around the room; nervous, all right.

"I appreciate your bearing with me all this time," Jewel began. "First, I'd like to say that there's not one person in this room that I'd like to lose . . . not just to Cathalene, but to anybody. Every one of you has made an enormous contribution to Bijoux's growth and success. And anyone who leaves will be missed more than I can say. But I also want you to know that whoever *does* choose to leave Bijoux will not go under a cloud. You'll go because it's right for you. And Edward and I will fully support your decision and wish you well."

How was it going? she wondered, as she paused to take a sip of coffee. It was hard to tell. But there was a look of surprise on most of the faces. She had caught them off guard. Good.

"I don't expect to change anyone's mind—anyone whose mind is already made up," she amended. "But before you hand in your resignations I'd like to talk for a few minutes about what Bijoux will be like if you choose to stay. Because change *is* in the air." Jewel glanced at Edward for support, and he smiled, urging her on.

"I, for one, am trying to change . . . to cool out, listen more. But it's not going to be easy. I'm going to need constant prodding, reminders that I'm not *always* right." Jewel paused, as another round of laughter circled the room, this time more comfortable, more relaxed. "So I expect you all to fight me, every step of the way . . . except when I'm being totally reasonable, of course," she joked. "Sometimes I'll give in to your ideas. But not every time. I can't change *completely.*" More laughter. "And when I *don't* go with your ideas, it won't be because I haven't considered them up, down, and sideways."

"Okay," Jewel sighed and rubbed her hands together. "The bottom line. I'm trying to change. But you'll have to meet me halfway. I even thought I'd read some of those books on Japanese management." She smiled and put her hands together and bowed. Then she sat. "I've said part of what I want to. Before I go on, does anyone have any comments, or questions?"

"Not really," Jill Cross answered. "I'd prefer you to finish first."

"All right. Are you all agreed?"

Heads bobbed up and down.

"Well, then I have some announcements to make: some changes that will be going into effect by the beginning of the year. First, those of you who stay will be given profit sharing in the company. And at some point down the road, when the stock market's stronger, Edward and I would like to take the company public. You'd all receive stock options if and when that happens."

Jewel noted an exchange of glances. Were they coming around yet? She couldn't tell without feedback, but it was clear that no one was ready to talk.

"Next, I'm going to start taking it a little easier. Spend a lot more time in the country with my children. If you can believe it." She laughed along with the others. "There has been a very recent change in my personal life that also has an effect on the company: my husband and I are getting a divorce."

Edward, who was jotting something on a pad, looked up, shocked. Jewel smiled, to assure him that she was all right.

"Allen will be stepping down as Bijoux's president, with my grati-tude and thanks. Edward will continue as design director. But I'm appointing him CEO, to take my place." She looked at Edward. "That is, if you'll accept."

"Oh, I'll accept all right," he said. "But what about you, Jewel?"

"Since I'm going to be taking more time off, I'll step down to president. And I promise to be every bit as hands-on as Allen ever was."

She waited until the laughter died down. This was the moment, and she felt the tension buzz through her like a bowstring.

"There's one last change. The new executive VP, and our new partner, will be Sascha Robinovsky." She paused, giving time to surprised voices. "He's leaving Tiffany to join us as soon as the formal arrangements can be made." Jewel looked over at Edward. He was grinning from ear to ear, and he brandished both fists, thumbs-up.

"Sascha and I go back a long way," Jewel explained. "Most of you don't know that we were married once. That he's the father of my daughters."

Mike Marshall whistled. "God, Jewel, you're really full of surprises today."

"I wanted to tell you directly—before the gossip began. What I want you to understand, you, meaning all of my designers, is that Sascha's presence will in no way diminish the role any of you play at Bijoux. Sascha will be one of us. He'll have his own floor space, just like the rest of us. His work won't be featured in ads any more often than yours, or mine."

"Wow! This is really something," Leilani said. "Sascha Robinovsky —as part of Bijoux. It's terrific news."

"Yeah, to be around him, to see him work up close. This is fabu-lous," Rita said.

"Maybe," Tom Tinker grumbled. "But we've been a team. Now we're getting a star, with a capital *S*. What's that going to do to the teamwork?"

"Sascha got along well with the other designers at Tiffany," Ed-ward said. "That's not going to change."

"I have my doubts too," Rody Abrams said. "Not that I don't think Bijoux's reputation will soar with Sascha here. But I'm not sure where *I'll* fit in."

"Sascha will push us all," Jewel said. "But I don't think there's a designer in this room who can't stand up to the heat he'll generate. Look, I'm not going to try and twist anyone's arm. Those of you who stay will do so because you want to. It's as simple as that."

"Well, I'm not leavin', Jewel," Rita Roberts said. "I love it here at Bijoux."

"Thank you, Rita. I'm really happy to hear that. But Edward and I would like to have resignations by Monday afternoon, from all those people who want to leave. You can tell us now, if your mind is already made up. Or you can let us know after the weekend . . . if you need more time to think it over," Jewel said. "Right *now* though, let's have a show of hands from those of you who're definitely staying on."

Almost immediately, Rita, Leilani, Mike, Meg, Katrina and Christof, and Erik Sanders all raised their hands. That left Rody Abrams, Tom Tinker, Charles Feldman, and Jill Cross either undecided, or ready to hand in their resignations. But that was only four people. With such a strong core group remaining, it meant the inevitable fallout defections of craftspeople and gem buyers would not happen.

That meant she had won!

Back in Jewel's office, Edward collapsed onto the sofa. "Jewel," he said, "you are some piece of work. When did you decide about Sascha?"

"About fifteen minutes before I walked in there."

"Well, darlin', you did good. *What* a morning! I must say, you handled it beautifully. I've never seen you use so much tact."

"Oh, thank you very much," Jewel said.

"But what's this about you and Allen? I can't believe it," Edward said.

"You remember Sara Richards? Well, the latest is she's knocked up. Poor Allen thinks it was an accident. Anyway, we talked the whole thing over last night. It's for the best, for both of us. You know that."

Edward nodded. "I suppose so. But I still think you're taking it awfully well."

"Thank you," Jewel said perkily. "I do too."

Jewel had Nushka bring Amber and Beryl to the city early Saturday morning so they could accompany her while she looked for a new co-op. She and Allen sat them down when they first arrived and broke the news to Nushka and the girls. Beryl took the news in shock. Amber, in anger. Nushka burst out crying.

"I'm never going to stop being your father, girls," Allen insisted, after the news had begun to sink in. "I adopted you, remember? I've helped raise you. You'll still spend time with me, here. I'll still come to Connecticut. We're going to continue to be a family. Your mother and I will always be friends. This isn't going to be a conventional divorce, please understand that."

"Nothing this family does is ever conventional," Amber mumbled.

"But there's going to be the baby," Beryl said. "This is going to be hard to get used to. I mean, Daddy, if you're our adopted father does that make the baby our brother, or half brother, or stepbrother?"

"I don't know," Allen smiled, a bit sadly. "You got me. But what makes you think it'll be a boy?"

"Well, you already have two girls. You're due," Beryl said with the unassailable logic of her fifteen years.

Even Amber cracked a smile before they all burst into tears again.

By Sunday afternoon, thanks to the soft real estate market, Jewel had found herself an apartment that she liked. It was an old, sprawling eight-room place on Central Park West, across the park from Allen. It was covered with a hideous selection of wallpaper, but it had real possibilities. Jewel knew Edward would love throwing himself into the project of making it liveable.

"We can see Daddy's place from here," Beryl exclaimed with forced perkiness as they explored the empty rooms. "We could even get lanterns and send semaphore signals!"

"I don't know," Amber said. "Binoculars or a good telescope would be better. Then we could spy."

"Let's go get something to eat, girls," Jewel called out from the front hall. "It's nearly time for you to head back to school. Shall we do Chinese?"

"Yeah, I'm starved," Beryl said. She put on her camel hair coat and wrapped a gold-and-white scarf, the Sheldon Arms colors, around her neck. "Mom, I'm having a whole lot of trouble getting used to all this."

"Oh, I know, baby," Jewel said, putting her arm around her younger daughter. "We all are. Even Allen. I think we have to try to be strong for his sake, most of all."

Amber came over and unexpectedly joined in the hug. "This is all so awful. And, Mother . . . I really feel sorry for you. Daddy having a child by somebody else. It's shocking."

Jewel smiled. It was the first sympathetic thing Amber had said to her since she had told the girls about Sascha. "Well, maybe it'll all turn out for the best. I've decided to spend most of my time in Connecticut . . . and turn you into day students. I'll come into the city only two or three days a week. I can set up a studio in the guest house." She sighed. "I'm tired of working so hard. And you two will be off to college in another couple of years. I want to spend as much time as possible with you before then."

"Do you mean it, Mother?" Amber asked.

Jewel nodded. *She's getting pretty again,* Jewel thought. *She's growing out of all that.* "I'm sorry I've been such a lousy mother. I want to make up for it, if I can."

"You *haven't* been a lousy mother," the girls both said at once.

"You've just been really busy," Beryl said.

"And we're proud of you. You're such a success," Amber added.

What words to a mother's ears. Jewel smiled. "Thank you. I never thought I'd hear you say that."

"If we're going to have time to eat, we'd better get going," Beryl said.

Jewel rang for the elevator and put her arms around her daughters. Things were finally looking up.

The atmosphere at Bijoux on Monday morning was the calm after the storm. There were smiles everywhere. She might be able to learn to like this kind of thing, Jewel thought. As long as the work got done.

Edward tapped on her door and came in. "I've got the final score-cards here," he said, holding up a couple of envelopes. "Letters of resignation from Tom and Jill. Sorry to see them go, but what the hell —nine to two, that's a big win in any league. Cathalene thinks so too. She called me this mornin', and she's pissed as hell. I wish my French was better," he grinned.

"I had a feeling they might go," Jewel said. "I'll drop them both a note and wish them well. What about Rody?"

"Oh, Rody wrestled with it all weekend, I expect. But he's stayin'. Guess he's curious about the great Sascha after all."

"Sascha's given his notice to Tiffany. He'll be joining us the beginning of February." Jewel smiled. "I guess I can start breathing again. I believe I neglected to mention that I never talked to him before the big meeting. I called, but he wasn't in. I just left a message. I didn't know till Saturday that he was in for sure."

Edward whistled. "The balls of a riverboat gambler," he said admiringly. "I'll see you, darlin'. The CEO has work to do."

A few minutes later, Meg buzzed. "Somebody named Hadley McNeill on the phone. Want me to get rid of him?"

"No!" Jewel cried. "Put him on."

"Madeleine, how are you?"

"Fine. *Where* are you?"

"In New York. Just got back yesterday. Look, Madeleine, I'd like to talk to you. Can we have lunch?"

"I'm booked. How about dinner?"

"Dinner? That's even better. You like Indian food?"

"I love it! Where?"

"How about the New Hadley Curry House? I'm staying down on Eleventh Street, and there's no better Indian chef between here and Bombay." Hadley gave her the address, and Jewel wrote it down carefully.

She was afraid it would be one of those days that dragged by, but in a few minutes she found herself at her worktable, lost in a new design. Every once in a while, when she thought about it, she was aware that she was smiling.

Hadley had a lot to tell her, did he? Well, she could give him a run for his money in *that* department.

33

The limousine cruised down Park, turned west, and slid into the darker, narrower streets that made up Greenwich Village. The streets were probably no darker and narrower than uptown, Jewel supposed; but they *seemed* that way, exotic little alleys. Over the last years, she had spent very little time in this part of town, she realized. It was strange.

But what wasn't strange, these days? Divorcing Allen, yet still living with him until her place was ready. Leaving the office at five, with others still there, to get ready for dinner with Hadley McNeill. Dressing in her dressing room, while across the bedroom Allen dressed in his, then kissing him good-bye and sending him off to Sara.

"Here we are . . . number twenty-four," John said, pulling up in front of an impeccably remodeled brownstone. "What time shall I fetch you?"

"Take the rest of the evening off, John," Jewel said. "I'll take a cab home."

"Thank you, ma'am. Enjoy your evening."

"Thanks, John. I intend to."

Jewel climbed the stairs to the main entrance slowly. Before she could press the buzzer, the door flew open.

"I saw you pull up," Hadley said. "Welcome, Madeleine." He kissed her lightly on both cheeks. "A chauffeured limo, no less! Dinner's almost ready, if you can bear to eat so soon. Otherwise, I'll put it on hold."

"I'm starving," Jewel said, as he took her coat. "What are we having?"

"All my specialties . . . samosas, chapati, shrimp curry, dhal, raita . . . and chocolate cake for dessert."

"Chocolate cake? Just what part of India were you in, anyway?"

"The chocolate cake is from the Hungarian bakery around the corner," Hadley grinned. "I never developed an affection for Indian desserts."

He led the way back to the kitchen, moving nimbly on his crutches.

The kitchen was an angular, gray, postmodern room that seemed well suited to preparation of such precious new American dishes as crawfish with raspberry vinaigrette, not for the huge, homey Indian meal (pots were simmering away on all six gas burners) that Hadley had put together.

"It all smells wonderful," Jewel said. She was reminded of her first date with Sascha, when he had made a Russian meal. Was it because she was so thin that men were always prompted to cook for her?

"What a feast," she sighed. "But I'm not sure I'll make it to the chocolate cake."

"I'm glad you could come, Madeleine, er, Jewel. That's what everybody calls you now?" She nodded. "Being as you're a married lady, I was surprised you were free for dinner."

Jewel smiled but said nothing. There was no point in telling him about Allen. At least not yet.

Hadley propped one crutch against the counter and managed to choreograph the progress of the various pots using only the other. "Beer is the traditional drink with this meal, but I can give you wine, or something else, if you like."

"Beer's fine," Jewel said. "I haven't had one for years."

"In India," Hadley explained, getting two beers from the refrigerator, "we drank a lot of it. It was preferable to bottled water or soda. It mellowed out the extraordinary contradictions of the country . . . made them easier to live with."

Jewel sat on a bar stool, and Hadley handed her an Indian Eagle beer. "Are you going back? When you get well, I mean?"

Hadley shook his head. "No, I don't think so. Not to work at least. That phase of my life is over. It was starting to be over even before the accident."

"What are you going to do?"

"Don't know yet. There are a lot of options. Money's not the problem, not for a while anyway." Hadley sat on the bar stool next to her and touched his glass to hers. "Well, as they say in India, here's looking at you, kid."

They drank. The beer was cold and tasted good. Then the samosas were ready, and Hadley scooped several onto a plate for her.

"So," she said, blowing on a samosa to cool it, "tell me about your trip. How was your witch doctor? Did he help you?"

"*She.* Her name is Nania, and she's a kahuna, one of the Hawaiian healers that go back to ancient times. Anyway, the answer is, yes, she did." He swiveled on his stool so that he was facing her directly, and Jewel was surprised to see the flush of excitement in his handsome face. "You're going to have to bear with me, Madeleine, because this may sound like the ravings of a lunatic. But this is what I was talking about on the phone when I said I wanted to talk to you."

"All right," she said. "Shoot."

"Nania's incredible," Hadley continued, as he checked the rice. "I'd love you to see her. She doesn't even touch you, or hardly. She works with her hands a few inches above your body, but you can feel the energy of her hands. You can *feel* this incredible heat. Then she actually does hands-on at the more blocked, difficult spots. I swear, she brought more feeling and energy back into my legs. She helped me . . . alleviated a lot of the pain." He stopped, smiling. "Do you think I'm nuts?"

"I don't know what to think. But if you feel some improvement . . ."

"Can't you see it? Can't you tell?"

Hadley had been sitting down when she saw him last. She couldn't tell the difference, but she nodded anyway.

"I know it's a lot to lay on you at once. But just keep an open mind, that's all I ask. The whole time I was there, I kept thinking, *Madeleine! I've got to tell her about all this.* I almost called you, then thought better of it. As crazy as this sounds in person, I knew you'd probably hang up on me if I tried to hit you with this over long distance. You'd have *really* thought I was nuts." He shook his head, chuckling at himself. "Maybe I *am* nuts, I don't know. But I know I can walk better than I've been able to since that damned bus fell on me."

He picked up her hand and squeezed it. "Look, I devoted a year and a half to conventional medicine and listened to the sober opinions that I'd never walk again. They're all scared to death of malpractice. They don't like to get your hopes up. But, Madeleine, you have to hope. There's nothing else." He lowered the heat under the curry pot and gave it a quick stir.

"I've come around to all this slowly," he continued. "After meditating, searching. I can either stop here, or try to go further . . . by checking out all the healing techniques that are out there. See if they work. So people laugh. Hell, I laughed too when I took my first step out there without crutches." He threw his hands up in the air and pantomimed a little jig. Jewel laughed.

"See," he said, "you're laughing too. Isn't it great?"

"Hadley," she said, "you're amazing. But do you really believe in miracles?"

"Miracles—I don't know. Metaphysics, maybe. Nania says the scar tissue is inhibiting the healing process. She wants me to go to Brazil. Apparently the healers there are very powerful. They work for free because they claim to channel their healing energy from higher beings . . . I know, I know." He paused, picking up on her skepticism. "God, you look absolutely appalled, Madeleine. I know it all *sounds* crazy, but it's worth a shot. Over the years, I've learned that you can shut out an awful lot by being too smart."

The food was ready. Hadley busied himself with ladling it into serving dishes, which he loaded onto a tea cart. "Here," he said, "if you'll roll this into the dining room for me, I'll bring some more beer."

In the austere, gray dining room, Hadley had draped the table with a Tabriz Oriental carpet and put the place settings on top of that. Candles towered out of scrolled brass Indian candlesticks.

"This is beautiful," Jewel said. "I can't believe you did all this."

"Well, I'm not working right now . . . I had plenty of time. I find cooking relaxing—rather Zen-like." Hadley fixed a plate of steaming curry for Jewel and one for himself and sat down across from her. "I realize I've been talking nonstop. And Madeleine, *Jewel,* I want you to know how special this is—to have you here. But I'm afraid you may be beginning to regret it. Poor old Hadley, gone off the deep end."

"No, I don't think that," Jewel said. "But it's all way out of my experience. Though I'm not as against what you're saying as you

probably think. But kahunas, Brazilians channeling higher beings
. . . you're going to have to give me a little time."

He grinned, and held up a hand. "Take all the time you need. You
still may not wind up in the same place I am. But I don't think that
matters. Who knows where my head will be in a year? I might be
signing up for medical school."

"I don't think so," Jewel smiled.

"I don't think so either. But I'm definitely on this, you'll pardon the
cliché, voyage of discovery. I keep running up more sail, and man,
the places it takes you! If you're not worried about making a fool of
yourself."

That was exactly what Jewel did worry about. It had been a guiding
principle of her life for as long as she could remember. But Hadley's
unselfconscious enthusiasm was infectious. For the past twenty minutes Jewel had been debating whether to tell him about her experience in the hospital: her "dream" that she was now convinced *wasn't*
a dream. She had not told anyone, because of her terror of making a
fool of herself. But if there was anyone who would understand, it was
Hadley.

"Actually," she began, "something happened to me. Something
very strange . . ."

She told him everything; and in the telling it came alive for her, the
warmth, the loving presence, the feeling of peace and belonging, the
healing water, the green stone. How she had not wanted to come
back, how the friendly beings had pushed her, gently making her see
how she was needed, and what *she* still needed, in life.

Hadley listened without interruption, nodding encouragement.
When she finished, his eyes were shining. He reached across the table
and squeezed her hand. "Then you *do* know," he said. He grinned
suddenly. "Man, aren't we a couple of space cadets."

They cleared the remains of the Indian feast. While Hadley covered the leftovers and loaded the dishwasher, Jewel made tea and
provided him with the quick version of her life since the last time
they'd met. For the first time she could remember, she spoke can-
didly, without trying to edit and improve the facts as she went.

They took their tea into the living room. Jewel sat on the sofa,
Hadley opposite her in a chrome and canvas director's chair.
". . . Which brings us almost up to the present," she finished. "Ex-
cept for one little detail: Allen and I are getting a divorce."

"Oh, Mad . . . Jewel, I'm sorry."

She shrugged. "Oh, it's all wonderfully modern and friendly. We're still under the same roof for a while, till my place is ready."

"Is there anyone else in your life?"

"No, just my daughters. I think I'm going to enjoy being single again. I need the time to reflect . . . work out some things," she said carefully. "And speaking of that, I have to tell you how sorry I am about everything that happened—with your father."

A dark look passed over Hadley's face. "Yeah, it hit me pretty hard. And I'm afraid Anna's anger fed mine. She was out of control."

Jewel folded her hands in her lap. "I can't entirely blame her. Looking at it from her, your, point-of-view, what I did was . . . Oh, Had, I'm so sorry. But it happened. I can't make excuses or lay blame. I can tell you now that hurting you was the worst of it, for me—even though you had already hurt me by falling in love with that Lydia."

"A severe lack of judgment on my part," he said. "She was there, and you weren't. That's all there was to it really. I made an ass of myself. Remember? I tried to tell you that time on the phone." He shook his head. "We were all children then."

Jewel nodded, thinking back. "Anyway, I was shook up by what happened. And I was sorry to lose Anna."

"Anna's crazy," he said glumly. "Or, at least, she's unhinged when it comes to you. Hell, I was devastated, for a while. I wanted you back . . . and then I found out about you and Dad. When you're that age, you see everything in black and white. But Anna, I don't know. She's always had this complex thing going with Dad. She couldn't blame *him* for what happened. She had to lay it all on you. I think a whole bunch of raw wires got crossed in her head."

Jewel sighed, shaking her head slowly. "Well, for a long time I missed her, Hadley. Anna was a sister to me, a best friend."

Hadley came over and sat on the sofa next to her. "She's gone and there's not a damn thing either of us can do about it. She's all locked up in a thousand little compartments now, and most of them you wouldn't want to peek inside." He sighed. "I simply outgrew my hatred. Oh, there was a time when I fantasized some sort of show-down with you, where I'd tell you how rotten you were. I even started to write you. But finally I decided to just let it go. Put you out of my mind. Which I succeeded in doing until . . ."

"You ran into me?"

"No, actually, that's the weird thing. I hadn't thought about you in years. I didn't know where you were or what you were doing. Then, when I got back to New York this fall, I started seeing people I thought were you." He laughed. "The *old* you, the way you used to look. It made me think about it all over again. And I realized it was completely in the past. I didn't care anymore. As I said, we were all so fucking young."

"Yes, we were," Jewel said. "I'm glad to have had this chance to talk to you. I'm glad we can leave it all back there."

"What about now? I don't want to rush you, but what are the possibilities of us seeing each other again?"

Jewel smiled. "I don't know. I like you, Hadley. I still find you attractive. But we're two different people now. We've both changed enormously."

"So we'll start fresh," he said. "And see what happens."

"You'd have to be willing to go very slow. There are a lot of things I'm dealing with right now."

"I'll go slow. Hell, I haven't been with a woman for nearly three years." He grinned, and she had to grin back.

"Look, I'm going to Brazil in a couple of days," he said suddenly. "Why don't you come? We can both visit the healers. It would be quite an experience to share."

"This is *slow?*" Jewel laughed, exasperated.

"Well. We could have separate bedrooms. It'd be a great place to get to know each other again."

"Oh, Hadley, I can't get away now. There's too much happening. We're having a huge party to announce Sascha's joining Bijoux. Then there's Christmas."

"But if it weren't for all that, would you go? I'm talking theoretically."

"Theoretically, I'd have to think about it. Part of my future plan is to think things through a bit more."

"Don't think too much. It's not good to ruin the spontaneity of the moment." Hadley ran his finger up and down Jewel's cheek. "Look, I know we have to get to know the people we are now. We'll take it easy, I promise. But I'll tell you this . . . when I was in Hawaii I thought about you a lot. I had this flash that we're going to be together. And that was before I knew you were getting a divorce."

Jewel shook her head. "You're impossible! I like you, Hadley, but

357

you *may* have gone off the deep end. Besides, if we started up again, Anna might murder us both," she said. "Do you realize how furious she'd be?"

"Fuck Anna," Hadley said. "She'll self-destruct one of these days. Nobody can sustain the amount of hatred she does without having it affect them sooner or later. Madeleine, whatever happens or doesn't happen with us will have *nothing* to do with her. Remember that."

"Okay. You're right."

"Now," he said, "tell me about your daughters. I want to get to know a bit more about the competition."

They drank tea, ate chocolate cake, and talked until past midnight. Hadley kissed her lightly when it was time to go, and then he walked her out to catch a taxi.

"Life takes funny turns, doesn't it?" he said.

"Yes. Maybe one of these days I'll catch on."

"I'll call you from Brazil and see you when I get back. If you want."

Jewel nodded. A cab pulled up to the curb.

"Bon voyage!" she said, opening the door. "Good luck with the healers. I really mean it."

"Thanks." He leaned over and kissed her again, a bit more seriously, before she got into the cab.

As she rode uptown, Jewel reflected on the evening. She had no idea whether she and Hadley would go anywhere; it was too soon to tell. And she didn't know what she wanted anyway. For now though, she had to admit she felt good.

34

The café at the Russian Tea Room, on West Fifty-seventh Street next to Carnegie Hall, was as picturesque as a Paris salon of the thirties. It was a large, L-shaped private room with rich crimson banquettes, shimmering brass samovars, and carved-wood side curtains framing the windows and doorways, each with a gilded clock at the center. Its walls were crowded with paintings and drawings: costumes from *Petrushka;* a cubist picture by Braque; a Toulouse-Lautrec pastel of a couple dressed for the opera; a sketch of Nureyev by Jamie Wyeth.

Tonight the room was crowded with people in elegant dress and glittering jewelry for the gala press reception celebrating the association of Sascha Robinovsky with Bijoux. The fashionable world and the journalists who record its doings turned out in force. The air was filled with the effervescent buzz of small talk and champagne bubbles, the scribbling of felt-tip pens in notebooks, and the bright flashes and clicking shutters of cameras.

The greatest concentration of these last was in the corner where Sascha stood with his arm around Jewel. Standing shyly nearby were Amber and Beryl, dressed in creations that Harry Harper had designed for them as the cornerstone of his new line for teens.

"Get a picture of my daughters too," Jewel instructed the photographers, as she gathered them to her. "And be sure to mention Harry Harper . . . he'll die if you don't."

Harry Harper, a few feet away, pantomimed strangling himself with his own hands. "I'll kill myself anyway, Jewel," he threatened.

"That's not my dress you're wearing tonight. Although you do look stunning. Much as I hate to admit it."

Jewel was done up in a short, silver-lamé-and-lace cocktail dress, and was wearing a diamond-studded silver necklace that Sascha had presented to her that evening before the party.

"A fine necklace for a fine neck," he had told her, recalling the time long ago when he had said the same thing.

"Darlings," Jewel said to her daughters. "I think you should go over and talk to Alexei and Yuri and Tanya." She nodded toward Sascha's children, sitting across the room with Aïna, who was engaged in animated Russian conversation with one of the waiters. "After all, you're half siblings. Get to know them a bit."

Amber sighed and rolled her eyes, but took her sister's hand. "Come on, Berry, let's mingle."

"They are fine girls," Sascha said, nodding proudly. "Good stock."

Jewel looked at her watch. "Excuse me, Sascha, I've got to make a call." But as she began to weave across the room, Edward intercepted her.

"This is the place to be tonight," he said, slipping an arm around her waist. "It's a smash. Everybody's here. Except," he added, peering around the room and then lowering his voice to an arch stage whisper, *"her."*

"Who?" Jewel asked, distracted.

" 'Who?' she asks. Who else? The vanquished—Cathalene." It had been Edward's idea to invite her, along with Jill Cross and Tom Tinker, to show that Bijoux rose above any hard feelings. Jewel had balked at first, but finally came around. She could afford to be magnanimous.

"Oh, she won't show," Jewel said. "But I chatted with Jill and Tom a few minutes ago, to show how nice I am."

"Oh, I just love our new Jewel!" Edward exclaimed. "Say, darlin', we've been so crazed I keep forgettin' to ask you, what are the Christmas plans? Connecticut?"

Jewel nodded. "The girls chose me over Allen, but he may come up during the day for a bit, *alone,* at my request. Nushka's going to her family. You and Peter will come, won't you? It'll keep us from getting maudlin."

"Of course, darlin'. And what about your friend Hadley?"

"Oh, I don't know. I told you, I'm *not* rushing into anything." Jewel looked at her watch. "He's supposed to be getting back from Brazil tonight. He should have been here by now. I'm going to call the airport."

"You're not rushing into anything? Look at yourself, fretting like a mother hen."

She started to protest, then saw the expression in Edward's eyes change. She turned and followed his gaze. At the far side of the room, coming through the door, was Cathalene Columbier.

Trailing behind her were Anna Ferguson and Wyatt McNeill.

"Oh, that *bitch* Cathalene," Jewel said through clenched teeth.

"Now, now, give them a chance," Edward counseled.

"Yes, darling, all right." How bad could it be? At least the meeting with Anna was on Jewel's turf this time.

Cathalene, her hair a mass of newly permed curls, greeted Edward with a kiss on each of his cheeks. "Don't you look wonderful, Edward! But you are always such a snappy dresser." She turned her eyes to Jewel. "Hello, Jewel," she said, giving two pecks to the air in the broad vicinity of Jewel's cheeks. "I brought some old friends of yours."

"Just to show there are no hard feelings?"

"Exactly." Cathalene smiled like a kitten and melted into the crowd.

Jewel grabbed Edward's hand. "Don't leave me for a second," she said. "Stay on my heels. I need you." Together they prepared to meet the enemy forces.

Wyatt came forward to give her a kiss, as Anna hung frostily back. "Cathalene and I talked Anna into coming tonight," he said, sotto voce. "I want to see you two friends again."

"Wyatt, this is Edward Randolph, my partner." As the two men shook hands, Jewel looked past Wyatt's shoulder. Anna, sleek in a simple, black dinner suit and a cold blaze of diamonds, looked even thinner than when Jewel had seen her last. The hollowness of her throat and cheeks made the bones of her face stand out starkly, accentuated by the tight chignon into which she had pulled back her auburn hair. Anna was glaring at her; there was no hint of friendship in her eyes. A waiter in a red tunic trimmed with Russian braid passed by, and Jewel plucked a champagne glass from the tray.

"I don't know, Wyatt," Jewel said doubtfully, taking a swallow. "I don't think there's much hope."

"Well, give it a shot," Wyatt said, giving her shoulder an encouraging squeeze. "Mr. Randolph, what about a drink?"

"Oh, I don't think . . ." Edward looked at Jewel.

She gave him a nod. "I can handle it," she said, forcing a smile.

"A drink? Why, that sounds like a first-rate idea, Mr. McNeill," Edward answered.

There was a three-yard avenue of strangely cleared space between Jewel and Anna. They faced each other across it, like two gunfighters in a Western. Then Jewel stepped forward and extended her hand.

"Hello, Anna," she said. "I'm glad you came."

Anna allowed her fingertips to brush Jewel's limply, then pulled her hand away, as if avoiding lethal germs. "Yes, well, you have quite a lot to celebrate. Getting Sascha Robinovsky to Bijoux. But then, I believe you used to sleep with him too, didn't you? You must be a marvelous asset to your personnel department."

"Can't we maintain some semblance of civility?" Jewel sighed. "We both have our grievances. Mine are more recent—your trying to bring down my company while I was laid out with a stroke. But the world's big enough for both of us. Let's give it a try. I mean, you didn't come here tonight just to pick a fight, did you?"

"Oh, that's good, coming from you," Anna said disgustedly. "You and Daddy, still plotting behind my back. And God knows what else."

"What are you talking about?"

"Daddy dragged me here tonight. *You* put him up to it."

"I've seen your father exactly once in all these years, by accident, in public," Jewel said. "Edward and I invited Cathalene out of professional courtesy. I didn't think you'd show up, and I certainly didn't ask Wyatt to bring you," Jewel said, trying to keep her temper. "Look, Anna, don't you think this hostility's gone on long enough? Aren't you ready to bury it?"

Anna's eyes narrowed. "I'll never bury it," she hissed. "I told you a long time ago, I think you're the most *malignant* person I've ever met. You're evil. And nothing's happened to make me change my mind."

That was enough. Jewel could barely keep her voice even. "I'm not evil, Anna. Doesn't hating me get *boring* after a while? If I were you, I'd try to get on with my life. Focus on something *positive* for a change. Now if you'll excuse me, I don't think there's much point in continuing this."

As Jewel turned away, Anna stuck out her black stiletto-heeled pump, and Jewel tripped over it. With her left side still weak, Jewel was not able to recover her balance and went pitching forward toward the floor.

A split second before she landed, she felt strong arms catch her and lift her up again.

"Hadley!"

"I've been here a few minutes," he said. "But I saw you with Anna and thought I'd better not barge in. You okay?"

"Yes, I'm all right."

Hadley glared at his sister. "What the hell are you up to, Anna?"

"It's all right, Had," Jewel assured him.

Anna's eyes were burning. Her lips began to tremble, and her pale skin glowed an unhealthy red. "What are *you* doing here, Hadley?" she demanded in a voice that was tight and shrill. "What's going on between you two?"

"We'll talk about it later," Hadley said warningly.

"You've got him again!" she screamed at Jewel. "You evil slut, you can't keep your hands off my family! Why won't you leave us *alone!*" Something inside Anna seemed to snap, some imaginary cord that had been too tightly strung for too many years. With a terrible scream, she flung her glass of bourbon onto the floor and lunged toward Jewel, swinging her fists with insane wildness.

Hadley stepped between them, pushing his sister back, as Wyatt plunged hastily through the suddenly quiet crowd.

"Anna!" he said in a stricken voice. "Oh God, Madeleine, I'm sorry. Come on, Hadley, let's get her out of here. Anna, honey . . . come on."

But with a sudden twist, Anna pulled away from Hadley's grasp. She reached to the floor and snatched up a shard of shattered glass. It cut deeply into her hand, and she raised it, dripping blood.

"At least I can make you *ugly!*" Anna shrieked, and her hand lashed out toward Jewel's face. Jewel recoiled, but the sharp glass sliced her cheek just below her right eye.

"You'll pay for everything you've done," Anna yelled hysterically, "you'll pay in hell! See if they want you now . . ."

"Mother!" Amber's horrified cry pierced the room.

Anna hesitated as her arm swung back for another strike, and Hadley grabbed it while Wyatt secured his arms around her. Anna was now sobbing hysterically as she watched her own blood trickle down her wrist and soak into the sleeve of her suit.

A waiter wrapped Anna's hand in a towel. Stumbling, sobbing, she allowed her father to steer her toward the door. Cathalene, white-faced, hurried after them.

Hadley helped Jewel to a banquette, and Sascha soaked a napkin in vodka and dabbed with it at the cut in her cheek. "It's not too bad," he said with a deep sigh of relief. "No need for stitches."

But Jewel was staring at Hadley. "Hadley, where are your crutches?"

Hadley smiled. "In Brazil." He held up the carved wooden cane he was carrying. "Next time I'll leave this there."

"We'd better get her to a hospital," Allen Prescott said, hovering nervously. Never good with the sight of blood, his face was ashen and he was trembling violently. "I'd feel better if a doctor looked at this."

"No," Jewel said. "Really, Allen, I'm all right. All I need is a Band-Aid."

Amber and Beryl had been rooting through Jewel's purse.

"Band-Aids," Amber said breathlessly.

"We found them in your wallet!" Beryl exclaimed.

Jewel kissed them. "Thank you, darlings. They've probably been there since you were babies. I don't think either of you has needed one for years. Let's hope they still work."

Hadley opened one and covered the cut.

"You'd better go help your father, Had," she said. "I'm okay. He needs you more right now."

He started to protest, then nodded. "I'll call you later."

Jewel stood up. The guests were still gathered around in shocked silence. She smiled. "And you reporters thought these press parties in the jewelry business were dull. Well, with Bijoux there's always more to it than free champagne." A wave of relieved laughter swept the room. After a moment, Jewel held up her hand. "Obviously, I can't tell you what to write. And I wouldn't try. But there's not much of a story in this little episode. Just strain and nerves gotten a bit out of hand. No harm done. There'll be no charges or nonsense like that. The real story tonight is Sascha Robinovsky and Bijoux, and the party's still going strong."

The crowd broke into applause. Sascha raised both his arms and gestured heartily, summoning people around him. "And I have plans," he boomed, "that will keep you pounding at your typewriters for weeks!"

Edward put his hands on Jewel's arms and looked at her closely as Sascha the Pied Piper drew the crowd away. "Are you sure you're all right, darlin'?"

"I don't know. How do I look?"

"You look gorgeous."

"That's the main thing, then. But I don't think I'll make it a late night."

The day before Christmas Eve, New York City was in the midst of an unexpected blizzard. The snow had begun falling during the night. Already eight inches deep, it was still coming down in frantic, tiny flakes. The traffic on Fifth Avenue, outside of Jewel's window at Bijoux, was at a standstill. The icy streets had caused cars to slide into one another all morning. Jewel was beginning to think that she and the girls should take the train to Connecticut, which, of course, would be a madhouse. But better than risking the treacherous roads.

She buzzed Meg. "Meg, can you see about getting train tickets to Danbury? I'm afraid this snow isn't going to let up anytime soon."

"Yeah. The latest weather flash is four to six inches *more.*"

"How can they do this to us? With Christmas almost here?" Jewel said indignantly. "I still haven't finished my last-minute shopping."

"Oh," said Meg, "Hadley McNeill's just arrived. Shall I send him right in?"

"Of course." Jewel glanced into the large wall mirror and smoothed her hair back. Her cheek below her eye was still bandaged.

Hadley entered the office, smiling. He brushed some snow off his overcoat and hung it, and his cane, on the coat rack. "Hello. Isn't this a great storm? I love New York when it snows. Have you ever noticed how friendly people get?" He came over and reached across her desk to kiss her cheek.

"Hi, Hadley. I thought we had a lunch date." She looked at her watch. "It's only eleven."

He shrugged. "I walked up from downtown. Made it faster than I thought I would. Want me to come back in an hour?"

"No." Jewel shook her head. "I don't feel much like working.

You're right. It *is* pretty. Of course, it's going to wreak havoc with our Christmas travel."

"Don't look at the bad side. It'll all work out fine."

"What's the word for a male Pollyanna?" Jewel smiled.

"Hey, I'm merely in a good mood. This is the first time I've seen you alone since I got back from Brazil."

Jewel nodded, the picture of Anna's contorted face flashing across her mind.

"How's Anna doing?"

Hadley had reported from the hospital that she was heavily sedated.

"I don't know. Not great. I honestly think if she'd had a gun that night she'd have shot us both down. Anna's been on the edge for years. Not just you, a lot of things—the drinking, and the extreme mood swings. I tried to talk to Mother and Dad about it years ago, but they never wanted to see it. Now we're all having to face it. Even Randy, when he's sober enough. And who knows . . . maybe the place we've got her in now will help her."

"I hope so," Jewel sighed. "It's all such a pity. I know you said that whatever happens between us has nothing to do with Anna. But Hadley, she's *always* going to be there, hating me. I don't think I could take it."

His face clouded. "Well, let's not talk about that now. Are you hungry?"

"Not really. I had coffee and a Danish half an hour ago."

"Then want to go for a walk? Up to the Park?"

Jewel smiled. Hadley's enthusiasm for the snow amused her. "All right. But I warn you . . . I'm not a great lover of the outdoors. The cold makes my nose bright red."

Hadley laughed. "Okay, a short walk. Then we'll eat, or get some coffee or something."

Out on the street, people were darting around, carrying crammed shopping bags, trying not to slip on the icy spots. Hadley took Jewel's arm and guided her carefully across the street, to where it was less crowded. The snow had blanketed the usual cacophony, and a quiet, surreal peace had descended over the city. There were few cars on the streets now, and only a smattering of brave cabdrivers.

"I still haven't heard about Brazil," Jewel said as they headed uptown toward Central Park.

Hadley shook his head. "It blew my mind. I have a friend who's a filmmaker. We may get together and do a documentary on these people. I mean, it's incredible down there. This guy Armando just reached *into* my leg. No drugs, nothing. I was *awake,* I saw it. He pulled out this mass of scar tissue. Then he sort of smoothed it over with his hand. When he'd finished, all you could see where he'd been working was like a little paper cut."

"It's amazing—"

"And," he interrupted, "another guy, Fabio, works with light and energy. You can *see* sparks fly from his hands, from his whole body . . . like a human light bulb. He worked on getting the energy in my legs balanced and flowing. I mean, it's fucking unbelievable, what they do. God, I'd love to get you down there, to let them work on you."

"Well—" Jewel started to say.

"Look," he interrupted again, "have you thought any more about us while I was away?"

Jewel nodded. "Yes."

"And what?"

"Well, next trip to Brazil I may come too."

"Yeah?" he said. "This is looking promising."

"Calm down." She smiled. "Slow, right? Separate bedrooms and all that."

"Well, yeah, if that's what you want."

"I didn't say it's what I want. It's what would be best."

"Okay, sure, separate bedrooms. No problem."

Jewel wiped a snowflake off her eyelash. "God, it's freezing. Let's go someplace and warm up."

"Okay." Hadley broke into a wide grin. "But I'd like to remind you —in Rio, it's summer now."

Jewel rolled her eyes and pulled him out of the snow, into the nice, cozy warmth of a small café.

"Let's plan the trip over coffee," she said.

"I'd rather plan it in bed with you. I mean, Christmas is almost here. And I can tell you what I want most."

"I know," Jewel laughed. "You're absolutely relentless."

"That's me," he said, leaning over to kiss her while the waitress waited patiently to show them to a table.

MEREDITH RICH is the author of the novels *Little Sins, Virginia Clay,* and *Bare Essence,* which was adapted as a major network miniseries and later as a weekly prime-time series. Under another name she has published numerous magazine articles and four nonfiction books on business and health.

A former New Yorker and Virginian, she now lives in northern New Mexico with her husband, a writer and cartoonist, and her two daughters.

She is active in the movement to save the environment, and is committed to world peace.